THE RISE
of the
TERRAN FEDERATION

Edited By John F. Carr

Pequod Press

THE RISE OF THE TERRAN FEDERATION

A Terro-Human Future History Collection

First Edition

Printed in the United States of America

First Printing 2017

V 10 9 8 7 6 5 4 3 2 1

ISBN: 978-0-937912-70-6

Pequod Press
P.O. Box 80
Boalsburg, PA 16827
www.PequodPress.com

TERRO-HUMAN FUTURE HISTORY

The Rise of the Terran Federation
Federation
Uller Uprising
Four-Day Planet
Cosmic Computer
Little Fuzzy
Fuzzy Sapiens
Fuzzies and Other People
Caveat Fuzzy
Fuzzy Ergo Sum
The Fuzzy Conundrum
Space Viking
Space Viking's Throne
The Last Space Viking
The Merlin Gambit
Empire

DEDICATION

To David Johnson who, with his Zarthani.net website and enthusiasm, kept Piper fandom growing into the Twenty-First Century!

ACKNOWLEDGEMENTS

Much of this book could not have been fully realized without the scholarship and dedication of John Anderson, who has carried on a lively correspondence with the author for over 30 years, as well as David Johnson who has kept Beam's torch burning at his Zarthani.net website and the ongoing efforts of Wolfgang Diehr who runs the PIPER-L@HOME.EASE.LSOFT.COM list. And, most importantly, H. Beam Piper, without whose writings and historical scholarship, none of this could have been done.

Special thanks go to Pequod Editor Victoria Alexander; as well as thanks to the copyediting team: Larry Hopkins, Dwight Decker and Wolfgang Diehr.

TERRO-HUMAN FUTURE HISTORY CHRONOLOGY

The Atomic Era is reckoned as beginning on the 2nd of December 1942, Christian era, with the first self-sustaining nuclear reactor, put into operation by Enrico Fermi at the University of Chicago. Unlike earlier dating-systems, it begins with a Year Zero, 12/2/1942 to 12/1/1943 CE. With allowances for December overlaps, 1943 CE is thus equal to Year Zero AE, and 1944 CE to 1 AE, and each century accordingly begins with the "double-zero" year, and ends with the ninety-nine year—H. Beam Piper.

(*All dates in the Chronology are based on Atomic Era dating—jfc*)

0	First self-sustaining nuclear fission reactor in Chicago.
27	First unmanned rocket, the *Kilroy*, lands on the moon.
31	The United Nations collapses.
31	Terran Federation formed.
32	The Thirty Days' War (World War III).
53	First human exploration of Mars; the *Cyrano* Expedition.
55 – 100	Further exploration of Mars, Venus, asteroids and moons of Jupiter.
92	Contragravity is developed.
95 – 105	First Federation begins to crack under strains of colonial claims and counter-claims of member states.
105	Venus secedes from the First Terran Federation.
106	World War IV (First Interplanetary War). Entire Northern Hemisphere devastated by nuclear bombardments.
109	World War IV ends.
110	First Terran Federation is re-centered in the Southern Hemisphere. Australia, New Zealand, South Africa, Brazil, Argentina, Uruguay agree to abolish nation states, creating a completely unified world. This marks the beginning of a new civilization. Lingua Terra begins taking shape.

119	South Africa, Australia, New Zealand, Brazil and Argentina form the Second Terran Federation.
127	Reformed Second Terran Federation establishes a single-world sovereignty when Britain becomes the last nation to join.
172	Keene-Gonzales-Dillingham Theory of Non-Einsteinian Relativity developed.
174	Venus secedes from the First Terran Federation.
183	The First Terran Federation is dissolved and the Second Terran Federation is established. New Federation imposes system-wide pax.
183	Dillingham hyperdrive developed.
192	First expedition to Alpha Centauri.
200	Atomic Era dating adopted.
200 – 800	Period of exploration, colonization and expansion.
350	Marduk colonized.
380	Fenris Company chartered and Fenris settled.
390	Chartered Fenris Company goes bankrupt, most colonists evacuated.
480	Anton Gerrit, leader of the Loki enslavement, captured on Fenris.
500	Federation forces intervene on Fenris with nuclear weapons.
526	Native revolt on Uller against Chartered Uller Company.
629	Zarathustra is discovered and settled.

TABLE OF CONTENTS

PREFACE

John F. Carr

THE TERRO-HUMAN FUTURE HISTORY

There remain questions (about Piper's death). His extensive notes have never been found; yet I know that he kept a well-organized set of loose leaf notebooks with entries color-coded; a star map of Federation and Empire; a history of the System States War; and other materials including some of my own letters which answered historical questions he had posed. Somewhere out there is a gold mine.

It isn't all lost. I have his letters; and some of his notes can be deduced from his writing. Beam firmly believed that history repeated itself; or at least that one can use real history to construct a future history. The casual reader will not easily deduce the historical models Beam employed. He was familiar with forgotten details: as an example, one of the battle scenes in Lord Kalvan of Otherwhen is drawn directly from the obscure Battle of Barnet in the Wars of the Roses. He knew the grand sweep of history, but he also knew the small tales; the intrigues and petty jealousies, heroism and cowardice, honor and betrayals.

This, I think, is why his stories have such a ring of truth. They seem real because many were real. Such things as happen in Piper's statecraft have happened time and time again to real politicians.

Jerry Pournelle

Federation

H. Beam Piper had a lifelong love affair with history. Off and on during the last few years of his life he was working on a major work, "Only the Arquebus," a historical novel about Gonzalo de Córdoba and the Italian wars of the early sixteenth century. Jerry Pournelle still remembers many an evening spent with Piper in his hotel room discussing historical figures and events and how they might apply to the future. Piper had many keen insights into the past and often expressed a longing that he wished he'd been alive in the simpler days of the Christian Era, when Clausewitzian politics and nuclear wars were a faraway nightmare.

In a March 22, 1963 letter to Jerry Pournelle, Beam gives a plot summary of his historical novel, "Age of the Arquebus:" "Having just finished a story in the VII Century A.E. (*Fuzzy Sapiens* jfc), I have now dug out the historical novel on which I have been working intermittently, when I have not been pressed by necessity to get something quickly saleable done, for the last couple of years. This is early Sixteenth Century C.E. (Christian Era jfc)—1502-1503, to be exact—and Ferdinand of Spain and Louis XII of France are fighting over the kingdom of Naples."

In several of his works Piper created characters that were historians or studied history as a hobby. In "The Edge of the Knife," a story about a college history professor who can sometimes see into the future, the professor says: "History follows certain patterns. I'm not a Toynbeean, but any historian can see that certain forces generally tend to produce similar effects." In *Space Viking*, Otto Harkaman, a Space Viking ship captain whose hobby is the study of history, says: "I study history. You know, it's odd; practically everything that happened on any of the inhabited planets had happened on Terra before the first spaceship." Vilfredo Pareto, a famous mid-twentieth century sociologist, said almost the same thing: almost every form of government or political-science possibility existed at one time or another among the Italian city-states of the Renaissance.

Piper also used historical events as plot models and for inspiration for his future history. In *Uller Uprising*, the first published work in Piper's Terro-Human Future History, he used the Sepoy Mutiny, a revolt in nineteenth century British-held India, when Bengalese soldiers were issued cartridges coated with what they "believed" to be the fat of cows (sacred to Hindus) and pigs (anathema to Muslims). This is confirmed by Piper in "The Edge of the Knife," an interesting story that fits sideways into his future history, where the history professor who sees into the future compares the planetary rebellion in Fourth Century A.E. (the *Uller Uprising*) to the Sepoy Mutiny. He also compares the early expansion of the Federation to the Spanish conquest of the New World.

Another historical analog used by Piper was the War in the Pacific during World War II. In *Cosmic Computer*, the planet Poictesme, the former headquarters of the Third Terran force during the System States War, has become in the post-war period a deserted backwater. Most of those remaining on Poictesme earn their living by salvaging and recycling old army vehicles and stores—a way of life that continued for some time on many of the Pacific atolls and islands after the war had ended. The survivors have created a belief system based on Merlin, the legendary super-computer that was reputed to have won the war for the Federation against the System States, which is reminiscent of the Cargo Cults much in vogue among the more isolated Pacific Islanders after the parachute drops of W.W. II.

Piper also paid great attention to historical detail, more so than any other previous SF writer since Olaf Stapeldon. In *Space Viking*, Piper gives the names of over fifty different planets and goes into historical, sociological and political detail on about twenty of them. This detail ranges from a short clause to pages of exposition concerning Federation history, past wars and historical figures, as well as comments on their political and sociological foibles.

Piper himself had a cyclical view of human history; one based on his study of history and influenced by Arnold Toynbee, the great English historian whose *A Study of History* had a great impact on the mid-twentieth century view of history. [For example, when Piper was working on story ideas for his short story "A Slave is A Slave," Mike Knerr writes in his unpublished biography, "PIPER": "Piper dug out his copy of Toynbee's *A Study of History*, searching for something to write about."]

Piper's Terro-Human Future History, which covers the eras of the Terran Federation, the Second Federation, the Interregnum and at least four Galactic Empires, has much of the depth of Toynbee's study of human civilization. Furthermore, it can be demonstrated that Piper's civilizations pass through many of the same phases, the *universal state*, the *time of rebellion*, the *time of troubles* and the *interregnum*, that Toynbee used to describe past civilizations, such as the Greek's, Persian's and Roman's.

Where Piper and Toynbee diverge is on Toynbee's insistence that "psychic forces" determine the course of history. In *A Study of History* Toynbee writes: "The Human protagonist in the divine drama not only serves God by enabling him to renew His creation, but also serves his fellow man by pointing the way for others to follow." Piper himself was a confirmed Agnostic. Although fascinated by parapsychology, and a believer in reincarnation, Piper was outwardly antagonistic toward organized religion, be it Buddhism or Christianity. There is no institution in Piper's work analogous to the early Roman Catholic Church, which Toynbee saw as the womb of western culture after the Fall of Rome.

Throughout Piper's future history, religion is played down or is the butt of satire, as in *Space Viking*, where he gives the following description of the pious Gilgameshers: "Their society seemed to be a loose theo-socialism, and their religion an absurd potpourri of most of the major monotheisms of the Federation period, plus doctrinal and ritualistic innovations of their own.

It is clear from Piper's conception of his own Terro-Human Future History that he believed that no human civilization would ever be more than a short stanza before the next verse of human history. Lucas Trask, the protagonist of *Space Viking*, sums up his and Piper's view of human history: "It may just be that there is something fundamentally unworkable about government itself. As long as *Homo Sapiens Terra* is a wild animal, which he always has been and always will be until he evolves into something different in a million years or so, maybe a workable system of government is a political science impossibility..." To Piper this is a political reality which he accepts as neither good nor bad—just a law, like the Second Law of Thermodynamics.

Piper's Terro-Human Future History spans thousands of years through the First and Second Federation, the System States Alliance, the Interstellar Wars, the Neo-Barbarian Age, the Sword-World Invasions, the formation of the League of Civilized Worlds, the First, Second, Third and Fourth Galactic Empires, the first of which is described as containing 3,365 worlds, 1.5 trillion people and 15 intelligent races. Unfortunately, Piper's death prematurely ended his exploration into his History of the Future. Most of his stories and novels concern themselves with the Terran Federation.

The Federation included a volume of over two hundred billion cubic light years and held over five million planets that could sustain life in a natural or artificial environment. Although internal evidence in the novels leaves us to suspect that only a few thousand or so of these worlds were inhabited by man during the Federation period, there were still new worlds being colonized up until the time of the System States War in the ninth century A.E., before the Federation's decline and fall. The universal Lingua Terra of the Federation was an English-Spanish-Afrikaans-Portuguese mixture of the old Terran (earth) tongues. Time is kept according to Galactic Standard (G.S.), based on Terran time in seconds, minutes and hours.

By the First Century, A.E., *Homo Sapiens* has become racially homogeneous. In *Four-Day Planet*, Piper states: "The amount of intermarriage that's gone on since the First Century, (had made) any resemblance between people's names and their appearance purely coincidental." In that sense, Piper was way ahead of his time.

Lingua Terra was also universal; by the Seventeenth Century A.E., it was spoken, in one form or another, by every descendant of the race that had gone out from the Sol System in the Third Century. It also appears that by the time of *Space Viking* all racial differences had been lost, although there is some mention of new racial differentiation due to environmental conditions. On Agni, a hot-star planet, the inhabitants were said to be tough for Neo-Barbarians and to have very dark skin.

Where are the American-Sino-Soviet superpowers in Piper's Terro-Human Future History? And what has happened to the cultural domination of Europe and North America?

The answer to this question lies in Piper's earliest short stories and novelettes, many predating the creation of his Terro-Human Future History. Throughout his body of work, Piper shows a predilection for certain themes: nuclear war, the cyclical nature of civilization, the threat of barbarians from within society and from without, the citizen patriot, reincarnation, time travel, para-psychological phenomenon, etc. In many of his stories published in the 1940s and '50s the threat of a global nuclear holocaust is clearly on his mind—as it was on the mind of any sane person who lived during that era of nuclear brinkmanship.

Piper's first short story, "Time and Time Again," contains his first mention of a Third World War, one that takes place in 1975 (only one year prior to the date given to the "Third World War" in his History of the Future letter to Peter Weston). "In Flight From Tomorrow" (originally titled "Immunity"), which was published in 1950, is the first story using Atomic Era (A.E.) dating and the first one to explore the rise and fall of civilization on earth. There are some glaring inconsistencies with later stories, which makes it impossible to place "Flight From Tomorrow" in the Terro-Human Future History, and the central idea—that man could over time "adapt" to radioactivity—is wrong, although that was not obvious at the time the story was written. It is certainly one of the more interesting stories in the Piper canon, and contains many of the ideas which we find in later Terro-Human Future Histories stories.

"Day of the Moron" could almost be called a part of the Terro-Human Future History; in this early story, Piper is clearly working out some of the background he later uses in his future history. However, there is no internal evidence that would make it a part of his Terro-Human Future History (nor does Piper place it there in his "future history letter").

It isn't until we get to *Uller Uprising* that we find the origin story of the Terro-Human Future History. *Uller Uprising* has an interesting history of its own; it first appeared as one of three short novels in a Twayne Triplet (a series of three novels along a similar theme published in one large book by Twayne) in 1952. A shorter version, by some 20,000 words, was later published in 1953 in *Space Science Fiction*. It's very unusual for a book to be serialized after its initial book publication. All the stories in *The Petrified Planet* were based on a science essay by noted scientist

Dr. John D. Clark, chief chemist at the Naval Air Rocket Test Station. There are several so-called Piperisms, the curse Niflheim, for example, that come right out of Clark's essay.

But while *Uller Uprising* is a treasure trove of information on the Fourth Century, A.E., it doesn't tell us much about the early Terran Federation. Instead we have to go to "The Edge of the Knife" about a history professor who *sees* into the future. The professor gets vision from the Third World War through the Third Imperium, storing his data in file folders, much as Piper was reputed to do. However, this story is most valuable for data on the early Federation:

He sighed and sat down at Marjorie's typewriter and began transcribing his notes. Assassination of Khalid ib'n Hussein, the pro-Western leader of the newly formed Islamic Caliphate; period of anarchy in the Middle East; inter-factional power-struggles; Turkish intervention. He wondered how long that would last; Khalid's son, Tallal ib'n Khalid, was at school in England when his father was—would be—killed. He would return, and eventually take his father's place, in time to bring the Caliphate into the Terran Federation when the general war came. There were some notes on that already; the war would result from an attempt by the Indian Communists to seize East Pakistan. The trouble was that he so seldom "remembered" an exact date.

Later in "Edge of the Knife":

There would be an Eastern (Axis) inspired uprising in Azerbaijan by the middle of next year; before autumn, the Indian Communists would make their fatal attempt to seize East Pakistan. The Thirty Days' War would be the immediate result. By that time, the Lunar base would be completed and ready; the enemy missiles would be supplied. Delivered without warning, it should have succeeded except that every rocket port had its secret duplicate and triplicate. That was Operation Triple Cross; no wonder Major Cutler had been so startled at the words, last evening. The enemy would be utterly overwhelmed under the rain of missiles from across space, but until the moon rockets began to fall, the United States would suffer grievously.

The end result, according to Piper, is World War III—the nightmare, in the 1950s and '60s, we all dreaded come to life. The new order is the Pan Federation, otherwise known as the First Federation, formed after the Thirty Days War. According to a security officer, who talks to our future visionary: "It's all pretty hush-hush, but this term Terran Federation (is) for a proposed organization to take the place of the U.N. if that organization breaks up..."

In "The Mercenaries," mention is made of the Islamic Kaliphate and a Fourth Komintern, which almost puts this story, which first appears in *Astounding* in 1949, into the Terro-Human Federation canon. Obviously, H. Beam Piper was already synthesizing his "view of the near future" as early as 1946 in "Time and Time Again" with the Hartley Presidency. Piper scholar David Johnson has rewritten "The Mercenaries" (see "Condottieri" in this volume) so that it does fit into the T-HFH. I suspect, like Asimov and Heinlein, had he lived into the 1980s, Piper would have found a way to unite all his yarns into one grand "universe."

FIRST FEDERATION

There are clues throughout Piper's early Terro-Human Future History stories about the Federation and its organization. In *Space Viking*, the First Terran Federation was said to be based on "Corporate State, First Century Pre-Atomic Era on Terra. Benny the Moose." Benny the Moose was one of Mussolini's nicknames. In Italy Mussolini created major corporations, embracing trade unions and syndicates. He set up the National Council of Corporations under his personal chairmanship. Thus, the First Federation might be compared to a Mercantile State under the aegis of a Director or President.

Since the "abolition of all national states under a single world sovereignty" ("Edge of the Knife") doesn't take place until sometime after World War IV and 127 A.E.—when the Second Federation establishes a single-world sovereignty—the First Federation is apparently a confederation, though stronger than the United Nations it supplants. This would seem a logical progression, from the ineffective League of Nations, to a United Nations subordinate to the nation-states and finally to a loosely joined nation-states under a weak Terran Federation. The breakup of the UN just before WWIII apparently includes the pullout of the USSR and India (Red China wasn't a member during Piper's lifetime), paralleling the collapse of the League of Nations from the fascist aggressions of the 1930s. "Khalid's death...would hasten the complete dissolution of the United Nations, already weakened by the crisis over the Eastern demands for the demilitarization and internationalization of the United States Lunar Base" ("Edge of the Knife").

The Terran Federation is formed just before World War III (Thirty Days War), and so its seat at first is probably in New York in former United Nations' Offices. There was little time to find new facilities, and besides the UN buildings they even appropriate its emblem, "a wreathed globe on a 'light blue' field." But after the nuclear exchange, Federation headquarters probably moves to St. Louis, as described in "Hunter Patrol." There, "New York was bombed flat. Where the old U.N. buildings were, it's still hot ...donated a big tract of land outside St. Louis." Being nearer the center of the contiguous states, it would also be more equidistant from Great Britain and Japan, the other major members of the early (northern-dominated) Terran Federation.

The Federation headquarters presumably remain in St. Louis until it's destroyed in World War IV (First Interplanetary War), making it the Terran Federation capital for almost a century (A.E. 32 to A.E. 106). Since Washington was also destroyed in WWIII ("Operation Triple Cross"), the US government probably moves there as well, making it the American capital, as well as the First Federation Capital.

After Word War IV, Piper never mentions the new location of the Second Federation capital, but it might well be Montevideo. The University of Montevideo is mentioned as a great—if not the greatest—center of learning in several places; when Conn Maxwell mentions he studied there in "Graveyard of Dreams."

Without the foot-dragging and interference, from the former communist states, which so often stymied common policies and action in the United Nations, the new Terran Federation would be free to become a more closely cooperative international organization.

"Omnilingual" takes place in 53 A.E. (1996 A.D.) during the early exploration phase of the First Federation. It chronicles the first human expedition to Mars as well as the discovery of extinct Martian civilization. As stated in Piper's "The Future History" letter: The "First Terran Federation begins to crack under strains of colonial claims and counter-claims of member states."

Piper never wrote any stories covering the events on earth after the Thirty Days War, or World War III, as it's called in the later stories, or World War IV. However, in "The Return" there is a convincing portrait of earth devastated by a long-ago nuclear war. Nature has run riot and the human survivors are slowly beginning to rebuild civilization again. There are some interesting parallels and it could be argued that this story fits into the Terro-Human Future History several centuries after the System States War.

THE ATOMIC WARS

There are only a few mentions by Piper of the Fourth World War. He also gives a reference to "the Atomic Wars" in "When in the Course...." The plural seems to indicate this includes World War III and World War IV, also called the Mars-Venus Revolt. According to "The Edge of the Knife" the enemy in WWIII is "utterly overwhelmed under the rain of missiles from across space." This certainly means the "obliteration of [its] civilization," as described in "The Answer:" only "leaving hundreds, where millions had been before." However, Piper never states whether it is only the Soviet Union which is destroyed, or if its Axis partners (China and India) are also annihilated.

We learn in "The Edge of the Knife" that the "United States would suffer grievously," but survive, as would the Kaliphate. Tallal, the son of Khalid, "would return, and eventually take his father's place, in time to bring the Kaliphate into the Terran Federation." The end result of the Atomic Wars is that the majority of the world's population (at least those who survived the nuclear holocaust) migrated into the Southern Hemisphere.

The survivors of the Atomic Wars not only flooded the countries of South America and Australia with their peoples, but they quickly asserted their cultural autonomy. The result is that the Terran Federation is dominated by United States interests and values. Despite their multinational makeup, the crew of *Cyrano*, as described in "Omnilingual" appears quite Americanized.

Another aspect of the Americanization is the development of a common language, Lingua Terra, which is based on English, even though Spanish is the dominant language of the Southern Hemisphere. However, American cultural dynamism appears to have dominated both the Federation and the former countries of South America and Africa. However, there is little specific information in Piper's works about what happened to most of Africa during the Atomic Wars. We do know that most of Northern Africa was bombed into oblivion, and that Southern Africa survived; however, little is revealed about the rest of the continent.

SOL-SYSTEM COLONIES

Piper provides us very little information about the First Terran Federation colonies on Mars and Luna. In "The Future History," Piper mentions—after the first landing on Mars—that there are "Further explorations of Mars, Venus, Asteroid Belt and the Moons of Jupiter." He then tells us that the First Federation begins to break apart due to the "strains of colonial claims and counter-claims of member states."

Many of the migrants are probably former refuges from the devastated Northern Hemisphere, the former United States prominent among them. It appears they brought their nationalist fervor with them to the new Sol-System colonies.

In "When in the Course...," Roger Barron, who comes from Venus, suggests there is a possible Northern Hemisphere origin for that planetary colony. Luna, Mars, and Venus might be in effect the last bastion of Northern Hemispheric culture, including its bellicose nature. This could be one factor in the Mars-Venus Revolt (First Interplanetary War) which resulted in the complete nuclear destruction of the Northern

Hemisphere. It's quite possible that the 'exiled' descendants of the once-dominant North resent the growing power and influence of the now-unified Southern Hemisphere. Or, maybe the survivors of the Axis states made a failed attempt to regain their former territories.

Before the war, Mars and Venus are 'colonies,' but afterwards they become 'Member Republics' of the Terran Federation, so a stalemate is implied since the Federation does not appear to have been destroyed. A decisive victory by the Terran Federation would have put an end to all colonial ambitions. The Second Federation (which is later referred to as the Federation) emerges out of the ashes of World War IV.

THE SECOND FEDERATION

The Second Terran Federation has a government with a "Parliament," whose executive is "the President of the Federation," which govern under the Federation Constitution. This sounds much like some combination of the American and British political systems. It might resemble the government of the Confederate States of America, which had a president, but whose constitution contained special clauses on states' rights. The original Terran Federation charter may therefore contain provisions guaranteeing certain national rights. However, the combination of President and Parliament in the Second Terran Federation could in fact come from the political systems of the Southern Hemisphere. South America has US-style Presidents, while South Africa, Australia, and New Zealand are former British colonies with Parliaments

How did civilization repair itself after the Third World War? Certainly, by 54 A.E. (1996 A.D.) civilization had repaired itself enough to successfully mount a major archeological expedition to Mars, as described in "Omnilingual." (Like many visionary science-fiction writers of his time, Piper would have been aghast at how little the space program has come since Sputnik.) His own definition of Lingua Terra provides the loci of early Federation civilization, especially since most of the nations are in the Southern Hemisphere. We can safely assume that the English language influence comes from U.S. and British refugees from the Northern Hemisphere, as well as Australia. In *Four-Day* planet two major newspapers are mentioned, the *La Prensa* from Buenos Aires and the *Melbourne Times*.

The government of the First Federation was based on the Corporate State—quite distinct from the Second Federation. By the time of the Second Federation, Piper compares the Federation government to that of Georgian England, a representative government with colonies and member states, rather than a strict monarchy. There are also charter companies (like the British East India Company) that discover and develop new planetary colonies, such as the Chartered Zarathustran Company which attempts to exterminate the Fuzzies in *Little Fuzzy*.

Piper, in "Edge of the Knife," compares Federation colonial expansion to: "And when Mars and Venus are colonized, there will be the same historic situations, at least in general shape, as arose when the European powers were colonizing the New Worlds, or for that matter, when the Greek city-states were throwing out colonies across the Aegean." Later he compares the early Federation with the Spanish Conquest, with events like the Uller Uprising and the Loki Enslavement. Many Federation planets have their own colonial governors who can only be overthrown by direct military intervention, and who are governed through and with the consent of a legislature.

Most of Piper's Terro-Human Federation stories, with the exception of "Graveyard of Dreams" and the novel it inspired, *Cosmic Computer*, involve the Federation's exploration and subjugation of new planets. *Cosmic Computer* takes place after the disastrous System States War (a thinly disguised version of our own Civil War), when the Federation has clearly entered its Toynbeean "time of troubles." In the follow-up novel, *Space Viking*, which takes place in the "interregnum," Piper writes that the System States War led to a period of instability and the eventual dissolution of the Second Federation. The Space Vikings, whose ancestors fled after the defeat of the System States Alliance, flee far beyond the boundaries of the Federation and create a dozen worlds named after famous swords.

The Terran Federation itself is well mapped by the novels, *Four-Day Planet, Uller Uprising, Little Fuzzy, Fuzzy Sapiens, Fuzzies and Other*

People, Cosmic Computer and half a dozen short stories; however, only one novel, *Space Viking*, and three short stories exist to describe the next four to five thousand years. Furthermore, since *Space Viking* takes place several hundred years before the First Galactic Empire, there are some rather large holes in Piper's Terro-Human Future History.

Eventually, the Interstellar Wars begin and the Second Federation is thrown into chaos, with only a few older worlds, like Marduk and Odin, retaining any vestiges of civilization and star-faring space craft. In *Space Viking*, the descendants of the System States Alliance who fled from the Terran Federation return to prey on the worlds of the Old Federation which have over the centuries descended into barbarism.

Sadly, Piper's premature death deprived us of the full expanse of his History of the Future as well as some cracking-good yarns.

Among hard-core H. Beam Piper enthusiasts, there are two camps regarding the following story, "Genesis." Some want to include this yarn as the founding story for Piper's Paratime series, while others see it as the seminal story for Piper's Terro-Human Future History. Piper, however, was mum on the subject.

In his Paratime series, Piper divided Paratime into five different levels based on the Martian's varying success in attempting to colonize Terra some 75,000 to 100,000 thousand years ago. Here's how Piper describes the Martian colonization effort in Lord Kalvan of Otherwhen:

"Twelve thousand years ago, facing extinction on an exhausted planet, the First Level race had discovered the existence of a second, lateral, time dimension and a means of physical transposition to and from a near-infinity of worlds of alternate probability parallel to their own. So the conveyers had gone out by stealth, bringing back wealth to Home Time-Line, a little from this one, a little from that, never enough to be missed anywhen....

"Second Level that had been civilized almost as long as the First, but there had been dark-age interludes. Except for paratemporal transposition, most of its sectors equaled First Level, and from many, Home Time Line had learned much. The Third Level civilizations were more recent, but still of respectable antiquity and advancement. Fourth Level had started late and progressed slowly; some Fourth Level genius was first domesticating animals long after the steam engine was obsolescent all over the Third. And Fifth Level on a few sectors, subhuman brutes, speechless and fireless, were cracking nuts and each other's heads with stones, and on most of it nothing even vaguely humanoid had appeared.

"Fourth Level was the big one. The others had devolved from low-probability genetic accidents; it was the maximum probability. It was divided into many sectors and subsectors, on most of which human civilization had first appeared in the valleys of the Nile and Tigris-Euphrates, and on the Indus and Yangtze."

Therefore, "Genesis" is plausibly the origin story for the Paratime series as described above. However, "Genesis" also has equally strong ties to Piper's Terro-Human Future History. One of the most contentious propositions in Piper's future history is the interfertility of both human and Freyans (the females of Freya being described as the most beautiful women in the galaxy). The Freyans are first mentioned in Piper's first published future history novel, Uller Uprising*:* "And I've always been in sympathy with extraterrestrial races; one of my great-grandmothers was a Freyan… "

The second Martian-origin link to Piper's future history is the story "Omnilingual," *which tells the story of an expedition from Terra discovering the remains of a dead civilization. There is internal evidence that the former inhabitants were very similar in appearance to* Homo sapiens.

*Some Piper fans have believed that Piper's primary market (*Astounding Science Fiction*) failed to buy Piper's unsold story,* "When in the Course…," *due to Freyan/human interfertility. In John W. Campbell's rejection letter for* "When in the Course," *he provides several telling reasons for rejecting the story, but does not mention the problem of parallel evolution.*

Interspecies fertility is a hard lump to swallow, but there have been "explanations" in other SF works: the most prominent is panspermia, the idea that some much earlier race seeded the universe or galaxy with the necessary DNA for the development of intelligent life. The other most-likely explanation is that the species are from the same stock, that is, refugees from another world. This last is the explanation that Piper offers for both the Paratime and the Terro-Human Future History. Thus, one could make a reasonable argument that "Genesis" is the origin story for both series—or take your choice?

GENESIS

H. Beam Piper

1

50,254 B.A.E.

Aboard the ship, there was neither day nor night; the hours slipped gently by, as vistas of star-gemmed blackness slid across the visiscreens. For the crew, time had some meaning—one watch on duty and two off. But for the thousand-odd colonists, the men and women who were to be the spearhead of migration to a new and friendlier planet, it had none. They slept, and played, worked at such tasks as they could invent, and slept again, while the huge ship followed her plotted trajectory.

Kalvar Dard, the army officer who would lead them in their new home, had as little to do as any of his followers. The ship's officers had all the responsibility for the voyage, and, for the first time in over five years, he had none at all. He was finding the unaccustomed idleness more wearying than the hectic work of loading the ship before the blast off from Doorsha. He went over his landing and security plans again, and found no probable emergency unprepared for. Dard wandered about the ship, talking to groups of his colonists, and found morale even better than he had hoped. He spent hours staring into the forward visiscreens, watching the disc of Tareesh, the planet of his destination, grow larger and plainer ahead.

Now, with the voyage almost over, he was in the cargo-hold just aft of the Number Seven bulkhead, with six girls to help him, checking construction material which would be needed immediately after landing. The stuff had all been checked two or three times before, but there was no harm in going over it again. It furnished an occupation to fill in the time; it gave Kalvar Dard an excuse for surrounding himself with half a dozen charming girls, and the girls seemed to enjoy being with him. There was tall blonde Olva, the electromagnetician; pert little Varnis, the machinist's helper; Kyna, the surgeon's-aide; dark-haired Analea; Dorita, the accountant; plump little Eldra, the armament technician. At the moment, they were all sitting on or around the desk in the corner of the store-room, going over the inventory when they were not just gabbling.

"Well, how about the rock-drill bits?" Dorita was asking earnestly, trying to stick to business. "Won't we need them almost as soon as we're off?"

"Yes, we'll have to dig temporary magazines for our explosives, small arms and artillery ammunition, and storage-pits for our fissionables and radioactives," Kalvar Dard replied. "We'll have to have safe places for that stuff ready before it can be unloaded; and if we run into hard rock near the surface, we'll have to drill holes for blasting-shots."

"The drilling machinery goes into one of those prefabricated sheds,"

Eldra considered. "Will there be room in it for all the bitts, too?"

Kalvar Dard shrugged. "Maybe. If not, we'll cut poles and build racks for them outside. The bitts are nono-steel; they can be stored in the open."

"If there are poles to cut," Olva added.

"I'm not worrying about that," Kalvar Dard replied. "We have a pretty fair idea of conditions on Tareesh; our astronomers have been making telescopic observations for the past fifteen centuries. There's a pretty big Arctic ice-cap, but it's been receding slowly, with a wide belt of what's believed to be open grassland to the south of it, and a belt of what's assumed to be evergreen forest south of that. We plan to land somewhere in the northern hemisphere, about the grassland-forest line.

And since Tareesh is richer in water that Doorsha, you mustn't think of grassland in terms of our wire-grass plains, or forests in terms of our brush thickets. The vegetation should be much more luxuriant."

"If there's such a large polar ice-cap, the summers ought to be fairly cool, and the winters cold," Varnis reasoned. "I'd think that would mean fur-bearing animals. Colonel, you'll have to shoot me something with a nice soft fur; I like furs."

Kalvar Dard chuckled. "Shoot you nothing. You can shoot your own furs. I've seen your carbine and pistol scores," he began.

* * * * *

There was a sudden suck of air, disturbing the papers on the desk. They all turned to see one of the ship's rocket-boat bays open; a young Air Force lieutenant named Seldar Glav, who would be staying on Tareesh with them to pilot their aircraft, emerged from an open airlock.

"Don't tell me you've been to Tareesh and back in that thing," Olva greeted him.

Seldar Glav grinned at her. "I could have been, at that; we're only twenty or thirty planetary calibers away, now. We ought to be entering Tareeshan atmosphere by the middle of the next watch. I was only checking the boats, to make sure they'll be ready to launch.... Colonel Kalvar, would you mind stepping over here? There's something I think you should look at, sir."

Kalvar Dard took one arm from around Analea's waist and lifted the other from Varnis' shoulder, sliding off the desk. He followed Glav into the boat-bay; as they went through the airlock, the cheerfulness left the young lieutenant's face.

"I didn't want to say anything in front of the girls, sir," he began, "but I've been checking boats to make sure we can make a quick getaway. Our meteor-security's gone out. The detectors are deader than the Fourth Dynasty, and the blasters won't synchronize.... Did you hear a big thump, about a half an hour ago, Colonel?"

"Yes, I thought the ship's labor-crew was shifting heavy equipment in the hold aft of us. What was it, a meteor-hit?"

"It was. Just aft of Number Ten bulkhead. A meteor about the size of the nose of that rocket-boat."

Kalvar Dard whistled softly. "Great Gods of Power! The detectors must be dead, to pass up anything like that.... Why wasn't a boat-stations call sent out?"

"Captain Vlazil was unwilling to risk starting a panic, sir," the Air Force officer replied. "Really, I'm exceeding my orders in mentioning it to you, but I thought you should know...."

Kalvar Dard swore. "It's a blasted pity Captain Vlazil didn't try thinking! Gold-braided quarter-wit! Maybe his crew might panic, but my people wouldn't.... I'm going to call the control-room and have it out with him. By the Ten Gods...!"

* * * * *

He ran through the airlock and back into the hold, starting toward the intercom-phone beside the desk. Before he could reach it, there was another heavy jar, rocking the entire ship. He, and Seldar Glav, who had followed him out of the boat-bay, and the six girls, who had risen on hearing their commander's angry voice, were all tumbled into a heap.

Dard surged to his feet, dragging Kyna up along with him; together, they helped the others to rise. The ship was suddenly filled with jangling bells, and the red danger-lights on the ceiling were flashing on and off.

"Attention! Attention!" the voice of some officer in the control-room blared out of the intercom-speaker. "The ship has just been hit by a large meteor! All compartments between bulkheads Twelve and Thirteen are sealed off. All persons between bulkheads Twelve and Thirteen, put on oxygen helmets and plug in at the nearest phone connection. Your air is leaking, and you can't get out, but if you put on oxygen equipment immediately, you'll be all right. We'll get you out as soon as we can, and in any case, we are only a few hours out of Tareeshan atmosphere. All persons in Compartment Twelve, put on...."

Kalvar Dard was swearing evilly. "That does it! That does it for good! Anybody else in this compartment, below the living quarter level?"

"No, we're the only ones," Analea told him.

"The people above have their own boats; they can look after themselves. You girls, get in that boat, in there. Glav, you and I'll try to warn the people above...."

There was another jar, heavier than the one which had preceded it, throwing them all down again. As they rose, a new voice was shouting over the public-address system: "*Abandon ship! Abandon ship!* The converters are backfiring, and rocket-fuel is leaking back toward the engine-rooms! An explosion is imminent! Abandon ship, all hands!"

Kalvar Dard and Seldar Glav grabbed the girls and literally threw them through the hatch, into the rocket-boat. Dard pushed Glav in ahead of him, then jumped in. Before he had picked himself up, two or three of the girls were at the hatch, dogging the cover down.

"All right, Glav, blast off!" Dard ordered. "We've got to be at least a hundred miles from this ship when she blows, or we'll blow with her!"

"Don't I know!" Seldar Glav retorted over his shoulder, racing for the controls. "Grab hold of something, everybody; I'm going to fire all jets at once!"

An instant later, while Kalvar Dard and the girls clung to stanchions and pieces of fixed furniture, the boat shot forward out of its housing. When Dard's head had cleared, it was in free flight.

"How was that?" Glav yelled. "Everybody all right?" He hesitated for a moment. "I think I blacked out for about ten seconds."

Kalvar Dard looked the girls over. Eldra was using a corner of her smock to stanch a nosebleed, and Olva had a bruise over one eye. Otherwise, everybody was in good shape.

"Wonder we didn't all black out, permanently," he said. "Well, put on the visiscreens, and let's see what's going on outside. Olva, get on the radio and try to see if anybody else got away."

"Set course for Tareesh?" Glav asked. "We haven't fuel enough to make it back to Doorsha."

"I was afraid of that," Dard nodded. "Tareesh it is; northern hemisphere, daylight side. Try to get about the edge of the temperate zone, as near water as you can...."

2

They were flung off their feet again, this time backward along the boat. As they picked themselves up, Seldar Glav was shaking his head, sadly. "That was the ship going up," he said; "the blast must have caught us dead astern."

"All right." Kalvar Dard rubbed a bruised forehead. "Set course for Tareesh, then cut out the jets till we're ready to land. And get the screens on, somebody; I want to see what's happened."

The screens glowed; then full vision came on. The planet on which they would land loomed huge before them, its north pole toward them, and its single satellite on the port side. There was no sign of any rocket-boat in either side screen, and the rear-view screen was a blur of yellow flame from the jets.

"Cut the jets, Glav," Dard repeated. "Didn't you hear me?"

"But I did, sir!" Seldar Glav indicated the firing-panel. Then he glanced at the rear-view screen. "The gods help us! It's yellow flame; the jets are burning out!"

Kalvar Dard had not boasted idly when he had said that his people would not panic. All the girls turned white; one or two gave low cries of consternation, but that was all.

"What happens next?" Analea wanted to know. "Do we blow, too?"

"Yes, as soon as the fuel-line burns up to the tanks."

"Can you land on Tareesh before then?" Dard asked.

"I can try. How about the satellite? It's closer."

"It's also airless. Look at it and see for yourself," Kalvar Dard advised. "Not enough mass to hold an atmosphere."

Glav looked at the army officer with new respect. He had always been inclined to think of the Frontier Guards as a gang of scientifically illiterate dirk-and-pistol bravos. He fiddled for a while with instruments on the panel; an automatic computer figured the distance to the planet, the boat's velocity, and the time needed for a landing.

"We have a chance, sir," he said. "I think I can set down in about thirty minutes; that should give us about ten minutes to get clear of the boat, before she blows up."

"All right; get busy, girls," Kalvar Dard said. "Grab everything we'll need. Arms and ammunition first; all of them you can find. After that, warm clothing, bedding, tools and food."

With that, he jerked open one of the lockers and began pulling out weapons. He buckled on a pistol and dagger, and handed other weapon-belts to the girls behind him. He found two of the heavy big-game rifles and several bandoliers of ammunition for them. He tossed out carbines, and boxes of carbine and pistol cartridges. He found two bomb-bags, each containing six light anti-personnel grenades and a big demolition-bomb. Glancing, now and then, at the forward screen, he caught glimpses of blue sky and green-tinted plains below.

"All right!" the pilot yelled. "We're coming in for a landing! A couple of you stand by to get the hatch open."

There was a jolt, and all sense of movement stopped. A cloud of white smoke drifted past the screens. The girls got the hatch open; snatching up weapons and bedding-wrapped bundles they all scrambled up out of the boat.

There was fire outside. The boat had come down upon a grassy plain; now the grass was burning from the heat of the jets. One by one, they ran forward along the top of the rocket-boat, jumping down to the ground clear of the blaze. Then, with every atom of strength they possessed they ran away from the doomed boat.

* * * * *

The ground was rough, and the grass high, impeding them. One of the girls tripped and fell; without pausing, two others pulled her to her feet, while another snatched up and slung the carbine she had dropped.

Then, ahead, Kalvar Dard saw a deep gully, through which a little stream trickled.

They huddled together at the bottom of it, waiting, for what seemed like a long while. Then a gentle tremor ran through the ground, and swelled to a sickening, heaving shock. A roar of almost palpable sound swept over them, and a flash of blue-white light dimmed the sun above. The sound, the shock, and the searing light did not pass away at once; they continued for seconds that seemed like an eternity. Earth and stones pelted down around them; choking dust rose. Then the thunder and the earth-shock were over; above, incandescent vapors swirled, and darkened into an overhanging pall of smoke and dust.

For a while, they crouched motionless, too stunned to speak. Then shaken nerves steadied and jarred brains cleared. They all rose weakly. Trickles of earth were still coming down from the sides of the gully, and the little stream, which had been clear and sparkling, was roiled with mud. Mechanically, Kalvar Dard brushed the dust from his clothes and looked to his weapons.

"That was just the fuel-tank of a little Class-3 rocket-boat," he said. "I wonder what the explosion of the ship was like." He thought for a moment before continuing. "Glav, I think I know why our jets burned out. We were stern-on to the ship when she blew; the blast drove our flame right back through the jets."

"Do you think the explosion was observed from Doorsha?" Dorita inquired, more concerned about the practical aspects of the situation. "The ship, I mean. After all, we have no means of communication, of our own."

"Oh, I shouldn't doubt it; there were observatories all around the planet watching our ship," Kalvar Dard said. "They probably know all about it, by now. But if any of you are thinking about the chances of rescue, forget it. We're stuck here."

"That's right. There isn't another human being within fifty million miles," Seldar Glav said. "And that was the first and only space-ship ever built. It took fifty years to build her, and even allowing twenty for research that wouldn't have to be duplicated, you can figure when we can expect another one."

"The answer to that one is, never. The ship blew up in space; fifty years' effort and fifteen hundred people gone, like that." Kalvar Dard snapped his fingers. "So now, they'll try to keep Doorsha habitable for a few more thousand years by irrigation, and forget about immigrating to Tareesh."

"Well, maybe, in a hundred thousand years, our descendants will build a ship and go to Doorsha, then," Olva considered.

"Our descendants?" Eldra looked at her in surprise. "You mean, then...?"

* * * * *

Kyna chuckled. "Eldra, you are an awful innocent, about anything that doesn't have a breech-action or a recoil-mechanism," she said. "Why do you think the women on this expedition outnumbered the men seven to five, and why do you think there were so many obstetricians and pediatricians in the med. staff? We were sent out to put a human population on Tareesh, weren't we? Well, here we are."

"But.... Aren't we ever going to...?" Varnis began. "Won't we ever see anybody else, or do anything but just live here, like animals, without machines or ground-cars or aircraft or houses or anything?" Then she began to sob bitterly.

Analea, who had been cleaning a carbine that had gotten covered with loose earth during the explosion, laid it down and went to Varnis, putting her arm around the other girl and comforting her. Kalvar Dard picked up the carbine she had laid down.

"Now, let's see," he began. "We have two heavy rifles, six carbines, and eight pistols, and these two bags of bombs. How much ammunition, counting what's in our belts, do we have?"

They took stock of their slender resources, even Varnis joining in the task, as he had hoped she would. There were over two thousand rounds for the pistols, better than fifteen hundred for the carbines, and four hundred for the two big-game guns. They had some spare clothing, mostly space-suit undergarments, enough bed-robes, one hand-axe, two flashlights, a first-aid kit, and three atomic lighters. Each one had a combat-dagger. There was enough tinned food for about a week.

"We'll have to begin looking for game and edible plants, right away,"

Glav considered. "I suppose there is game, of some sort; but our ammunition won't last forever."

"We'll have to make it last as long as we can; and we'll have to begin improvising weapons," Dard told him. "Throwing-spears and throwing-axes. If we can find metal, or any recognizable ore that we can smelt, we'll use that; if not, we'll use chipped stone. Also, we can learn to make snares and traps, after we learn the habits of the animals on this planet. By the time the ammunition's gone, we ought to have learned to do without firearms."

"Think we ought to camp here?"

Kalvar Dard shook his head. "No wood here for fuel, and the blast will have scared away all the game. We'd better go upstream; if we go down, we'll find the water roiled with mud and unfit to drink. And if the game on this planet behaves like the game-herds on the wastelands of Doorsha, they'll run for high ground when frightened."

Varnis rose from where she had been sitting. Having mastered her emotions, she was making a deliberate effort to show it.

"Let's make up packs out of this stuff," she suggested. "We can use the bedding and spare clothing to bundle up the food and ammunition."

They made up packs and slung them, then climbed out of the gully. Off to the left, the grass was burning in a wide circle around the crater left by the explosion of the rocket-boat. Kalvar Dard, carrying one of the heavy rifles, took the lead. Beside and a little behind him, Analea walked, her carbine ready. Glav, with the other heavy rifle, brought up in the rear, with Olva covering for him, and between, the other girls walked, two and two.

Ahead, on the far horizon, was a distance-blue line of mountains. The little company turned their faces toward them and moved slowly away, across the empty sea of grass.

3

They had been walking, now, for five years. Kalvar Dard still led, the heavy rifle cradled in the crook of his left arm and a sack of bombs slung from his shoulder, his eyes forever shifting to right and left searching for hidden danger. The clothes in which he had jumped from the rocket-boat were patched and ragged; his shoes had been replaced by high laced buskins of smoke-tanned hide. He was bearded, now, and his hair had been roughly trimmed with the edge of his dagger.

Analea still walked beside him, but her carbine was slung, and she carried three spears with chipped flint heads; one heavy weapon, to be thrown by hand or used for stabbing, and two light javelins to be thrown with the aid of the hooked throwing-stick Glav had invented. Beside her trudged a four-year old boy, hers and Dard's, and on her back, in a fur-lined net bag, she carried their six-month-old baby.

In the rear, Glav still kept his place with the other big-game gun, and Olva walked beside him with carbine and spears; in front of them, their three-year-old daughter toddled. Between vanguard and rearguard, the rest of the party walked: Varnis, carrying her baby on her back, and Dorita, carrying a baby and leading two other children. The baby on her back had cost the life of Kyna in childbirth; one of the others had been left motherless when Eldra had been killed by the Hairy People.

* * * * *

That had been two years ago, in the winter when they had used one of their two demolition-bombs to blast open a cavern in the mountains. It had been a hard winter; two children had died, then—Kyna's firstborn, and the little son of Kalvar Dard and Dorita. It had been their first encounter with the Hairy People, too.

Eldra had gone outside the cave with one of the skin water-bags, to fill it at the spring. It had been after sunset, but she had carried her pistol, and no one had thought of danger until they heard the two quick shots, and the scream. They had all rushed out, to find four shaggy, manlike things tearing at Eldra with hands and teeth, another lying dead, and a sixth huddled at one side, clutching its abdomen and whimpering. There had been a quick flurry of shots that had felled all four of the assailants, and Seldar Glav had finished the wounded creature with his dagger, but Eldra was dead. They had built a cairn of stones over her body, as they had done over the bodies of the two children killed by the cold. But, after an examination to see what sort of things they were, they had tumbled the bodies of the Hairy People over the cliff. These had been too bestial to bury as befitted human dead, but too manlike to skin and eat as game.

Since then, they had often found traces of the Hairy People, and when they met with them, they killed them without mercy. These were great shambling parodies of humanity, long-armed, short-legged, and twice as heavy as men, with close-set reddish eyes and heavy bone-crushing jaws. They may have been incredibly debased humans, or perhaps beasts on the very threshold of manhood. From what he had seen of conditions on this planet, Kalvar Dard suspected the latter to be the case. In a million or so years, they might evolve into something like humanity. Already, the Hairy ones had learned the use of fire, and of chipped crude stone implements—mostly heavy triangular choppers to be used in the hand, without helves.

Twice, after that night, the Hairy People had attacked them—once while they were on the march, and once in camp. Both assaults had been beaten off without loss to themselves, but at cost of precious ammunition. Once they had caught a band of ten of them swimming a river on logs; they had picked them all off from the bank with their carbines. Once, when Kalvar Dard and Analea had been scouting alone, they had come upon a dozen of them huddled around a fire and had wiped them out with a single grenade.

Once, a large band of Hairy People hunted them for two days, but only twice had they come close, and both times, a single shot had sent them all scampering. That had been after the bombing of the group around the fire. Dard was convinced that the beings possessed the rudiments of a language, enough to communicate a few simple ideas, such as the fact that this little tribe of aliens were dangerous in the extreme.

* * * * *

There were Hairy People about now; for the past five days, moving northward through the forest to the open grasslands, the people of Kalvar Dard had found traces of them. Now, as they came out among the seedling growth at the edge of the open plains, everybody was on the alert.

They emerged from the big trees and stopped among the young growth, looking out into the open country. About a mile away, a herd of game was grazing slowly westward. In the distance, they looked like the little horse-like things, no higher than a man's waist and heavily maned and bearded, that had been one of their most important sources of meat. For the ten thousandth time, Dard wished, as he strained his eyes, that somebody had thought to secure a pair of binoculars when they had abandoned the rocket-boat. He studied the grazing herd for a long time.

The seedling pines extended almost to the game-herd and would offer concealment for the approach, but the animals were grazing into the wind, and their scent was much keener than their vision. This would preclude one of their favorite hunting techniques, that of lurking in the high grass ahead of the quarry. It had rained heavily in the past few days, and the under mat of dead grass was soaked, making a fire-hunt impossible. Kalvar Dard knew that he could stalk to within easy carbine-shot, but he was unwilling to use cartridges on game; and in view of the proximity of Hairy People, he did not want to divide his band for a drive hunt.

"What's the scheme?" Analea asked him, realizing the problem as well as he did. "Do we try to take them from behind?"

"We'll take them from an angle," he decided. "We'll start from here and work in, closing on them at the rear of the herd. Unless the wind shifts on us, we ought to get within spear-cast. You and I will use the spears; Varnis can come along and cover for us with a carbine. Glav, you and Olva and Dorita stay here with the children and the packs. Keep a sharp lookout; Hairy People around, somewhere." He unslung his rifle and exchanged it for Olva's spears. "We can only eat about two of them before the meat begins to spoil, but kill all you can," he told Analea; "we need the skins."

Then he and the two girls began their slow, cautious, stalk. As long as the grassland was dotted with young trees, they walked upright, making good time, but the last five hundred yards they had to crawl, stopping often to check the wind, while the horse-herd drifted slowly by. Then they were directly behind the herd, with the wind in their faces, and they advanced more rapidly.

"Close enough?" Dard whispered to Analea.

"Yes; I'm taking the one that's lagging a little behind."

"I'm taking the one on the left of it." Kalvar Dard fitted a javelin to the hook of his throwing-stick. "Ready? Now!"

He leaped to his feet, drawing back his right arm and hurling, the throwing-stick giving added velocity to the spear. Beside him, he was conscious of Analea rising and propelling her spear. His missile caught the little bearded pony in the chest; it stumbled and fell forward to its front knees. He snatched another light spear, set it on the hook of the stick and darted it at another horse, which reared, biting at the spear with its teeth. Grabbing the heavy stabbing-spear, he ran forward, finishing it off with a heart-thrust. As he did, Varnis slung her carbine, snatched a stone-headed throwing axe from her belt, and knocked down another horse, then ran forward with her dagger to finish it.

By this time, the herd, alarmed, had stampeded and was galloping away, leaving the dead and dying behind. He and Analea had each killed two; with the one Varnis had knocked down, that made five. Using his dagger, he finished off one that was still kicking on the ground, and then began pulling out the throwing-spears. The girls, shouting in unison, were announcing the successful completion of the hunt; Glav, Olva, and Dorita were coming forward with the children.

It was sunset by the time they had finished the work of skinning and cutting up the horses and had carried the hide-wrapped bundles of meat to the little brook where they had intended camping. There was firewood to be gathered, and the meal to be cooked, and they were all tired.

"We can't do this very often, anymore," Kalvar Dard told them, "but we might as well, tonight. Don't bother rubbing sticks for fire; I'll use the lighter."

He got it from a pouch on his belt—a small, gold-plated, atomic lighter, bearing the crest of his old regiment of the Frontier Guards. It was the last one they had, in working order. Piling a handful of dry splinters under the firewood, he held the lighter to it, pressed the activator, and watched the fire eat into the wood.

The greatest achievement of man's civilization, the mastery of the basic, cosmic, power of the atom—being used to kindle a fire of natural fuel, to cook unseasoned meat killed with stone-tipped spears. Dard looked sadly at the twinkling little gadget, then slipped it back into its pouch. Soon it would be worn out, like the other two, and then they would gain fire only by rubbing dry sticks, or hacking sparks from bits of flint or pyrites. Soon, too, the last cartridge would be fired, and then they would perforce depend for protection, as they were already doing for food, upon their spears.

And they were so helpless. Six adults, burdened with seven little children, all of them requiring momently care and watchfulness. If the cartridges could be made to last until they were old enough to fend for themselves.... If they could avoid collisions with the Hairy People.... Someday, they would be numerous enough for effective mutual protection and support; someday, the ratio of helpless children to able adults would redress itself. Until then, all that they could do would be to survive; day after day, they must follow the game-herds.

4

For twenty years, now, they had been following the game. Winters had come, with driving snow, forcing horses and deer into the woods, and the little band of humans to the protection of mountain caves. Springtime followed, with fresh grass on the plains and plenty of meat for the people of Kalvar Dard. Autumns followed summers, with fire-hunts, and the smoking and curing of meat and hides. Winters followed autumns, and spring times came again, and thus until the twentieth year after the landing of the rocket-boat.

Kalvar Dard still walked in the lead, his hair and beard flecked with gray, but he no longer carried the heavy rifle; the last cartridge for that had been fired long ago. He carried the hand-axe, fitted with a long helve, and a spear with a steel head that had been worked painfully from the receiver of a useless carbine. He still had his pistol, with eight cartridges in the magazine, and his dagger, and the bomb-bag, containing the big demolition-bomb and one grenade. The last shred of clothing from the ship was gone, now; he was clad in a sleeveless tunic of skin and horse-hide buskins.

Analea no longer walked beside him; eight years before, she had broken her back in a fall. It had been impossible to move her, and she stabbed herself with her dagger to save a cartridge. Seldar Glav had broken through the ice while crossing a river, and had lost his rifle; the next day he died of the chill he had taken. Olva had been killed by the Hairy People, the night they had attacked the camp, when Varnis' child had been killed.

They had beaten off that attack, shot or speared ten of the huge sub-men, and the next morning they buried their dead after their custom, under cairns of stone. Varnis had watched the burial of her child with blank, uncomprehending eyes, then she had turned to Kalvar Dard and said something that had horrified him more than any wild outburst of grief could have.

"Come on, Dard; what are we doing this for? You promised you'd take us to Tareesh, where we'd have good houses, and machines, and all sorts of lovely things to eat and wear. I don't like this place, Dard; I want to go to Tareesh."

From that day on, she had wandered in merciful darkness. She had not been idiotic, or raving mad; she had just escaped from a reality that she could no longer bear.

Varnis, lost in her dream-world, and Dorita, hard-faced and haggard, were the only ones left, beside Kalvar Dard, of the original eight. But the band had grown, meanwhile, to more than fifteen. In the rear, in Seldar Glav's old place, the son of Kalvar Dard and Analea walked. Like his father, he wore a pistol, for which he had six rounds, and a dagger, and in his hand he carried a stone-headed killing-maul with a three-foot handle which he had made for himself. The woman who walked beside him and carried his spears was the daughter of Glav and Olva; in a net-bag on her back she carried their infant child. The first Tareeshan born of Tareeshan parents; Kalvar Dard often looked at his little grandchild during nights in camp and days on the trail, seeing, in that tiny fur-swaddled morsel of humanity, the meaning and purpose of all that he did. Of the older girls, one or two were already pregnant, now; this tiny threatened beachhead of humanity was expanding, gaining strength. Long after man had died out on Doorsha and the dying planet itself had become an arid waste, the progeny of this little band would continue to grow and to dominate the younger planet, nearer the sun. Someday, an even mightier civilization than the one he had left would rise here....

All day the trail had wound upward into the mountains. Great cliffs loomed above them, and little streams spumed and dashed in rocky gorges below. All day, the Hairy People had followed, fearful to approach too close, unwilling to allow their enemies to escape. It had started when they had rushed the camp, at daybreak; they had been beaten off, at cost of almost all the ammunition, and the death of one child. No sooner had the tribe of Kalvar Dard taken the trail, however, than they had been pressing after them. Dard had determined to cross the mountains, and had led his people up a game-trail, leading toward the notch of a pass high against the skyline.

The shaggy ape-things seemed to have divined his purpose. Once or twice, he had seen hairy brown shapes dodging among the rocks and stunted trees to the left. They were trying to reach the pass ahead of him. Well, if they did.... He made a quick mental survey of his resources. His pistol, and his son's, and Dorita's, with eight, and six, and seven rounds. One grenade, and the big demolition bomb, too powerful to be thrown by hand, but which could be set for delayed explosion and dropped over a cliff or left behind to explode among pursuers. Five steel daggers, and plenty of spears and slings and axes. Himself, his son and his son's woman, Dorita, and four or five of the older boys and girls, who would make effective front-line fighters. And Varnis, who might come out of her private dream-world long enough to give account for herself, and even the tiniest of the walking children could throw stones or light spears. Yes, they could force the pass, if the Hairy People reached it ahead of them, and then seal it shut with the heavy bomb. What lay on the other side, he did not know; he wondered how much game there would be, and if there were Hairy People on that side, too.

Two shots slammed quickly behind him. He dropped his axe and took a two-hand grip on his stabbing-spear as he turned. His son was hurrying forward, his pistol drawn, glancing behind as he came.

"Hairy People. Four," he reported. "I shot two; she threw a spear and killed another. The other ran."

The daughter of Seldar Glav and Olva nodded in agreement.

"I had no time to throw again," she said, "and Bo-Bo would not shoot the one that ran."

Kalvar Dard's son, who had no other name than the one his mother had called him as a child, defended himself. "He was running away. It is the rule: *use bullets only to save life, where a spear will not serve.*"

Kalvar Dard nodded. "You did right, son," he said, taking out his own pistol and removing the magazine, from which he extracted two cartridges. "Load these into your pistol; four rounds aren't enough. Now we each have six. Go back to the rear, keep the little ones moving, and don't let Varnis get behind."

"That is right. *We must all look out for Varnis, and take care of her,*" the boy recited obediently. "That is the rule."

He dropped to the rear. Kalvar Dard holstered his pistol and picked up his axe, and the column moved forward again. They were following a ledge, now; on the left, there was a sheer drop of several hundred feet, and on the right a cliff rose above them, growing higher and steeper as the trail slanted upward. Dard was worried about the ledge; if it came to an end, they would all be trapped. No one would escape. He suddenly felt old and unutterably weary. It was a frightful weight that he bore—responsibility for an entire race.

Suddenly, behind him, Dorita fired her pistol upward. Dard sprang forward—there was no room for him to jump aside--and drew his pistol. The boy, Bo-Bo, was trying to find a target from his position in the rear. Then Dard saw the two Hairy People; the boy fired, and the stone fell, all at once.

It was a heavy stone, half as big as a man's torso, and it almost missed Kalvar Dard. If it had hit him directly, it would have killed him instantly, mashing him to a bloody pulp; as it was, he was knocked flat, the stone pinning his legs.

At Bo-Bo's shot, a hairy body plummeted down, to hit the ledge. Bo-Bo's woman instantly ran it through with one of her spears. The other ape-thing, the one Dorita had shot, was still clinging to a rock above.

Two of the children scampered up to it and speared it repeatedly, screaming like little furies. Dorita and one of the older girls got the rock off Kalvar Dard's legs and tried to help him to his feet, but he collapsed, unable to stand. Both his legs were broken.

This was it, he thought, sinking back. "Dorita, I want you to run ahead and see what the trail's like," he said. "See if the ledge is passable. And find a place, not too far ahead, where we can block the trail by exploding that demolition-bomb. It has to be close enough for a couple of you to carry or drag me and get me there in one piece."

"What are you going to do?"

"What do you think?" he retorted. "I have both legs broken. You can't carry me with you; if you try it, they'll catch us and kill us all. I'll have to stay behind; I'll block the trail behind you, and get as many of them as I can, while I'm at it. Now, run along and do as I said."

She nodded. "I'll be back as soon as I can," she agreed.

The others were crowding around Dard. Bo-Bo bent over him, perplexed and worried. "What are you going to do, father?" he asked. "You are hurt. Are you going to go away and leave us, as mother did when she was hurt?"

"Yes, son; I'll have to. You carry me on ahead a little, when Dorita gets back, and leave me where she shows you to. I'm going to stay behind and block the trail, and kill a few Hairy People. I'll use the big bomb."

"The *big* bomb? The one nobody dares throw?" The boy looked at his father in wonder.

"That's right. Now, when you leave me, take the others and get away as fast as you can. Don't stop till you're up to the pass. Take my pistol and dagger, and the axe and the big spear, and take the little bomb, too. Take everything I have, only leave the big bomb with me. I'll need that."

Dorita rejoined them. "There's a waterfall ahead. We can get around it, and up to the pass. The way's clear and easy; if you put off the bomb just this side of it, you'll start a rock-slide that'll block everything."

"All right. Pick me up, a couple of you. Don't take hold of me below the knees. And hurry."

A hairy shape appeared on the ledge below them; one of the older boys used his throwing-stick to drive a javelin into it. Two of the girls picked up Dard; Bo-Bo and his woman gathered up the big spear and the axe and the bomb-bag.

They hurried forward, picking their way along the top of a talus of rubble at the foot of the cliff, and came to where the stream gushed out of a narrow gorge. The air was wet with spray there, and loud with the roar of the waterfall. Kalvar Dard looked around; Dorita had chosen the spot well. Not even a sure-footed mountain-goat could make the ascent, once that gorge was blocked.

"All right; put me down here," he directed. "Bo-Bo, take my belt, and give me the big bomb. You have one light grenade; know how to use it?"

"Of course, you have often showed me. I turn the top, and then press in the little thing on the side, and hold it in till I throw. I throw it at least a spear-cast, and drop to the ground or behind something."

"That's right. And use it only in greatest danger, to save everybody. Spare your cartridges; use them only to save life. And save everything of metal, no matter how small."

"Yes. Those are the rules. I will follow them, and so will the others. And we will always take care of Varnis."

"Well, goodbye, son." He gripped the boy's hand. "Now get everybody out of here; don't stop till you're at the pass."

"You're not staying behind!" Varnis cried. "Dard, you promised us! I remember, when we were all in the ship together—you and I and Analea and Olva and Dorita and Eldra and, oh, what was that other girl's name, Kyna! And we were all having such a nice time, and you were telling us how we'd all come to Tareesh, and we were having such fun talking about it...."

"That's right, Varnis," he agreed. "And so I will. I have something to do, here, but I'll meet you on top of the mountain, after I'm through, and in the morning we'll all go to Tareesh."

She smiled—the gentle, childlike smile of the harmlessly mad—and turned away. The son of Kalvar Dard made sure that she and all the children were on the way, and then he, too, turned and followed them, leaving Dard alone.

Alone, with a bomb and a task. He'd borne that task for twenty years, now; in a few minutes, it would be ended, with an instant's searing heat. He tried not to be too glad; there were so many things he might have done, if he had tried harder. Metals, for instance. Somewhere there surely must be ores which they could have smelted, but he had never found them. And he might have tried catching some of the little horses they hunted for food, to break and train to bear burdens. And the alphabet—why hadn't he taught it to Bo-Bo and the daughter of Seldar Glav, and laid on them an obligation to teach the others? And the grass-seeds they used for making flour sometimes; they should have planted fields of the better kinds, and patches of edible roots, and returned at the proper time to harvest them. There were so many things, things that none of those young savages or their children would think of in ten thousand years....

Something was moving among the rocks, a hundred yards away. He straightened, as much as his broken legs would permit, and watched. Yes, there was one of them, and there was another, and another. One rose from behind a rock and came forward at a shambling run, making bestial sounds. Then two more lumbered into sight, and in a moment the ravine was alive with them. They were almost upon him when Kalvar Dard pressed in the thumbpiece of the bomb; they were clutching at him when he released it. He felt a slight jar....

When they reached the pass, they all stopped as the son of Kalvar Dard turned and looked back. Dorita stood beside him, looking toward the waterfall too; she also knew what was about to happen. The others merely gaped in blank incomprehension, or grasped their weapons, thinking that the enemy was pressing close behind and that they were making a stand here. A few of the smaller boys and girls began picking up stones.

Then a tiny pin-point of brilliance winked, just below where the snow-fed stream vanished into the gorge. That was all, for an instant, and then a great fire-shot cloud swirled upward, hundreds of feet into the air; there was a crash, louder than any sound any of them except Dorita and Varnis had ever heard before.

"He did it!" Dorita said softly.

"Yes, he did it. My father was a brave man," Bo-Bo replied. "We are safe, now."

Varnis, shocked by the explosion, turned and stared at him, and then she laughed happily. "Why, there you are, Dard!" she exclaimed. "I was wondering where you'd gone. What did you do, after we left?"

"What do you mean?" The boy was puzzled, not knowing how much he looked like his father, when his father had been an officer of the Frontier Guards, twenty years before.

His puzzlement worried Varnis vaguely. "You.... You are Dard, aren't you?" she asked. "But that's silly; of course you're Dard! Who else could you be?"

"Yes. I am Dard," the boy said, remembering that it was the rule for everybody to be kind to Varnis and to pretend to agree with her. Then another thought struck him. His shoulders straightened. "Yes. I am Dard, son of Dard," he told them all. "I lead, now. Does anybody say no?"

He shifted his axe and spear to his left hand and laid his right hand on the butt of his pistol, looking sternly at Dorita. If any of them tried to dispute his claim, it would be she. But instead, she gave him the nearest thing to a real smile that had crossed her face in years.

"You are Dard," she told him; "you lead us, now."

"But of course Dard leads! Hasn't he always led us?" Varnis wanted to know. "Then what's all the argument about? And tomorrow he's going to take us to Tareesh, and we'll have houses and ground-cars and aircraft and gardens and lights, and all the lovely things we want. Aren't you, Dard?"

"Yes, Varnis; I will take you all to Tareesh, to all the wonderful things," Dard, son of Dard, promised, for such was the rule about Varnis.

Then he looked down from the pass into the country beyond. There were lower mountains, below, and foothills, and a wide blue valley, and, beyond that, distant peaks reared jaggedly against the sky. He pointed with his father's axe.

"We go down that way," he said.

* * * * *

So they went, down, and on, and on, and on. The last cartridge was fired; the last sliver of Doorshan metal wore out or rusted away. By then, however, they had learned to make chipped stone, and bone, and reindeer-horn, serve their needs. Century after century, millennium after millennium, they followed the game-herds from birth to death, and birth replenished their numbers faster than death depleted. Bands grew in numbers and split; young men rebelled against the rule of the old and took their women and children elsewhere.

They hunted down the hairy Neanderthalers, and exterminated them ruthlessly, the origin of their implacable hatred lost in legend. All that they remembered, in the misty, confused, way that one remembers a dream, was that there had once been a time of happiness and plenty, and that there was a goal to which they would someday attain. They left the mountains—were they the Caucasus? The Alps? The Pamirs?—and spread outward, conquering as they went. We find their bones, and their stone weapons, and their crude paintings, in the caves of Cro-Magnon and Grimaldi and Altimira and Mas-d'Azil; the deep layers of horse and reindeer and mammoth bones at their feasting-place at Solutre. We wonder how and whence a race so like our own came into a world of brutish sub-humans.

Just as we wonder, too, at the network of canals which radiate from the polar caps of our sister planet, and speculate on the possibility that they were the work of hands like our own. And we concoct elaborate jokes about the "Men From Mars"—*ourselves*.

In this sequel to "Genesis," written by Wolfgang Diehr (author of two successful Fuzzy sequels), gives his answer to the parallel evolution thesis. It makes for a most interesting story. . . .

SECOND GENESIS

Wolfgang Diehr

I

24,752 P.A.E.

The spaceship gleamed brightly, even in the dim light of late evening. It was designed to hold over one hundred twenty people not counting the crew plus food and water for twelve months or half a year as Doorshans reckoned time. Air was less of a problem since a number of live plants were also loaded on in case the anticipated voyage exceeded the five-month estimate. Every type of seed was carefully stored in the cargo hold.

Many of the plants were capable of producing edible fruits and vegetables, though it was unlikely they would be needed for that purpose during the journey. Water reclamation devices would convert liquid waste into irrigation for the plants. Solid waste would be jettisoned, thus reducing the over-all weight of the craft and cargo, if ever so slightly. And, taking pains to be prepared for every contingency, concentrated vitamin supplements sufficient for a year were carefully stocked.

Captain Marthok Darthi looked appraisingly at the exterior of what could be his last command. It was intended to be a colony ship to Tareesh, the nearest habitable world. Doorsha, his home planet, was dying and had been doing so for millennia.

Marthok, tall and stout with short red hair and a well-trimmed mustache, turned away from the ship and addressed the shorter, balding man that approached from his left.

"Still no word from the astronomy detail?" Colonel Orsohn asked.

"No change," the Captain said, shaking his head. "The meteor damage to the first ship must have caused it to crash possibly killing all hands and passengers. If any survived they must have lost all technology in the incident and had to start over from scratch."

Marthok released a long breath. The previous colony ship had left thousands of years ago and the ancient astronomers had tracked their progress through every second of the long voyage. A meteor had struck the first ship as it edged into Tareesh's atmosphere. Now, many millennia later, powerful telescopes and other equipment sought evidence of a Doorshan civilization fifty million miles away. After nearly twelve thousand solar cycles no sign of cities or even organized settlements were in evidence. Over fifteen hundred of Doorshan's best and brightest killed by a chunk of space debris.

"It took fifty years to get that first colony ship ready," Marthok continued. "I'm surprised we were able to put together this second ship in just twenty five years, Orsohn."

"Technology improves, becomes more sophisticated. After twelve millennia it should be child's play to build a space ship."

Captain Marthok agreed.

"The other ship was at least six times larger," pointed out the Air Force Colonel. "You know your ancient history, I see. Well, Captain Marthok, we are operating with limited resources. Building the canals was costly and draining and only delayed the inevitable."

"Too bad, this ship will only hold about a hundred and forty odd people." Marthok rubbed his jaw and added, "Pretty small genetic base for starting a colony."

"Oh, not at all," the shorter man countered. "No two passengers are closer than fourth cousins genetically speaking. As long as the descendants keep track of their lineage and procreate in sufficient numbers the stock should stay healthy and viable. I dare say you could manage with half that number provided sufficient care was taken."

"Will there be any other ships after this one departs, Orsohn?"

"Unlikely. We had to search far and wide to find these volunteers after what happened to the first ship. The test ship we sent out last year that vanished didn't help either. We scrapped the bottom of a lot of barrels to fill this ship. I, like most others, intended to stay behind to turn off the lights."

"Doorsha will only support life for another fifty, maybe a hundred years," the Captain said. "If you can call what we're doing here *living*."

"I do know. Like most others staying behind I underwent sterilization," Orsohn said.

"What? Why?" Marthok asked.

"No point in fathering children on a dead world." Orsohn looked up into the sky. The stars were now bright and vivid in the thin air. Night came quickly on a world with a thinning atmosphere and precious little moisture. "I don't want my children, or grandchildren, to die with the planet. Better that they not be born at all. Besides I live on through my only son that will be on that ship." Orsohn put special emphasis on the last statement.

"Why not come with us?" Marthok asked.

"I am too old to waste food and water and fuel on. I am over forty years old, after all."

Marthok swore blasphemously. "We need brains just as much as muscle, Orsohn, only more so. And on Tareesh you would be over eighty, you know, with its much shorter year. Besides, all the really bright young people are refusing to go. They cite the previous ship disaster as their excuse. I think this new star drive engine we installed frightens most of them. By the Ten Gods, we even had to pardon a few criminals to fill the roster for this trip!"

"Space travel is a young man's game, Captain. Besides, the star drive has never been tested."

"We had to beg for the radioactive isotopes that power it as it was," admitted the Captain. "There are precious few resources left in this world."

"Which is the reason you are leaving it and I am not. I have too little time left to me to be considered a resource," Orsohn replied.

"What will you do then?" demanded Marthok. "Sit around and wait to die?"

"Well, when our resources finally dry up a number of us intend to shut ourselves up in a chamber and make a toast with *kolnack*."

"You plan to suicide?" Marthok winced at the thought. "I prefer to meet death with a pistol in hand. And not pointed at myself, either."

"And that is why you are going on the ship. Look at it this way; someday your descendants might come back for a visit and find my mummified remains."

"There's a cheery thought," Marthok said dryly, then he changed the subject. "We launch the sixth of *Doma*."

"So soon?"

"We have a limited window of opportunity, you know. Tareesh will be out of range if we wait too long. It cycles around the sun in half the time Doorsha does."

"Please, Captain. I do know something about planetary movements. But since you are not long for this world, you must join me at my home for dinner on the fifth…unless you have already made plans…."

"I'll be there, Orsohn, and I'll bring that bottle of *garfar* I've been saving for a special occasion, but only if you stop calling me 'captain.'"

"Agreed, but only if you will call me 'father.'"

* * * * *

The trip had taken five months. At full burn, the voyage would have taken half that time but caution was the watchword of this voyage. There was a chance that Tareesh would be too dangerous to settle on so fuel would be needed should they have to seek out a different world. Of course no other suitable planet existed within the confines of the solar system; that was what the star drive was for.

Tareesh was considered the best candidate for successful colonization with its climate, atmosphere and ecosystem despite the oppressive gravity as compared to Doorsha. Shuttles and probes would be sent down to the surface to take soil-samples, test the air for inimical gasses and collect microscopic organisms for study. If the results proved less than optimistic, the star drive would be fired up and the ship would make all speed for the nearest planetary system that Doorshan scientists proclaimed likely to support life. The nearest such system was estimated to be 2.45 Doorshan light-years away or in star drive terms a three to four week journey.

The first colony ship to approach Tareesh had no star rive, so could only hope and pray to the Ten Gods that this new world would prove hospitable. Unfortunately, they never had the chance to find out. A meteor struck the ship and destroyed it. Tareesh had cycled around the sun at least twenty-five thousand times since the meteor incident. It was unknown if any of the lifeboats had escaped to the world below, or if any survivors still existed eking out a meager existence without the aid of modern Doorshan technology.

Captain Marthok Darthi was anxiously watching the visiscreen as the image of Tareesh and its lone satellite, Laneesh, grew larger. All but essential personnel had been ordered to board the lifeboats. The lesson of the first colony ship was ever present in his mind and he wanted to be able to evacuate his people in an eye-blink should something go wrong.

Mass sensors, far more efficient than those of the first ship, were set for maximum sensitivity. If anything larger than a pebble came within a thousand *nors* of the hull, alarms would go off and automatic systems would alter course so as to avoid collision.

"We should have gone directly to Malnori," Lieutenant Moorson Karn grumbled.

"Two and a half light-years is a long detour, Karn," Captain Marthok said.

"Four weeks to another star verses five months to a neighboring planet," Moorson argued. "Why couldn't we have used the star drive? We would have been to Tareesh in an eye-blink."

This was an old argument that either participant could have recited by heart but it released tension to have it.

"We could have overshot by millions of miles, maybe all the way to the sun," explained Captain Marthok for the *nth* time. "Star drive isn't accurate to less than sixty million miles, making it good for interstellar travel but insanely dangerous in a planetary system."

"I know, I know," the Lieutenant sighed. "Seems to me they could have perfected it before sending us out with the damn thing."

"Time was running out. We were down to years instead of centuries, or even decades. If we do go to Malnori we will need fuel enough for the interplanetary end of the trip. And if there are no suitable planets there…."

"On to the next target, which is, um, Fenlara."

"And that will be our last stop, no matter what," Marthok finished. "Our fuel will be exhausted as will our food and water."

"Well, since we are coming up on Tareesh now," the Lieutenant observed. "I guess it would be pointless to debate the strategy that brought us here."

Marthok looked about at the crew as they studied various monitors and gages, taking notes and pressing buttons. One man, Sub-lieutenant Hos, was particularly busy at his station.

Marthok walked over to look over the young man's shoulder. What he saw held little meaning for him so he inquired, "Is something wrong, Hos?"

"I am not certain, Captain," said the Sub-lieutenant. "We are approaching the radiation belt that rings Tareesh."

"As expected. Our shielding is more than adequate to protect us from any danger."

"Yes, sir, but I can't be certain if it is not affecting our instrumentation."

"What makes you say that?" Lieutenant Moorson asked.

"According to my readings, Tareesh is undergoing a magnetic inversion."

"Captain!" Ensign Barsuum yelled from the helm control. "The star drive has activated on its own. We are entering otherspace!"

"Shut it down," the Captain ordered. "Now!"

Barsuum rapidly typed out commands on his console. "The controls won't respond, sir."

"Can we still launch the lifeboats?" Lieutenant Moorson asked.

"Too late for that," Captain Marthok said. "Once the star drive initiated, anything leaving the ship would become lost in otherspace.

Without a star drive to control re-entry to space normal the life boats would be trapped forever." He had been drilled mercilessly on all aspects of the Star Drive almost to the exclusion of everything else. "Tareesh's magnetic field inversion must have buggered the engine controls."

"We are now in otherspace and at speed, sir."

"What is our heading?"

"Unknown, sir," the ensign replied. "Navigation is um, malfunctioning, too."

"Damn," the Captain said under his breath. "Karn, order the people out of the life boats before some idiot panics and gets himself lost in otherspace. Barsuum, get a team on the controls and navigation. I want them operational ten minutes ago."

It took considerably longer than the negative time requested to get the ship back under control. Navigation was restored twelve hours into otherspace, but the star drive controls defied all efforts at repair. It was a nervous three weeks before the controls were repaired and the ship was able to enter normal space.

"Where in the seven hells of Darshlon are we?" Marthok demanded as he looked at the visiscreen. The screen displayed constellations completely unfamiliar to the captain and crew.

"Well, we can't even estimate how far we are from the jump point, and we don't know in which direction," answered Wehls, the astrometrics chief. "Navigation was off-line when we entered otherspace so it failed to record the starting position and direction as it was designed to do. We went a lot further in the time we were traveling than we thought possible."

"How do you figure that?"

"The nearest G0 type sun that we can find with a nine planet system is eighteen light-years away. We are too far out to even be sure that that system was our starting point."

"Can't we make a reasonable estimate based on time in otherspace?" Marthok asked. "Speed is constant there, or that is what I was told."

"Speed is constant there, sir," supplied Wehls. "But time may not be."

"Explain."

"We were in otherspace for five hundred and sixteen hours. Based on that time estimate, we should be 4.3 Doorshan light years from Tareesh. At that distance we should be able to spot a G0 type star. But the nearest one is eighteen light-years away."

"So otherspace travel is faster than we thought?"

"No, sir. All our data tells us that that is impossible, at least at our current level of technology. What is possible is that time works differently in otherspace than in normal space. The three weeks we spent in otherspace may be the equivalent of several months, maybe even years, in normal space."

Years? Marthok mentally filed the information away for later. "Don't we have charts on the computer that would allow us to extrapolate our location?"

"We did, but a lot of the data on the computer was corrupted during the magnetic inversion."

"Are we lost in space?" Marthok looked into the screen again. "I want options. Since Doorsha has a G0 type sun. Put astronomy on locating every G0 sun for fifty light years. Work with the data retrieval team. Even partial data is better than nothing. Maybe between the two teams we can get a fix on where we are. While you're at it, look for any sign of an inhabitable world in our current neighborhood."

"Yes, sir." Wehls rushed off, as Lieutenant Moorson Karn walked over.

"Make it good news or go away," Marthok said.

"I overheard you barking at Wehls. I already located three more G0 type suns."

"Becoming a precog?"

"After six months under your command, I know what to expect. I put astronomy on finding G0 suns as soon as we dropped out of otherspace. K0 type suns, too."

"I should have thought of that one myself. Good thinking, Karn. What are the stats of the suns you found so far?"

"The nearest one, a K0, is three light-years off from our current location, but lacks any promising planets for colonization based on their positions around the star. Too close or too far from the primary to be good candidates. The next one is four point five light years away, and has two possible candidates, though one might be too warm for comfort."

"And the third, Karn?"

"Only one likely planet in an orbit similar to Varna. It is fifteen light years away."

Marthok recalled that Varna was the second world from the sun in the home system.

"A system with two possibilities is better than one, especially when it is closer. Set course and prepare the star drive."

"Astronomy would like a chance to map this region before we change location."

"How long do they need, Lieutenant?"

"About a day."

"They have half that. Move some people around if you have to and speed them up, but we are running on limited resources and I won't waste a second anywhere. And get Science Department working on what the hell happened back on Tareesh. I don't want a repeat of that."

"Yes, sir."

"One more thing; I give commands, I do not 'bark.'"

Astronomy Department took slightly longer than the ordered half-day but Lieutenant Moorson convinced Captain Marthok that the extra time was vital for a safe hyper-jump pointing out that accurate star-charts would reduce the risk of emerging from otherspace inside a sun.

"Also, the two planets are far enough apart that, with care, we might be able to make a jump from one planet to the other within the confines of the planetary system," explained the lieutenant.

"What? How do you figure that?"

"The first planet, the warmer one, is about ninety-million miles from its sun and there are no celestial bodies between the planet and us," Moorson Karn continued. "Buross in Quantum Mechanics Department says we can fine-tune the jump to be accurate to thirty-million miles with a few minor adjustments on the star drive and the sensors."

"How minor?"

"We did them already."

Captain Marthok Darthi debated with himself whether or not to dress down the lieutenant for taking the initiative without consulting him first then decided against it. Initiative was in short supply and should be encouraged, not quashed.

"What about jumping to the other planet?"

"It has an orbit of slightly over a hundred million miles from the sun," Moorson continued. "Its current orbital location puts it at about a hundred and seventy million miles from the first target, and far enough over from the sun that we won't come within twenty million miles of it."

"I thought space normal bodies had no effect on otherspace," Captain Marthok said, remembering his training back on Doorsha.

"We are a little concerned about intense gravitation and magnetic fields after what happened near Tareesh. Intense gravity can affect light, so maybe it could affect otherspace as well."

Marthok nodded. He was glad to be surrounded by officers at least as intelligent as himself. "Speaking of Tareesh, does Science Department have any theories about what happened there?"

"Several, sir, but the most likely one is that every so often, say thirty-thousand Doorshan years, a planet will undergo a magnetic shift of its poles. What was a positive charge will become a negative charge and vice versa. It was our bad timing to close in on Tareesh when it was at the apex of that shift. The odds against it happening again as we approach another planet are about as good as the whole crew suddenly sprouting horns and a tail."

"Good work, Karn," said the captain. "How soon until we are ready to go?"

"Just give the command, sir."

"Activate ship-wide," Marthok ordered the Communications Officer. "All hands prepare for jump to otherspace."

* * * * *

The ship emerged from otherspace a scant five million miles from the target planet, a gray, brown world. Weary, yet hopeful, crewmen turned all telescopes and sensors to the planet's surface.

"It's a desert world, sir," Lieutenant Moorson explained. "Hardly any water worth mentioning. Not even at the poles. Gravity is high, also. Higher than Tareesh."

"Tareesh had about three times the gravity of Doorsha," commented Marthok. "We had to train for years to strengthen our bones and muscles just to survive there. This world is too inimical for us even if it had water. Set course for the second target."

"Might I suggest we do a sensor sweep of the next target before we jump?"

"Can we get any meaningful readings at this distance?"

"Enough to make some educated guesses."

"Do it."

Three hours of telescopic and sensor sweeps showed the planet had to be at least half covered with water and possessing a Doorsha-like gravity well. Plant growth could not be seen through the planet's heavy cloud cover, but sensor data suggested free oxygen in the atmosphere as well as nitrogen and other gasses.

"We will have to get a lot closer for more accurate readings," Lieutenant Moorson said.

"Looks good enough to risk the jump," Marthok replied. "Let's take a closer look. Karn, would you like to do the honors?"

"Yes, sir!" Moorson Karn turned to the Communications Officer and said, "Activate ship-wide. All hands prepare for jump to otherspace."

Re-entry from otherspace left the ship twenty-nine million miles from the planet, which was about three months travel by standard propulsion. The hyper-jump was an eye blink in comparison. Precious fuel was expended to bring the ship closer to the prospective world, during which time the science departments scanned and viewed what could become their new home. The perpetual cloud cover prevented direct examination of the surface, so probes were launched when the ship achieved an outer orbit.

"This is not good," Captain Marthok said without preamble. Telemetry from the probes displayed a storm-wracked landscape devoid of any visible vegetation or animal life. Torrential rains pounded the landmasses on every continent driven by hurricane force winds.

"The planet looks like it is in the early stages of its development," suggested Bradry. The young technician was also an amateur geologist.

"What does that mean?" Moorson Karn asked.

"It means this planet isn't done cooking, yet," the Captain replied.

"I would estimate that this world won't be ready for habitation for another hundred million years," Bradry added. "Give or take twenty million."

"Karn, I want an inventory of supplies and fuel, an analysis on projected power consumption to our next target and a list of non-essential personnel," the Captain ordered in a low voice as he pulled the younger man off to the side.

"Why the personnel li—" started the Lieutenant, then he caught himself and looked a little pale. "Oh. I see, Captain. You think it will come to that?"

"I hope not. Have the probes collect up as much water as they can carry before we retrieve them. We might be able to use it, for its components if not for drinking. Issue out vitamin supplements, too. As of now everybody is on half rations until we make planetfall. If we last that long."

"Will do, sir."

* * * * *

The voyage to the next G0 star was particularly difficult for the captain and crew. On half rations tempers were short and a few fights broke out among the passengers. Two men killed each other in one especially brutal brawl. Marthok ordered their bodies jettisoned immediately. There were no facilities for storing the dead and the Doorshans could not even imagine using the bodies for food.

Another passenger, one of the pardoned criminals, forced himself on one of the women. When he was caught the captain held a brief trial with himself as the judge, jury and executioner. Moorson Karn was given the unenviable task of defending the rapist, but with the victim clearly identifying the man his guilt was assured. Once convicted the man was immediately sentenced to death and jettisoned into otherspace with full ship-wide audio and visual of the proceedings. This was to ensure that everybody knew the penalty for deviant behavior while aboard ship.

The ship exited otherspace after two weeks of travel. As luck would have it they appeared in space normal twenty-eight million miles from the target planet.

"We don't have enough fuel to do a full burn and we're too low on food for a slow approach," reported Lieutenant Moorson.

"We'll have to dump anything we don't need or can afford to spare," Captain Darthi said. "Karn, take a security team and go through everybody's quarters and sift through their belongings. Personal keepsakes, anything over three changes of clothing, cosmetics, non-essential books... all out the airlock. Start with my quarters first and put it on ship-wide. Then start in on the furniture in the mess hall and recreation areas. Rip out cupboards in the mess hall. If there are any empty crates or containers of any kind, dump them."

"Yes, sir. Sir, how many probes will we need when we get to target planet?"

"Hmm...good point. Either it will sustain us or it won't. We don't have fuel or supplies to go anywhere else. Dump all but one probe then gut and jettison one lifeboat."

"Sir?"

"Was I unclear? We can stuff more people into each lifeboat now that they will all have less baggage. I suspect we may be lighter on the body count by the time we get there as well."

"Understood, sir. I'll get right on it now, sir." he raced off to perform what would surely be an unpopular duty.

It was a full day before the Lieutenant reported back with his progress; a day filled with outraged calls from the passengers and crew demanding what in the Seven Hells the captain thought he was doing.

"Mission accomplished, sir," Karn said, as he entered the command center. "I loaded up all the personal belongings onto the lifeboat and aimed it at the planet."

"Why?" Marthok asked.

"People were more inclined to cooperate if there was a chance that they could recover their things later."

"It'll be more likely to burn up in the atmosphere without a pilot to guide it, assuming it even makes it that far."

"It won't. I siphoned the fuel leaving just enough to give it a good sendoff. The lifeboats are useless beyond five hundred thousand miles, anyway. I diplomatically omitted that information," the lieutenant said. "I also ripped out all the non-load bearing partitions and walls and jettisoned them, along with some extra cooking utensils."

There was that initiative again. "What is the estimated effect on our inertia?"

"Less than two percent according to Navigation. We need to either drop a lot more weight, which I don't think we can do, or find another way to up our acceleration."

"I hate to do this, but dump the heavy construction equipment."

"The dozers and lifters? How will we build new homes?"

"With sweat and blood, which is more than we'll have if we don't make it to the planet. Besides, we'll still have hand tools." Captain Marthok Darthi collapsed into a convenient chair and let out a long breath. "Do we have any useful intel on the planet, yet?"

"Yes, sir," Lieutenant Moorson Karn replied. "Gravity and atmosphere are very similar to that of Tareesh. Vegetation is sparse, but present, at least on the side facing us. We'll have more intelligence after the planet revolves a bit. Traces of methane in the atmosphere suggest the likelihood of animal life forms as well. Ambient temperature ranges from subzero at the poles to fifty-five *daartaks* at the equator. There are three major landmasses. The rest, about two-thirds or so, is covered by water or a reasonable equivalent."

"Sounds like our best bet, yet."

"Yes, sir." Karn thought for a moment then spoke up again. "Sir, do you intend to try using the star drive to get us any closer to the planet?"

"Oh, gods, no! The power is all but exhausted on the damn thing and at this range it would be insane to try a jump to the planet. I considered trying to jump off to the side of the target, but we could end up thirty million miles out on the opposite direction." Marthok rose and looked absently at a visiscreen. "The star drive is just so much junk, now."

"Then, if I may make a suggestion, why don't we dump it?"

"Dump it?" The realization hit like a cannonball. "Of course! Damn thing weighs tons and it was designed to be ejected should it become unstable. Karn, make it happen then get a new estimate from Navigation."

"What about the construction equipment then?"

"Dump it anyway. The more weight we take off the better our chances."

"Then we won't need the charging equipment for it, either."

"Right, but pull the power cells just in case we figure out a way to use them for fuel."

* * * * *

"How many were involved?"

"Four men and one woman, sir." Lieutenant Moorson shifted uncomfortably from foot to foot as he gave his report. "It seems the woman had promised certain…favors…to the four men if they would get her more food."

Marthok shook his head in disgust. Five passengers broke into the nursery and started eating the fruits and vegetables that were being carefully nurtured there. The lot of them were caught before too much damage could be done, but now, as captain of the ship, Marthok Darthi would have to make an extreme example of the offenders.

"Stuff them into the airlock put it on ship-wide and space them."

"Sir?"

"Karn, we no longer have the time or resources to be squeamish," he said with some regret. "The food they ate will come out of somebody else's mouth. To make up for it they forfeit food, water and air for the rest of the voyage. Since we don't need the dead weight, out they go. The woman, too. That will leave slightly more for the rest."

"I understand, sir," the Lieutenant said gloomily. "It gets harder every day, doesn't it?"

"What does?"

"Deciding who lives or dies, making decisions that affect the future of our race."

"It does. Someday that task may fall to you. I just hope I am setting a good example for you to follow."

* * * * *

Over the next month, Karn oversaw numerous plans to increase fuel efficiency. The power cells harvested from the construction equipment were jerry-rigged into ships power reducing the drain on the engines for life support. The lieutenant also evacuated several rooms and cut power to them, doubling up the occupants in the remaining chambers and conserving heat. Lighting was lowered all ship-wide, and shut off altogether in rarely used areas, forcing the crew to rely on hand held lights when working in the darkened places.

Rations were cut to a third, causing a lot of grumbling among the passengers and crew but the memory of five people getting jettisoned kept things from getting violent. Karn posted extra guards on the seed stores lest somebody try for another little snack.

The captain and lieutenant held daily, if the term could be applied in space, meetings with the science departments looking for a way to either stretch the fuel or accelerate the ship. During one such meeting, Buross ventured one daring plan.

"We are within two days burn of this planet here," Buross indicated a dot on the chart that depicted the local planetary system.

"It's in the opposite direction of where we plan to go," pointed out Wehls.

"Precisely," nodded the man. "We come in at three-quarter burn at the equator, let the gravity grab us enough to pull us around with its rotation, then kick it into high burn after it pulls us around into the right direction. The slingshot effect should double our speed, shooting us to our target in half the time. We can cut engines and coast the rest of the way. Fuel will only be used for maneuvering and deceleration when we hit planetfall."

"Risky," observed Karn. "If we are off by even a fraction of a degree, we could miss by millions of miles."

"At this point it is likely our best bet," the Captain said. "Buross, work with Barsuum and Wehls and get the calculations as fine-tuned as possible." Marthok turned to Moorson, "Karn, on the nine remaining lifeboats we will evenly distribute the seeds, food, water and personnel. I want even distribution of men and women on each ship. If even one boat makes it we have a shot at keeping the race alive. Everything else gets stuffed into cargo crates and dropped by parasail when the ship gets low enough."

"No telling where it could end up," Karn observed.

"No choice. We pulled all the power cells from the cargo lifts. And keep the weapons in the armory until we are ready to make planetfall. I don't want to risk a mutiny so close to the end of this joyride."

Captain Marthok's caution proved justified. With only two weeks left until planetfall a group of six men tried to break into the armory. Four of them were killed in the battle as was one of the guards. The captain questioned the survivors and found that the men wanted to take a lifeboat and make a dive for the planet with a few women they intended to abduct. Marthok had the two men, along with the five bodies, immediately jettisoned.

"The idiots would have died a long slow death trying to reach a planet well out of range for the lifeboat," muttered Marthok loud enough for Moorson to hear. "We did the gene pool a favor by removing them from it."

"Think we got rid of the last of the malcontents?" Moorson asked, after taking a drink from his cup.

"I don't know whether I should hope so or not," grunted Marthok. His cup was empty but he made no move to get up and refill it. All but one drinking cup for each person on board had been jettisoned. When people were spaced the dishes and flatware were spaced with them. "We need people to make the new colony work but every person we space leaves that much more food, water and air for the rest."

"Well, we could stop spacing them for being criminals and just space them for being the kind of people who commit crimes," the Lieutenant jested. “That would cut down on the surplus personnel real quick.”

“If only we had a machine to help us identify them,” Marthok said with a wry smile. “Something that would show if they were lying or not when we questioned them.”

“Well, in the meanwhile we’ll just have to catch them in the act, sir.” Karn stood up from the table and refilled his cup of *biddaa*. All but two bottles of *garfar* had also been jettisoned long ago. The alcoholic beverage was being saved for a toast after planetfall. “Refill your *biddaa*?”

“No. I’ve used my ration for the day,” Marthok said with some regret.

“Seven more rations just became available, you know,” said Karn wryly.

“I am going to pretend you didn’t just say that.”

* * * * *

“I have some good news and some bad news, sir.”

“Just for variety give us the good news first, Wehls,” Captain Marthok said wearily.

“We will be arriving at the planet two days sooner than we had calculated.”

“Great! How did that happen?” asked Karn.

“The slingshot effect worked better than we had expected boosting our velocity higher than anticipated. Which brings us to the bad news….

“We’re going too fast for the remaining fuel to slow us down before we make planetfall,” Marthok finished. “I half expected something like that to happen.”

“You surprise me, sir.”

“I studied physics at university, Wehls. How do we overcome Davert’s Rule?”

Karn looked over at his captain. “What is Davert’s Rule?”

“‘An object in motion will remain in motion until acted upon by an external agency,’” supplied Buross. “But that isn’t the problem here, begging your pardon, sir. It’s the mass/inertia to thrust ratio. The ship has X amount of mass at Y amount of velocity which has to be countered with Z amount of reverse thrust to make safe planetfall. We don’t have enough

Z to counter the X and Y."

"How much can we cut the Y with our Z?" Moorson asked.

"I would estimate a sixty percent speed reduction if we do a full reverse burn with our remaining fuel, Lieutenant Moorson," Wehls said.

"Can we eject the lifeboats at that speed and still make safe planetfall?" Marthok asked Karn.

Karn was the best pilot on board but this was outside of his usual experience. In fact it was outside of everybody's experience. "It'll be tricky, sir. Hit the atmosphere dead on and friction will vaporize the boat like a meteor. Fly in at too shallow an angle and the boat could skim the atmosphere, like a stone skipping on water, sending it back out into space with a one way ticket. Counting myself, there are only three pilots on board that I think would have even an infinitesimal chance of making it down in one piece."

"We can only put fifteen bodies on a boat, plus supplies. Fifteen if we pack it and still leave the pilot unhindered," Captain Marthok considered aloud. "That makes forty-five people with a halfway decent chance of surviving planetfall. The rest will need a miracle to make it down." Marthok shook his head wearily. It was time to decide who lives and who dies once more. "All right, here's how we are going to do this...."

* * * * *

During the next sleep-cycle, handpicked security teams redistributed the seeds, some plants and food supplies into three of the lifeboats. Weapons and ammunition went into the lifeboat intended for Karn and Marthok. Personnel were assigned to lifeboats based on three criteria: knowledge and skills, physical ability and psychological history. Karn as the best pilot had the lifeboat with the most essential personnel, while Ensign Mikroy, the least qualified pilot, was to ferry the least qualified passengers. Marthok hated having to do that to the ensign; he was fond of her and thought she had promise. But pilots were at a premium and the survival of the race came first.

The pilots had three days to practice the drop on the simulation machine. Captain Marthok Darthi was now glad that he hadn't jettisoned the simulator with other heavy equipment. Lieutenant Moorson supervised the pilots while on duty and practiced on the machine during his off hours. Marthok took on Karn's normal duties so as to insure minimal distraction from the pilot training.

The pilots were also put back on full rations for the remainder of the voyage. Marthok had no interest in trusting the lives of the passengers and crew to pilots who were too weak or addled from malnutrition to operate a lifeboat at peak efficiency. As such, they had to be segregated from the rest of the passengers and crew to prevent a possible riot over their preferential treatment.

The night before the attempt to make planetfall Marthok ordered a banquet in the main hall. All the food that could not be fit into the lifeboats was prepared and served to the entire crew and the passengers. The crowd took it as a celebration but Marthok saw it as the last meal of a condemned man; most of the people present would likely die during planetfall.

Scans and telescopic data of the planet were collected right up to the last hour before the lifeboats were to be loaded and launched. The planet was Tareesh-like in almost every way. There was less vegetation in evidence but the atmosphere, abundant water and animal life appeared—at a distance—to be close enough to Tareesh's eco-system to be very encouraging. Unfortunately, the ship was going too fast to launch the probe so they were denied information on what the chemical balance of the soil might be.

When the ship reached optimal safe distance the lifeboats were launched one at a time at three minute intervals. The first boat came in at too shallow a dive and bounced off the atmosphere as Moorson Karn had predicted could happen. The next two, perhaps taking the misfortune of the first lifeboat into account, tried for a steeper trajectory. At first they seemed to handle the stresses of the descent well enough until the hulls began to glow first red, then white, then seemed to disintegrate before the horrified eyes of the pilots to follow.

The fourth lifeboat launched and came in at a smooth trajectory that was neither too shallow nor too deep, followed by the fifth. Both boats looked to have their descent under complete control until the fourth spun about from turbulence. The pilot fought to regain control only to sheer sideways and collide with the fifth boat, destroying both instantly.

"By the Gods!" Marthok yelled, as he watched through the visiscreen on the command lifeboat. Hitting the communications link he ordered the remaining lifeboats to launch at five minute intervals so as to avoid another collision.

Moorson Karn, in the sealed off pilot's section, received the order and reset his panel. He, too, had observed the disastrous launchings.

"Out! Now!" Marthok yelled at the passengers as he gathered up his pack. "Grab the food, water and seeds. Forget everything else."

Two lifeboats made it to the planet's surface relatively intact. One hit the ocean about five hundred paces from the shore while the other, piloted by Karn, had a rough landing on the land. Marthok was the first out of his seat barking orders before the craft had even come to a full stop.

"Move it, move it! We don't know how much damage this thing took when we landed," the Captain shouted. "It could catch fire at any moment so get going."

Contrary to his own advice Marthok turned and rushed to the cockpit to check on Moorson Karn. He found the lieutenant slumped in his seat with an open wound on his forehead. The Captain checked for a pulse and was pleased to find one, then unstrapped the unconscious man and dragged him out of the lifeboat.

Outside, Marthok could see the other craft as it slowly sank. The passengers were trying to swim for shore, but the long privation of reduced rations had sapped much of their strength. Doorsha was a planet of relatively low gravity, and very little water. The high gravity, while bad enough, was less a problem than the Doorshan's unfamiliarity with swimming. Marthok Darthi could only watch helplessly as more than half of the swimmers foundered and sank below the waves. Only four women and two men made it to the shoreline.

A sudden explosion from behind threw Marthok off his feet. The lifeboat had indeed caught fire and ignited the fuel causing an explosion and destroying the one craft as the other sank out of sight below the waves. Standing and brushing himself off, he first checked Karn, then quickly took a headcount. There were numerous minor injuries caused by the flying shrapnel of the exploding lifeboat and one fatality. Wehls had taken a piece of metal through his chest; he was dead before he hit the ground.

* * * * *

"Well, that's how it breaks down, sir," Barsuum said. Like most of the crew the ensign was trained in two specialties. On ship he was a helmsman, on planet he was an agriculturalist. "The soil is pretty much identical to Doorsha's except for the nitrate levels. That also explains the sparse vegetation, I think."

"Wouldn't the local flora be adapted to the lower nitrate levels?" asked Moorson Karn.

"I would have thought so but it may be that the levels were much higher at one point, then something, maybe a natural disaster of some sort, bled off the nitrates. It is also possible that this was once an overgrown area. The flora may have grown out of control, leached the nitrates from the soil and then died off."

"How does nature keep the balance?" Karn asked.

"Animal waste and decaying corpses, mostly."

"Now that you mention it, I haven't seen so much as a hoof print, assuming whatever indigenous critters there are on this planet even have hooves, since we got here. Yet sensor scans found lots of evidence of animal life," said Marthok. "After two days, not so much as a flyer or a creeper."

"It might be concentrated on the other two landmasses we spotted from space," Buross suggested. "Still, there could be some animal life elsewhere on this continent. If the vegetation were destroyed by, say, a fire, then all the animals would be driven off. This close to the ocean it would be easy to see how a flood could wash away all signs of past growth. Without new vegetation to lure the herbivores back nothing else would come back, either."

"Then we will have to find them as well as edible plants and fresh water." Marthok turned to Karn. "Feel up to walking, yet?"

"Absolutely. Especially if we are looking for the other two lifeboats."

"Good. Everybody, we're moving out."

* * * * *

Several weeks of walking and searching failed to reveal any sign of the other lifeboats. The twenty men and women that had started the trek were reduced to seventeen. One man, crazed from near starvation, attacked Captain Marthok earning him a bullet from Moorson Karn. Another failed to use caution before eating some wild berries. The mild toxicity of the fruit might not have caused more than an upset stomach on a healthy adult but men and women, weakened from months of lean rations, proved far too susceptible to the relatively weak poison.

A woman who had allowed herself to fall back too far from the group fell prey to a man-sized predator. Marthok and Karn expended several rounds of precious ammunition bringing the carnivore down. While a small detail buried the unfortunate victim, Buross and Karn skinned and gutted the beast then spit it over an open flame.

The flesh of the beast was strange to the Doorshan refugees as they were accustomed to artificially created meat grown from yeast like cultures. The vast majority of animal life was long extinct on Doorsha. It was unknown whether their bodies would be able to properly digest and process the alien meat as all the testing equipment was destroyed with the lifeboat. Marthok determined that it would either sustain them or not so there was no point being too careful.

"This is our last stop on our cosmic journey," the Captain pointed out. "If the local flora and fauna can't keep us alive, well, then we'll be dead long before we can plant and harvest any crops from our seeds."

"We should save some of the bones from the beast," Karn suggested.

"For what?"

"Clubs, bone-knives. We could also try to figure out how to tan the hide and harvest the gut."

"Good point. Our clothes and weapons won't last forever, and we don't even have the beginnings of a metal working culture on this world. Karn, you are in charge of resources from now on. Nothing gets used or discarded without your approval."

"Okay, Chief," Moorson said with a salute.

Marthok turned to Karn with a raised eyebrow. "Chief?"

"I figure that we are a tribe, now. As our leader that makes you the chief."

"Humph. 'Chief Marthok Darthi of the Doorsha tribe.' I like it. That makes you sub-chief, then. First in line for the throne."

The group came to a valley that was hemmed in by mountains on three sides. Two small rivers flowed in at one end from opposite directions and merged together to form a larger stream. There were some trees and wild growth covering the valley floor. A few large beasts wandered aimlessly about grazing on the wild grass. No predators were in evidence though some could be hiding in the underbrush.

"How are we set for ammunition," Chief Marthok asked.

"Barsuum and Buross have twenty pistol rounds each and I have thirteen rifle rounds and two grenades," Sub-Chief Karn replied. "You?"

"Eleven rifle, fifteen pistol and three grenades." Marthok looked over the members of the tribe. "We're too weak from the trek and lean rations to try to use the bone clubs you fashioned. I doubt that would work anyways. And we don't have the time to make spears. We'll have to use up some ammunition and bring one of those grazers down."

"Some of those trees might have fruit or nuts. After we get the meat we'll see what else we can scare up."

The animal took three rifle rounds to bring down. The rest, startled by the gunshots, stampeded in all directions. One bull trampled Marthok in its panic. Karn was the first by his side.

"It's…all up to you…now…Chief Moorson," gasped out the dying chief. "The survival…of the race…is in your…very good hands."

"Yes, sir," the new chief said. "Doorsha tribe will continue on."

Marthok nodded then sighed as the breath left his body for the last time.

* * * * *

True to his word, Moorson Karn led the Doorsha tribe and made great strides to insure the survival of the Doorshan race. The valley was cultivated and beasts were domesticated over the years that followed. The hearty Doorshan seeds quickly adapted to the relative warmth and humidity of the new world giving birth to lush growths that rapidly spread over the entire continent.

The tribe suffered great gains and terrible losses. Children born to the tribe initially suffered an appalling mortality rate owning to the high gravity of the planet as compared to Doorsha. Only the strongest of infants made it to adulthood. The offspring of those children proved as hearty as their parents and the mortality rate dropped and the tribe grew.

Eventually the ammunition was used up forcing the tribe to rely on what they could fashion from stone and wood and bone. Lacking paper or the means to make any, the tribe was unable to hand down their history beyond oral traditions. Over the decades, then the centuries, the planet of their birth was forgotten.

Slowly, the population grew and spread out. Language and customs evolved and changed. Lacking any real competition the march of technological advancement was slow. It was many thousands of years before the people re-invented gunpowder and an effective means to use it. Eventually a feudal society developed. Multiple princedoms quarreled and went to war among themselves for power, prestige or property.

It was during the beginning of one such quarrel that the descendants of the first spaceship from Doorsha, now called Mars, found their way to the world of the second ship. The people that had survived and flourished on Tareesh, now known as Terra, had forgotten their Martian heritage even as the people of the second colony had. The Terrans named the planet of the second colony 'Freya' and were amazed at the inexplicable similarities between themselves and the people of this new world. None suspected the common heritage that they shared.

II

"A spacecraft, you say?" repeated Captain Plumber of the survey ship, *City of Mallorysport.*

"Well, it seems a bit small for a spaceship," Lieutenant Voxx replied. "My guess is that it's a lifeboat of some kind."

"What kind of condition is it in?"

"Surprisingly good. I haven't sent a party to check it out yet but scans show a small hull breach on the starboard side. From the size of it I would estimate it could hold about ten to twelve people."

Plumber scratched his jaw as he considered what to do. "Think it might be an old Space Viking relic? They got around quite a bit for about five hundred-odd years two thousand years ago...."

"Hull configuration is all wrong, sir. I request permission to take a party down and investigate."

"Well make it quick," waved the captain dismissively. "We have to get to Yggdrasil and we're falling behind schedule."

Lieutenant Voxx took three men with him in a shuttle down to the asteroid's surface. The Abbott drive smoothly dropped the craft down mere paces from the ancient lifeboat.

"Look at these markings on the hull," said Voxx as he approached the craft. *Over three thousand years in space and we still can't make a comfortable vac-suit,* thought the lieutenant absently as he tried to scratch an itch through the thick space suit. "I saw something like this in an old historical vid."

"I'll take some pictures of it," offered Sergeant Twopersons. "Maybe we can find something in the library to compare it to."

"Good idea, Sergeant."

"I think this is an emergency release," Corporal Romanov called out. "Whatever powered this thing is long depleted."

"Can you pry it open?" the Lieutenant asked.

"Dugan, bring the sonic torch from the shuttle," called out the corporal. Ten minutes later the hatch was off and the four men were in.

"What is this stuff?' the Sergeant asked.

"Books, clothes, something that looks likes perfume bottles," Voxx offered.

"Got a photo album here, sir."

The men gathered around Dugan and carefully turned the brittle pages. The photos depicted a family in various scenes and combinations. Several of the pictures clearly showed a landscape of red sand in the background.

"This look familiar to anybody?" Voxx asked.

"Nope."

"Can't say I've seen it before."

"Kind of looks like Mars."

"Mars?" Voxx looked closer at a picture, then at the writing on a book cover.

"Great Ghu!" he shouted. The feedback from the vac-suit radios made the other three men wince. "These books are written in Martian. Back in the first or second century A.E. a team of scientist found the last remnants of the old Martian people and their books or something."

"People?" Twopersons prompted.

"Well, mummified remains, actually." Voxx held up the book in his gloved hand. "But the writing in the books was exactly like this."

"What is it doing here in the Freyan system?" Private Dugan asked.

"It means they were here!"

"Maybe they still are," Twopersons offered.

"Still here?" Voxx looked blankly at Twopersons.

"The Freyans, Lieutenant."

"It is a possibility, sir," Voxx replied. "All the tests show that the lifeboat and its contents are at least thirty-thousand years old. Likely older, but airless space makes a good preservative."

"Then the Freyans should be well ahead of us technologically," the Captain argued. "If they had hyperdrive fifty thousand years ago they would be so far ahead of us now we would look like apes to them."

"Actually, the presence of the lifeboat suggests that they ran into difficulty."

"How so?"

Normally the captain was not so obtuse, thought Voxx. "The boat was loaded with non-essential personal belongings. That would suggest they were trying to lighten the load on their ship. Fuel conservation."

"Well, if they shot a lifeboat out to save fuel they might have been just passing through...."

"If you were jettisoning stuff to save power, sir, what is the first thing you would do?"

Plumber took a breath and let it out slowly. "Find a hospitable planet to set down on then send out an emergency signal."

"Only their ship might have crashed or they had to abandon it and restart civilization almost from scratch." Voxx could barely contain his excitement. "This is a remarkable find."

"And we can't tell anybody about it," the Captain replied.

"What? Why not?"

"The New Federation is in a fragile state right now," Captain Plumber explained patiently. "The memory of the Empire is still strong on many planets. After centuries of barbarism and interplanetary war we are only now getting back to peaceful coexistence. Interstate war destroyed the Old Federation, while stagnation and ennui brought down the Empire. We are a long way from being one big happy family. Baldur is already making rumblings about seceding from the Federation. They maintain that Mars colonized Terra and that the original Terrans we supplanted were the Neanderthals. If we bring back proof that the Freyans are direct descendants they will argue that they were right and all Nifflheim will break loose."

"They probably *are* right," the confused Lieutenant said. "That would explain how Cro-Magnon man seemed to appear out of nowhere in the fossil record. But how can that cause trouble?"

"They'll secede. First of all they'll claim that the Freyans are the true Martians and make Ghu only knows what kind of crazy demands and proclamations," Plumber said, in a strained voice. "There is a huge movement there to Terraform, or Martioform if you will, Mars to make it habitable again. Next a huge movement or maybe a new religion will sprout up, maybe even a holy war of some kind. That would be the first domino. Thor will be right on their tail and the whole New Federation could fall apart again."

"I see." Voxx broke protocol and collapsed into a seat. Plumber ignored the lapse. "What do we do with the lifeboat then? Destroy it?"

"Nifflheim, no! That kind of knee-jerk reaction always causes more problems than it fixes. By now your party has told every single person on the ship about the lifeboat and its contents. And some of the crew is part Freyan. No, we stick it in the cargo hold and haul it back to Odin. They'll go over it with a fine tooth comb, declare it a fake then shove it into storage somewhere until the day comes when the truth can be safely told."

Voxx considered it. "Will people believe that?"

"History is replete with scientific hoaxes especially where the Martians are concerned," said the captain with a dismissive gesture. "There were those phony Martian cave writings on Terra for example, or the so-called 'Fuzzy Spaceship' on Zarathustra."

"Well, there goes my place in history," Voxx sighed.

"Don't worry; I'll see to it that you will get full credit for the discovery even if not in our lifetimes."

"I appreciate that, sir. You know, I am not a Martianist, but I can't help but think we really are descendants of a Martian colony on Terra. Just like the Freyans."

"Oh, I think we are, too. That would explain why Freyans successfully interbreed with Terrans," Plumber nodded. "And one day everybody will know it."

John Anderson and I have been corresponding about H. Beam Piper for well over 30 years. If it were possible to earn a Ph.D. in Piperology, John would own one!

In this piece on "The Early Terran Federation," he goes into great detail about the origins and beginning of the Federation. I do not always agree with his conclusions, but I always find them thought provoking and illuminating. Unfortunately, Piper didn't live long enough to flesh out his creation, but John has done a great job in helping bring his Terro-Human Future History to life.

THE EARLY HISTORY OF THE TERRAN FEDERATION

John Anderson

1) **Corporate State**

The First Terran Federation is said to be "based on the Corporate State" (*Federation*, pg. xxix), but the only mention of one that I'm aware of is in Space Viking: "Corporate State, First Century Pre-Atomic on Terra. Benny the Moose." (*Space Viking*, pg. 85) "Pre-Atomic" would disqualify the Terran Federation (and even the UN), and in any case I believe this refers to the Italy of Benito Mussolini. The comparison in *Space Viking* is to Eglonsby on Amaterasu, run by "the President of the Council of Syndics" (ibid). The Council is "elected by the Syndicates they represent. There is the Syndicate of Labor, the Syndicate of Manufacturers, the Syndicate of Small Businesses, the..." (ibid) In Italy, Mussolini "created major corporations, embracing trade unions or syndicates... he set up the National Council of Corporations (in effect, his substitute for a Parliament), under his personal chairmanship." (*The Rise and Fall of the Soviet Empire*, pg. 512) "Benny the Moose" would seem to be a 1930s gangster-style version of the fascist dictator's name, similar to (the much later) "Big Moogie Blisko and Zikko the Nose" (*Empire*, pg. 146). For all I know, Mussolini was compared to America's gangsters, like "Big Al" Capone. However, with the advent of interplanetary commerce, the First Terran Federation could possibly be termed a Corporate State (and more so the Second, with its prevalence of Chartered Companies and much more extensive interstellar commerce), though Mercantile State might be a better term.

2) **Confederation**

Since the "abolition of all national states under a single world sovereignty" doesn't take place until sometime around "2050 to 2070" AD (*Empire*, pg. 21-22), the first Terran Federation is apparently only a loose federation (confederation), though a stronger body than the old United Nations. This would seem a logical progression; from the ineffective League of Nations, through a UN subordinate to nation-states, to nation-states under a weak Terran Federation.

The breakup of the UN just before WWIII apparently includes the pullout of the USSR and India (Red China wasn't a member during Piper's lifetime), paralleling the collapse of the League of Nations from the fascist aggressions of the 1930s. "Khalid's death... would hasten the complete dissolution of the United Nations, already weakened by the crisis over the Eastern demands for the demilitarization and internationalization of the United States Lunar Base" (ibid, pg. 30). Without these contentious communist states, which have often stymied common policies and action, the new Terran Federation would be free to become a more closely cooperative organization than the UN.

Since Britain is "the last nation to join the Terran Federation" (ibid, pg. 225), the Southern Hemispheric nations join right away, but they "managed to stay out of the Third and Fourth World Wars." (*Uller Uprising*, pg. 55) That they are able to remain neutral seems to support a confederation; only the Northern nations choose to fight under the Terran Federation aegis, as only some countries fought for the UN in Korea. In contrast, a Terran Federation having a strong central government could presumably force all member nations to support the cause in some fashion, contributing either troops, money, or materiel to the war effort.

The Second Terran Federation has such a government, with a "Parliament," whose executive is "the President of the Federation." (*Four-Day Planet*, pg. 193), both of which govern under the "Federation Constitution" (ibid, pg. 196). This sounds like a combination of the American and British political systems. It could thus originate in the first Terran Federation, since that body is created by the "Politico-Strategic Planning Board" (*Empire*, pg. 48) of the US. If so, its British element would imply that the United Kingdom joins the Terran Federation either during or soon after WWIII. But it will likely be a limited body at first, possibly coordinating such common matters as defense.

It might then resemble at first the government of the Confederate States of America, which had a president, but whose constitution contained special clauses on states' rights. The original Terran Federation charter may therefore contain provisions guaranteeing certain "national rights." However, the combination of President and Parliament in the Second Terran Federation could in fact come from the political systems of the Southern Hemisphere. South America has US-style Presidents, while South Africa, Australia, and New Zealand are former British colonies with Parliaments.

WWIII SURVIVORS

1. CLUES

There are several other mentions by Piper of a Fourth World War. He also gives a few references to "the Atomic Wars" (*Federation*, pg. 211 for example); the plural seems to indicate this includes WWIII and WWIV at least, and possibly even the Mars-Venus Revolt. Since there is a WWIV, it behooves us to try to ascertain the survivors of WWIII, in order to project the later conflict's participants. "The enemy" in WWIII is "utterly overwhelmed under the rain of missiles from across space" (*Empire*, pg. 56).1 take this to mean "the obliteration of [its] civilization" (*Worlds of H. Beam Piper*, pg. 174), and only "leaving hundreds, where millions had been before" (I read this in Piper somewhere, but can't find the reference now). However, it is unclear whether only the Soviet Union is meant, or if its Axis partners—China and India—are also annihilated. The "United States would suffer grievously" (*Empire*, pg. 56), but survives, as apparently does Britain, "the last nation to join" the Terran Federation, and possibly also the Caliphate. Tallal, the son of Khalid, "would return, and eventually take his father's place, in time to bring the Caliphate into the Terran Federation" (ibid, pg. 16-17). "Eventually" may imply that after defeating the various revolts the Caliphate is reunified by him. He is also presumably pro-Western, both because he was schooled in England (ibid), and because the East caused his father's fall and his country's chaos. As far as I can tell, the fate of the other major northern nations (France, Japan, Germany, Italy) is nowhere revealed, though if there are Fourth World War alliance systems, then at least one of these also survives.

In this regard, the mention in "Omnilingual" of archaeological digs in Pakistan (Mohenjo-Daro) and Italy (Minturnae), as well as the presence of the Japanese woman Sachiko Koremitsu, may imply these nations' survival. But what is interesting and likely significant is that the names of all the expedition's members indicate a democratic and Northern Hemispheric origin. Most seem Anglo-American—Hubert Penrose, Martha Dane, Gloria Standish, Tony Lattimer—while the rest are Western allies, like Sachiko of Japan and Selim the Turco-German. This implies the survival of Britain (Hubert Penrose at least sounds British); if so, then UK involvement means the Commonwealth joins the TF either during or soon after WWIII. (This might then support the British-style Parliament in the First TF, as surmised above.) The Expedition's roster also implies that the Southern Hemisphere has not yet become the center of Terran civilization, since there is a conspicuous lack, 22 years after WWIII, of Hispanic or Afrikaner members.

Anglo-American dominance would thus seem natural, since the US won the space race by reaching Luna and building the moon-base, and Britain is a close ally and also an advanced nation. Selim von Olmhorst may represent both Middle Eastern and European participation; his lone figure could signify that these areas have not yet recovered fully from WWIII. The Expedition shows a similar lack of Chinese and Hindu members, which implies that either these communist nations were destroyed with the USSR in WWIII, or they survived, but never joined the Terran Federation.

2. **THE NORTHERN HEMISPHERE**

The Northern Hemisphere still seems predominant after WWIII; therefore "the end of civilization in the Northern Hemisphere and the rise of the new civilization in South America and South Africa and

Australia" (*Uller Uprising*, pg. 150) apparently occurs at a later date. This is presumably during and after the debacle in the United States in A. E. 114 (ibid, pg. 169), which seems linked to the hemisphere-wide destruction, and together probably constitute WWIV. The obliteration of an entire hemisphere would likely take a world war to accomplish, and this event occurs only after the development of "the Bethe-cycle bomb, and the sub-neutron bomb, and the omega-ray bomb, and the nega-matter bomb." (ibid, pg. 150) From "The Answer," we know the nega-matter bomb is not developed until "fifteen years" (*Worlds of H. Beam Piper*, pg. 174) after WWIII (which occurs in 1969 in the story; the bomb is therefore tested in 1984). It is thus apparently not used in combat until WWIV, and General Lanningham goes to South America after the American fiasco (*Uller Uprising*, pg. 169). This indicates that there is no place left in the Northern Hemisphere for him to go, implicitly linking the "debacle" in AE 114 with the hemisphere-wide destruction.

Together with the post-WWIII nega-matter bomb, these facts support a WWIV occurring at that date. Though not a THFH story, corroborating evidence can be found in *Lone Star Planet*. New Texas is settled "after the Fourth World—or First Interplanetary—War. Sometime around 2100." (*Four-Day Planet/Lone Star Planet*, pp. 229-230) 2100 AD thus being after WWIV, it is also after 2056 AD, which is AE 114. If WWIV involves competing alliances, which seems likely (and as the previous ones did), then the lack of Chinese and Hindu members in the first Mars Expedition is apparently explained by these two nations not sharing the fate of the USSR in WWIII, and never having joined the Federation. In order for this to be true, the "enemy" which is "utterly overwhelmed" in WWIII would therefore be only America's main enemy of the Cold War, the Soviet Union. This is in fact supported by: "Those who saw, in the towering steam-column above it, a tempting target for enemy—which still meant Soviet—bombers and guided missiles." (*Worlds of H. Beam Piper*, pg. 199, emphasis added) China and India thus probably survive, and remain communist dictatorships, later becoming the opposing side to the democratic Terran Federation in WWIV. Their destruction in 2056 AD would bring to an end the last of the totalitarian regimes; this is supported by "Nobody…is stupid enough, today, to want to be a dictator. That ended by the middle of the Twenty-First Century. Everybody knows what happened to Mussolini, and Hitler, and Stalin, and all their imitators." (*Crisis in 2140*, pg. 13)

3. UNIFIED TERRA

a. Preventing WWV

Thus, Terra is probably not fully united until after WWIV, which occurs in 2056 AD; this is within the range of the "completely unified world" of "2050 to 2070" (*Empire*, pp. 21-22). Before this, it is "incompletely" unified, as the Terran Federation still consists of nation-states, and the major nations of China and India (with probably a few satellite communist states in Asia) do not belong. The "abolition of all national states under a single world sovereignty" (ibid) would seem to occur because the Northern nations destroy about 70% of Terra's land surface in WWIV (including North America, Europe, Asia, and at least the northern two-thirds of Africa); a WWV would probably mean the end of the remaining 30%. Though there is no longer an opposing bloc to the (Southern) Terran Federation, the surviving nations resolve to ensure beyond doubt they never go down the road leading to world war, which happens when there are "Too many thermonuclear weapons and too many competing national sovereignties." (*Lord Kalvan of Otherwhen*, pg. 3) "You either went on to the inevitable catastrophe, or you realized, in time, that nuclear armament and nationalism cannot exist together on the same planet" (*Uller Uprising*, pg. 186-7). The League of Nations, the United Nations, and Terran Federation were all based on the principles of national self-determination and collective security. But nations use force to secure their rights, a fundamental contradiction to collective security. This is not an insurmountable problem, until nuclear weapons are developed.

When nations use nukes to secure their rights, self-determination is no longer an issue; national survival itself comes into question. The South sees the trend of the previous World Wars (WWI: bad for Europe. WWII: bad for Europe and East Asia. WWIII: very bad for Europe, East Asia, possibly South/Southwest Asia, really bad for central North America, and extremely bad for East Europe/North Asia. WWIV: extremely bad for all Europe, all Asia, all North America, and North Africa), and draws the proper conclusion. Complete unification therefore saves (Southern) Terra from a WWV, since "we put an end to that folly in time; we made one nation out of all our people, and swore never to commit such crimes again" (ibid, pg. 64). This would then be the next political progression in the series (see Confederation, above), "from the ineffective League of Nations, through a UN subordinate to nation-states, to nation-states under a weak Terran Federation," to a fully-unified planet under a strong Terran Federation.

b) **Lingua Terra**

Possibly the fear of nuclear war, after the horrific devastation of WWIV, is a new breach in the Terran Federation. With the destruction of the dominant Northern Hemispheric powers, the Southern nations would find themselves in a leaderless Federation. A political struggle for control might begin, especially as to where the new capital should be located (see TF HQ, below). The tension could be between a Spanish-Portuguese bloc (Catholic South America, Romance languages), and an Anglo-Afrikaner alliance (Protestant Australia-New Zealand-South Africa, Germanic languages). Though all these nations are Western—and the Southern Hemisphere has been far less warlike than the Northern—there is a history of conflict between these religious/linguistic groups. But with WWIV still fresh in everyone's minds, they all realize where this will take them if they don't squelch it immediately. One aspect of a unified state is a common language, so Lingua Terra might well be devised specifically to solidify the union of these somewhat disparate peoples. Another aspect would be the refugee problem.

With the destruction of the Northern Hemisphere, there would probably be a multitude of people fleeing South, as does General Lanningham. They would represent a variety of languages and cultures, which might threaten the stability of the Southern nations. A common language could also help alleviate the assimilation process, since everyone—not just the refugees—would be required to learn it. Some Northern survivors, however, would undoubtedly go to the extraterrestrial colonies (see Toward a Unified Solar System, below).

c) **Terran Federation Headquarters**

The TF is formed just before WWIII, and so its seat at first is probably in New York. There is little time to find new facilities, and besides the UN buildings they even appropriate its emblem, a "wreathed globe" on a "light blue" field (*Federation*, pg., 84). But after the nuclear exchange, Terran Federation HQ probably moves to St. Louis, as in "Hunter Patrol." There, "New York was bombed flat. Where the old U.N. buildings were, it's still hot…donated a big tract of land outside St. Louis" (*Worlds of H. Beam Piper*, pg. 85). Being nearer the center of the contiguous states, it would also be more equidistant from Great Britain and Japan, the other major members of the early (Northern-dominated) Terran Federation. It presumably remains here until destroyed in WWIV, making it the Federation capital for 82 years (AE 32 to AE 114). Since Washington is also destroyed in WWIII (see Operation Triple Cross, below), the US government probably moves here as well, making it the American capital, as well as the "World Capital, St. Louis" (ibid, pg. 82). However, this is not strictly true in a global sense, as China and India probably never join the TF. After WWIV, I don't recall any mention by Piper as to where TF HQ is subsequently located, but it might be Montevideo. The University of Montevideo is mentioned as a great—if not the greatest—center of learning in several places; when Conn Maxwell mentions he studied there, "The mate gave him a quick look of surprised respect" (*Federation*, pg. 174). It would make sense for the Terran Federation capital to be situated on the larger and more populous South American landmass, and using the existing capital of smaller Uruguay would show that large nations like Brazil and Argentina will not be allowed to dominate the union. Montevideo is on the Rio de la Plata, a major river estuary in a temperate climate—the largest such site in the Southern Hemisphere—which are also points in its favor.

Though something of a stretch, this could be supported by University of Montevideo alumnus Conn Maxwell, who was aided by "the head of our Modem History Department" in gaining "access to non-public material, some of it still classified...I have locations and maps and plans of every Federation installation built here..." (*Cosmic Computer*, pg. 15). The feeling I get is that these materials are located at the University or not far away. If the former, it might make sense if such documents were not moved too far from their original location, which is presumably at the military headquarters in the Terran Federation capital. Having worked on government projects, I presume part of the "help" the History Department head gives him is in getting a security clearance, which requires a background check. (If he didn't have clearance, the Terran Federation could have accused Conn—not to mention the department head—of espionage. On the other hand, the System States were defeated 40 years previously, so the government no longer has an external threat. If security is now somewhat lax, it may be understandable. Besides, it would take at least a year to do a check on Conn, whose home is 6 months away from Terra. Apparently, Professor Kellton's "letter"—ibid—was enough.) Conn leaves Terra from the "La Plata Spaceport" (ibid, pg. 1), which would thus be near Montevideo, indicating it as an important urban center. The second-largest "temperate river" site (though only so along the coast) is Adelaide near the Murray River, in South Australia. This later seems to become an opposing political pole to the democratic center on Terra, as "Adelaide had a Federation-wide reputation for left-wing neo-Marxist 'liberalism.'" (*Federation*, pg. 131) This could be a remnant of my postulated "new breach," but may actually have its origin in the southern movement of refugees from communist China and India after WWIV. The founding of new headquarters for the premier international organization after WWIII and WWIV seems to be a continuation of previous world wars. The League of Nations took up residence in Geneva after WWI and the UN in New York after WWII.

4) **Toward a Unified Solar System**

Since the Terran Federation "colonies on Mars and Luna" (*Empire*, pg. 22) are founded before WWIV, I assume they are Northern Hemispheric, and indeed mainly Anglo-American in population. Many refugees from the now-destroyed Northern nations may go to the colonies, rather than the Southern Hemisphere. The timeline in Empire has Venus settled in AE 116; it may be part of—and help alleviate—this migration, only two years after WWIV. This could be supported by "one of the Second Century Martian Colonial poets, Eirrarsson, or somebody like that." (*Federation*, pg. 179) His name suggests a northern European or North American origin, and the "colonies inside the Sol System, before the Interstellar Era, that hadn't turned out any better than Poictesme" (ibid) could include some on Mars from this presumed sudden influx of immigrants. Roger Barron comes from Venus (ibid, pg. 209), also suggesting a Northern origin for that planetary colony.

Luna, Mars, and Venus might be in effect the last bastion of Northern Hemispheric culture, including its competitive—not to say warlike—nature. This could be one factor in the Mars-Venus Revolt (only S0 years after WWIV); the "exiled" descendants of the once-dominant North resent the growing power and influence of the now-unified South. Luna may in fact be sympathetic to the revolt of its 'cousins', but is close enough to Terra to prevent its secession.

But with the defeat of the revolt (as I presume it is, since I believe it to be based on the failed Latin League Revolt against Rome), the last elements of aggressive Northern nationalism are also defeated. Before the revolt, Mars and Venus are "colonies," while afterward they become "Member Republics" of the Terran Federation, so a colonial victory may seem implied. But Federation success seems to be supported by Piper as quoted by John Carr: "the new Terran Federation imposes System-wide pax" in the 2nd Century AE. It doesn't seem likely for a defeated Terra to be able to "impose" anything, therefore it is probably victorious. The System States War might support this. "The Federation... fought it because if the System States had won, half of them would be at war among themselves now." (*Federation*, pg. 197) To my knowledge, there is no mention of Mars and Venus subsequently fighting each other, or Terra, again. On the contrary, the Second Terran Federation seems to become a truly universal state at last, strong yet benign, and ruled from a now-dominant Terra, a condition which lasts for many centuries. Terran pre-eminence seems supported by "the good men all left to colonize, and the stuffed shirts and yes-men and herd-followers and safety-firsters stayed on Terra and tried to govern the Galaxy." (*Space Viking*, pg. 9) Though through a revolt, the colonies showed they have matured politically, enough to warrant (theoretically) equal status in the Federation. In my view, the organizing of the Second Terran Federation in AE 183 parallels Rome's reorganization of the Latin League after its defeat of same, in which the dominance of Rome was recognized. (Though now I am far outside the scope of this paper. Back to WWIII.)

WWIII Strategic Nuclear Exchange

1) Goals and Strikes

It is implied in "The Edge of the Knife" that when (and we are now certain of this being) the Soviets enter the war, they do so by launching a nuclear sneak attack designed to destroy America, the core of the Terran Federation. This would seem to be based on the Clausewitz principle, "Strike for the heart;" taking out your strongest enemy will win you the war. To do otherwise would throw "away the advantage of surprise and priority of attack" (*Worlds of H. Beam Piper*, pg. 174), and "Delivered without warning, it should have succeeded" (*Empire*, pg. 56). Therefore the Russians expect victory from a sudden strike. Their motivation seems to be fear of the moon-base.

The USSR lost the moon race, and once completed, "the Lunar fortress... would ensure world supremacy" (*Worlds of H. Beam Piper*, pg. 30) for America. The idea of a race to annex the Moon and its importance as a missile base seems to come from the 1950 movie *Destination Moon* (although it was perhaps a common idea then). In the film, the nation that can claim the Moon and set up a missile-launching site will control the world. Since they do attack, the Soviets apparently don't know the base is "completed and ready" (*Empire*, pg. 56). And since their strike was "aimed primarily at the rocketports from which it was supplied" (ibid), their war plan's nuclear goal is seemingly threefold, or in Russian, a "troika:"

1. Severance of the link between the US and the moon-base, preventing its completion.
2. Crippling or destruction of America. But since they are apparently the only other nation with a space program, the defeat of America will enable the Soviets to:
3. Conquer the now cut-off moon-base and annex Luna, giving world supremacy to the USSR.

The USSR couldn't beat America to the moon, so they'll take it from her. Their method is a classic case of "divide and conquer" (another Clausewitz axiom?), and Soviet completion of the base will allow Peter the Great's supposed death-bed wish—for his heirs to conquer the world—to finally come true. Lyndon Johnson's worst fear—"I, for one, don't want to go to bed by the light of a Communist moon." (*The Right Stuff*, pp. 400-401)—would thus become a reality if Luna turns Red. To insure success, the Soviets would probably want to "git th'ar fustest, and fire the most shots and score the most hits with them" (*Lord Kalvan of Otherwhen*, pg. 102). They would therefore concentrate the nukes to maximize their strike.

This implies that the US and USSR are the main—if not the only—nations involved in the strategic nuclear exchange, possibly supported by "until the moon-rockets began to fall [on the USSR], the United States would suffer grievously" (ibid, emphasis added). This makes sense, as at this time, only these two nations had large quantities of nuclear weapons. (Tactical nukes are another matter; they will probably be used freely in ground combat, which would include areas like central Europe, between NATO and Warsaw Pact forces; and Korea, between the US and China/USSR).

Though no expert, I presume this would include atomic bombs, nuclear artillery, and short-range missiles. According to *The War Atlas* (map 9), the first nuclear test of the UK was in 1952, France in 1960, and China in 1964. Thus, all three had at least a few nukes in Piper's time;

if they are involved in the exchange as well, they will presumably suffer far less damage than the main two combatants. This would then support their surviving the war. India probably does not have them, as Piper calls their invasion of Bangladesh an "attempt" (*Empire*, pg. 55).

This implies the invasion fails, while with nuclear weapons we can assume it would have succeeded (at least initially). It is therefore interesting that India conducted its first nuclear test in 1974 (*The War Atlas*, map 9 again), the very year of Piper's WWIII. I assume it takes some time between testing and weapons deployment, making Piper's presumed projection of a non-nuclear India in WWIII a true one, and supporting Indian survival of the war as well.

2) **Operation Triple Cross**

America's primary rocketports are probably knocked out in the initial strike, but this part of the Soviet plan is effectively thwarted, as "every rocketport had its secret duplicate and triplicate." (*Empire*, pg. 56) These sites of Operation Triple Cross are thus unscathed, preventing the moon-base from being cut off from the US, but probably also provide America with a second-strike capability. The "United-States would suffer grievously" quote seems to imply that the US takes it on the chin, unable to retaliate, until rescued by Luna. But since the base is "completed and ready," it is hard to see how Operation Triple Cross "saved the country" (*Empire*, pg. 47) if the only purpose of the secret rocketports is to keep the supply lines to Luna open.

Also, since the moon-base contains nuclear missiles, the rocketports must have them—or at least the parts to make them—as well. And third, it would be against common sense for America to put all its nuclear eggs in one basket, especially when that basket is so far away, however secure that might make it.

Assuming this is correct, then the rest of the Soviet first strike hits America's other military installations and major cities (including ports) hard. These probably include "New York and Washington and Detroit and Mobile and San Francisco" (*Worlds of H. Beam Piper*, pg. 173). Nuking the ports as well as industrial cities such as Detroit would prevent the

US from re-supplying its overseas forces or reinforcing its allies, a crucial lesson the Soviets would have learned from WWII. Separating America from its allies would also come under the "divide and conquer" strategy, and might necessitate revising the second step of the Soviet nuclear plan of "Separating America from its overseas allies, and crippling its industry and government." Nuking Washington in a surprise attack might "decapitate" the American leadership, paralyzing any possible retaliation. Since only the President can authorize the use of nuclear weapons, his death, plus the loss of Congress, the Pentagon, and the Supreme Court could leave no obvious successor to take command. The US response might therefore be delayed, which would explain the "taking it on the chin" feeling. This is therefore the critical moment—a "crossroad of destiny;" what happens next will determine the fate of the US, the Terran Federation, and future of the world. Any lower-ranking US military or political leaders surviving the strike would probably scramble to recruit the best man in the nation, and give him emergency powers to deal with the crisis; this would probably be a former President or great statesman.

Once authorized, the secondary Operation Triple Cross rocketports return fire, giving the gloating Soviets an unpleasant surprise. A retaliatory strike, it probably hits the known Russian nuclear missile sites and major industrial cities as well. This could be the "First Cross" of the operation.

The USSR has covert missile sites as well, which probably locate, target, and eliminate America's now-revealed secondary Operation Triple Cross sites. But then the secret tertiary ones likely come on line—the "Second Cross"—to keep the attack going. This allows the US to continue giving as good (or bad) as they get, doubtless to the Russians' rage and dismay.

The Ivans may even scrape up enough nukes to destroy these as well, thinking they certainly have won this time, but if any totalitarian telescopes are trained on Luna, they will have dire news for any surviving Commissars. A missile-armada is seen lifting away from the unexpectedly "armed, and fully operational" base on Luna, targeted on what remains of the Motherland. In disbelief the Soviets stare doom unstoppable in the face; the utter ruin of their grandiose plans for world conquest and of the Revolution itself becomes apparent. Panic may set in at last; most who know probably attempt to flee, but if any nukes remain a few could resolve to go down fighting, for what few hours remain until the moon-rockets arrive. The Sword of Damocles, America's "Third Cross" falls; the USSR is FUBAR.

This scenario seems to make sense in that it allows the US to retaliate (almost) immediately, rather than having to take it for many hours until the moon-rockets arrive, as well as providing America with "Regular defense in depth; we couldn't have done nearly as well ourselves." (*Lord Kalvan of Otherwhen*, pg. 93) This could be supported by Poictesme, where defense in depth is also seen. During the System States War, "most of the important installations were built in duplicate, even triplicate, as a precaution against space attack." (*Cosmic Computer*, pg. 15) It would also support the survival of China and India, as the US would presumably not "waste" any strategic nukes on them while being hammered by the Soviets. All its efforts would go toward defeating the USSR; by the time that's accomplished, America may have exhausted its nuclear arsenal. It would then take some time to build more (and resupply the moon-base), since at least most of its industrial cities and rocketports have been destroyed.

Another aspect to take into account is when Piper set up this scenario. The DEW (Distant Early Warning) Line and Mid-Canada Line of radar stations were built to prevent a surprise attack over the Pole. But, the development of ballistic missile submarines renewed the possibility of a sneak attack, so this interpretation of the exchange could still be valid. (However, it could necessitate changing the "First Cross" to a submarine strike, and the third set of rocketports might then not be used, keeping unbroken the link with Luna.)

3) **Moon-Missile Transit Time**

How long do the moon-rockets take? From the *History Channel* recently, ICBMs fly at "17,000 miles per hour." That seems about right, as it is just below "escape velocity, about 17,500 miles per hour. At that speed, instead of arcing over and slamming...back into the atmosphere, it could break the bonds of Earth's gravity and slip into orbit" (*The Race*, pg. 17). Of course, the missiles won't need either level of thrust to escape the Moon's low gravity, but they probably still fly at a higher speed. This would be because America is in dire straits when they are launched; you wouldn't want your *cavalry* to tarry on the way to the rescue. Luna being about 240,000 miles away, the moon-rockets would then take approximately 13.7 hours to reach their targets at *escape velocity*, and 14.1 for normal ICBM speed. Perhaps even less time would be required, as the incoming missiles could pick up acceleration from Earth's gravity.

Assuming a direct trajectory to the USSR, they are thus launched when the Eastern Hemisphere is roughly facing away from Luna; the Soviets might not see the liftoff, nor their flight for the first few hours. Granting the higher (gravity–assisted) speed might make the flight-time closer to 12 hours, but the missiles could fly even faster if equipped with multiple stages. According to the movie *Apollo 13*, the upper-stage had to accelerate to 24,500 mph for Trans-Lunar Insertion. Using this speed would cut incoming flight-time to 9.8 hours. The rockets would be built to withstand the heat of reentry, and in fact may be armored in collapsium, as the Kilroy presumably was. In "The Mercenaries," Kato Sugihara says "I think that I have the key to the problem of collapsing matter to plate the hull of the spaceship." (*Worlds of H. Beam Piper*, pg. 36-7) The need for this may be due to "the problem of what goes on in the *hot layer* surrounding the Earth" (ibid). Presumably this means radiation belts beyond the atmosphere, which I believe have since been proven to be nowhere near as dangerous as was feared early on. But it may also be to protect spaceships from being *hulled* by meteors, which would kill the astronauts. Though they contain no crew, it would not seem illogical for the moon-missiles to be similarly protected, if only for the high-speed atmospheric reentry. The Soviets apparently do not launch any nukes at the moon-base, presumably because, as stated above, 1) they do not know it has been completed, and 2) they want it intact, in order to dominate Terra.

4. **Red Refugees**

Though they might not see the launch and early flight of the moon-missiles, the Soviets could be informed by spies, or if Piper projected their having surveillance satellites. Since it is such a threat, one would think the Russians would keep as close an eye as possible on American moon-base activity. If so, an "early warning" of the launch (or, for that matter, when the Operation Triple Cross rocketports begin retaliating) could give the surviving Soviet leadership time to save what they can, including their lives; but more importantly, scientific and military data, equipment, and personnel. The logical places to flee from Siberia and the Russian Far East would be nearby China, the next strongest communist state, and from Soviet Central Asia to western China or India. European Russia is likely to be much harder hit than the Asiatic region, since it is smaller, far more populous and industrial, with greater amounts of military sites. Any survivors from this area would probably go West or South.

This could be where one of Paula Quinton's ancestors came from, as she says, "I'm also part Spanish, part Russian, part Italian, part English... the usual modem Argentine mixture." (*Uller Uprising*, pg. 55) If it includes weapons experts and rocket scientists, this "exodus of expertise" could help explain how China and India later become such a threat to the Terran Federation, even as the USSR did to the US after capturing German scientists and equipment at the end of WWII.

A Soviet *jump start* of their industry and technology would allow China and India to catch up fairly quickly with the Terran Federation. Since WWIV involves the end of civilization in the Northern Hemisphere, this "Sino-Hindic Axis" apparently becomes far more formidable than the USSR ever was alone. As their goal is the moon-base, I would also postulate that the Soviets have prepared a "Lunar Expeditionary Force" at one of their secret missile sites, ready to occupy the moon once America is defeated.

It is probably destroyed by Operation Triple Cross, though elements might survive to flee the country, perhaps becoming the nuclei of later Chinese and Indian space forces (one can almost imagine the Chinese saying "Our Russians are better than their Russians," even as "our Germans" were allegedly better than the Soviet ones). This would make sense, because the Fourth World War is also called the "First Interplanetary War." In addition to Terra, therefore, WWIV will see Lunar combat at least, and perhaps some fighting on Mars and Venus as well.

H. Beam Piper, from the very start of his career, tended to reuse good ideas, events, social themes and technologies (such as contragravity, collapsed matter and hyperspace travel) that he either created, or borrowed from other authors—after putting on his own unique spin. Not surprising, a number of his early short stories have elements, such as social events, governments, wars and cataclysms that are similar to those he used later when his stories (other than the Paratime yarns) were set in his future history.

David Johnson, one of the premier Piper scholars and popularizers, has taken it upon himself to modify several of Piper's early works that "almost" fall within the purviews of his future history and set them firmly in the Terro-Human Future History. It was his efforts that convinced me to put together new collections of Piper short stories along with those of his ardent admirers.

Here, David has taken Piper's "The Mercenary" and recast it into Piper's Terro-Human Future History.

THE CONDOTTIERI

H. Beam Piper with David Johnson

22 A.E.

Duncan MacLeod hung up the suit he had taken off, and sealed his shirt, socks and underwear in a laundry envelope bearing his name and identity-number, tossing this into one of the wire baskets provided for the purpose. Then, naked except for the plastic identity disk around his neck, he went over to the desk, turned in his locker key, and passed into the big room beyond.

Four or five young men, probably soldiers on their way to town, were coming through from the other side. Like MacLeod, they wore only the plastic disks they had received in exchange for the metal ones they wore inside the reservation, and they were being searched by attendants who combed through their hair, probed into ears and nostrils, peered into mouths with tiny searchlights, and employed a variety of magnetic and electronic detectors.

To this search MacLeod submitted wearily. He had become quite a connoisseur of security measures in fifteen years' research and development work for a dozen different nations, but the Tonto Basin Research Establishment of the Philadelphia Project exceeded anything he had seen before. There were gray-haired veterans of the old Manhattan Project here, men who had worked with Fermi at Chicago, or with Oppenheimer at Los Alamos, twenty years before, and they swore in amused exasperation when they thought of how the relatively mild regulations of those days had irked them. And yet, the very existence of the Manhattan Project had been kept a secret from all but those engaged in it, and its purpose from most of them. Today, in 1965, there might have been a few wandering tribesmen in Somaliland or the Kirghiz Steppes who had never heard of the Philadelphia Project, or of the Red Triumph Five-Year Plan, but every literate person in the world knew that the great power-blocs were racing desperately to launch the first spaceship to reach the Moon and build the Lunar fortress that would insure world supremacy.

He turned in the nonmagnetic identity disk at the desk on the other side of the search room, receiving the metal one he wore inside the reservation, and with it the key to his inside locker. He put on the clothes he had left behind when he had passed out, and filled his pockets with the miscellany of small articles he had not been allowed to carry off the reservation. He knotted the garish necktie affected by the civilian workers and in particular by members of the MacLeod Research Team to advertise their nonmilitary status, lit his pipe, and walked out into the open gallery beyond.

Karen Hilquist was waiting for him there, reclining in one of the metal chairs. She looked cool in the belted white coveralls, with the white turban bound around her yellow hair, and very beautiful. When he saw her, his heart gave a little bump, like a Geiger responding to an ionizing particle. It always did that, although they had been together for twelve years, and married for ten. Then she saw him and smiled, and he came over, fanning himself with his sun helmet, and dropped into a chair beside her.

"Did you call our center for a jeep?" he asked. When she nodded, he continued: "I thought you would, so I didn't bother."

For a while, they sat silent, looking with bored distaste at the swarm of steel-helmeted Army riflemen and tommy-gunners guarding the transfer platforms and the vehicles gate. A string of trucks had been passed under heavy guard into the clearance compound: they were now unloading supplies onto a platform, at the other side of which other trucks were backed waiting to receive the shipment. A hundred feet of bare concrete and fifty armed soldiers separated these from the men and trucks from the outside, preventing contact.

"And still they can't stop leaks," Karen said softly. "And we get blamed for MacLeod nodded and started to say something, when his attention was drawn by a commotion on the driveway. A big Tucker limousine with an O.D. paint job and the single-starred flag of a brigadier general was approaching, horning impatiently. In the back seat MacLeod could see a heavy-shouldered figure with the face of a bad-tempered great Dane—General Daniel Nayland, the military commander of Tonto Basin. The inside guards jumped to attention and saluted; the barrier shot up as though rocket-propelled, and the car slid through; the barrier slammed down behind it. On the other side, the guards were hurling themselves into a frenzy of saluting.

Karen made a face after the receding car and muttered something in Hindustani. She probably didn't know the literal meaning of what she had called General Nayland, but she understood that it was a term of extreme opprobrium.

Her husband contributed: "His idea of Heaven would be a huge research establishment, where he'd be a five-star general, and Galileo, Newton, Priestley, Dalton, Maxwell, Planck and Einstein would be tech sergeants."

"And Marie Curie and Lise Meitner would be Wac corporals," Karen added. "He really hates all of us, doesn't he?"

"He hates our Team," MacLeod replied. "In the first place, we're a lot of civilians, who aren't subject to his regulations and don't have to salute him. We're working under the United Nations' Free Scientists Convention, not under contract with the United States Government, and as the United States participates in the Convention on a treaty basis, our compact has the force of a treaty obligation. It gives us what amounts to extraterritoriality, like Europeans in China during the Nineteenth Century. So we have our own transport, for which he must furnish petrol, and our own armed guard, and we fly our own flag over Team Center, and that gripes him as much as anything else. That and the fact that we're foreigners. So wouldn't he love to make this espionage rap stick on us!"

"And our compact specifically gives the United States the right to take action against us in case we endanger the national security," Karen added. She stuffed her cigarette into the not-too-recently-emptied receiver beside her chair, her blue eyes troubled. "You know, some of us could get shot over this, if we're not careful. Dunc, does it really have to be one of our own people who—?"

"I don't see how it could be anybody else," MacLeod said. "I don't like the idea any more than you do, but there it is."

"Well, what are we going to do? Is there nobody whom we can trust?"

"Among the technicians and guards, yes. I could think of a score who are absolutely loyal. But among the Team itself—the top researchers—there's nobody I'd take a chance on but Kato Sugihara."

"Can you even be sure of him? I'd hate to think of him as a traitor, but—"

"I have a couple of reasons for eliminating Kato," MacLeod said. "In the first place, outside nucleonic and binding-force physics, there are only three things he's interested in: jitterbugging, hand-painted neckties, and Southern-style cooking. If he went over to the Axis, he wouldn't be able to get any of those. Then, he only spends about half his share of the Team's profits, and turns the rest back into the Team Fund. He has a credit of about a hundred thousand dollars, which he'd lose by leaving us. And then, there's another thing. Kato's father was killed on Guadalcanal, in 1942, when he was only five. After that he was brought up in the teachings of Bushido by his grandfather, an old-time samurai. Bushido is open to some criticism, but nobody can show where double-crossing your own gang is good Bushido. And today, Japan is allied with the United States, and in any case, he wouldn't help the Axis. The Japanese'll forgive Russia for that Mussolini back-stab in 1945 after the Irish start building monuments to Cromwell."

A light-blue jeep, lettered *MacLeod Research Team* in cherry-red, was approaching across the wide concrete apron. MacLeod grinned.

"Here it comes. Fasten your safety belt when you get in; that's Ahmed driving."

Karen looked at her watch. "And it's almost time for dinner. You know, I dread the thought of sitting at the table with the others, and wondering which of them is betraying us."

"Only nine of us, instead of thirteen, and still one is a Judas," MacLeod said. "I suppose there's always a place for Judas, at any table."

The MacLeod Team dined together, apart from their assistants and technicians and students. This was no snobbish attempt at class-distinction: matters of Team policy were often discussed at the big round table, and the more confidential details of their work. People who have only their knowledge and their ideas to sell are wary about bandying either loosely, and the six men and three women who faced each other across the twelve-foot diameter of the teakwood table had no other stock-in-trade.

They were nine people of nine different nationalities, or they were nine people of the common extra-nationality of science. That Duncan MacLeod, their leader, had grown up in the Transvaal and his wife had been born in the Swedish university town of Upsala was typical not only of their own group but of the hundreds of independent research-teams that had sprung up after the Second World War. The scientist-adventurer may have been born of the relentless struggle for scientific armament supremacy among nations and the competition for improved techniques among industrial corporations during the late 1950s and early '60s, but he had been begotten when two masses of uranium came together at the top of a steel tower in New Mexico in 1945. And, because scientific research is pre-eminently a matter of pooling brains and efforts, the independent scientists had banded together into teams whose leaders acquired power greater than that of any *condottiere* captain of Renaissance Italy.

Duncan MacLeod, sitting outwardly relaxed and merry and secretly watchful and bitterly sad, was such a free-captain of science. One by one, the others had rallied around him, not because he was a greater physicist than they, but because he was a bolder, more clever, less scrupulous adventurer, better able to guide them through the maze of international power-politics and the no less ruthless if less nakedly violent world of Big Industry.

There was his wife, Karen Hilquist, the young metallurgist who, before she was twenty-five, had perfected a new hardening process for SKF and an incredibly tough gun-steel for the Bofors works. In the few minutes since they had returned to Team Center, she had managed to change her coveralls for a skirt and blouse, and do something intriguing with her hair.

And there was Kato Sugihara, looking younger than his twenty-eight years, who had begun to demonstrate the existence of whole orders of structure below the level of nuclear particles.

There was Suzanne Maillard, her gray hair upswept from a face that had never been beautiful but which was alive with something rarer than mere beauty: she possessed, at the brink of fifty, a charm and smartness that many women half her age might have envied, and she knew more about cosmic rays than any other person living.

And Adam Lowiewski, his black mustache contrasting so oddly with his silver hair, frantically scribbling equations on his doodling-pad, as though his racing fingers could never keep pace with his brain, and explaining them, with obvious condescension, to the boyish-looking Japanese beside him. He was one of the greatest of living mathematicians by anybody's reckoning—*the* greatest, by his own.

And Sir Neville Lawton, the electronics expert, with thinning red-gray hair and meticulously-clipped mustache, who always gave the impression of being in evening clothes, even when, as now, he was dressed in faded khaki.

And Heym ben-Hillel, the Israeli quantum and wave-mechanics man, his heaping dinner plate an affront to the Laws of Moses, his white hair a fluffy, tangled chaos, laughing at an impassively-delivered joke the English knight had made.

And Rudolf von Heldenfeld, with a thin-lipped killer's mouth and a frozen face that never betrayed its owner's thoughts—he was the specialist in magnetic currents and electromagnetic fields.

And Farida Khouroglu, the Turkish girl whom MacLeod and Karen had found begging in the streets of Istanbul, ten years ago, and who had grown up following the fortunes of the MacLeod Team on every continent and in a score of nations. It was doubtful if she had ever had a day's formal schooling in her life, but now she was secretary of the Team, with a grasp of physics that would have shamed many a professor. She had grown up a beauty, too, with the large dark eyes and jet-black hair and paper-white skin of her race. She and Kato Sugihara were very much in love.

A good team; the best physics-research team in a power-mad, knowledge-hungry world. MacLeod thought, toying with the stem of his wineglass, of some of their triumphs: The West Australia Atomic Power Plant. The Ibero-American Confederation's Segovia Plutonium Works, which had got them all titled as Grandees of the restored Spanish Monarchy. The sea-water chemical extraction plant in Basra. The hard-won victory over a seemingly insoluble problem in the Belgian Congo uranium mines— He thought, too, of the dangers they had faced together, in a world where soldiers must use the weapons of science and scientists must learn the arts of violence. Of the treachery of the Indian Communists, for whom they had once worked; of the intrigues and plots which had surrounded them in Spain; of the many attempted kidnappings and assassinations; of the time in Calcutta when they had fought with pistols and tommy guns and snatched-up clubs and flasks of acid to defend their laboratories.

A good team—before the rot of treason had touched it. He could almost smell the putrid stench of it, and yet, as he glanced from face to face, he could not guess the traitor. And he had so little time—

Kato Sugihara's voice rose to dominate the murmur of conversation around the table.

"I think I am getting somewhere on my photon-neutrino-electron interchange-cycle," he announced. "And I think it can be correlated to the collapsed-matter research."

"So?" von Heldenfeld looked up in interest. "And not with the problem of what goes on in the 'hot layer' surrounding the Earth?"

"No, Suzanne talked me out of that idea," the Japanese replied. "That's just a secondary effect of the effect of cosmic rays and solar radiations on the order of particles existing at that level. But I think that I have the key to the problem of collapsing matter to plate the hull of the spaceship."

"That's interesting," Sir Neville Lawton commented. "How so?"

"Well, you know what happens when a photon comes in contact with the atomic structure of matter," Kato said. "There may be an elastic collision, in which the photon merely bounces off. Macroscopically, that's the effect we call reflection of light. Or there may be an inelastic collision, when the photon hits an atom and knocks out an electron—the old photoelectric effect. Or, the photon may be retained for a while and emitted again relatively unchanged—the effect observed in luminous paint. Or, the photon may penetrate, undergo a change to a neutrino, and either remain in the nucleus of the atom or pass through it, depending upon a number of factors. All this, of course, is old stuff; even the photon-neutrino interchange has been known since the mid-'50s, when the Gamow neutrino-counter was developed. But now we come to what you have been so good as to christen the Sugihara Effect—the neutrino picking up a negative charge and, in effect, turning into an electron, and then losing its charge, turning back into a neutrino, and then, as in the case of metal heated to incandescence, being emitted again as a photon.

"At first, we thought this had no connection with the spaceship insulation problem we are charged to work out, and we agreed to keep this effect a Team secret until we could find out if it had commercial possibilities. But now, I find that it has a direct connection with the collapsed-matter problem. When the electron loses its negative charge and reverts to a neutrino, there is a definite accretion of interatomic binding-force, and the molecule, or the crystalline lattice or whatever tends to contract, and when the neutrino becomes a photon, the nucleus of the atom contracts."

Heym ben-Hillel was sitting oblivious to everything but his young colleague's words, a slice of the flesh of the unclean beast impaled on his fork and halfway to his mouth.

"Yes! Certainly!" he exclaimed. "That would explain so many things I have wondered about: And of course, there are other forces at work which, in the course of nature, balance that effect—"

"But can the process be controlled?" Suzanne Maillard wanted to know. "Can you convert electrons to neutrinos and then to photons in sufficient numbers, and eliminate other effects that would cause compensating atomic and molecular expansion?"

Kato grinned, like a tomcat contemplating the bones of a fish he has just eaten.

"Yes, I can. I have." He turned to MacLeod. "Remember those bullets I got from you?" he asked.

MacLeod nodded. He handloaded his .38-special, and like all advanced cases of handloading-fever, he was religiously fanatical about uniformity of bullet weights and dimensions. Unlike most handloaders, he had available the instruments to secure such uniformity.

"Those bullets are as nearly alike as different objects can be," Kato said. "They weigh 158 grains, and that means one-five-eight-point-zero-zero-zero-practically-nothing. The diameter is .35903 inches. All right; I've been subjecting those bullets to different radiation-bombardments, and the best results have given me a bullet with a diameter of .35892 inches, and the weight is unchanged. In other words, there's been no loss of mass, but the mass had contracted. And that's only been the first test."

"Well, write up everything you have on it, and we'll lay out further experimental work," MacLeod said. He glanced around the table. "So far, we can't be entirely sure. The shrinkage may be all in the crystalline lattice: the atomic structure may be unchanged. What we need is matter that is really collapsed."

"I'll do that," Kato said. "Farida, I'll have all my data available for you before noon tomorrow: you can make up copies for all Team members."

"Make mine on microfilm, for projection," von Heldenfeld said.

"Mine, too," Sir Neville Lawton added.

"Better make microfilm copies for everybody," Heym ben-Hillel suggested. "They're handier than type-script."

MacLeod rose silently and tiptoed around behind his wife and Rudolf von Heldenfeld, to touch Kato Sugihara on the shoulder.

"Come on outside, Kato," he whispered. "I want to talk to you."

The Japanese nodded and rose, following him outside onto the roof above the laboratories. They walked over to the edge and stopped at the balustrade.

"Kato, when you write up your stuff, I want you to falsify everything you can. Put it in such form that the data will be absolutely worthless, but also in such form that nobody, not even Team members, will know it has been falsified. Can you do that?"

Kato's almond-shaped eyes widened. "Of course I can, Dunc," he replied. "But why—?"

"I hate to say this, but we have a traitor in the Team. One of those people back in the dining room is selling us out to the Eastern Axis. I know it's not Karen, and I know it's not you, and that's as much as I do know, now."

The Japanese sucked in his breath in a sharp hiss. "You wouldn't say that unless you were sure, Dunc," he said.

"No. At about 1000 this morning, Dr. Weissberg, the civilian director, called me to his office. I found him very much upset. He told me that General Nayland is accusing us—by which he meant this Team—of furnishing secret information on our subproject to Axis agents. He said that British Intelligence agents at Smolensk had learned that the Red Triumph laboratories there were working along lines of research originated at MacLeod Team Center here. They relayed the information to Central Intelligence, and Central Intelligence passed it on to Army Intelligence, and now Counter Espionage is riding Nayland about it, and he's trying to make us the goat."

"He would love to get some of us shot," Kato said. "And that could happen. They took a long time getting tough about espionage in this country, but when Americans get tough about something, they get tough right. But look here; we handed in our progress-reports to Felix Weissberg, and he passed them on to Nayland. Couldn't the leak be right in Nayland's own HQ?"

"That's what I thought, at first," MacLeod replied. "Just wishful thinking, though. Fact is, I went up to Nayland's HQ and had it out with him; accused him of just that. I think I threw enough of a scare into him to hold him for a couple of days. I wanted to know just what it was the Axis was supposed to have got from us, but he wouldn't tell me. That, of course, was classified-stuff."

"Well?"

"Well then, Karen and I got our digestive tracts emptied and went in to town, where I could use a phone that didn't go through a military switch-board, and I put through a call to the President's son. He owes us a break, after the work we did in Puerto Rico. I told him all I wanted was some information to help clear ourselves, and he told me to wait a half an hour and then call Counter Espionage Office in Washington and talk to General Hammond."

"Ha! If the President's for us, what are we worried about?" Kato asked. "I always knew his son was the power back of the Puerto Rican job and his father was the front-man: I'll bet it's the same with the Government."

"The President's for us as long as our nose is clean. If we let it get dirty, we get it bloodied, too. We have to clean it ourselves," MacLeod told him. "But here's what Hammond gave me: The Axis knows all about our collapsed-matter experiments with zinc, titanium and nickel. They know about our theoretical work on cosmic rays, including Suzanne's work up to about a month ago. They know about that effect Sir Neville and Heym discovered two months ago." He paused. "And they know about the photon-neutrino-electron interchange."

Kato responded to this with a gruesome double-take that gave his face the fleeting appearance of an ancient samurai war mask.

"That wasn't included in any report we ever made," he said. "You're right: the leak comes from inside the Team. It must be Sir Neville, or Suzanne, or Heym ben-Hillel, or Adam Lowiewski, or Rudolf von Heldenfeld, or—No! No, I can't believe it could be Farida!" He looked at MacLeod pleadingly. "You don't think she could have?"

"No, Kato. The Team's her whole life, even more than it is mine. She came with us when she was only twelve, and grew up with us. She doesn't know any other life than this, and wouldn't want any other. It has to be one of the other five."

"Well, there's Suzanne," Kato began. "She had to clear out of France because of political activities, after the collapse of the Fourth Republic and the establishment of the Rightist Directoire in '57. And she worked with Joliot-Curie, and she was at the University of Louvain in the early

'50s, when that place was crawling with Commies."

"And that brings us to Sir Neville," MacLeod added. "He dabbles in spiritualism; he and Suzanne do planchette-seances. A planchette can be manipulated. Maybe Suzanne produced a communication advising Sir Neville to help the Axis."

"Could be. Then, how about Lowiewski? He's a Pole who can't go back to Poland, and Poland's an Axis country." Kato pointed out. "Maybe he'd sell us out for amnesty, though why he'd want to go back there, the way things are now—?"

"His vanity. You know, missionary-school native going back to the village wearing real pants, to show off to the savages. Used to be a standing joke, down where I came from." MacLeod thought for a moment. "And Rudolf: he's always had a poor view of the democratic system of government. He might feel more at home with the Axis. Of course, the Ruskis killed his parents in 1945—"

"So what?" Kato retorted. "The Americans killed my father in 1942, but I'm not making an issue out of it. That was another war; Japan's an Allied country, now. So's Germany—How about Heym, by the way? Remember when the Axis wanted us to come to Russia and do the same work we're doing here?"

"I remember that after we turned them down, somebody tried to kidnap Karen," MacLeod said grimly. "I remember a couple of Russians got rather suddenly dead trying it, too."

"I wasn't thinking of that. I was thinking of our round-table argument when the proposition was considered. Heym was in favor of accepting. Now that, I would say, indicates either Communist sympathies or an over trusting nature," Kato submitted. "And a lot of grade-A traitors have been made out of people with trusting natures."

MacLeod got out his pipe and lit it. For a long time, he stared out across the mountain-ringed vista of sagebrush, dotted at wide intervals with the bulks of research-centers and the red roofs of the villages.

"Kato, I think I know how we're going to find out which one it is," he said. "First of all, you write up your data, and falsify it so that it won't do any damage if it gets into Axis hands. And then—"

The next day started in an atmosphere of suppressed excitement and anxiety, which, beginning with MacLeod and Karen and Kato Sugihara, seemed to communicate itself by contagion to everybody in the MacLeod Team's laboratories. The top researchers and their immediate assistants and students were the first to catch it; they ascribed the tension under which their leader and his wife and the Japanese labored to the recent developments in the collapsed-matter problem. Then, there were about a dozen implicitly-trusted technicians and guards, who had been secretly gathered in MacLeod's office the night before and informed of the crisis that had arisen. Their associates could not miss the fact that they were preoccupied with something unusual.

They were a variegated crew; men who had been added to the Team in every corner of the world. There was Ahmed Abd-el-Rahman, the Arab jeep-driver who had joined them in Basra. There was the wiry little Greek whom everybody called Alex Unpronounceable. There was an Italian, and two Chinese, and a cashiered French Air Force officer, and a Malay, and the son of an English earl who insisted that his name was Bertie Wooster. They had sworn themselves to secrecy, had heard MacLeod's story with a polylingual burst of pious or blasphemous exclamations, and then they had scattered, each to the work assigned him.

MacLeod had risen early and submitted to the ordeal of the search to leave the reservation and go to town again, this time for a conference at the shabby back-street cigar store that concealed a Counter Espionage center. He had returned just as Farida Khouroglu was finishing the microfilm copies of Kato's ingeniously-concocted pseudo-data. These copies were distributed at noon, while the Team was lunching, along with carbons of the original type-script.

He was the first to leave the table, going directly to the basement, where Alex Unpronounceable and the man who had got his alias from the works of P.G. Wodehouse were listening in on the telephone calls going in and out through the Team-center switch-board, and making recordings. For two hours, MacLeod remained with them. He heard Suzanne Maillard and some woman who was talking from a number in the Army married-officers' settlement making arrangements about a party. He heard Rudolf von Heldenfeld make a date with some girl. He listened to a violent altercation between the Team chef and somebody at Army Quartermaster's HQ about the quality of a lot of dressed chicken. He listened to a call that came in for Adam Lowiewski, the mathematician.

"This is Joe," the caller said. "I've got to go to town late this afternoon, but I was wondering if you'd have time to meet me at the Recreation House at Oppenheimer Village for a game of chess. I'm calling from there, now."

"Fine; I can make it," Lowiewski's voice replied. "I'm in the middle of a devil's own mathematical problem; maybe a game of chess would clear my head. I have a new queen's-knight gambit I want to try on you, anyhow."

Bertie Wooster looked up sharply. "Now there; that may be what we're—"

The telephone beside MacLeod rang. He scooped it up; named himself into it.

It was Ahmed Abd-el-Rahman. "Look, chief; I tail this guy to Oppenheimer Village," the Arab, who had learned English from American movies, answered. "He goes into the rec-joint. I slide in after him, an' he ain't in sight. I'm lookin' around for him, see, when he comes bargin' outa the Don Ameche box. Then he grabs a table an' a beer. What next?"

"Stay there; keep an eye on him," MacLeod told him. "If I want you, I'll call."

MacLeod hung up and straightened, feeling under his packet for his .38-special.

"That's it, boys," he said. "Lowiewski. Come on."

"Hah!" Alex Unpronounceable had his gun out and was checking the cylinder. He spoke briefly in description of the Polish mathematician's ancestry, physical characteristics, and probable post-mortem destination. Then he put the gun away, and the three men left the basement.

For minutes that seemed like hours, MacLeod and the Greek waited on the main floor, where they could watch both the elevators and the stairway. Bertie Wooster had gone up to alert Kato Sugihara and Karen.

Then the door of one of the elevators opened and Adam Lowiewski emerged, with Kato behind him, apparently lost in a bulky scientific journal he was reading. The Greek moved in from one side, and MacLeod stepped in front of the Pole.

"Hi, Adam," he greeted. "Have you looked into that batch of data yet?"

"Oh, yes. Yes." Lowiewski seemed barely able to keep his impatience within the bounds of politeness. "Of course, it's out of my line, but the mathematics seems sound." He started to move away.

"You're not going anywhere," MacLeod told him. "The chess game is over. The red pawns are taken—the one at Oppenheimer Village, and the one here."

There was a split second in which Lowiewski struggled—almost successfully—to erase the consternation from his face.

"I don't know what you're talking about," he began. His right hand started to slide under his left coat lapel.

MacLeod's Colt was covering him before he could complete the movement. At the same time, Kato Sugihara dropped the paper-bound periodical, revealing the thin-bladed knife he had concealed under it. He stepped forward, pressing the point of the weapon against the Pole's side. With the other hand, he reached across Lowiewski's chest and jerked the pistol from his shoulder-holster. It was one of the elegant little .32 Beretta 1954 Model automatics.

"Into the elevator," MacLeod ordered. An increasing pressure of Kato's knife emphasized the order. "And watch him; don't let him get rid of anything," he added to the Greek.

"If you would explain this outrage—" Lowiewski began. "I assume it is your idea of a joke—"

Without even replying, MacLeod slammed the doors and started the elevator upward, letting it rise six floors to the living quarters. Karen Hilquist and the aristocratic black-sheep who called himself Bertie Wooster were waiting when he opened the door. The Englishman took one of Lowiewski's arms; MacLeod took the other. The rest fell in behind as they hustled the captive down the hall and into the big sound-proofed dining room. They kept Lowiewski standing, well away from any movable object in the room; Alex Unpronounceable took his left arm as MacLeod released it and went to the communicator and punched the all-outlets button.

"Dr. Maillard; Dr. Sir Neville Lawton; Dr. ben-Hillel; Dr. von Heldenfeld; Mlle. Khouroglu," he called. "Dr. MacLeod speaking. Come at once, repeat at once, to the round table—Dr. Maillard; Dr. Sir Neville Lawton—"

Karen said something to the Japanese and went outside. For a while, nobody spoke. Kato came over and lit a cigarette in the bowl of MacLeod's pipe. Then the other Team members entered in a body. Evidently Karen had intercepted them in the hallway and warned them that they would find some unusual situation inside; even so, there was a burst of surprised exclamations when they found Adam Lowiewski under detention.

"Ladies and gentlemen," MacLeod said, "I regret to tell you that I have placed our colleague, Dr. Lowiewski, under arrest. He is suspected of betraying confidential data to agents of the Eastern Axis. Yesterday, I learned that data on all our work here, including Team-secret data on the Sugihara Effect, had got into the hands of the Axis and was being used in research at the Smolensk laboratories. I also learned that General Nayland blames this Team as a whole with double-dealing and selling this data to the Axis. I don't need to go into any lengthy exposition of General Nayland's attitude toward this Team, or toward Free Scientists as a class, or toward the research-compact system. Nor do I need to point out that if he pressed these charges against us, some of us could easily suffer death or imprisonment."

"So he had to have a victim in a hurry, and pulled my name out of the hat," Lowiewski sneered.

"I appreciate the gravity of the situation," Sir Neville Lawton said. "And if the Sugihara Effect was among the data betrayed, I can understand that nobody but one of us could have betrayed it. But why, necessarily, should it be Adam? We all have unlimited access to all records and theoretical data."

"Exactly. But collecting information is the smallest and easiest part of espionage. Almost anybody can collect information. Where the spy really earns his pay is in transmitting of information. Now, think of the almost fantastic security measures in force here, and consider how you would get such information, including masses of mathematical data beyond any human power of memorization, out of this reservation."

"Ha, nobody can take anything out," Suzanne Maillard said. "Not even one's breakfast. Is Adam accused of sorcery, too?"

"The only material things that are allowed to leave this reservation are sealed cases of models and data shipped to the different development plants. And the Sugihara Effect never was reported, and wouldn't go out that way," Heym ben-Hillel objected.

"But the data on the Sugihara Effect reached Smolensk," MacLeod replied. "And don't talk about Darwin and Wallace: it wasn't a coincidence. This stuff was taken out of the Tonto Basin Reservation by the only person who could have done so, in the only way that anything could leave the reservation without search. So I had that person shadowed, and at the same time I had our telephone lines tapped, and eavesdropped on all calls entering or leaving this center. And the person who had to be the spy-courier called Adam Lowiewski, and Lowiewski made an appointment to meet him at the Oppenheimer Village Recreation House to play chess."

"Very suspicious, very suspicious," Lowiewski derided. "I receive a call from a friend at the same time that some anonymous suspect is using the phone. There are only five hundred telephone conversations a minute on this reservation."

"Immediately, Dr. Lowiewski attempted to leave this building," MacLeod went on. "When I intercepted him, he tried to draw a pistol. This one." He exhibited the Beretta. "I am now going to have Dr. Lowiewski searched, in the presence of all of you." He nodded to Alex and the Englishman.

They did their work thoroughly. A pile of Lowiewski's pocket effects was made on the table; as each item was added to it, the Pole made some sarcastic comment.

"And that pack of cigarettes: unopened," he jeered. "I suppose I communicated the data to the manufacturers by telepathy, and they printed it on the cigarette papers in invisible ink."

"Maybe not. Maybe you opened the pack, and then resealed it," Kato suggested. "A heated spatula under the cellophane; like this."

He used the point of his knife to illustrate. The cellophane came unsealed with surprising ease: so did the revenue stamp. He dumped out the contents of the pack: sixteen cigarettes, four cigarette tip-ends, four bits snapped from the other ends—and a small aluminum microfilm capsule.

Lowiewski's face twitched. For an instant, he tried vainly to break loose from the men who held him. Then he slumped into a chair. Heym ben-Hillel gasped in shocked surprise. Suzanne Maillard gave a short, feline-like cry. Sir Neville Lawton looked at the capsule curiously and said: "Well, my sainted Aunt Agatha!"

"That's the capsule I gave him, at noon," Farida Khouroglu exclaimed, picking it up. She opened it and pulled out a roll of colloidex projection film. There was also a bit of cigarette paper in the capsule, upon which a notation had been made in Cyrillic characters.

Rudolf von Heldenfeld could read Russian. "'Data on new development of photon-neutrino-electron interchange. 22 July, '65. Vladmir.' Vladmir, I suppose, is this *schweinhund's* code name," he added.

The film and the paper passed from hand to hand. The other members of the Team sat down; there was a tendency to move away from the chair occupied by Adam Lowiewski. He noticed this and sneered.

"Afraid of contamination from the moral leper?" he asked. "You were glad enough to have me correct your stupid mathematical errors."

Kato Sugihara picked up the capsule, took a final glance at the cigarette pack, and said to MacLeod: "I'll be back as soon as this is done." With that, he left the room, followed by Bertie Wooster and the Greek.

Heym ben-Hillel turned to the others: his eyes had the hurt and puzzled look of a dog that has been kicked for no reason. "But why did he do this?" he asked.

"He just told you," MacLeod replied. "He's the great Adam Lowiewski. Checking math for a physics-research team is beneath his dignity. I suppose the Axis offered him a professorship at Stalin University." He was watching Lowiewski's face keenly. "No," he continued. "It was probably the mathematics chair of the Soviet Academy of Sciences."

"But who was this person who could smuggle microfilm out of the reservation?" Suzanne Maillard wanted to know. "Somebody has invented teleportation, then?"

MacLeod shook his head. "It was General Nayland's chauffeur. It had to be. General Nayland's car is the only thing that gets out of here without being searched. The car itself is serviced at Army vehicles pool; nobody could hide anything in it for a confederate to pick up outside. Nayland is a stuffed shirt of the first stuffing, and a tinpot Hitler to boot, but he is fanatically and incorruptibly patriotic. That leaves the chauffeur. When Nayland's in the car, nobody even sees him; he might as well be a robot steering-device. Old case of Father Brown's Invisible Man. So, since he had to be the courier, all I did was have Ahmed Abd-el-Rahman shadow him, and at the same time tap our phones. When he contacted Lowiewski, I knew Lowiewski was our traitor."

* * * * *

Sir Neville Lawton gave a strangling laugh. "Oh, my dear Aunt Fanny! And Nayland goes positively crackers on security. He gets goose pimples every time he hears somebody saying 'E = mc²', for fear an Axis spy might hear him. It's a wonder he hasn't put the value of Planck's Constant on the classified list. He sets up all these fantastic search rooms and barriers, and then he drives through the gate, honking his bloody horn, with his chauffeur's pockets full of top secrets. Now I've seen everything!"

"Not quite everything," MacLeod said. "Kato's going to put that capsule in another cigarette pack, and he'll send one of his lab girls to Oppenheimer Village with it, with a message from Lowiewski to the effect that he couldn't get away. And when this chauffeur takes it out, he'll run into a Counter Espionage road-block on the way to town. They'll shoot him, of course, and they'll probably transfer Nayland to the Mississippi Valley Flood Control Project, where he can't do any more damage. At least, we'll have him out of our hair."

"If we have any hair left," Heym ben-Hillel gloomed. "You've got Nayland into trouble, but you haven't got us out of it."

"What do you mean?" Suzanne Maillard demanded. "He's found the traitor and stopped the leak."

"Yes, but we're still responsible, as a team, for this betrayal," the Israeli pointed out. "This Nayland is only a symptom of the enmity which politicians and militarists feel toward the Free Scientists, and of their opposition to the research-compact system. Now they have a scandal to use. Our part in stopping the leak will be ignored; the publicity will be about the treason of a Free Scientist."

"That's right," Sir Neville Lawton agreed. "And that brings up another point. We simply can't hand this fellow over to the authorities. If we do, we establish a precedent that may wreck the whole system under which we operate."

"Yes: it would be a fine thing if governments start putting Free Scientists on trial and shooting them," Farida Khouroglu supported him. "In a few years, none of us would be safe."

"But," Suzanne cried, "you are not arguing that this species of an animal be allowed to betray us unpunished?"

"Look," Rudolf von Heldenfeld said. "Let us give him his pistol, and one cartridge, and let him remove himself like a gentleman. He will spare himself the humiliation of trial and execution, and us all the embarrassment of having a fellow scientist pilloried as a traitor."

"Now there's a typical Prussian suggestion," Lowiewski said.

Kato Sugihara, returning alone, looked around the table. "Did I miss something interesting?" he asked.

"Oh, very," Lowiewski told him. "Your Junker friend thinks I should perform *seppuku*."

Kato nodded quickly. "Excellent idea!" he congratulated von Heldenfeld. "If he does, he'll save everybody a lot of trouble. Himself included." He nodded again. "If he does that, we can protect his reputation, after he's dead."

"I don't really see how," Sir Neville objected. "When the Counter Espionage people were brought into this, the thing went out of our control."

"Why, this chauffeur was the spy, as well as the spy-courier," MacLeod said. "The information he transmitted was picked up piecemeal from different indiscreet lab-workers and students attached to our team. Of course, we are investigating, mumble-mumble. Naturally, no one will admit, mumble-mumble. No stone will be left unturned, mumble-mumble. Disciplinary action, mumble-mumble."

"And I suppose he got that microfilm piecemeal, too?" Lowiewski asked.

"Oh, that?" MacLeod shrugged. "That was planted on him. One of our girls arranged an opportunity for him to steal it from her, after we began to suspect him. Of course, Kato falsified everything he put into that report. As information, it's worthless."

"Worthless? It's better than that," Kato grinned. "I'm really sorry the Axis won't get it. They'd try some of that stuff out with the big betatron at Smolensk, and a microsecond after they'd throw the switch, Smolensk would look worse than Hiroshima did."

"Well, why would our esteemed colleague commit suicide, just at this time?" Karen Hilquist asked.

"Maybe plutonium poisoning." Farida suggested. "He was doing something in the radiation-lab and got some Pu in him, and of course, shooting's not as painful as that. So—"

"Oh, my dear!" Suzanne protested. "That but stinks! The great Adam Lowiewski, descending from his pinnacle of pure mathematics, to perform a vulgar experiment? With actual *things*?" The Frenchwoman gave an exaggerated shudder. "Horrors!"

"Besides, if our people began getting radioactive, somebody would be sure to claim we were endangering the safely of the whole establishment, and the national-security clause would be invoked, and some nosy person would put a Geiger on the dear departed," Sir Neville added.

"Nervous collapse." Karen said. "According to the laity, all scientists are crazy. Crazy people kill themselves. Adam Lowiewski was a scientist.

Ergo Adam Lowiewski killed himself. Besides, a nervous collapse isn't instrumentally detectable."

Heym ben-Hillel looked at MacLeod, his eyes troubled.

"But, Dunc; have we the right to put him to death, either by his own hand or by an Army firing squad?" he asked. "Remember he is not only a traitor; he is one of the world's greatest mathematical minds. Have we a right to destroy that mind?"

Von Heldenfeld shouted, banging his fist on the table: "I don't care if he's Gauss and Riemann and Lorenz and Poincare and Minkowski and Whitehead and Einstein, all collapsed into one! The man is a stinking traitor, not only to us, but to all scientists and all sciences! If he doesn't shoot himself, hand him over to the United States, and let them shoot him! Why do we go on arguing?"

Lowiewski was smiling, now. The panic that had seized him in the hallway below, and the desperation when the cigarette pack had been opened, had left him.

"Now I have a modest proposal, which will solve your difficulties," he said. "I have money, papers, clothing, everything I will need, outside the reservation. Suppose you just let me leave here. Then, if there is any trouble, you can use this fiction about the indiscreet underlings, without the unnecessary embellishment of my suicide—"

Rudolf von Heldenfeld let out an inarticulate roar of fury. For an instant he was beyond words. Then he sprang to his feet.

"Look at him!" he cried. "Look at him, laughing in our faces, for the dupes and fools he thinks we are!" He thrust out his hand toward MacLeod. "Give me the pistol! He won't shoot himself; I'll do it for him!"

"It would work, Dunc. Really, it would," Heym ben-Hillel urged.

"No," Karen Hilquist contradicted. "If he left here, everybody would know what had happened, and we'd be accused of protecting him. If he kills himself, we can get things hushed up: dead traitors are good traitors. But if he remains alive, we must disassociate ourselves from him by handing him over."

"And wreck the prestige of the Team?" Lowiewski asked.

"At least you will not live to see that!" Suzanne retorted.

Heym ben-Hillel put his elbows on the table and his head in his hands. "Is there no solution to this?" he almost wailed.

"Certainly: an obvious solution," MacLeod said, rising. "Rudolf has just stated it. Only I'm leader of this Team, and there are, of course, jobs a team-leader simply doesn't delegate." The safety catch of the Beretta clicked a period to his words.

"No!" The word was wrenched almost physically out of Lowiewski. He, too, was on his feet, a sudden desperate fear in his face. "No! You wouldn't murder me!"

"The term is *execute*," MacLeod corrected. Then his arm swung up, and he shot Adam Lowiewski through the forehead.

For an instant, the Pole remained on his feet. Then his knees buckled, and he fell forward against the table, sliding to the floor.

MacLeod went around the table, behind Kato Sugihara and Farida Khouroglu and Heym ben-Hillel, and stood looking down at the man he had killed. He dropped the automatic within a few inches of the dead renegade's outstretched hand, then turned to face the others.

"I regret," he addressed them, his voice and face blank of expression, "to announce that our distinguished colleague, Dr. Adam Lowiewski, has committed suicide by shooting, after a nervous collapse resulting from overwork."

Sir Neville Lawton looked critically at the motionless figure on the floor.

"I'm afraid we'll have trouble making that stick, Dunc," he said. "You shot him at about five yards; there isn't a powder mark on him."

"Oh, sorry; I forgot." MacLeod's voice was mockingly contrite. "It was Dr. Lowiewski's expressed wish that his remains be cremated as soon after death as possible, and that funeral services be held over his ashes. The big electric furnace in the metallurgical lab will do, I think."

"But…but there'll be all sorts of formalities—" the Englishman protested.

"Now you forget. Our compact," MacLeod reminded him. "We

stand upon our extraterritorial immunity: we certainly won't allow any stupid bureaucratic interference with our deceased colleague's wishes. We have a regular M.D. on our payroll, in case anybody has to have a death certificate to keep him happy, but beyond that—" He shrugged.

"It burns me up, though!" Suzanne Maillard cried. "After the spaceship is built, and the Lunar Base is established, there will be publicity, and people will eulogize this species of an Iscariot!"

Heym ben-Hillel, who had been staring at MacLeod in shocked unbelief, roused himself.

"Well, why not? Isn't the creator of the Lowiewski function transformations and the rules of inverse probabilities worthy of eulogy?" He turned to MacLeod. "I couldn't have done what you did, but maybe it was for the best. The traitor is dead; the mathematician will live forever."

"You miss the whole point," MacLeod said. "Both of you. It wasn't a question of revenge, like gangsters bumping off a double-crosser. And it wasn't a question of whitewashing Lowiewski for posterity. We are the MacLeod Research Team. We owe no permanent allegiance to, nor acknowledge the authority of, any national sovereignty or any combination of nations. We deal with national governments as with equals. In consequence, we must make and enforce our own laws.

"You must understand that we enjoy this status only on sufferance. The nations of the world tolerate the Free Scientists only because they need us, and because they know they can trust us. Now, no responsible government official is going to be deceived for a moment by this suicide story we've confected. It will be fully understood that Lowiewski was a traitor, and that we found him out and put him to death. And, as a corollary, it will be understood that this Team, as a Team, is fully trustworthy, and that when any individual Team member is found to be untrustworthy, he will be dealt with promptly and without public scandal. In other words, it will be understood, from this time on, that the MacLeod Team is worthy of the status it enjoys and the responsibilities concomitant with it.

"The Edge of the Knife" is one of H. Beam Piper's more interesting stories, since it combines his interest in history with that of parapsychology. Piper's agent, Kenneth White, first sent this story to John W. Campbell at Astounding Science Fiction *who rejected it on the basis that it was not a psionics story, his them current hobby horse. His agent finally placed it with* Amazing Stories.

The professor in the story is afflicted with precognition, but it's not of any use since his visions arrives unexpectedly and only provides quick glimpses of the future. As Professor Chalmers' puts it: "I have the ability to prehend future events. I can, by concentrating, bring into my mind the history of the world, at least in general outline, for the next five thousand years." *The worst effect of these insights is that they are so real they interfere with his teaching job. To say nothing of his sanity!*

These visions of Professor Chalmers also provide us with some fascinating glimpses into Piper's Terro-Human Future History, since Piper was not with us long enough to write the stories he alluded to in these visions.

THE EDGE OF THE KNIFE

H. Beam Piper

30 A.E.

Chalmers stopped talking abruptly, warned by the sudden attentiveness of the class in front of him. They were all staring; even Guellick, in the fourth row, was almost half awake. Then one of them, taking his silence as an invitation to questions found his voice.

"You say Khalid ib'n Hussein's been assassinated?" he asked incredulously. "When did that happen?"

"In 1973, at Basra." There was a touch of impatience in his voice; surely they ought to know that much. "He was shot, while leaving the Parliament Building, by an Egyptian Arab named Mohammed Noureed, with an old U. S. Army M3 submachine-gun. Noureed killed two of Khalid's guards and wounded another before he was overpowered. He was lynched on the spot by the crowd; stoned to death. Ostensibly, he and his accomplices were religious fanatics; however, there can be no doubt whatever that the murder was inspired, at least indirectly, by the Eastern Axis."

The class stirred like a grain-field in the wind. Some looked at him in blank amazement; some were hastily averting faces red with poorly suppressed laughter. For a moment he was puzzled, and then realization hit him like a blow in the stomach-pit. He'd forgotten, again.

"I didn't see anything in the papers about it," one boy was saying.

"The newscast, last evening, said Khalid was in Ankara, talking to the President of Turkey," another offered.

"Professor Chalmers, would you tell us just what effect Khalid's death had upon the Islamic Caliphate and the Middle Eastern situation in general?" a third voice asked with exaggerated solemnity. That was Kendrick, the class humorist; the question was pure baiting.

"Well, Mr. Kendrick, I'm afraid it's a little too early to assess the full results of a thing like that, if they can ever be fully assessed. For instance, who, in 1911, could have predicted all the consequences of the pistol-shot at Sarajevo? Who, even today, can guess what the history of the world would have been had Zangarra not missed Franklin Roosevelt in 1932? There's always that if."

He went on talking safe generalities as he glanced covertly at his watch. Only five minutes to the end of the period; thank heaven he hadn't made that slip at the beginning of the class. "For instance, tomorrow, when we take up the events in India from the First World War to the end of British rule, we will be largely concerned with another victim of the assassin's bullet, Mohandas K. Gandhi. You may ask yourselves, then, by how much that bullet altered the history of the Indian sub-continent. A word of warning, however: The events we will be discussing will be either contemporary with or prior to what was discussed today. I hope that you're all keeping your notes properly dated. It's always easy to become confused in matters of chronology."

He wished, too late, that he hadn't said that. It pointed up the very thing he was trying to play down, and raised a general laugh.

As soon as the room was empty, he hastened to his desk, snatched pencil and notepad. This had been a bad one, the worst yet; he hadn't heard the end of it by any means. He couldn't waste thought on that now, though. This was all new and important; it had welled up suddenly and without warning into his conscious mind, and he must get it down in notes before the "memory"—even mentally, he always put that word into quotes—was lost. He was still scribbling furiously when the instructor who would use the room for the next period entered, followed by a few of his students. Chalmers finished, crammed the notes into his pocket, and went out into the hall.

Most of his own Modern History IV class had left the building and were on their way across the campus for science classes. A few, however, were joining groups for other classes here in Prescott Hall, and in every group, they were the center of interest. Sometimes, when they saw him, they would fall silent until he had passed; sometimes they didn't, and he caught snatches of conversation.

"Oh, brother! Did Chalmers really blow his jets this time!" one voice was saying.

"Bet he won't be around next year."

Another quartet, with their heads together, were talking more seriously.

"Well, I'm not majoring in History, myself, but I think it's an outrage that some people's diplomas are going to depend on grades given by a lunatic!"

"Mine will, and I'm not going to stand for it. My old man's president of the Alumni Association, and...."

That was something he had not thought of, before. It gave him an ugly start. He was still thinking about it as he turned into the side hall to the History Department offices and entered the cubicle he shared with a colleague. The colleague, old Pottgeiter, Medieval History, was emerging in a rush; short, rotund, gray-bearded, his arms full of books and papers, oblivious, as usual, to anything that had happened since the Battle of Bosworth or the Fall of Constantinople. Chalmers stepped quickly out of his way and entered behind him. Marjorie Fenner, the secretary they also shared, was tidying up the old man's desk.

"Good morning, Doctor Chalmers." She looked at him keenly for a moment. "They give you a bad time again in Modern Four?"

Good Lord, did he show it that plainly? In any case, it was no use trying to kid Marjorie. She'd hear the whole story before the end of the day.

"Gave myself a bad time."

Marjorie, still fussing with Pottgeiter's desk, was about to say something in reply. Instead, she exclaimed in exasperation.

"Ohhh! That man! He's forgotten his notes again!" She gathered some papers from Pottgeiter's desk, rushing across the room and out the door with them.

For a while, he sat motionless, the books and notes for General European History II untouched in front of him. This was going to raise hell. It hadn't been the first slip he'd made, either; that thought kept recurring to him. There had been the time when he had alluded to the colonies on Mars and Venus. There had been the time he'd mentioned the secession of Canada from the British Commonwealth, and the time he'd called the U. N. the Terran Federation. And the time he'd tried to get a copy of Franchard's *Rise and Decline of the System States*, which wouldn't be published until the Twenty-eighth Century, out of the college library. None of those had drawn much comment, beyond a few student jokes about the history professor who lived in the future instead of the past. Now, however, they'd all be remembered, raked up, exaggerated, and added to what had happened this morning.

He sighed and sat down at Marjorie's typewriter and began transcribing his notes. Assassination of Khalid ib'n Hussein, the pro-Western leader of the newly formed Islamic Caliphate; period of anarchy in the Middle East; interfactional power-struggles; Turkish intervention. He wondered how long that would last; Khalid's son, Tallal ib'n Khalid, was at school in England when his father was—would be—killed. He would return, and eventually take his father's place, in time to bring the Caliphate into the Terran Federation when the general war came. There were some notes on that already; the war would result from an attempt by the Indian Communists to seize East Pakistan. The trouble was that he so seldom "remembered" an exact date. His "memory" of the year of Khalid's assassination was an exception.

Nineteen seventy-three—why, that was this year. He looked at the calendar. October 16, 1973. At very most, the Arab statesman had two and a half months to live. Would there be any possible way in which he could give a credible warning? He doubted it. Even if there were, he questioned whether he should—for that matter, whether he *could*—interfere....

He always lunched at the Faculty Club; today was no time to call attention to himself by breaking an established routine. As he entered, trying to avoid either a furtive slink or a chip-on-shoulder swagger, the crowd in the lobby stopped talking abruptly, then began again on an obviously changed subject. The word had gotten around, apparently. Handley, the head of the Latin Department, greeted him with a distantly polite nod. Pompous old owl; regarded himself, for some reason, as a sort of unofficial Dean of the Faculty. Probably didn't want to be seen fraternizing with controversial characters. One of the younger men, with a thin face and a mop of unruly hair, advanced to meet him as he came in, as cordial as Handley was remote.

"Oh, hello, Ed!" he greeted, clapping a hand on Chalmers' shoulder. "I was hoping I'd run into you. Can you have dinner with us this evening?" He was sincere.

"Well, thanks, Leonard. I'd like to, but I have a lot of work. Could you give me a raincheck?"

"Oh, surely. My wife was wishing you'd come around, but I know how it is. Some other evening?"

"Yes, indeed." He guided Fitch toward the dining-room door and nodded toward a table. "This doesn't look too crowded; let's sit here."

After lunch, he stopped in at his office. Marjorie Fenner was there, taking dictation from Pottgeiter; she nodded to him as he entered, but she had no summons to the president's office.

The summons was waiting for him, the next morning, when he entered the office after Modern History IV, a few minutes past ten.

"Doctor Whitburn just phoned," Marjorie said. "He'd like to see you, as soon as you have a vacant period."

"Which means right away. I shan't keep him waiting."

She started to say something, swallowed it, and then asked if he needed anything typed up for General European II.

"No, I have everything ready." He pocketed the pipe he had filled on entering, and went out.

The president of Blanley College sat hunched forward at his desk; he had rounded shoulders and round, pudgy fists and a round, bald head. He seemed to be expecting his visitor to stand at attention in front of him. Chalmers got the pipe out of his pocket, sat down in the desk-side chair, and snapped his lighter.

"Good morning, Doctor Whitburn," he said very pleasantly.

Whitburn's scowl deepened. "I hope I don't have to tell you why I wanted to see you," he began.

"I have an idea." Chalmers puffed until the pipe was drawing satisfactorily. "It might help you get started if you did, though."

"I don't suppose, at that, that you realize the full effect of your performance, yesterday morning, in Modern History Four," Whitburn replied. "I don't suppose you know, for instance, that I had to intervene at the last moment and suppress an editorial in the *Black and Green*, derisively critical of you and your teaching methods, and, by implication, of the administration of this college. You didn't hear about that, did you? No, living as you do in the future, you wouldn't."

"If the students who edit the *Black and Green* are dissatisfied with anything here, I'd imagine they ought to say so," Chalmers commented. "Isn't that what they teach in the journalism classes, that the purpose of journalism is to speak for the dissatisfied? Why make exception?"

"I should think you'd be grateful to me for trying to keep your behavior from being made a subject of public ridicule among your students. Why, this editorial which I suppressed actually went so far as to question your sanity!"

"I should suppose it might have sounded a good deal like that, to them. Of course, I have been preoccupied, lately, with an imaginative projection of present trends into the future. I'll quite freely admit that I should have kept my extracurricular work separate from my class and lecture work, but—"

"That's no excuse, even if I were sure it were true! What you did, while engaged in the serious teaching of history, was to indulge in a farrago of nonsense, obvious as such to any child, and damage not only your own standing with your class but the standing of Blanley College as well. Doctor Chalmers, if this were the first incident of the kind it would be bad enough, but it isn't. You've done things like this before, and I've warned you before. I assumed, then, that you were merely showing the effects of overwork, and I offered you a vacation, which you refused to take. Well, this is the limit. I'm compelled to request your immediate resignation."

Chalmers laughed. "A moment ago, you accused me of living in the future. It seems you're living in the past. Evidently you haven't heard about the Higher Education Faculty Tenure Act of 1963, or such things as tenure-contracts. Well, for your information, I have one; you signed it yourself, in case you've forgotten. If you want my resignation, you'll have to show cause, in a court of law, why my contract should be voided, and I don't think a slip of the tongue is a reason for voiding a contract that any court would accept."

Whitburn's face reddened. "You don't, don't you? Well, maybe it isn't, but insanity is. It's a very good reason for voiding a contract voidable on grounds of unfitness or incapacity to teach."

He had been expecting, and mentally shrinking from, just that. Now that it was out, however, he felt relieved. He gave another short laugh.

"You're willing to go into open court, covered by reporters from papers you can't control as you do this student sheet here, and testify that for the past twelve years you've had an insane professor on your faculty?"

"You're.... You're trying to blackmail me?" Whitburn demanded, half rising.

"It isn't blackmail to tell a man that a bomb he's going to throw will blow up in his hand." Chalmers glanced quickly at his watch. "Now, Doctor Whitburn, if you have nothing further to discuss, I have a class in a few minutes. If you'll excuse me...."

He rose. For a moment, he stood facing Whitburn; when the college president said nothing, he inclined his head politely and turned, going out.

Whitburn's secretary gave the impression of having seated herself hastily at her desk the second before he opened the door. She watched him, round-eyed, as he went out into the hall.

He reached his own office ten minutes before time for the next class. Marjorie was typing something for Pottgeiter; he merely nodded to her, and picked up the phone. The call would have to go through the school exchange, and he had a suspicion that Whitburn kept a check on outside calls. That might not hurt any, he thought, dialing a number.

"Attorney Weill's office," the girl who answered said.

"Edward Chalmers. Is Mr. Weill in?"

She'd find out. He was; he answered in a few seconds.

"Hello, Stanly; Ed Chalmers. I think I'm going to need a little help. I'm having some trouble with President Whitburn, here at the college. A matter involving the validity of my tenure-contract. I don't want to go into it over this line. Have you anything on for lunch?"

"No, I haven't. When and where?" the lawyer asked.

He thought for a moment. Nowhere too close the campus, but not too far away.

"How about the Continental; Fontainebleau Room? Say twelve-fifteen."

"That'll be all right. Be seeing you."

Marjorie looked at him curiously as he gathered up the things he needed for the next class.

Stanly Weill had a thin dark-eyed face. He was frowning as he set down his coffee-cup.

"Ed, you ought to know better than to try to kid your lawyer," he said. "You say Whitburn's trying to force you to resign. With your contract, he can't do that, not without good and sufficient cause, and under the Faculty Tenure Law, that means something just an inch short of murder in the first degree. Now, what's Whitburn got on you?"

Beat around the bush and try to build a background, or come out with it at once and fill in the details afterward? He debated mentally for a moment, then decided upon the latter course.

"Well, it happens that I have the ability to prehend future events. I can, by concentrating, bring into my mind the history of the world, at least in general outline, for the next five thousand years. Whitburn thinks I'm crazy, mainly because I get confused at times and forget that something I know about hasn't happened yet."

Weill snatched the cigarette from his mouth to keep from swallowing it. As it was, he choked on a mouthful of smoke and coughed violently, then sat back in the booth-seat, staring speechlessly.

"It started a little over three years ago," Chalmers continued. "Just after New Year's, 1970. I was getting up a series of seminars for some of my postgraduate students on extrapolation of present social and political trends to the middle of the next century, and I began to find that I was getting some very fixed and definite ideas of what the world of 2050 to 2070 would be like. Completely unified world, abolition of all national states under a single world sovereignty, colonies on Mars and Venus, that sort of thing. Some of these ideas didn't seem quite logical; a number of them were complete reversals of present trends, and a lot seemed to depend on arbitrary and unpredictable factors. Mind, this was before the first rocket landed on the Moon, when the whole moon-rocket and lunar-base project was a triple-top secret. But I knew, in the spring of 1970, that the first unmanned rocket would be called the *Kilroy*, and that it would be launched some time in 1971. You remember, when the news was released, it was stated that the rocket hadn't been christened until the day before it was launched, when somebody remembered that old 'Kilroy-was-here' thing from the Second World War. Well, I knew about it over a year in advance."

Weill had been listening in silence. He had a naturally skeptical face; his present expression mightn't really mean that he didn't believe what he was hearing.

"How'd you get all this stuff? In dreams?"

Chalmers shook his head. "It just came to me. I'd be sitting reading, or eating dinner, or talking to one of my classes, and the first thing I'd know, something out of the future would come bubbling up in me. It just kept pushing up into my conscious mind. I wouldn't have an idea of something one minute, and the next it would just be part of my general historical knowledge; I'd know it as positively as I know that Columbus discovered America in. 1492. The only difference is that I can usually remember where I've read something in past history, but my future history I know without knowing how I know it."

"Ah, that's the question!" Weill pounced. "You don't know how you know it. Look, Ed, we've both studied psychology, elementary psychology at least. Anybody who has to work with people, these days, has to know some psychology. What makes you sure that these prophetic impressions of yours aren't manufactured in your own subconscious mind?"

"That's what I thought, at first. I thought my subconscious was just building up this stuff to fill the gaps in what I'd produced from logical extrapolation. I've always been a stickler for detail," he added, parenthetically. "It would be natural for me to supply details for the future. But, as I said, a lot of this stuff is based on unpredictable and arbitrary factors that can't be inferred from anything in the present. That left me with the alternatives of delusion or precognition, and if I ever came near going crazy, it was before the *Kilroy* landed and the news was released. After that, I knew which it was."

"And yet, you can't explain how you can have real knowledge of a thing before it happens. Before it exists," Weill said.

"I really don't need to. I'm satisfied with knowing that I know. But if you want me to furnish a theory, let's say that all these things really do exist, in the past or in the future, and that the present is just a moving knife-edge that separates the two. You can't even indicate the present. By the time you make up your mind to say, 'Now!' and transmit the impulse to your vocal organs, and utter the word, the original present moment is part of the past. The knife-edge has gone over it. Most people think they know only the present; what they know is the past, which they have already experienced, or read about. The difference with me is that I can see what's on both sides of the knife-edge."

Weill put another cigarette in his mouth and bent his head to the flame of his lighter. For a moment, he sat motionless, his thin face rigid.

"What do you want me to do?" he asked. "I'm a lawyer, not a psychiatrist."

"I want a lawyer. This is a legal matter. Whitburn's talking about voiding my tenure contract. You helped draw it; I have a right to expect you to help defend it."

"Ed, have you been talking about this to anybody else?" Weill asked.

"You're the first person I've mentioned it to. It's not the sort of thing you'd bring up casually, in a conversation."

"Then how'd Whitburn get hold of it?"

"He didn't, not the way I've given it to you. But I made a couple of slips, now and then. I made a bad one yesterday morning."

He told Weill about it, and about his session with the president of the college that morning. The lawyer nodded.

"That was a bad one, but you handled Whitburn the right way," Weill said. "What he's most afraid of is publicity, getting the college mixed up in anything controversial, and above all, the reactions of the trustees and people like that. If Dacre or anybody else makes any trouble, he'll do his best to cover for you. Not willingly, of course, but because he'll know that that's the only way he can cover for himself. I don't think you'll have any more trouble with him. If you can keep your own nose clean, that is. Can you do that?"

"I believe so. Yesterday I got careless. I'll not do that again."

"You'd better not." Weill hesitated for a moment. "I said I was a lawyer, not a psychiatrist. I'm going to give you some psychiatrist's advice, though. Forget this whole thing. You say you can bring these impressions into your conscious mind by concentrating?" He waited briefly; Chalmers nodded, and he continued: "Well, stop it. Stop trying to harbor this stuff. It's dangerous, Ed. Stop playing around with it."

"You think I'm crazy, too?"

Weill shook his head impatiently. "I didn't say that. But I'll say, now, that you're losing your grip on reality. You are constructing a system of fantasies, and the first thing you know, they will become your reality, and the world around you will be unreal and illusory. And that's a state of mental incompetence that I can recognize, as a lawyer."

"How about the *Kilroy*?"

Weill looked at him intently. "Ed, are you sure you did have that experience?" he asked. "I'm not trying to imply that you're consciously lying to me about that. I am suggesting that you manufactured a memory of that incident in your subconscious mind, and are deluding yourself into thinking that you knew about it in advance. False memory is a fairly common thing, in cases like this. Even the little psychology I know, I've heard about that. There's been talk about rockets to the Moon for years. You included something about that in your future-history fantasy, and then, after the event, you convinced yourself that you'd known all about it, including the impromptu christening of the rocket, all along."

A hot retort rose to his lips; he swallowed it hastily. Instead, he nodded amicably.

"That's a point worth thinking of. But right now, what I want to know is, will you represent me in case Whitburn does take this to court and does try to void my contract?"

"Oh, yes; as you said, I have an obligation to defend the contracts I draw up. But you'll have to avoid giving him any further reason for trying to void it. Don't make any more of these slips. Watch what you say, in class or out of it. And above all, don't talk about this to anybody. Don't tell anybody that you can foresee the future, or even talk about future probabilities. Your business is with the past; stick to it."

The afternoon passed quietly enough. Word of his defiance of Whitburn had gotten around among the faculty—Whitburn might have his secretary scared witless in his office, but not gossipless outside it—though it hadn't seemed to have leaked down to the students yet. Handley, the Latin professor, managed to waylay him in a hallway, a hallway Handley didn't normally use.

"The tenure-contract system under which we hold our positions here is one of our most valuable safeguards," he said, after exchanging greetings. "It was only won after a struggle, in a time of public animosity toward all intellectuals, and even now, our professional position would be most insecure without it."

"Yes. I found that out today, if I hadn't known it when I took part in the struggle you speak of."

"It should not be jeopardized," Handley declared.

"You think I'm jeopardizing it?"

Handley frowned. He didn't like being pushed out of the safety of generalization into specific cases.

"Well, now that you make that point, yes. I do. If Doctor Whitburn tries to make an issue of—of what happened yesterday—and if the court decides against you, you can see the position all of us will be in."

"What do you think I should have done? Given him my resignation when he demanded it? We have our tenure-contracts, and the system was instituted to prevent just the sort of arbitrary action Whitburn tried to take with me today. If he wants to go to court, he'll find that out."

"And if he wins, he'll establish a precedent that will threaten the security of every college and university faculty member in the state. In any state where there's a tenure law."

Leonard Fitch, the psychologist, took an opposite attitude. As Chalmers was leaving the college at the end of the afternoon, Fitch cut across the campus to intercept him.

"I heard about the way you stood up to Whitburn this morning, Ed," he said. "Glad you did it. I only wish I'd done something like that three years ago.... Think he's going to give you any real trouble?"

"I doubt it."

"Well, I'm on your side if he does. I won't be the only one, either."

"Well, thank you, Leonard. It always helps to know that. I don't think there'll be any more trouble, though."

He dined alone at his apartment, and sat over his coffee, outlining his work for the next day. When both were finished, he dallied indecisively, Weill's words echoing through his mind and raising doubts. It was possible that he had been manufacturing the whole thing in his subconscious mind. That was, at least, a more plausible theory than any he had constructed to explain an ability to produce real knowledge of the future. Of course, there was that business about the *Kilroy*. That had been too close on too many points to be dismissed as coincidence. Then, again, Weill's words came back to disquiet him. Had he really gotten that before the event, as he believed, or had he only imagined, later, that he had?

There was one way to settle that. He rose quickly and went to the filing-cabinet where he kept his future-history notes and began pulling out envelopes. There was nothing about the *Kilroy* in the Twentieth Century file, where it should be, although he examined each sheet of notes carefully. The possibility that his notes on that might have been filed out of place by mistake occurred to him; he looked in every other envelope. The notes, as far as they went, were all filed in order, and each one bore, beside the future date of occurrence, the date on which the knowledge—or must he call it delusion?—had come to him. But there was no note on the landing of the first unmanned rocket on Luna.

He put the notes away and went back to his desk, rummaging through the drawers, and finding nothing. He searched everywhere in the apartment where a sheet of paper could have been mislaid, taking all his books, one by one, from the shelves and leafing through them, even books he knew he had not touched for more than three years. In the end, he sat down again at his desk, defeated. The note on the *Kilroy* simply did not exist.

Of course, that didn't settle it, as finding the note would have. He remembered—or believed he remembered—having gotten that item of knowledge—or delusion—in 1970, shortly before the end of the school term. It hadn't been until after the fall opening of school that he had begun making notes. He could have had the knowledge of the robot rocket in his mind then, and neglected putting it on paper.

He undressed, put on his pajamas, poured himself a drink, and went to bed. Three hours later, still awake, he got up, and poured himself another, bigger, drink. Somehow, eventually, he fell asleep.

The next morning, he searched his desk and book-case in the office at school. He had never kept a diary; now he was wishing that he had. That might have contained something that would be evidence, one way or the other. All day, he vacillated between conviction of the reality of his future knowledge and resolution to have no more to do with it. Once he decided to destroy all the notes he had made, and thought of making a special study of some facet of history, and writing another book, to occupy his mind.

After lunch, he found that more data on the period immediately before the Thirty Days' War was coming into his consciousness. He resolutely suppressed it, knowing as he did that it might never come to him again. That evening, too, he cooked dinner for himself at his apartment, and laid out his class-work for the next day. He'd better not stay in, that evening; too much temptation to settle himself by the living-room fire with his pipe and his notepad and indulge in the vice he had determined to renounce. After a little debate, he decided upon a movie; he put on again the suit he had taken off on coming home, and went out.

The picture, a random choice among the three shows in the neighborhood, was about Seventeenth Century buccaneers; exciting action and a sound-track loud with shots and cutlass-clashing. He let himself be drawn into it completely, and, until it was finished, he was able to forget both the college and the history of the future. But, as he walked home, he was struck by the parallel between the buccaneers of the West Indies and the space-pirates in the days of the dissolution of the First Galactic Empire, in the Tenth Century of the Interstellar Era. He hadn't been too clear on that period, and he found new data rising in his mind; he hurried his steps, almost running upstairs to his room. It was long after midnight before he had finished the notes he had begun on his return home.

Well, that had been a mistake, but he wouldn't make it again. He determined again to destroy his notes, and began casting about for a subject which would occupy his mind to the exclusion of the future. Not the Spanish Conquistadores; that was too much like the early period of interstellar expansion. He thought for a time of the Sepoy Mutiny, and then rejected it—he could "remember" something much like that on one of the planets of the Beta Hydrae system, in the Fourth Century of the Atomic Era. There were so few things, in the history of the past, which did not have their counter-parts in the future. That evening, too, he stayed at home, preparing for his various classes for the rest of the week and making copious notes on what he would talk about to each. He needed more whiskey to get to sleep that night.

Whitburn gave him no more trouble, and if any of the trustees or influential alumni made any protest about what had happened in Modern

History IV, he heard nothing about it. He managed to conduct his classes without further incidents, and spent his evenings trying, not always successfully, to avoid drifting into "memories" of the future....

He came into his office that morning tired and unrefreshed by the few hours' sleep he had gotten the night before, edgy from the strain, of trying to adjust his mind to the world of Blanley College in mid-April of 1973. Pottgeiter hadn't arrived yet, but Marjorie Fenner was waiting for him; a newspaper in her hand, almost bursting with excitement.

"Here; have you seen it, Doctor Chalmers?" she asked as he entered.

He shook his head. He ought to read the papers more, to keep track of the advancing knife-edge that divided what he might talk about from what he wasn't supposed to know, but each morning he seemed to have less and less time to get ready for work.

"Well, look! Look at that!"

She thrust the paper into his hands, still folded, the big, black headline where he could see it.

KHALID IB'N HUSSEIN ASSASSINATED

He glanced over the leading paragraphs. Leader of Islamic Caliphate shot to death in Basra...leaving Parliament Building for his palace outside the city...fanatic, identified as an Egyptian named Mohammed Noureed... old American submachine-gun...two guards killed and a third seriously wounded...seized by infuriated mob and stoned to death on the spot....

For a moment, he felt guilt, until he realized that nothing he could have done could have altered the event. The death of Khalid ib'n Hussein, and all the millions of other deaths that would follow it, were fixed in the matrix of the space-time continuum. Including, maybe, the death of an obscure professor of Modern History named Edward Chalmers.

"At least, this'll be the end of that silly flap about what happened a month ago in Modern Four. This is modern history, now; I can talk about it without a lot of fools yelling their heads off."

She was staring at him wide-eyed. No doubt horrified at his cold-blooded attitude toward what was really a shocking and senseless crime.

"Yes, of course; the man's dead. So's Julius Caesar, but we've gotten over being shocked at his murder."

He would have to talk about it in Modern History IV, he supposed; explain why Khalid's death was necessary to the policies of the Eastern Axis, and what the consequences would be. How it would hasten the complete dissolution of the old U. N., already weakened by the crisis over the Eastern demands for the demilitarization and internationalization of the United States Lunar Base, and necessitate the formation of the Terran Federation, and how it would lead, eventually, to the Thirty Days' War. No, he couldn't talk about that; that was on the wrong side of the knife-edge. Have to be careful about the knife-edge; too easy to cut himself on it.

Nobody in Modern History IV was seated when he entered the room; they were all crowded between the door and his desk. He stood blinking, wondering why they were giving him an ovation, and why Kendrick and Dacre were so abjectly apologetic. Great heavens, did it take the murder of the greatest Moslem since Saladin to convince people that he wasn't crazy?

Before the period was over, Whitburn's secretary entered with a note in the college president's hand and over his signature; requesting Chalmers to come to his office immediately and without delay. Just like that; expected him to walk right out of his class. He was protesting as he entered the president's office. Whitburn cut him off short.

"Doctor Chalmers,"—Whitburn had risen behind his desk as the door opened—"I certainly hope that you can realize that there was nothing but the most purely coincidental connection between the event featured in this morning's newspapers and your performance, a month ago, in Modern History Four," he began.

"I realize nothing of the sort. The death of Khalid ib'n Hussein is a fact of history, unalterably set in its proper place in time-sequence. It was a fact of history a month ago no less than today."

"So that's going to be your attitude; that your wild utterances of a month ago have now been vindicated as fulfilled prophesies? And I suppose you intend to exploit this—this coincidence—to the utmost. The involvement of Blanley College in a mess of sensational publicity means nothing to you, I presume."

"I haven't any idea what you're talking about."

"You mean to tell me that you didn't give this story to the local newspaper, the *Valley Times*?" Whitburn demanded.

"I did not. I haven't mentioned the subject to anybody connected with the *Times*, or anybody else, for that matter. Except my attorney, a month ago, when you were threatening to repudiate the contract you signed with me."

"I suppose I'm expected to take your word for that?"

"Yes, you are. Unless you care to call me a liar in so many words." He moved a step closer. Lloyd Whitburn outweighed him by fifty pounds, but most of the difference was fat. Whitburn must have realized that, too.

"No, no; if you say you haven't talked about it to the *Valley Times*, that's enough," he said hastily. "But somebody did. A reporter was here not twenty minutes ago; he refused to say who had given him the story, but he wanted to question me about it."

"What did you tell him?"

"I refused to make any statement whatever. I also called Colonel Tighlman, the owner of the paper, and asked him, very reasonably, to suppress the story. I thought that my own position and the importance of Blanley College to this town entitled me to that much consideration." Whitburn's face became almost purple. "He...he laughed at me!"

"Newspaper people don't like to be told to kill stories. Not even by college presidents. That's only made things worse. Personally, I don't relish the prospect of having this publicized, any more than you do. I can assure you that I shall be most guarded if any of the *Times* reporters talk to me about it, and if I have time to get back to my class before the end of the period, I shall ask them, as a personal favor, not to discuss the matter outside."

Whitburn didn't take the hint. Instead, he paced back and forth, storming about the reporter, the newspaper owner, whoever had given the story to the paper, and finally Chalmers himself. He was livid with rage.

"You certainly can't imagine that when you made those remarks in class you actually possessed any knowledge of a thing that was still a month in the future," he spluttered. "Why, it's ridiculous! Utterly preposterous!"

"Unusual, I'll admit. But the fact remains that I did. I should, of course, have been more careful, and not confused future with past events. The students didn't understand...."

Whitburn half-turned, stopping short.

"My God, man! You *are* crazy!" he cried, horrified.

The period-bell was ringing as he left Whitburn's office; that meant that the twenty-three students were scattering over the campus, talking like mad. He shrugged. Keeping them quiet about a thing like this wouldn't have been possible in any case. When he entered his office, Stanly Weill was waiting for him. The lawyer drew him out into the hallway quickly.

"For God's sake, have you been talking to the papers?" he demanded. "After what I told you...."

"No, but somebody has." He told about the call to Whitburn's office, and the latter's behavior. Weill cursed the college president bitterly.

"Any time you want to get a story in the *Valley Times*, just order Frank Tighlman not to print it. Well, if you haven't talked, don't."

"Suppose somebody asks me?"

"A reporter, no comment. Anybody else, none of his damn business. And above all, don't let anybody finagle you into making any claims about knowing the future. I thought we had this under control; now that it's out in the open, what that fool Whitburn'll do is anybody's guess."

Leonard Fitch met him as he entered the Faculty Club, sizzling with excitement.

"Ed, this has done it!" he began, jubilantly. "This is one nobody can laugh off. It's direct proof of precognition, and because of the prominence of the event, everybody will hear about it. And it simply can't be dismissed as coincidence...."

"Whitburn's trying to do that."

"Whitburn's a fool if he is," another man said calmly. Turning, he saw that the speaker was Tom Smith, one of the math professors. "I figured the odds against that being chance. There are a lot of variables that might affect it one way or another, but ten to the fifteenth power is what I get for a sort of median figure."

"Did you give that story to the *Valley Times?*" he asked Fitch, suspicion rising and dragging anger up after it.

"Of course, I did," Fitch said. "I'll admit, I had to go behind your back and have some of my postgrads get statements from the boys in your history class, but you wouldn't talk about it yourself...."

Tom Smith was standing beside him. He was twenty years younger than Chalmers, he was an amateur boxer, and he had good reflexes. He caught Chalmers' arm as it was traveling back for an uppercut, and held it.

"Take it easy, Ed; you don't want to start a slugfest in here. This is the Faculty Club; remember?"

"I won't, Tom; it wouldn't prove anything if I did." He turned to Fitch. "I won't talk about sending your students to pump mine, but at least you could have told me before you gave that story out."

"I don't know what you're sore about," Fitch defended himself. "I believed in you when everybody else thought you were crazy, and if I hadn't collected signed and dated statements from your boys, there'd have been no substantiation. It happens that extrasensory perception means as much to me as history does to you. I've believed in it ever since I read about Rhine's work, when I was a kid. I worked in ESP for a long time. Then I had a chance to get a full professorship by coming here, and after I did, I found that I couldn't go on with it, because Whitburn's president here, and he's a stupid old bigot with an air-locked mind...."

"Yes." His anger died down as Fitch spoke. "I'm glad Tom stopped me from making an ass of myself. I can see your side of it." Maybe that was the curse of the professional intellectual, an ability to see everybody's side of everything. He thought for a moment. "What else did you do, beside hand this story to the *Valley Times?* I'd better hear all about it."

"I phoned the secretary of the American Institute of Psionics and Parapsychology, as soon as I saw this morning's paper. With the time-difference to the East Coast, I got him just as he reached his office. He advised me to give the thing the widest possible publicity; he thought that would advance the recognition and study of parapsychology. A case like this can't be ignored; it will demand serious study...."

"Well, you got your publicity, all right. I'm up to my neck in it."

There was an uproar outside. The doorman was saying, firmly:

"This is the Faculty Club, gentlemen; it's for members only. I don't care if you gentlemen are the press, you simply cannot come in here."

"We're all up to our necks in it," Smith said. "Leonard, I don't care what your motives were, you ought to have considered the effect on the rest of us first."

"This place will be a madhouse," Handley complained. "How we're going to get any of these students to keep their minds on their work...."

"I tell you, I don't know a confounded thing about it," Max Pottgeiter's voice rose petulantly at the door. "Are you trying to tell me that Professor Chalmers murdered some Arab? Ridiculous!"

He ate hastily and without enjoyment, and slipped through the kitchen and out the back door, cutting between two frat-houses and circling back to Prescott Hall. On the way, he paused momentarily and chuckled. The reporters, unable to storm the Faculty Club, had gone off in chase of other game and had cornered Lloyd Whitburn in front of Administration Center. They had a jeep with a sound-camera mounted on it, and were trying to get something for telecast. After gesticulating angrily, Whitburn broke away from them and dashed up the steps and into the building. A campus policeman stopped those who tried to follow.

His only afternoon class was American History III. He got through it somehow, though the class wasn't able to concentrate on the Reconstruction and the first election of Grover Cleveland. The halls were free of reporters, at least, and when it was over he hurried to the Library, going to the faculty reading-room in the rear, where he could smoke. There was nobody there but old Max Pottgeiter, smoking a cigar, his head bent over a book. The Medieval History professor looked up.

"Oh, hello, Chalmers. What the deuce is going on around here? Has everybody gone suddenly crazy?" he asked.

"Well, they seem to think I have," he said bitterly.

"They do? Stupid of them. What's all this about some Arab being shot? I didn't know there were any Arabs around here."

"Not here. At Basra." He told Pottgeiter what had happened.

"Well! I'm sorry to hear about that," the old man said. "I have a friend at Southern California, Bellingham, who knew Khalid very well. Was in the Middle East doing some research on the Byzantine Empire; Khalid was most helpful. Bellingham was quite impressed by him; said he was a wonderful man, and a fine scholar. Why would anybody want to kill a man like that?"

He explained in general terms. Pottgeiter nodded understandingly: assassination was a familiar feature of the medieval political landscape, too. Chalmers went on to elaborate. It was a relief to talk to somebody like Pottgeiter, who wasn't bothered by the present moment, but simply boycotted it. Eventually, the period-bell rang. Pottgeiter looked at his watch, as from conditioned reflex, and then rose, saying that he had a class and excusing himself. He would have carried his cigar with him if Chalmers hadn't taken it away from him.

After Pottgeiter had gone Chalmers opened a book—he didn't notice what it was—and sat staring unseeing at the pages. So the moving knife-edge had come down on the end of Khalid ib'n Hussein's life; what were the events in the next segment of time, and the segments to follow? There would be bloody fighting all over the Middle East—with consternation, he remembered that he had been talking about that to Pottgeiter. The Turkish army would move in and try to restore order. There would be more trouble in northern Iran, the Indian Communists would invade Eastern Pakistan, and then the general war, so long dreaded, would come. How far in the future that was he could not "remember," nor how the nuclear-weapons stalemate that had so far prevented it would be broken. He knew that today, and for years before, nobody had dared start an all-out atomic war. Wars, now, were marginal skirmishes, like the one in Indonesia, or the steady underground conflict of subversion and sabotage that had come to be called the Subwar. And with the United States already in possession of a powerful Lunar base.... He wished he could "remember" how events between the murder of Khalid and the Thirty Day's War had been spaced chronologically. Something of that had come to him, after the incident in Modern History IV, and he had driven it from his consciousness.

He didn't dare go home where the reporters would be sure to find him. He simply left the college, at the end of the school-day, and walked without conscious direction until darkness gathered. This morning, when he had seen the paper, he had said, and had actually believed, that the news of the murder in Basra would put an end to the trouble that had started a month ago in the Modern History class. It hadn't: the trouble, it seemed, was only beginning. And with the newspapers, and Whitburn, and Fitch, it could go on forever....

It was fully dark, now; his shadow fell ahead of him on the sidewalk, lengthening as he passed under and beyond a street-light, vanishing as he entered the stronger light of the one ahead. The windows of a cheap cafe reminded him that he was hungry, and he entered, going to a table and ordering something absently. There was a television screen over the combination bar and lunch-counter. Some kind of a comedy program, at which an invisible studio-audience was laughing immoderately and without apparent cause. The roughly dressed customers along the counter didn't seem to see any more humor in it than he did. Then his food arrived on the table and he began to eat without really tasting it.

After a while, an alteration in the noises from the television penetrated his consciousness; a news-program had come on, and he raised his head. The screen showed a square in an Eastern city; the voice was saying:

"... Basra, where Khalid ib'n Hussein was assassinated early this morning—early afternoon, local time. This is the scene of the crime; the body of the murderer has been removed, but you can still see the stones with which he was pelted to death by the mob...."

A close-up of the square, still littered with torn-up paving-stones. A Caliphate army officer, displaying the weapon—it was an old M3, all right; Chalmers had used one of those things, himself, thirty years before, and he and his contemporaries had called it a "grease-gun." There were some recent pictures of Khalid, including one taken as he left the plane on his return from Ankara. He watched, absorbed; it was all exactly as he had "remembered" a month ago. It gratified him to see that his future "memories" were reliable in detail as well as generality.

"But the most amazing part of the story comes, not from Basra, but from Blanley College, in California," the commentator was saying, "where, it is revealed, the murder of Khalid was foretold, with uncanny accuracy, a month ago, by a history professor, Doctor Edward Chalmers...."

There was a picture of himself, in hat and overcoat, perfectly motionless, as though a brief moving glimpse were being prolonged. A glance at the background told him when and where it had been taken—a year and a half ago, at a convention at Harvard. These telecast people must save up every inch of old news-film they ever took. There were views of Blanley campus, and interviews with some of the Modern History IV boys, including Dacre and Kendrick. That was one of the things they'd been doing with that jeep-mounted sound-camera, this afternoon, then. The boys, some brashly, some embarrassedly, were substantiating the fact that he had, a month ago, described yesterday's event in detail.

There was an interview with Leonard Fitch; the psychology professor was trying to explain the phenomenon of precognition in layman's terms, and making heavy going of it. And there was the mobbing of Whitburn in front of Administration Center. The college president was shouting denials of every question asked him, and as he turned and fled, the guffaws of the reporters were plainly audible.

An argument broke out along the counter.

"I don't believe it! How could anybody know all that about something before it happened?"

"Well, you heard that-there professor, what was his name. An' you heard all them boys...."

"Ah, college-boys; they'll do anything for a joke!"

"After refusing to be interviewed for telecast, the president of Blanley College finally consented to hold a press conference in his office, from which telecast cameras were barred. He denied the whole story categorically and stated that the boys in Professor Chalmers' class had concocted the whole thing as a hoax...."

"There! See what I told you!"

"... stating that Professor Chalmers is mentally unsound, and that he has been trying for years to oust him from his position on the Blanley faculty but has been unable to do so because of the provisions of the Faculty Tenure Act of 1963. Most of his remarks were in the nature of a polemic against this law, generally regarded as the college professors' bill of rights. It is to be stated here that other members of the Blanley faculty have unconditionally confirmed the fact that Doctor Chalmers did make the statements attributed to him a month ago, long before the death of Khalid ib'n Hussein...."

"Yah! How about *that*, now? How'ya gonna get around *that*?"

Beckoning the waitress, he paid his check and hurried out. Before he reached the door, he heard a voice, almost stuttering with excitement:

"Hey! Look! That's *him*!"

He began to run. He was two blocks from the cafe before he slowed to a walk again.

That night, he needed three shots of whiskey before he could get to sleep.

A delegation from the American Institute of Psionics and Parapsychology reached Blanley that morning, having taken a strato-plane from the East Coast. They had academic titles and degrees that even Lloyd Whitburn couldn't ignore. They talked with Leonard Fitch, and with the students from Modern History IV, and took statements. It wasn't until after General European History II that they caught up with Chalmers—an elderly man, with white hair and a ruddy face; a young man who looked like a heavy-weight boxer; a middle-aged man in tweeds who smoked a pipe and looked as though he ought to be more interested in grouse-shooting and flower-gardening than in clairvoyance and telepathy. The names of the first two meant nothing to Chalmers. They were important names in their own field, but it was not his field. The name of the third, who listened silently, he did not catch.

"You understand, gentlemen, that I'm having some difficulties with the college administration about this," he told them. "President Whitburn has even gone so far as to challenge my fitness to hold a position here."

"We've talked to him," the elderly man said. "It was not a very satisfactory discussion."

"President Whitburn's fitness to hold his own position could very easily be challenged," the young man added pugnaciously.

"Well, then, you see what my position is. I've consulted my attorney, Mr. Weill and he has advised me to make absolutely no statements of any sort about the matter."

"I understand," the eldest of the trio said. "But we're not the press, or anything like that. We can assure you that anything you tell us will be absolutely confidential." He looked inquiringly at the middle-aged man in tweeds, who nodded silently. "We can understand that the students in your modern history class are telling what is substantially the truth?"

"If you're thinking about that hoax statement of Whitburn's, that's a lot of idiotic drivel!" he said angrily. "I heard some of those boys on the telecast, last night; except for a few details in which they were confused, they all stated exactly what they heard me say in class a month ago."

"And we assume,"—again he glanced at the man in tweeds—"that you had no opportunity of knowing anything, at the time, about any actual plot against Khalid's life?"

The man in tweeds broke silence for the first time. "You can assume that. I don't even think this fellow Noureed knew anything about it, then."

"Well, we'd like to know, as nearly as you're able to tell us, just how you became the percipient of this knowledge of the future event of the death of Khalid ib'n Hussein," the young man began. "Was it through a dream, or a waking experience; did you visualize, or have an auditory impression, or did it simply come into your mind...."

"I'm sorry, gentlemen." He looked at his watch. "I have to be going somewhere, at once. In any case, I simply can't discuss the matter with you. I appreciate your position; I know how I'd feel if data of historical importance were being withheld from me. However, I trust that you will appreciate my position and spare me any further questioning."

That was all he allowed them to get out of him. They spent another few minutes being polite to one another; he invited them to lunch at the Faculty Club, and learned that they were lunching there as Fitch's guests. They went away trying to hide their disappointment.

The Psionics and Parapsychology people weren't the only delegation to reach Blanley that day. Enough of the trustees of the college lived in the San Francisco area to muster a quorum for a meeting the evening before; a committee, including James Dacre, the father of the boy in Modern History IV, was appointed to get the facts at first hand; they arrived about noon. They talked to some of the students, spent some time closeted with Whitburn, and were seen crossing the campus with the Parapsychology people. They didn't talk to Chalmers or Fitch. In the afternoon, Marjorie Fenner told Chalmers that his presence at a meeting, to be held that evening in Whitburn's office, was requested. The request, she said, had come from the trustees' committee, not from Whitburn; she also told him that Fitch would be there. Chalmers promptly phoned Stanly Weill.

"I'll be there along with you," the lawyer said. "If this trustees' committee is running it, they'll realize that this is a matter in which you're entitled to legal advice. I'll stop by your place and pick you up.... You haven't been doing any talking, have you?"

He described the interview with the Psionics and Parapsychology people.

"That was all right.... Was there a man with a mustache, in a brown tweed suit, with them?"

"Yes. I didn't catch his name...."

"It's Cutler. He's an Army major; Central Intelligence. His crowd's interested in whether you had any real advance information on this. He was in to see me, just a while ago. I have the impression he'd like to see this whole thing played down, so he'll be on our side, more or less and for the time being. I'll be around to your place about eight; in the meantime, don't do any more talking than you have to. I hope we can get this straightened out, this evening. I'll have to go to Reno in a day or so to see a client there...."

The meeting in Whitburn's office had been set for eight-thirty; Weill saw to it that they arrived exactly on time. As they got out of his car at Administration Center and crossed to the steps, Chalmers had the feeling of going to a duel, accompanied by his second. The briefcase Weill was carrying may have given him the idea; it was flat and square-cornered, the size and shape of an old case of dueling pistols. He commented on it.

"Sound recorder," Weill said. "Loaded with a four-hour spool. No matter how long this thing lasts, I'll have a record of it, if I want to produce one in court."

Another party was arriving at the same time—the two Psionics and Parapsychology people and the Intelligence major, who seemed to have formed a working partnership. They all entered together, after a brief and guardedly polite exchange of greetings. There were voices raised in argument inside when they came to Whitburn's office. The college president was trying to keep Handley, Tom Smith, and Max Pottgeiter from entering his private room in the rear.

"It certainly is!" Handley was saying. "As faculty members, any controversy involving establishment of standards of fitness to teach under a tenure-contract concerns all of us, because any action taken in this case may establish a precedent which could affect the validity of our own contracts."

A big man with iron-gray hair appeared in the doorway of the private office behind Whitburn; James Dacre. "These gentlemen have a substantial interest in this, Doctor Whitburn," he said. "If they're here as representatives of the college faculty, they have every right to be present."

Whitburn stood aside. Handley, Smith and Pottgeiter went through the door; the others followed. The other three members of the trustees' committee were already in the room. A few minutes later, Leonard Fitch arrived, also carrying a briefcase.

"Well, everybody seems to be here," Whitburn said, starting toward his chair behind the desk. "We might as well get this started."

"Yes. If you'll excuse me, Doctor." Dacre stepped in front of him and sat down at the desk. "I've been selected as chairman of this committee; I believe I'm presiding here. Start the recorder, somebody."

One of the other trustees went to the sound recorder beside the desk—a larger but probably not more efficient instrument than the one Weill had concealed in his briefcase—and flipped a switch. Then he and his companions dragged up chairs to flank Dacre's, and the rest seated themselves around the room. Old Pottgeiter took a seat next to Chalmers. Weill opened the case on his lap, reached inside, and closed it again.

"What are they trying to do, Ed?" Pottgeiter asked, in a loud whisper. "Throw you off the faculty? They can't do that, can they?"

"I don't know, Max. We'll see...."

"This isn't any formal hearing, and nobody's on trial here," Dacre was saying. "Any action will have to be taken by the board of trustees as a whole, at a regularly scheduled meeting. All we're trying to do is find out just what's happened here, and who, if anybody, is responsible...."

"Well, there's the man who's responsible!" Whitburn cried, pointing at Chalmers. "This whole thing grew out of his behavior in class a month ago, and I'll remind you that at the time I demanded his resignation!"

"I thought it was Doctor Fitch, here, who gave the story to the newspapers," one of the trustees, a man with red hair and a thin, eye-glassed face, objected.

"Doctor Fitch acted as any scientist should, in making public what he believed to be an important scientific discovery," the elder of the two Parapsychology men said. "He believed, and so do we, that he had discovered a significant instance of precognition—a case of real prior knowledge of a future event. He made a careful and systematic record of Professor Chalmers' statements, at least two weeks before the occurrence of the event to which they referred. It is entirely due to him that we know exactly what Professor Chalmers said and when he said it."

"Yes," his younger colleague added, "and in all my experience I've never heard anything more preposterous than this man Whitburn's attempt, yesterday, to deny the fact."

"Well, we're convinced that Doctor Chalmers did in fact say what he's alleged to have said, last month," Dacre began.

"Jim, I think we ought to get that established, for the record," another of the trustees put in. "Doctor Chalmers, is it true that you spoke, in the past tense, about the death of Khalid ib'n Hussein in one of your classes on the sixteenth of last month?"

Chalmers rose. "Yes, it is. And the next day, I was called into this room by Doctor Whitburn, who demanded my resignation from the faculty of this college because of it. Now, what I'd like to know is, why did Doctor Whitburn, in this same room, deny, yesterday, that I'd said anything of the sort, and accuse my students of concocting the story after the event as a hoax."

"One of them being my son," Dacre added. "I'd like to hear an answer to that, myself."

"So would I," Stanly Weill chimed in. "You know, my client has a good case against Doctor Whitburn for libel."

Chalmers looked around the room. Of the thirteen men around him, only Whitburn was an enemy. Some of the others were on his side, for one reason or another, but none of them were friends. Weill was his lawyer, obeying an obligation to a client which, at bottom, was an obligation to his own conscience. Handley was afraid of the possibility that a precedent might be established which would impair his own tenure-contract. Fitch, and the two men from the Institute of Psionics and Parapsychology were interested in him as a source of study-material. Dacre resented a slur upon his son; he and the others were interested in Blanley College as an institution, almost an abstraction. And the major in mufti was probably worrying about the consequences to military security of having a prophet at large. Then a hand gripped his shoulder, and a voice whispered in his ear:

"That's good, Ed; don't let them scare you!"

Old Max Pottgeiter, at least, was a friend.

"Doctor Whitburn, I'm asking you, and I expect an answer, why did you make such statements to the press, when you knew perfectly well that they were false?" Dacre demanded sharply.

"I knew nothing of the kind!" Whitburn blustered, showing, under the bluster, fear. "Yes, I demanded this man's resignation on the morning of October Seventeenth, the day after this incident occurred. It had come to my attention on several occasions that he was making wild and unreasonable assertions in class, and subjecting himself, and with himself the whole faculty of this college, to student ridicule. Why, there was actually an editorial about it written by the student editor of the campus paper, the *Black and Green*. I managed to prevent its publication...." He went on at some length about that. "If I might be permitted access to the drawers of my own desk," he added with elephantine sarcasm, "I could show you the editorial in question."

"You needn't bother; I have a carbon copy," Dacre told him. "We've all read it. If you did, at the time you suppressed it, you should have known what Doctor Chalmers said in class."

"I knew he'd talked a lot of poppycock about a man who was still living having been shot to death," Whitburn retorted. "And if something of the sort actually happened, what of it? Somebody's always taking a shot at one or another of these foreign dictators, and they can't miss all the time."

"You claim this was pure coincidence?" Fitch demanded. "A ten-point coincidence: Event of assassination, year of the event, place, circumstances, name of assassin, nationality of assassin, manner of killing, exact type of weapon used, guards killed and wounded along with Khalid, and fate of the assassin. If that's a simple and plausible coincidence, so's dealing ten royal flushes in succession in a poker game. Tom, you figured that out; what did you say the odds against it were?"

"Was all that actually stated by Doctor Chalmers a month ago?" one of the trustees asked, incredulously.

"It absolutely was. Look here, Mr. Dacre, gentlemen." Fitch came forward, unzipping his briefcase and pulling out papers. "Here are the signed statements of each of Doctor Chalmers' twenty-three Modern History Four students, all made and dated before the assassination. You can refer to them as you please; they're in alphabetical order. And here." He unfolded a sheet of graph paper a yard long and almost as wide. "Here's a tabulated summary of the boys' statements. All agreed on the first point, the fact of the assassination. All agreed that the time was sometime this year. Twenty out of twenty-three agreed on Basra as the place. Why, seven of them even remembered the name of the assassin. That in itself is remarkable; Doctor Chalmers has an extremely intelligent and attentive class."

"They're attentive because they know he's always likely to do something crazy and make a circus out of himself," Whitburn interjected.

"And this isn't the only instance of Doctor Chalmers' precognitive ability," Fitch continued. "There have been a number of other cases...."

Chalmers jumped to his feet; Stanly Weill rose beside him, shoved the cased sound-recorder into his hands, and pushed him back into his seat.

"Gentlemen," the lawyer began, quietly but firmly and clearly. "This is all getting pretty badly out of hand. After all, this isn't an investigation of the actuality of precognition as a psychic phenomenon. What I'd like to hear, and what I haven't heard yet, is Doctor Whitburn's explanation of his contradictory statements that he knew about my client's alleged remarks on the evening after they were supposed to have been made and that, at the same time, the whole thing was a hoax concocted by his students."

"Are you implying that I'm a liar?" Whitburn bristled.

"I'm pointing out that you made a pair of contradictory statements, and I'm asking how you could do that knowingly and honestly," Weill retorted.

"What I meant," Whitburn began, with exaggerated slowness, as though speaking to an idiot, "was that yesterday, when those infernal reporters were badgering me, I really thought that some of Professor Chalmers' students had gotten together and given the *Valley Times* an exaggerated story about his insane maunderings a month ago. I hadn't imagined that a member of the faculty had been so lacking in loyalty to the college...."

"You couldn't imagine anybody with any more intellectual integrity than you have!" Fitch fairly yelled at him.

"You're as crazy as Chalmers!" Whitburn yelled back. He turned to the trustees. "You see the position I'm in, here, with this infernal Higher Education Faculty Tenure Act? I have a madman on my faculty, and can I get rid of him? No! I demand his resignation, and he laughs at me and goes running for his lawyer! And he is a madman! Nobody but a madman would talk the way he does. You think this Khalid ib'n Hussein business is the only time he's done anything like this? Why, I have a list of a dozen occasions when he's done something just as bad, only he didn't have a lucky coincidence to back him up. Trying to get books that don't exist out of the library, and then insisting that they're standard textbooks. Talking about the revolt of the colonies on Mars and Venus. Talking about something he calls the Terran Federation, some kind of a world empire. Or something he calls Operation Triple Cross, that saved the country during some fantastic war he imagined...."

"*What did you say?*"

The question cracked out like a string of pistol shots. Everybody turned. The quiet man in the brown tweed suit had spoken; now he looked as though he were very much regretting it.

"Is there such a thing as Operation Triple Cross?" Fitch was asking.

"No, no. I never heard anything about that; that wasn't what I meant. It was this Terran Federation thing," the major said, a trifle too quickly and too smoothly. He turned to Chalmers. "You never did any work for PSPB; did you ever talk to anybody who did?" he asked.

"I don't even know what the letters mean," Chalmers replied.

"Politico-Strategic Planning Board. It's all pretty hush-hush, but this term Terran Federation is a tentative name for a proposed organization to take the place of the U. N. if that organization breaks up. It's nothing particularly important, and it only exists on paper."

It won't exist only on paper very long, Chalmers thought. He was wondering what Operation Triple Cross was; he had some notes on it, but he had forgotten what they were.

"Maybe he did pick that up from somebody who'd talked indiscreetly," Whitburn conceded. "But the rest of this tommyrot! Why, he was talking about how the city of Reno had been destroyed by an explosion and fire, literally wiped off the map. There's an example for you!"

He'd forgotten about that, too. It had been a relatively minor incident in the secret struggle of the Subwar; now he remembered having made a note about it. He was sure that it followed closely after the assassination of Khalid ib'n Hussein. He turned quickly to Weill.

"Didn't you say you had to go to Reno in a day or so?" he asked.

Weill hushed him urgently, pointing with his free hand to the recorder. The exchange prevented him from noticing that Max Pottgeiter had risen, until the old man was speaking.

"Are you trying to tell these people that Professor Chalmers is crazy?" he was demanding. "Why, he has one of the best minds on the campus. I was talking to him only yesterday, in the back room at the Library. You know," he went on apologetically, "my subject is Medieval History; I don't pay much attention to what's going on in the contemporary world, and I didn't understand, really, what all this excitement was about. But he explained the whole thing to me, and did it in terms that I could grasp, drawing some excellent parallels with the Byzantine Empire and the Crusades. All about the revolt at Damascus, and the sack of Beirut, and the war between Jordan and Saudi Arabia, and how the Turkish army intervened, and the invasion of Pakistan...."

"When did all this happen?" one of the trustees demanded.

Pottgeiter started to explain; Chalmers realized, sickly, how much of his future history he had poured into the trusting ear of the old medievalist, the day before.

"Good Lord, man; don't you read the papers at all?" another of the trustees asked.

"No! And I don't read inside-dope magazines, or science fiction. I read carefully substantiated facts. And I know when I'm talking to a sane and reasonable man. It isn't a common experience, around here."

Dacre passed a hand over his face. "Doctor Whitburn," he said, "I must admit that I came to this meeting strongly prejudiced against you, and I'll further admit that your own behavior here has done very little to dispel that prejudice. But I'm beginning to get some idea of what you have to contend with, here at Blanley, and I find that I must make a lot of allowances. I had no idea.... Simply no idea at all."

"Look, you're getting a completely distorted picture of this, Mr. Dacre," Fitch broke in. "It's precisely as I believed; Doctor Chalmers is an unusually gifted precognitive percipient. You've seen, gentlemen, how his complicated chain of precognitions about the death of Khalid has been proven veridical; I'd stake my life that every one of these precognitions will be similarly verified. And I'll stake my professional reputation that the man is perfectly sane. Of course, abnormal psychology and psychopathology aren't my subjects, but...."

"They're not my subjects, either," Whitburn retorted, "but I know a lunatic by his ravings."

"Doctor Fitch is taking an entirely proper attitude," Pottgeiter said, "in pointing out that abnormal psychology is a specialized branch, outside his own field. I wouldn't dream, myself, of trying to offer a decisive opinion on some point of Roman, or Babylonian, history. Well, if the question of Doctor Chalmers' sanity is at issue here, let's consult somebody who specializes in insanity. I don't believe that anybody here is qualified even to express an opinion on that subject, Doctor Whitburn least of all."

Whitburn turned on him angrily. "Oh, shut up, you doddering old fool!" he shouted. "Look; there's another of them!" he told the trustees. "Another deadhead on the faculty that this Tenure Law keeps me from getting rid of. He's as bad as Chalmers, himself. You just heard that string of nonsense he was spouting. Why, his courses have been noted among the students for years as snap courses in which nobody ever has to do any work...."

Chalmers was on his feet again, thoroughly angry. Abuse of himself he could take; talking that way about gentle, learned, old Pottgeiter was something else.

"I think Doctor Pottgeiter's said the most reasonable thing I've heard since I came in here," he declared. "If my sanity is to be questioned, I insist that it be questioned by somebody qualified to do so."

Weill set his recorder on the floor and jumped up beside him, trying to haul him back into his seat.

"For God's sake, man! Sit down and shut up!" he hissed.

Chalmers shook off his hand. "No, I won't shut up! This is the only way to settle this, once and for all. And when my sanity's been vindicated, I'm going to sue this fellow...."

Whitburn started to make some retort, then stopped short. After a moment, he smiled nastily.

"Do I understand, Doctor Chalmers, that you would be willing to submit to psychiatric examination?" he asked.

"Don't agree; you're putting your foot in a trap!" Weill told him urgently.

"Of course, I agree, as long as the examination is conducted by a properly qualified psychiatrist."

"How about Doctor Hauserman at Northern State Mental Hospital?" Whitburn asked quickly. "Would you agree to an examination by him?"

"Excellent!" Fitch exclaimed. "One of the best men in the field. I'd accept his opinion unreservedly."

Weill started to object again; Chalmers cut him off. "Doctor Hauserman will be quite satisfactory to me. The only question is, would he be available?"

"I think he would," Dacre said, glancing at his watch. "I wonder if he could be reached now." He got to his feet. "Telephone in your outer office, Doctor Whitburn? Fine. If you gentlemen will excuse me...."

It was a good fifteen minutes before he returned, smiling.

"Well, gentlemen, it's all arranged," he said. "Doctor Hauserman is quite willing to examine Doctor Chalmers—with the latter's consent, of course."

"He'll have it. In writing, if he wishes."

"Yes, I assured him on that point. He'll be here about noon tomorrow—it's a hundred and fifty miles from the hospital, but the doctor flies his own plane—and the examination can start at two in the afternoon. He seems familiar with the facilities of the psychology department, here;

I assured him that they were at his disposal. Will that be satisfactory to you, Doctor Chalmers?"

"I have a class at that time, but one of the instructors can take it over—if holding classes will be possible around here tomorrow," he said. "Now, if you gentlemen will pardon me, I think I'll go home and get some sleep."

Weill came up to the apartment with him. He mixed a couple of drinks and they went into the living room with them.

"Just in case you don't know what you've gotten yourself into," Weill said, "this Hauserman isn't any ordinary couch-pilot; he's the state psychiatrist. If he gets the idea you aren't sane, he can commit you to a hospital, and I'll bet that's exactly what Whitburn had in mind when he suggested him. And I don't trust this man Dacre. I thought he was on our side, at the start, but that was before your friends got into the act." He frowned into his drink. "And I don't like the way that Intelligence major was acting, toward the last. If he thinks you know something you are not supposed to, a mental hospital may be his idea of a good place to put you away."

"You don't think this man Hauserman would allow himself to be influenced ...? No. You just don't think I'm sane. Do you?"

"I know what Hauserman'll think. He'll think this future history business is a classic case of systematized schizoid delusion. I wish I'd never gotten into this case. I wish I'd never even heard of you! And another thing; in case you get past Hauserman all right, you can forget about that damage-suit bluff of mine. You would not stand a chance with it in court."

"In spite of what happened to Khalid?"

"After tomorrow, I won't stay in the same room with anybody who even mentions that name to me. Well, win or lose, it'll be over tomorrow and then I can leave here."

"Did you tell me you were going to Reno?" Chalmers asked. "Don't do it. You remember Whitburn mentioning how I spoke about an explosion there? It happened just a couple of days after the murder of Khalid.

There was—will be—a trainload of high explosives in the railroad yard; it'll be the biggest non-nuclear explosion since the *Mont Blanc* blew up in Halifax harbor in World War One...."

Weill threw his drink into the fire; he must have avoided throwing the glass in with it by a last-second exercise of self-control.

"Well," he said, after a brief struggle to master himself. "One thing about the legal profession; you do hear the damnedest things!... Good night, Professor. And try—please try, for the sake of your poor harried lawyer—to keep your mouth shut about things like that, at least till after you get through with Hauserman. And when you're talking to him, don't, don't, for heaven's sake, *don't*, volunteer anything!"

The room was a pleasant, warmly-colored, place. There was a desk, much like the ones in the classrooms, and six or seven wicker armchairs. A lot of apparatus had been pushed back along the walls; the dust-covers were gay cretonne. There was a couch, with more apparatus, similarly covered, beside it. Hauserman was seated at the desk when Chalmers entered.

He rose, and they shook hands. A man of about his own age, smooth-faced, partially bald. Chalmers tried to guess something of the man's nature from his face, but could read nothing. A face well trained to keep its owner's secrets.

"Something to smoke, Professor," he began, offering his cigarette case.

"My pipe, if you don't mind." He got it out and filled it.

"Any of those chairs," Hauserman said, gesturing toward them.

They were all arranged to face the desk. He sat down, lighting his pipe. Hauserman nodded approvingly; he was behaving calmly, and didn't need being put at ease. They talked at random—at least, Hauserman tried to make it seem so—for some time about his work, his book about the French Revolution, current events. He picked his way carefully through the conversation, alert for traps which the psychiatrist might be laying for him. Finally, Hauserman said:

"Would you mind telling me just why you felt it advisable to request a psychiatric examination, Professor?"

"I didn't request it. But when the suggestion was made, by one of my friends, in reply to some aspersions of my sanity, I agreed to it."

"Good distinction. And why was your sanity questioned? I won't deny that I had heard of this affair, here, before Mr. Dacre called me, last evening, but I'd like to hear your version of it."

He went into that, from the original incident in Modern History IV, choosing every word carefully, trying to concentrate on making a good impression upon Hauserman, and at the same time finding that more "memories" of the future were beginning to seep past the barrier of his consciousness. He tried to dam them back; when he could not, he spoke with greater and greater care lest they leak into his speech.

"I can't recall the exact manner in which I blundered into it. The fact that I did make such a blunder was because I was talking extemporaneously and had wandered ahead of my text. I was trying to show the results of the collapse of the Ottoman Empire after the First World War, and the partition of the Middle East into a loose collection of Arab states, and the passing of British and other European spheres of influence following the Second. You know, when you consider it, the Islamic Caliphate was inevitable; the surprising thing is that it was created by a man like Khalid...."

He was talking to gain time, and he suspected that Hauserman knew it. The "memories" were coming into his mind more and more strongly; it was impossible to suppress them. The period of anarchy following Khalid's death would be much briefer, and much more violent, than he had previously thought. Tallal ib'n Khalid would be flying from England even now; perhaps he had already left the plane to take refuge among the black tents of his father's Bedouins. The revolt at Damascus would break out before the end of the month; before the end of the year, the whole of Syria and Lebanon would be in bloody chaos, and the Turkish army would be on the march.

"Yes. And you allowed yourself to be carried a little beyond the present moment, into the future, without realizing it? Is that it?"

"Something like that," he replied, wide awake to the trap Hauserman had set, and fearful that it might be a blind, to disguise the real trap. "History follows certain patterns. I'm not a Toynbeean, by any manner of means, but any historian can see that certain forces generally tend to produce similar effects. For instance, space travel is now a fact; our government has at present a military base on Luna. Within our lifetimes—certainly within the lifetimes of my students—there will be explorations and attempts at colonization on Mars and Venus. You believe that, Doctor?"

"Oh, unreservedly. I'm not supposed to talk about it, but I did some work on the Philadelphia Project, myself. I'd say that every major problem of interplanetary flight had been solved before the first robot rocket was landed on Luna."

"Yes. And when Mars and Venus are colonized, there will be the same historic situations, at least in general shape, as arose when the European powers were colonizing the New World, or, for that matter, when the Greek city-states were throwing out colonies across the Aegean. That's the sort of thing we call projecting the past into the future through the present."

Hauserman nodded. "But how about the details? Things like the assassination of a specific personage. How can you extrapolate to a thing like that?"

"Well...." More "memories" were coming to the surface; he tried to crowd them back. "I do my projecting in what you might call fictionalized form; try to fill in the details from imagination. In the case of Khalid, I was trying to imagine what would happen if his influence were suddenly removed from Near Eastern and Middle Eastern, affairs. I suppose I constructed an imaginary scene of his assassination...."

He went on at length. Mohammed and Noureed were common enough names. The Middle East was full of old U. S. weapons. Stoning was the traditional method of execution; it diffused responsibility so that no individual could be singled out for blood-feud vengeance.

"You have no idea how disturbed I was when the whole thing happened, exactly as I had described it," he continued. "And worst of all, to me, was this Intelligence officer showing up; I thought I was really in for it!"

"Then you've never really believed that you had real knowledge of the future?"

"I'm beginning to, since I've been talking to these Psionics and Parapsychology people," he laughed. It sounded, he hoped, like a natural and unaffected laugh. "They seem to be convinced that I have."

There would be an Eastern-inspired uprising in Azerbaijan by the middle of the next year; before autumn, the Indian Communists would make their fatal attempt to seize East Pakistan. The Thirty Days' War would be the immediate result. By that time, the Lunar Base would be completed and ready; the enemy missiles would be aimed primarily at the rocketports from which it was supplied. Delivered without warning, it should have succeeded—except that every rocketport had its secret duplicate and triplicate. That was Operation Triple Cross; no wonder Major Cutler had been so startled at the words, last evening. The enemy would be utterly overwhelmed under the rain of missiles from across space, but until the moon-rockets began to fall, the United States would suffer grievously.

"Honestly, though, I feel sorry for my friend Fitch," he added. "He's going to be frightfully let down when some more of my alleged prophecies misfire on him. But I really haven't been deliberately deceiving him."

And Blanley College was at the center of one of the areas which would receive the worst of the thermonuclear hell to come. And it would be a little under a year....

"And that's all there is to it!" Hauserman exclaimed, annoyance in his voice. "I'm amazed that this man Whitburn allowed a thing like this to assume the proportions it did. I must say that I seem to have gotten the story about this business in a very garbled form indeed." He laughed shortly. "I came here convinced that you were mentally unbalanced. I hope you won't take that the wrong way, Professor," he hastened to add. "In my profession, anything can be expected. A good psychiatrist can never afford to forget how sharp and fine is the knife-edge."

"The knife-edge!" The words startled him. He had been thinking, at that moment, of the knife-edge, slicing moment after moment relentlessly away from the future, into the past, at each slice coming closer and closer to the moment when the missiles of the Eastern Axis would fall. "I didn't know they still resorted to surgery, in mental cases," he added, trying to cover his break.

"Oh, no; all that sort of thing is as irrevocably discarded as the whips and shackles of Bedlam. I meant another kind of knife-edge; the thin, almost invisible, line which separates sanity from non-sanity. From madness, to use a deplorable lay expression." Hauserman lit another cigarette. "Most minds are a lot closer to it than their owners suspect, too. In fact, Professor, I was so convinced that yours had passed over it that I brought with me a commitment form, made out all but my signature, for you." He took it from his pocket and laid it on the desk. "The modern equivalent of the *lettre-de-cachet*, I suppose the author of a book on the French Revolution would call it. I was all ready to certify you as mentally unsound, and commit you to Northern State Mental Hospital."

Chalmers sat erect in his chair. He knew where that was; on the other side of the mountains, in the one part of the state completely untouched by the H-bombs of the Thirty Days' War. Why, the town outside which the hospital stood had been a military headquarters during the period immediately after the bombings, and the center from which all the rescue work in the state had been directed.

"And you thought you could commit me to Northern State!" he demanded, laughing scornfully, and this time he didn't try to make the laugh sound natural and unaffected. "You—confine *me*, anywhere? Confine a poor old history professor's body, yes, but that isn't me. I'm universal; I exist in all space-time. When this old body I'm wearing now was writing that book on the French Revolution, I was in Paris, watching it happen, from the fall of the Bastille to the Ninth Thermidor. I was in Basra, and saw that crazed tool of the Axis shoot down Khalid ib'n Hussein—and the professor talked about it a month before it happened. I have seen empires rise and stretch from star to star across the Galaxy, and crumble and fall. I have seen...."

Doctor Hauserman had gotten his pen out of his pocket and was signing the commitment form with one hand; with the other, he pressed a button on the desk. A door at the rear opened, and a large young man in a white jacket entered.

"You'll have to go away for a while, Professor," Hauserman was telling him, much later, after he had allowed himself to become calm again.

"For how long, I don't know. Maybe a year or so."

"You mean to Northern State Mental?"

"Well.... Yes, Professor. You've had a bad crack-up. I don't suppose you realize how bad. You've been working too hard; harder than your nervous system could stand. It's been too much for you."

"You mean, I'm nuts?"

"Please, Professor. I deplore that sort of terminology. You've had a severe psychological breakdown...."

"Will I be able to have books, and papers, and work a little? I couldn't bear the prospect of complete idleness."

"That would be all right, if you didn't work too hard."

"And could I say good-bye to some of my friends?"

Hauserman nodded and asked, "Who?"

"Well, Professor Pottgeiter...."

"He's outside now. He was inquiring about you."

"And Stanly Weill, my attorney. Not business; just to say good-bye."

"Oh, I'm sorry, Professor. He's not in town, now. He left almost immediately after.... After...."

"After he found out I was crazy for sure? Where'd he go?"

"To Reno; he took the plane at five o'clock."

Weill wouldn't have believed, anyhow; no use trying to blame himself for that. But he was as sure that he would never see Stanly Weill alive again as he was that the next morning the sun would rise. He nodded impassively.

"Sorry he couldn't stay. Can I see Max Pottgeiter alone?"

"Yes, of course, Professor."

Old Pottgeiter came in, his face anguished. "Ed! It isn't true," he stammered. "I won't believe that it's true."

"What, Max?"

"That you're crazy. Nobody can make me believe that."

He put his hand on the old man's shoulder. "Confidentially, Max, neither do I. But don't tell anybody I'm not. It's a secret."

Pottgeiter looked troubled. For a moment, he seemed to be wondering if he mightn't be wrong and Hauserman and Whitburn and the others right.

"Max, do you believe in me?" he asked. "Do you believe that I knew about Khalid's assassination a month before it happened?"

"It's a horribly hard thing to believe," Pottgeiter admitted. "But, dammit, Ed, you did! I know, medieval history is full of stories about prophecies being fulfilled. I always thought those stories were just legends that grew up after the event. And, of course, he's about a century late for me, but there was Nostradamus. Maybe those old prophecies weren't just *ex post facto* legends, after all. Yes. After Khalid, I'll believe that."

"All right. I'm saying, now, that in a few days there'll be a bad explosion at Reno, Nevada. Watch the papers and the telecast for it. If it happens, that ought to prove it. And you remember what I told you about the Turks annexing Syria and Lebanon?" The old man nodded. "When that happens, get away from Blanley. Come up to the town where Northern State Mental Hospital is, and get yourself a place to live, and stay there. And try to bring Marjorie Fenner along with you. Will you do that, Max?"

"If you say so." His eyes widened. "Something bad's going to happen here?"

"Yes, Max. Something very bad. You promise me you will?"

"Of course, Ed. You know, you're the only friend I have around here. You and Marjorie. I'll come, and bring her along."

"Here's the key to my apartment." He got it from his pocket and gave it to Pottgeiter, with instructions. "Everything in the filing cabinet on the left of my desk. And don't let anybody else see any of it. Keep it safe for me."

The large young man in the white coat entered.

David Johnson was so taken with "The Edge of the Knife" he wrote a sequel of sorts, calling it "The Spine of the Knife." This story provides us with a close-up view of both the beginning Terran Federation and World War III. It's a fascinating yarn, and one that H. Beam Piper never got around to writing.

THE SPINE OF THE KNIFE

David Johnson

40 A.E. Cranhurst Academy, England

Tallal ib'n Khalid slipped the leather jerkin over his lean torso, pulled on his soft-soled slippers, and examined Walid's knife. Its wooden eight-inch blade was edged in red grease paint, and its handle was wound with copper wire and covered with black velvet to afford a good grip. He nodded approvingly, gripped it with his thumb resting on the knife spine, and advanced to meet Shafra Bari.

As he had expected, the burly Yemeni was depending upon his greater brawn to overpower his antagonist. He advanced with a sidling, spread-eagled gait, his knife hand against his right hip and his left hand extended in front. Tallal nodded with satisfaction, still a wrist-grabber. Then he blinked. Why, the fellow was actually holding his knife reversed, his little finger to the guard and his thumb on the pommel!

Tallal went cautiously to meet him, made a feint at Bari's knife hand with his own left, and then side-stepped quickly to the right. As Bari's left hand grabbed at his right wrist, Tallal's left hand brushed against it and closed into a fist, with Bari's left thumb inside of it. He gave a quick downward twist with his wrist, pulling Bari off balance.

Caught by surprise, Bari stumbled, his knife flailing wildly away from Tallal. As he tumbled forward, Tallal pivoted on his left heel and drove the point of his knife toward the back of Bari's neck. At the same time he released Bari's thumb.

Suddenly, the Yemeni seemed to lunge forward, regaining control from his stumble. Twisting his torso around, his knife darted up, its spine clashing with the edge of Tallal's, then knocking the knife from his grasp! Bari continued his lunge, ducking his head as he hit the ground on his shoulder. Tallal turned to scramble after his lost knife, skittering across the floor of the gymnasium. As he leapt down to grab the knife a great weight slammed him to the floor, knocking the wind from him.

Tallal's head jerked up, Bari pulling his hair. The edge of the Yemeni's knife slid across Tallal's throat to leave a greasy, red streak.

"Hold!" shouted the sergeant. The Yemeni released Tallal and leapt to his feet, extending his hand to help Tallal from the floor.

As Tallal reached his feet, the sergeant turned to the row of cadets watching from the edge of the mat.

"Your knife can be both a defensive and an offensive weapon. Never forget that," the sergeant said. Tallal thought he detected the hint of a grin on Walid's face. "Dismissed," the sergeant concluded.

Bari stepped forward, offering his hand.

"I surprised you," he said as Tallal shook his hand. "You fought well, Cadet." Tallal shook his head slowly and frowned slightly.

"You are too kind, Cadet. I appreciate the lesson you have taught me today." The Yemeni bowed his head slightly and turned toward the double doors. Walid came up.

"My condolences, cousin," he said in Arabic, smiling broadly now. "I thought you would best him."

Tallal removed a kerchief from his pocket, wiped the greasepaint from the training knife, and then from his throat.

"Thank you for loaning your knife," he said, also in Arabic, handing the knife to Walid, pommel first. "I'm grateful it was just a training bout. Otherwise you'd be offering your condolences to the *Khalif*."

"By the grace of Allah may that never be the case, Tallal," Walid said, turning the knife in his hands. "I hope your father dies in his tent, an old man with you there to comfort your mother and sisters." He placed the knife in the sheath above his hip, the Cranhurst insignia stitched into the soft leather.

"I'm sure that'll be the case," Tallal said, unbuttoning the jerkin and pulling it from his arms. He reached out and put his hand on his cousin's shoulder. "I need a shower."

The two young men made their way through the double doors where the sergeant and the other cadets had gone out.

"It had never occurred to me that a knife could be used defensively," Tallal said. "When Bari used the spine of the knife to parry my blade I hardly realized what was happening. That's why I lost my knife."

"I wonder," Walid said. He paused then began again, "Do you suppose Sergeant Donahoe had coached Bari? That would be like him: to make his point by demonstration."

"Perhaps," Tallal mused. "Perhaps." The two cadets walked on toward the locker room in silence.

When Tallal arrived the next morning at their small study room in Prescott Hall, Walid was already seated, his notes from International Politics spread across the tabletop. He looked up as Tallal entered.

"Good morning, cousin," he said.

"Good morning," Tallal answered, hardly looking at Walid. He put his books and notes on the table and took a seat across from Walid but his gaze wandered to the room's small window and the parade ground outside. Walid frowned.

"Tallal?" Tallal blinked, looked back at Walid.

"I'm sorry, Walid. I've been thinking about Bari."

"The fight?" Walid's frown deepened. "Enough of that. You should be thinking about Brodie's theory of nuclear deterrence and the missiles of the Eastern Axis. The exam is next week!" Tallal nodded.

"Yes, about the fight...*and* about nuclear missiles." Walid continued to frown. "What if?" Tallal began, then paused. "What if it were possible to counter a nuclear attack, to use missiles to counter other missiles, as Bari used his knife-spine to counter my knife-edge?" Walid shook his head.

"It would be impossible to design a missile so accurate it could attack another missile already in flight!"

"Perhaps," agreed Tallal. "But if one could create a missile force that could survive an enemy's attack...."

"You mean like the U.S. Lunar Base?" Walid asked. Tallal's dark eyes focused in the distance beyond the wall behind Walid.

"Well, yes, for now, but eventually the Eastern Axis will build its own lunar base—or be able to attack the U.S. missiles on Luna with rockets from Earth." He turned to look out the window again. "No, I'm talking about something else, about a missile force with such redundancies that it could survive a direct attack and yet still be able to retaliate afterwards, as Bari did with me yesterday."

"Wouldn't the attacker simply deploy more missiles, to overwhelm the redundant missile force?" Walid asked.

"Yes," Tallal said. "If an attacker knew about the redundant missiles he would work to overwhelm them, but if he didn't know, if the redundancies were a secret...."

Walid nodded.

"The 'knife-spine' could 'turn' an attack. The attacker could be overcome by a counter-attack from the secret missiles." He shuddered. "But the devastation of the first attack. May Allah forgive us, it would be horrible!" This time Tallal nodded. "Grievous, yes, but victory nonetheless."

"Do you suppose anyone has such a knife-spine? A force of secret missiles?"

"Who can know?" Tallal asked. "The United States had the vision to establish its Lunar Base. Perhaps it's been prescient in other ways too."

"But the Lunar Base has provoked a confrontation. Even now the Eastern Axis makes its case at the United Nations, calling for demilitarization and internationalization of the Lunar Base."

Again Tallal nodded.

"That's what took father to Ankara to meet the President of Turkey. They'll support the United States at the United Nations."

"But why does the United States provoke the Eastern Axis so?" Walid asked. "Surely the Americans must have known the Lunar Base would be seen as an unacceptable escalation?"

"Yes, they must have known," Tallal agreed. "So perhaps it's meant to distract from the knife-spine...."

En route to Cheverton Estate, Northamptonshire, England, November 1973

The next morning he and Walid had a campus pass. Ali met them at the gate with a car to take them to the country house. From the back seat Tallal watched the grey countryside speed by the Daimler.

"Mrs. Somerton said that my uncle was expected up from London today and will join us for lunch," Walid said, seated beside him. Tallal turned to look at him but checked himself and returned his eyes to the passing hills. He took a deep breath.

"Will *Amir* Nayef's daughter be joining him?"

"She didn't say," Walid said. "But I'd expect as much. It wouldn't be like *'Amm* Nayef to leave his family at the embassy." Tallal smiled softly. Walid grinned, and continued quickly. "You don't fool me, cousin," he said. "I knew Tijan caught your attention when we were at Cheverton last month!" Tallal's smile widened.

"She is a remarkable young woman, you must admit."

"Bah! She's pretentious! She believes being educated makes her equal to a man."

"She's more than the equal to any man I know, yourself included," Tallal said, laughing now. "She's delightful company and marvelous to look at."

"You've been corrupted by these Britons," Walid said, laughing too. "You're captivated by Tijan because she's more Briton than Arab." Tallal shook his head.

"She's both Arab and Briton." He paused. "Allah willing, that's the sort of wife I'll want by my side if I'm to continue Father's efforts to modernize the Caliphate."

"Oh ho!" Walid said.

Cheverton Estate, Northamptonshire, England, November 1973

The car pulled up before Cheverton House. Ali got out and came round to open the door. Already, a pair of servants had come out of the house and were getting their luggage out of the boot. Tallal followed Walid out of the car, into the autumn chill. A slight rain had begun to fall.

Wallace, the grey-haired butler, was standing just outside the door of the house.

"Welcome, young sirs," he said in English, holding the door open for them both. Inside, he motioned to another servant who took their coats. "The Ambassador has already arrived," he said. "He would like to see you, as soon as you have settled yourselves."

"Which means right away," Walid said, also in English. "We shouldn't keep him waiting." Wallace started to say something, swallowed it, and then asked them if they were in need of refreshment as he led them toward the salon.

"No, we will wait until lunch," said Tallal, and followed his cousin into the salon.

The Sublime Caliph's Ambassador Extraordinary and Plenipotentiary to the Court of St. James sat hunched forward at his desk; he had square shoulders and square, thick fists, a round, bald head and a neatly-trimmed, black beard. He rose from the desk as Walid and Tallal came through the doorway into the salon.

"Peace be upon you, Your Royal Highness," Nayef ib'n Abdullah said, bowing slightly and touching hands and cheeks with Tallal.

"And peace and mercy upon you, kinsman," Tallal replied. Nayef greeted Walid in the same manner, calling him "nephew" and Walid calling him "uncle" in reply.

"Please sit." Nayef indicated four chairs in the center of the room.

"It is kind of you to invite us to lunch," Tallal said. Nayef looked from Tallal to Walid.

"I do not imagine they serve *mezze* at Cranhurst." Tallal and Walid smiled, shaking their heads softly.

"Shepard's pie and mutton," Walid said.

Nayef chuckled softly.

"And how go your studies?"

"Well," Tallal said. "We've military history and international politics this session."

The older man nodded.

"And physical combat," added Walid. "Tallal, er...the Crown Prince has been working on a synthesis of the two." He grinned at Tallal.

Nayef raised an eyebrow.

"It's nothing," Tallal said. "Just a wild fantasy." He lifted his gaze from his folded hands in his lap. "Have you had any news from home?"

"Indeed, I have," Nayef said. "I spoke with the *Khalif* last evening. We discussed his recent efforts in Ankara. He asked about you and bid me to send you his love."

Tallal smiled gently. "You are kind, kinsman, to bring me this news from my father. He traveled to Ankara to discuss the trouble in Syria?"

Nayef nodded. "President Ariburun shares our interest in thwarting the efforts of the Eastern Axis to foment unrest among the peoples of the Caliphate."

Tallal frowned. "Eastern Axis? Is it not Al Saud that would topple the Hashemite thrones?"

This time Nayef shook his head slowly from side to side. "Yes, the Saudis despite the apparent warmth they showed the *Khalif* during last year's *hajj* still dream of seizing our realms excepting the refugees from Palestine but they are not behind the seditionists in Syria. It is Egypt doing the bidding of its Eastern Axis patrons—"

"Bah!" interrupted Walid. "What good is there in learning about Spartans and Athenians or the simmering stand-off on the Korean peninsula when our own lands are beset with such intrigues?"

Tallal turned to look at him. "It's from the examples of history and of geopolitics that we understand our own challenges, cousin."

"Bah!" Walid said again, grinning this time. "You should be a professor! I struggle with my texts while you find strategic lessons in the gymnasium!"

Tallal's brow furrowed and he looked away from the older man.

Nayef watched him closely for a few heartbeats, then turned his gaze on Walid. "That is as it should be, nephew. Allah willing, your classmate will be *Khalif* himself one day many years from now." He rose from his chair. "Let us go to enjoy some *mezze*."

Tallal and Walid stood to follow him. Before they reached the door Tallal asked, "Has your family come up from London with you, kinsman."

Walid grinned.

"Yes," Nayef said as he stepped into the hall. "My wife and my daughter will join us for lunch." After a moment he added, "She would be angry if she knew I'd mentioned it but my daughter has been much looking forward to seeing you again, Highness."

Walid's grin grew brighter.

"The pleasure will be mine, kinsman," replied Tallal.

As they walked down the hall to the dining room Tallal wondered if Tijan were truly looking forward to seeing him again. Yes, she had been cordial when they had last been at Cheverton together and it had seemed as if she had seen him as a man rather than merely as her Crown Prince. That did not mean though that she was fond of him.

He was convinced that Nayef had a genuine affection for him but it was also clear that the old Bedouin always remembered that Tallal would one day be his chieftain. If Tallal were to marry his daughter Nayef's future and that of his family would continue to be secure. Nayef had never been anything other than a loyal retainer of Tallal's father but that did not mean he was beyond using his daughter as a means to secure his position into the future.

Tallal had to admit to himself, no matter how beautiful and interesting Tijan was, that he would never take her as his wife if she did not come to the marriage of her own will and out of love for him. He smiled softly. One thing of which he was certain was that Tijan herself would have it no other way. She might not have feelings for him but she would also not allow herself to be courted by him if she did not have some affection for him.

Tallal followed Nayef and Walid into the dining room. This was not the formal dining room but the smaller, more intimate family dining room. Tallal could see a servant leaving just as he came into the room and as Nayef moved to the other doorway his wife, Mihrimah al-Nayef, entered and greeted her husband with a clasp of hands. Behind her came Tijan, slightly taller than her mother, her blue print dress carefully pressed and her long, dark hair drawn up upon her head. She disappeared behind

Nayef's bulk as they hugged warmly.

Moving past her husband, Nayef's wife said, "Peace be upon you, Your Royal Highness."

"May peace and the blessings of Allah be upon you, *Amira*," Tallal responded, taking her offered hand. She turned to greet her nephew.

Tallal stepped forward and offered his hand to Tijan. "May peace be upon you, *Amira*," he said with a smile.

"May peace and mercy be upon you, Your Royal Highness," Tijan said, smiling in return.

Another servant spoke quietly to Nayef. "Lunch is served," Nayef said, motioning toward the table.

Silently cursing the requirements of etiquette, Tallal nevertheless took his place at the head of the table. Walid held a chair to Tallal's right for his aunt and after she was seated moved around the table to the other side, where Nayef had just seated his daughter across from her mother. Nayef sat at the other end of the table and Walid sat next to Tijan, his uncle on his left. Servants brought the first course.

"Tell us of your studies at Cranhurst, Highness," *Amira* Nayef said.

"We have international politics and military history this session," Tallal said. He glanced at Walid and then at Tijan. "And physical combat."

"And they go well?"

"Yes," Tallal said. He hoped Walid would not elaborate. "How go your own studies at Norham, *Amira*," he asked Tijan.

"Nothing quite so interesting, I'm afraid, Highness," she said with a frown. "Frankish literature, Persian poetry, and Baroque music."

"There are many young women in our lands who would envy you your education," her mother said.

"My apologies, Mother," Tijan said, bowing her head slightly. "And to you as well, Father. You are right, of course, Mother, but how I would love to study history or politics...or physical combat!"

"In truth, I envy you," Tallal said. "Yes, I enjoy my studies and understand that they will serve me well someday, Allah willing, but at times it would be good simply to study for the sake of knowledge, for beauty even."

"Hah," Walid said. "Perhaps you were pondering beauty the other day when Bari bested you!" He grinned. Tallal glared at him, then turned back to Tijan.

"We were practicing with knives and my opponent used his in a most unconventional manner." Tallal looked away from Tijan to the plate of food before him.

"Unconventional?" Tijan seemed genuinely interested.

"He used the spine of his knife, the edge opposite the sharpened portion of the blade, to deflect my knife. It was a maneuver I had never before encountered."

Amira Nayef asked, "Surely part of the point of your practice is to learn how to deal with such unconventional maneuvers?"

Tallal nodded.

Servants cleared the first course and set the platters for the second course. Tallal picked at his plate, not hungry even as he relished the familiarity of the humus and grilled lamb.

"Tallal has even found insights into grand strategy in his experience on the practice mat," Walid said, still grinning.

"Perhaps this is not an appropriate topic for conversation over lunch," Nayef said.

"Father, please," Tijan said. After a moment her father nodded.

"Tallal believes there could be an alternative to nuclear deterrence," Walid said.

"Deterrence? You mean a way to stop a nuclear war?" Tijan asked.

"Perhaps," Tallal said. "Ever since the United States launched *Orbiter* in 1963 and Russia followed with its own artificial satellite later that year the Western and Eastern blocs have known that they could inflict dreadful harm on each other's nations. What stops them from attacking each other is the fear of retaliation from the other side."

"Some say this brings great stability to international politics," Nayef said. "Yes, the Eastern and Western blocs might clash through proxies as they did in Indonesia early last decade but this Subwar is much to be preferred to an outright nuclear war."

"Surely that is not how the people of Indonesia saw it," Tijan said.

"Perhaps not," Tallal said. "But deterrence is not as stable as some would claim." Nayef nodded. "Each side dreams of a successful first strike against its adversary, an opening attack so devastating that it eliminates—or substantially reduces—the opponent's ability to retaliate."

"Which leads to an arms race," continued Walid. "The nuclear warheads get more powerful and so the missiles must get bigger. Three years after *Orbiter* the United States used an even larger rocket to launch the manned spacecraft *Zephyr*. It took the Russians two more years but eventually they did the same."

"And five years after *Zephyr* the missiles had gotten so powerful that the United States was able to launch *Kilroy* to Luna," finished Tallal.

"But what do all of these spacecraft and moon rockets have to do with knife fighting?" Tijan asked.

Nayef smiled, looking from Tallal to Walid.

"They are merely artifacts of the arms race," Walid said. "As each side makes larger missiles that can carry bigger nuclear warheads they can also use them to carry heavier payloads into space, like *Zephyr* or the extra fuel used by *Kilroy* to reach Luna." He looked across the table at Tallal. "His encounter with the spine of the knife has led Tallal to a possible solution to the unstable one-upmanship of this arms race."

"What is your solution," Tijan asked. Tallal looked at Nayef who nodded gently.

"Each side builds more missiles to counter the missiles of the other side," Tallal said. "If one side could build a missile force in secret, the other side would not know to match it. That advantage could prove decisive in an actual battle."

"You mean a nuclear war?" Tijan asked, leaning back from the table, her eyes widening.

"Yes," Tallal said. "If one side were to strike first the destruction would be horrible. But if the other side had a secret missile force it could retaliate decisively. The costs would be unimaginable but the victorious outcome would be preferred over devastation and defeat."

Amira Nayef shuddered. "It is a ghastly world in which we find ourselves living."

"It is, my wife," Nayef said. "It is these harsh circumstances which keep me here among the Britons instead of among family and friends in our tents in the desert."

"Building this secret force of missiles would be an extraordinary undertaking," Tijan said.

Tallal nodded. "It may very well be beyond the current capabilities of the Americans or the Russians. It would also be very difficult to keep such an undertaking secret."

"Some sort of diversion would help," Walid said. "Like a missile base on Luna."

"But the Eastern Axis decries the U.S. Lunar Base," Tijan said.

"Indeed," Tallal said. "While its diplomats make their calls for demilitarization and internationalization at the United Nations and its intelligence agencies point their satellite sensors and telescopes at Luna, they may not be paying attention to efforts underway elsewhere."

Servants cleared the main course and served the *baklava.*

"*Kilroy* itself was a closely-held secret," Walid said. "The world did not know about the lunar-base project until the moon-rocket was launched in 1971."

"Surely the spies of the Eastern Bloc knew of the Americans' plans for Luna," Tijan said.

"Most likely," admitted Tallal. "If there were a secret missile force they might discover it as well." He frowned.

"Perhaps there is no spine of the knife," Walid admitted.

"Perhaps not," Nayef said. "But it's an intriguing premise, Highness. It pleases me to see you take to your studies so well. The *Khalif* will be proud of you."

"Thank you, kinsman," Tallal said, blushing.

Nayef turned to look at Walid. "And you, nephew. You grasp these matters too. One day, Allah willing, you will serve your cousin well."

It was Walid's turn to blush.

"Thank you, Uncle," he said. Tallal grinned and stole a look at Tijan. She returned his smile.

"Now tell us, daughter," Nayef continued, "did I see your cello in your baggage this morning?" Tijan nodded. "Perhaps you will play us something from one of those dreadful Baroque composers after lunch?"

"Yes, father," Tijan said, turning to look at Tallal. "It would be my pleasure, if it would please Your Highness."

Tallal smiled softly.

"I can imagine nothing I would rather hear, *Amira*." Tijan smiled broadly.

"Please, daughter, let it be something lively," her mother said. "Perhaps a *courante*? We could use a bit of cheer after all this talk of war and destruction." Nayef nodded as he rose from his seat and came around the table to pull his wife's chair from the table.\

This provided Tallal the opportunity to do the same for Tijan. Walid, standing next to her, did his best to keep from grinning.

The knock on the guest room door woke Tallal. The door opened slowly. A short, bulky figure silhouetted by the soft light in the hallway knelt on the threshold. Rising from his bed Tallal recognized Nayef with a start. He turned on the lamp on his bedside table.

"Majesty," the big man said, a tremor in his voice.

"What is it, kinsman," Tallal asked, his own voice shaking. He pulled on his robe and stepped toward Nayef.

"There has been a tragedy, Majesty," Nayef said. *"Majesty" again.* "Your father, Khalid, God's peace be upon him, has been slain."

Tallal stepped back, his arms out before him. "What? No," he cried. "This cannot be!"

"I am afraid so, Majesty," Nayef said. "An assassin's bullet took him."

Tallal's body shuddered uncontrollably. After a moment he stilled. "When?" he asked, his voice steady now.

"A few hours ago, at Basra," Nayef said. Tallal stepped forward, reached down to Nayef.

"Rise, kinsman." He grasped the older man's hand. Nayef came to his feet. Tallal stepped forward, arms reaching. Nayef held him firmly for several moments. After a time Tallal withdrew from the embrace.

"I must go to Mother," he said.

"Yes," Nayef said. "A car is on its way. A plane will be waiting at Kirmington airfield. A military transport courtesy of Her Majesty's government. It will take us directly to Basra."

Us?" Tallal asked.

"Yes, Majesty," Nayef said. "I will return with you, and my family will accompany me. I will not be apart from them during this crisis. Walid will come too."

"Aye, that's sound, kinsman," Tallal said. "In truth, I welcome your companionship."

"I am yours, Majesty," Nayef said. "Though I wish it were under different circumstances."

"I too, kinsman. I too." Tallal said. "I welcome your service and trust you will serve me as you have served my father." Nayef nodded, then turned back toward the open doorway.

"If I may take your leave, Majesty, I must tell the others," he said. "The butler will be here presently to get you dressed." Tallal noticed for the first time that Nayef was still wearing his bedclothes.

En route (by air) to Basra, Iraq, November 1973

Tallal stared out the jet's window, watching the clouds below slide slowly past. The British had provided them with one of the planes used by senior military and government officials. This was no large troop transport but rather a military version of the sort of aircraft also used by business executives. The eight members of their party—Nayef had brought along two of his household servants and a secretary from the embassy staff—filled perhaps half the seats. A British military attaché and two officials from the Foreign Office who had been aboard the plane when Tallal and the others had arrived at the airfield sat at the front of the cabin near the door to the cockpit. The steward, a Royal Air Force enlisted man, was offering them water.

Walid snoozed in the seat beside him. Tallal could not sleep. He knew he would never see his father again. The report the embassy secretary had given him said Father had been shot to death while leaving the Parliament Building for the palace outside the city. The assassin was a religious fanatic, identified as an Egyptian named Mohammed Noureed. He had used an old American submachine-gun. Besides Father, two guards had been killed and a third seriously wounded. The killer was seized by an infuriated mob and stoned to death on the spot in the traditional manner. That was the report but Tallal found it difficult to accept that Father was dead. He wanted to believe, desperately, that Father would be there, on the apron to greet him when the plane landed in Basra.

But he would not be.

Outside the window the clouds had cleared. Below the green expanse between the great rivers, *al-Dijla* and *al-Furat*, drifted by. It seemed familiar to him but to his Father, who had been born at Taif, in the sparse deserts of the Hejaz, it had always been a marvel. Tallal thought of his mother; she would be devastated. And the assassin was from her homeland. Mother had feared for Father's life since he had proclaimed the Islamic Caliphate five years ago, changing his name to Khalid ib'n Hussein. "Khalid" for Khalid ib'n Walid, the Sword of God, Companion to the Prophet, and military leader of the first Caliphate. And "ib'n Hussein" for Tallal's great-grandfather, Hussein ib'n Ali, who had proclaimed the short-lived Sharifan Caliphate after the Ottoman Caliphate was abolished. Mother had known that there would be those who would never accept Father as *Khalif*. How terrible that she had been right!

Nayef had told him it was true that Father's assassin and his accomplices were religious fanatics but that there could be no doubt whatsoever that the murder was inspired, at least indirectly, by the Eastern Axis. In some manner that he did not yet understand, Father's death was necessary to the policies of the Eastern Axis.

King Ali ib'n Hussein Airport, al-Basra, Iraq, November 1973

The sun was setting as the plane touched down. The Prime Minister, *Amir* Yousef, and *Amir* Salim, the Defence Minister, met the plane on the apron. *Malik* Faisal had come from Baghdad and *Malik* Raad from Damascus as well. There were others, many of them advisors to his father that Tallal recognized. Offering their condolences they all called him

"Majesty," as Nayef had done ever since he'd come into Tallal's room at Cheverton.

"The Parliament is in session now to consider the Act of Succession, Majesty," *Amir* Yousef said. "They will accept your Oath of Accession as soon as we arrive."

"Thank you, *Amir* Yousef," Tallal said. "But I wish to see my mother first."

"Majesty," Yousef said. "Your mother and your sisters have gone into seclusion at the winter encampment of *Sheikh* Hamid." Hamid was one of his father's closest advisors. Tallal had visited his black tents in the hills above Basra many times. "The delay would be several hours."

"Surely, the Parliament can wait while a son goes to his mother after his father has been slain by an assassin's bullet," Tallal said. "Ask the Speaker to recess until tomorrow." Yousef looked at Salim and then Nayef. Both men nodded.

"As you command, Majesty," the prime minister said, bowing slightly.

Tallal turned to the two kings:

"Your Highnesses, would you share the hospitality of *Sheikh* Hamid with me?"

"As you wish, Majesty," Faisal said.

"I would welcome his hospitality and your company, Majesty," Raad said.

Tallal nodded and Yousef led him to a waiting military vehicle. Nayef joined them as Walid, Tijan, and her mother were escorted to another vehicle. The two kings and *Amir* Salim rode in the vehicle directly behind Tallal's. Nayef's staff and the British officials were taken to other vehicles farther back in the convoy.

Shammar Encampment, al-Basra, Iraq, November 1973

Hamid was at the Parliament in Basra, so his seneschal greeted Tallal's party—calling him Majesty like everyone else—and conducted them to the guest quarters.

"Son," his mother said, moving quickly across the room to greet him as he entered. She seemed older to Tallal, her eyes swollen and her hair disheveled as she embraced him.

"It warms my heart, Mother, to see you. How I wish the circumstances were different." His mother began to shiver in his arms. He held her gently. After a moment she stepped back. Her composure returned she seemed every bit the *Khalifa* she had been sitting behind Father in the Audience Hall of the palace.

"Your father loved you very much, Tallal, and he would be proud of the man you have become."

"My heart aches knowing I will not see him again," Tallal said.

"Mine as well, son. It is a terrible thing," she said. "But your father's people, your people, need you now." Tallal nodded.

"First I would see my sisters," he said. "I will give the Oath tomorrow."

"They've just managed to get to sleep," his mother said. "But they will delight in your arrival." She led him into the sleeping chamber.

Hall of the Senate, Basra, Iraq, November 1973

As Tallal knelt before him, the ancient President of the Senate, his voice trembling slightly, said, "Whereas it has pleased All-Merciful God to call to His Mercy our late Sublime and Sovereign Prince Khalid ib'n Hussein, Successor to the Prophet, Peace be upon Him, by whose decease the Succession is solely and rightfully come to the Exalted and Compassionate Prince Tallal ib'n Khalid.

"We, therefore, the Spiritual and Temporal Stewards of this Dominion, being here assisted with these His late Majesty's Consultative Council, with the Kings of Iraq and of Jordan and of Syria, with the Prince of Kuwait and the President of Lebanon, with other Principal Sages of Piety, with the High Mayor, Councilors, and Citizens of Basra, do now hereby with One Voice and Submission of Spirit and Heart proclaim that the Exalted and Compassionate Prince Tallal ib'n Khalid is now, by the death of our late Successor of venerable memory, become Caliph Tallal ib'n Khalid, by the Will of God, Successor to the Prophet, Praise be upon Him, and of all His Dominions, Commander of the Faithful, to whom His subjects do acknowledge all Loyalty and constant Dutifulness with hearty and humble Affection, beseeching Allah by whom Caliphs do reign, to bless the Sublime Prince Tallal ib'n Khalid with long and happy Years to reign over us."

Shammar Encampment, al-Basra, Iraq, November 1973

Tallal returned from the *masjid* with *Sheikh* Hamid and his retinue to the black tents of his winter encampment. After his mother and sisters joined them for a simple dinner, the Shammar chieftain insisted that Tallal stay in his own apartments, and retired with his wives to the guest quarters Tallal had shared with Walid the night before. Tallal missed his friend whom he'd seen only briefly during the reception following the Oath of Accession, before the procession to his father's burial site. He struggled to get to sleep, realizing at last that it was his father he truly missed.

He came into Hamid's audience chamber that morning tired and unrefreshed by the few hours' sleep he had gotten the night before, edgy from the strain of trying to adjust his mind to the Court of the Islamic Caliphate. Nayef hadn't arrived yet, but *Amir* Yousef was waiting for him, a cable in his hand, almost recoiling in dismay.

"I regret bringing such ill tidings, Majesty," he said as he entered.

He shook his head softly. It would take him some time to get used to such deference from men he'd known only as his elders.

"There has been an uprising in Syria," the prime minister said. "The rebels have seized the palace and hold *Malik* Raad's wife and children hostage. His Highness is already returning to Damascus."

"That's sound," Tallal said. "We will give him every assistance." Yousef glanced down at his folded hands. At that moment, the footmen parted the curtains of the entrance and Nayef entered, followed by his secretary and the British military attaché. They each bowed in turn as they approached Tallal and Yousef.

"Good morning, kinsman," Tallal said

"Would that it were, Majesty," Nayef said, glancing at Yousef. "I trust you've heard of the trouble in Syria?"

Tallal nodded.

Yousef softly cleared his throat.

"Welcome, *Amir* Nayef. I was about to inform His Majesty of Prime Minister Salam's request for reinforcements in Lebanon." He paused, turning back to Tallal. "And of the marshaling of Saudi forces in Tabouk and al-Jouf." Tallal tried to remember his Saudi geography.

"They threaten Jordan?" Yousef nodded. "This will make it difficult to support *Malik* Raad?" Again Yousef nodded.

"Your Majesty," Nayef said. "*Malik* Raad did not ask for aid when he departed for Damascus. He understands that the Caliphate faces many enemies." Yousef nodded softly. Tallal looked from Yousef to Nayef and then back to Yousef.

"What do you recommend?"

"*Amir* Salim is in the antechamber, Majesty," Yousef said. "Allow me to ask him to join us." Tallal nodded. Yousef turned and spoke to an aide, who quickly left by the entrance Nayef had come through. After a moment the defense minister entered the audience chamber, followed by Yousef's aide. Salim bowed and then approached Tallal and the others.

"Good morning, *Amir* Salim," Tallal said.

Salim frowned.

"Your Majesty." The defense minister nodded and looked at Yousef.

"His Majesty has asked for our recommendations."

Salim nodded again.

"Majesty, *Malik* Raad understands that were we to send him aid from the Saudi frontier it would leave Jordan undefended," Salim said.

"Will *Malik* Raad be able to quell the revolt on his own?" Tallal asked.

"*Malik* Raad is valiant, Majesty," Salim said. Glancing again at Yousef he added, "But the rebels have the greater numbers."

"Can we offer him no assistance?" Salim looked at Yousef. The prime minister smiled softly and nodded.

"Your father had a plan, Majesty," Salim said. "When he was in Ankara he reached an understanding with President Ariburun. The Turks are prepared to assist the Caliphate in Syria."

"Turkey will come to *Malik* Raad's aid?" Tallal asked.

Salim and Yousef nodded.

"You have but to give the word, Majesty," Nayef said.

"Then by all means, yes!"

"By your leave then, Majesty. I will inform the Foreign Minister." Nayef bowed and turned toward the exit, motioning to his secretary and the attaché to follow him. As the footmen parted the curtains the diplomat stopped and turned back to look at Salim.

"You must take His Majesty to *al-Borak*," he said. Salim started and looked quickly at Yousef. After a moment the prime minister nodded.

Al-Borak *Research Center, al-Dulaim, Iraq, November 1973*

The plane landed in darkness. Tallal was forced to admit he had no idea where they might be. Yousef and Salim had rebuffed his questions, begging his indulgence until he reached the secret facility. He assented but insisted that Walid come along. Salim in particular had not liked that idea.

"Ninety minutes," Walid said from the seat next to him as the plane taxied. "And, I think, to the northwest. I would say we're in al-Dulaim."

"Yes," agreed Tallal. "Though not quite to the Saudi frontier. What could it be?"

Walid simply shook his head. As the plane came to a stop, the defense minister rose from his seat.

"Your Majesty, if you will wait a moment while I prepare the reception."

Tallal nodded his assent and Salim moved to the hatch which the airman had opened. As the stairway extended to the ground Tallal could see through the viewport men in military uniform gathering on the apron. The uniform worn by one of them seemed unusual. Salim stepped through the doorway, headed down the stairway, and was greeted by one of the officers.

"That looks like an American officer," Walid said, stooping to look out the viewport.

"Is it?" Tallal raised his eyebrows. "Well, let's see what this is about."

He moved past the saluting airman and through the doorway. There was a light, cool breeze as he made his way down the stairway. It shook slightly as Walid stepped onto the landing behind him. As Tallal reached the apron Salim and the officer he had met, an air force major general, stepped forward to greet him.

"Majesty, may I present General Kalil al-Tay, commander of *al-Borak* Research Center," Salim said. The officer bowed.

"Your service is appreciated, General," Tallal said. "I look forward to learning about your facility."

"It is an honor to welcome Your Majesty," al-Tay said. Then, in English, he added, "May I also present Lieutenant Colonel Anthony Miles of the United States Air Force who is assisting us here." He turned and the officer in the unusual uniform stepped forward. Tall, red-haired; and light-skinned he stood out among the other men and not just because his uniform was different.

"Please accept my greetings on behalf of the United States Government, Your Majesty." Miles bowed slightly, then added, "It had been my good fortune to meet your father. Please also accept my official and personal condolences."

"Thank you, Colonel," Tallal said. Turning once again to al-Tay he asked, "What is your mission here, General?"

As Salim presented Walid to the other officers, al-Tay motioned toward a waiting car. "If you will join us, Majesty, it will be my honor to show you." Tallal moved toward the car, and stepped past another saluting airman holding the open door. Al-Tay got in beside him while the American colonel seated himself in the front passenger seat. Tallal noticed Salim and Walid and another officer getting into a car behind them.

"*Al-Borak* is a joint undertaking with the United States," al-Tay said. "Its mission is the first of its kind for the Caliphate."

"*Amir* Salim has told me the effort was initiated by my father," Tallal said.

"May the peace of the Prophet be upon him," al-Tay said. "Yes, Majesty, your father authorized our mission after being approached by the Americans about Operation Triple Cross. Perhaps Colonel Miles can explain about that." The American officer turned slightly in his seat to look at Tallal.\

"You are aware of our Lunar Base, Your Majesty?" Miles asked. Tallal nodded. "You're likely also aware of the...consternation it has caused the Eastern Axis." Again Tallal nodded. "The Lunar Base is supplied by launch facilities in the United States. Because the Base itself is unassailable those launch facilities have become key targets of the nuclear missiles of the Axis."

The car pulled up in front of a nondescript, concrete, two-story building with a large cargo portal, which was closed, and a small door before which stood a pair of military policemen. Another airman opened the car door and saluted as Tallal stepped out. Al-Tay and Miles got out of the car as the other car pulled in behind them.

"This way, Majesty," al-Tay said, walking around the car and gesturing toward the guarded door. The general returned the guards' salutes and one of them opened the door. Salim and Walid and the other officer came up behind them as al-Tay led Tallal through the doorway. Inside, another guard seated at a desk spoke into a phone while another airman saluted and motioned toward an opening elevator. It was large enough for the entire group to board. Once the door had closed the airman activated the control and the elevator began to move downward.

"As I was saying, Your Majesty," Miles continued. "The United States cannot allow the rocketports which supply the Lunar Base to be destroyed." The elevator continued to move downward, then slowed and came to a stop. After a moment the doors opened toward a long corridor. Tallal and the others followed al-Tay and Miles as they started down the corridor. Miles turned to look at Tallal. "In fact, while the missiles and their warheads are in place on Luna, key targeting components are still being assembled which must be sent up to Luna before the base is fully operational."

Tallal guessed they'd walked nearly half a kilometer before the party stepped into a large facility of which Tallal could make no sense. The expansive cylindrical space was open with some sort of large, central pillar surrounded by equipment and gantries. A series of catwalks and ducts and pipes and electrical conduits ran up the walls toward a ceiling which was not quite visible. Dozens of technicians seemed to be at work on platforms at several different levels above and below them.

"It's a rocket!" he exclaimed.

The tour of the launch facility was both impressive and surreal. It was officially conducted by General at-Tay but the American, Colonel Miles, did most of the talking. Tallal was surprised the Caliphate could accomplish such a thing, but as the tour progressed it became clear that the essential elements, including the rocket itself and most of the technical talent, had been provided by the Americans. From his brief interactions with personnel along the way, Tallal concluded the Caliphate civilian technicians and air force personnel were treated as partners and were learning a great deal but they were junior partners nonetheless.

The tour ended at the launch control center which had telephone and live television connections to the main U.S. launch control center in California. The group had been given an opportunity to refresh themselves and a light breakfast was served in a conference room just behind the control center. For the first time since they'd left the airplane Tallal and Walid had a few moments to themselves in one corner of the room.

"Can you believe it?" Walid asked. "A secret missile program just as you'd imagined!" Tallal shook his head.

"Not exactly." Tallal glanced across the room at Colonel Miles, who was talking with *Amir* Salim and General al-Tay. "This isn't a missile complex. Remember what we learned on the tour. The rocket here doesn't have a nuclear warhead but rather will carry a payload to the Lunar Base, some of these 'Howard gyroscopes' that American lieutenant described."

"Yes, yes," Walid said. "Some navigation and targeting components for the Lunar missiles that were more difficult to assemble than expected." His words came quickly, his voice rising slightly. "Close enough for me! If the primary launch facilities in the U.S. are destroyed, secret duplicate and triplicate rocketports like this one here in al-Dulaim will send those gyroscopes to Luna." He paused. "I wonder where the other sites might be."

"I suspect they won't tell us," Tallal said. "Praise be to Allah, let's hope we never have the chance to find out."

The Caliphal Palace, Basra, Iraq, December 1973

"It was gracious of your mother to invite my mother and me to lunch, Your Majesty," Tijan said.

Tallal smiled.

"Please, you may call me 'Tallal' when we are alone," he held the gate to the garden open for her. She smiled, and as she stepped past him he caught a faint hint of perfume.

"Then you must also call me 'Tijan' instead of '*Amira*.'" Her smile widened.

"It will be my pleasure, Tijan," he said. "I'm afraid that lunch was my sister Saliha's idea, though Mother was quick to assent."

"Do you have the sense that our parents like the idea of us spending time together?"

"It has occurred to me," Tallal said. "But surely it has been mere chance, with your father having been posted to London while I was at school in England."

"It has been my experience that the al-Hashemi leave little to chance," Tijan said. "He has never admitted it outright but I have gotten the sense from my father that he was sent to London by your father to watch over you." Tallal turned to look at her, frowning.

"That thought had not occurred to me," he said after a moment. He turned to look at the water trickling between the small, green palms. "It would seem to make sense. I had wondered why your father would miss a chance to stay at Court here in Basra. He's been close to my father since they were students together in England, like Walid and me. Indeed, it was your father's suggestion that my father change his name when the Arab Federation became the Caliphate."

"And thus, your name too, Tallal," Tijan said with a grin.

"I may no longer be 'Tallal ib'n Abdullah' but am still 'Tallal.'" His gaze returned to her.

"And now *Khalif*."

"Yes." He frowned again and lowered his eyes. "I miss my father." Tijan reached out, took his hand in hers. Tallal's heart leapt.

"I'm sorry, Tallal," she said. "Your father was a great leader, and a good man." After a moment she added, "You're a good man too." She smiled. "And perhaps, Allah willing, you'll also be a great leader."

"You believe so?"

"Do you?"

"I don't know," he said. "There's much that must be decided but it seems the men around me make the decisions."

"Aren't they the same men who served your father?"

"Yes," he admitted, after a moment.

"Then you should trust your father's judgment."

"Would my father have allowed the sack of Beirut by the Syrian rebels?"

"Did you allow it?"

"Yes! No." He turned around, clenched his hands into fists. "I don't know." He faced Tijan again, unclenched his fists. "I wanted to send military forces to assist Raad but Yousef and Salim and even your father advised against it."

"Why didn't they want to assist *Malik* Raad at Damascus?"

"It's not that they didn't want to assist Raad; it's that they didn't believe we could spare the forces from the Saudi frontier."

"And now *Malik* Raad and his family have been killed, may peace be upon them, while the rebels overrun Lebanon." She shuddered. "Did they have no other plans?"

"They had another plan, my father's plan." Tijan looked at him, waiting. "Your father, on my behalf, has asked the Turks to intervene in Syria."

"Will they?"

"The assault has already begun," Tallal said. "We should hear it in the news tomorrow, if the recovery effort for that terrible explosion in the United States is no longer the headline."

"And the Saudi frontier?"

"Jordan remains secure."

"What is it then that troubles you?" she asked. "I mean, besides the tragedies in Damascus and Beirut."

"I worry what will happen once the Turks have gained control of Syria."

"What do you mean?"

"Will they return it to our control?" Tijan frowned.

"These are questions for my father." After a moment she asked, "What might you do to make that more likely?"

"We need some counter to the Turks," Tallal said. "A strong ally who does not also support the Saudis. Like the Americans."

"How will you get the Americans to help us? What do we have that they might want?"

"Allah willing, there is something," Tallal said.

The Foreign Ministry, Basra, Iraq, March 1974

"I can assure Your Majesty that the United States shares the Caliphate's concern about Saudi Arabia's attack on Jordan." Tallal studied the American ambassador, sitting to Yousef's left along one side of the table. Reeve was balding and his glasses gave him a scholarly air—matched by genuine accomplishments in the academy according to the dossier *Sheikh* Sabah had shared with him beforehand—which reminded him of one of his instructors at Cranhurst.

"What most interests us are those specific actions the United States is prepared to undertake to demonstrate its concern about the Saudi invasion," the foreign minister said, on Tallal's right and across the table from the American ambassador.

"Surely Minister Salim's told you of the satellite reconnaissance of the Saudi forces in al-Jouf and Tabouk that we've shared with his staff," the military attaché, Lanningham, seated beside Reeve, said.

Sabah nodded.

"Yes, of course, Major," the Kuwaiti said. "But *Amir* Salim has also asked, on His Majesty's behalf, for similar reconnaissance of the Turkish forces in Syria and Lebanon." The attaché looked to the ambassador.

"It's our understanding, Foreign Minister, that Turkey's move into Syria and Lebanon came at the Caliphate's request." Reeve looked from Sabah to Nayef, seated next to the foreign minister.

Nayef's face remained impassive. From his seat beside Tallal, Yousef said, "If you have reached that 'understanding' then surely you must also understand that His Majesty's Government had no expectation that Syria and Lebanon would be annexed by Turkey." Reeve nodded.

"An unfortunate overstep, I'm sure, Prime Minister," Reeve said. "Nevertheless, it would be very difficult for the United States to step between two allies." Lanningham nodded. *There it was*, thought Tallal. Yousef gave a slight nod to Sabah.

"We understand this difficulty, Ambassador," the foreign minister said. "You must therefore also understand that under such circumstances it may be difficult for the Caliphate to continue its cooperation with the United States in the *al-Borak* undertaking." Reeve frowned.

"I see, Foreign Minister," he said, looking at Yousef and then at Tallal.

"That would be...unfortunate." Lanningham jumped in. "Turkey's also a participant in Operation Triple Cross," he said.

Reeve turned to the major and frowned.

"We are aware of this," Nayef said, looking back at Reeve. "But we also know that there has as yet been no launch facility constructed in Asia Minor."

"A site has been surveyed," Lanningham said. "The facility design exists!" Reeve reached out, placed his hand on Lanningham's arm.

Beside Nayef, *Amir* Salim spoke. "We know that the site in al-Dulaim was selected over the site in Turkey. Putting aside the near state of completion of *al-Borak* and the better suitability of its location for launching payloads to Luna over any place in Turkey—*al-Borak*'s latitude makes it even somewhat better suited to supplying your Lunar Base than is your own facility in California—it seems unlikely, particularly given the objections of the Eastern Axis, that you can afford the delay which would come with construction of a new facility in Turkey."

Reeve released Lanningham's arm, smiled at Sabah.

"I believe what Major Lanningham means, Foreign Minister, is to ask if there's some way we might help each other to resolve our mutual difficulties." Sabah nodded, glanced at Yousef. *Here it comes*, thought Tallal.

"I believe there was another matter you also wanted to discuss today," the Kuwaiti said.

Reeve frowned again.

"Indeed, Foreign Minister," the American said after a moment. "I'm sure His Majesty's Government is aware of the strain the Saudi action has placed upon the United Nations."

"Surely, Ambassador, this strain pales in comparison to the protests of the Eastern Axis over your Lunar Base," Sabah said.

Lanningham started to speak but Reeve interrupted him. "Perhaps so," Reeve said. After a moment he continued, "What's important is that we consider what institution might take the place of the U.N. if that organization breaks-up."

"If I may say so, Ambassador, that premise seems a bit...premature," Sabah said.

"On the contrary, Foreign Minister," Reeve said. "Already new institutions have emerged which look beyond the U.N. The Eastern Axis itself, for example. Or the recent accommodation between the British and the French."

"And the new Conclave convened by the African members of the Commonwealth and the French Union?" Nayef asked.

Reeve nodded.

"The U.S. has its own idea for a new institution?" Sabah asked.

"We're calling it the 'Terran Federation of States.'"

"It would succeed at collective security where the U.N. has failed," Lanningham added.

"If we join this 'Terran Federation' will you share reconnaissance of the Turks?" Sabah asked.

"I'm afraid it wouldn't be that simple, Foreign Minister," Reeve said. "The Turks have already expressed an interest in joining the Terran Federation."

Sabah looked at Yousef, who looked at Tallal. Tallal nodded.

"Could not the collective security provisions of the new Terran Federation be construed to prohibit one member from annexing the territory of another?" Sabah asked.

Reeve sat back in his chair, looked past Lanningham to the embassy counselor seated next to him. After a moment, the junior diplomat nodded.

"Yes, Foreign Minister," Reeve said. "There may have to be an arbitration process but it seems highly unlikely that the Terran Federation would begin with a contravention of its founding principles."

"Go on, Ambassador Reeve," Tallal said. "You have captured our attention."

"With pleasure, Your Majesty...."

Shammar Encampment, al-Basra, Iraq, June 1974

Tallal kicked the mare again as he rounded the last marker. A hot wind blew sand in his eyes and nose from Walid's horse ahead of him, and his mount faltered. Another kick and the horse regained her stride but it was clear now that they would not catch Walid. As Walid's horse crossed the marker into the small oasis, Tallal urged his horse to one last effort. They crossed under the banner just moments behind Walid, but already the young man was jumping off his horse, handing the reins to the hostler, and turning to greet him.

"Well raced," Walid said, grinning as Tallal dismounted and handed his horse to another hostler.

"I'd have had you if you'd not bumped us at the second marker," Tallal said.

Walid smiled more broadly. "Excuses!" He wrapped his arm around Tallal and they walked to the pavilion. Tijan and his sister Saliha rose from their seats as they stepped onto the carpet and into the shade. Tijan's bright green *hijab* fluttered softly in the breeze.

"Congratulations," she said to Walid. After a moment she added, "I wish I could have joined you."

A servant handed Tallal a large canteen of water.

"Your English riding lessons would do little good here in the desert!" Walid interjected, taking an offered canteen from another servant.

"I'd like to see you try," Tallal said. He removed his *keffiyeh*, swabbed his head with a wet towel from another servant.

"Thank you," Tijan said with a smile.

Walid laughed.

"You'll have to make it so now," he said, also removing his *keffiyeh* and toweling off his head. Tallal motioned toward the table which had been set.

"Will you join us for lunch?"

"With pleasure," Tijan said. Tallal held her chair for her. When Walid waited for him after seating Saliha, Tallal motioned for him to sit down. Walid remained standing until Tallal took his seat then seated himself.

"Oh, how the world changes," Walid said, passing a tray of figs to Saliha. "Women riding *seglawi* in the desert!"

"The world *is* changing," Tallal said. "Consider the uprising in Azerbaijan."

"Bah, it's just the Eastern Axis and the machinations of the Subwar," Walid said. "Nothing new about that."

Tijan frowned at Walid.

"When someone tells me something I don't understand I ask him what he means," Tijan said, looking to Tallal. "What do you mean?"

"The efforts of the Eastern Axis to break off Azerbaijan will likely push Iran into the Terran Federation too," Tallal said.

"Too?" Tijan asked.

Tallal blinked.

"Now you've done it," Walid said. "You'll have to tell her."

"It will likely be the case that the Caliphate will join the Terran Federation."

After a moment Tijan asked, "You found your leverage?"

Walid raised his eyebrows.

"Your 'spine of the knife'?"

Walid choked on his fig.

"Perhaps," Tallal said, glancing at Walid. After a moment he added, "We may have reached an accommodation."

"And that's why Turkey no longer talks of annexation in Syria?" Tallal smiled.

"Perhaps."

"And what 'world change' will the Caliphate and the Kingdom of Iran joining the Terran Federation bring?"

"It will only happen if the United Nations fails," Tallal said. Walid nodded.

"Yes, I see now," Walid said. "The U.N. has been completely ineffective in helping Iran to counter the Eastern Axis incursion in Azerbaijan."

Tijan looked from Walid back to Tallal. "But how can this be?" she asked.

"It began with the objections of the Eastern Axis to the Lunar Base," Walid said.

"No," Tallal said. "I think it goes back farther than that."

Walid flashed a grin at Tijan and asked, "What do you mean?"

"The Eastern Axis objected to the militarization of Luna and called for the internationalization of Luna. That mirrors an earlier move that also failed at the United Nations."

"Antarctica?" Tijan asked.

"Yes!" Tallal said, looking at Walid but nodding toward Tijan.

She blushed. "It's been fifteen years since the U.S. failed in its effort to internationalize Antarctica."

"That has no bearing on the current dispute over Luna with the Eastern Axis," Walid said.

"Not directly, no," Tallal agreed. "But the dispute then was not with the Eastern Axis. It was the British who thwarted the Americans at the U.N."

"And now there are competing territorial claims across the Southern Continent," Tijan said.

Again Tallal nodded.

"With Britain and the United States—and, yes, others like Argentina and Chile and even the Eastern Axis—establishing settlements in Antarctica that are as much political claims as they are research facilities."

"But Britain and the United States are allies today," Saliha said.

"Ostensibly, yes," Tallal said. "If the U.N. fails though it won't be because of the withdrawal of the Eastern Axis. It will be because other nations no longer support it."

"You're talking about the alignment between the British Commonwealth and the French Union," Walid said.

Tallal nodded.

"But that's just a customs union!"

"Which extends to six continents but excludes the United States," Tallal said. "And us too, of course."

"Hasn't Canada just withdrawn from the Commonwealth?" Tijan asked.

Again Tallal nodded.

"It will join the Terran Federation too," Walid said.

"But Britain objects?" Saliha asked.

Tallal smiled.

"Change indeed," Walid said, nodding softly.

The Caliphal Palace, Basra, Iraq, July 1974

"This next one, Majesty, will not sit well with the British," Yousef said, seated on the other side of the conference table in his office, as the Iranian foreign minister left the dais. Looking closely at the television screen, Tallal did not recognize the diplomat who had seated himself at the table on the dais. His dress and appearance suggested a northern European, which he knew would be unusual today, and the West German delegate had already signed the document. Nayef, seated next to Yousef, seemed to notice Tallal's frown.

"Ireland, Majesty, was an early supporter," he said.

"The Irish take great pleasure in defying Britain, Majesty," Salim added. The Irish diplomat had finished signing and was leaving the dais. *Sheikh* Sabah stepped into the frame and seated himself at the table. After a moment, Tallal smiled as Sabah, having signed the document, rose from his seat and shook hands with the American Secretary of State.

"This is an historic day for the Caliphate, Majesty," Yousef said, turning from the screen to look at him. Tallal nodded.

"Your father would be very pleased, Majesty," Nayef added.

"As am I," Tallal said. "Thank you all for your efforts to this end." His gaze took in Yousef and Nayef across the table as well as Salim seated next to him.

"*Sheikh* Sabah's role has been crucial as well, Majesty," Yousef said.

Tallal agreed.

On the screen the Japanese foreign minister was signing the document. He was followed by another diplomat.

When the Pakistani foreign minister stepped to the dais a few moments later Nayef said, "The only other former Commonwealth member, Majesty."

"No others besides Canada?" Tallal asked.

"No, Majesty," Nayef said, shaking his head.

"And no members of the French Union?" Tallal asked.

Nayef shrugged. "None, Majesty. Indeed Liberia is the only member of the African Conclave to join."

After the Pakistani came another East Asian diplomat, a Filipino, Tallal guessed. He was followed by another European. Tallal looked a question at Nayef.

"Foreign Minister Soares of Portugal, Majesty," Nayef said. "The final European nation to sign. Of course, that means the Portuguese territories in Africa too."

Tallal nodded his thanks, turned his attention back to the television screen. The Portuguese diplomat was followed by yet another East Asian delegate that Tallal did not recognize. Then the Turkish foreign minister stepped to the dais and seated himself at the table. Like the others before him the Turkish diplomat signed the document then rose from the table to shake hands with his American counterpart. He was followed by the representative from South Vietnam. After shaking hands with the Vietnamese diplomat the American Secretary of State stepped to the podium next to the table as the auditorium broke out in applause.

"My fellow delegates," began the American diplomat as the applause quieted. "The Compact of the Terran Federation of States which we have just signed here in St. Louis on this 21st day of July, is a firm foundation upon which we can build more effective collective security for our peoples. Upon all of us, in all our nations, is now laid the duty of turning into action these words which we have written. Upon our decisive action rests the hope of those who have come before us, those now living, and those who will follow us, for a world of secure nations which will work and cooperate in a strong, united alliance of states...."

They stood together at the balustrade, their arms about each other's waists, her head against his cheek. Behind, the thin leaved shrubbery rustled softly with the wind, and from the lower main terrace came music and laughing voices. The city of Basra spread in front of them, white minarets rising from the narrow spaces of streets and smaller buildings, with a shimmer of sun-reflecting cars below. Far away, the hills were raw umber in the afternoon light, and the bright yellow sun hung in a clear blue sky.

Tallal's eye caught a grey blur two miles to the southeast, and for an instant he was puzzled. Then he frowned. The sunlight on the six hundred-foot hull of the U.S.S. *Bainbridge*, back at the port of Basra after the joint exercise in the Arabian Sea. He didn't want to think about that now.

Instead, he pressed Tijan closer and whispered her name, "Tijan," and then, "*Khalifa* Tijan al-Tallal."

"Oh, no, Tallal!" Her protest was half joking and half apprehensive. "It's bad fortune to be called by your married name before the wedding."

"I've been calling you that in my mind since that night of the Duke of York's ball, when you were just arrived in London."

She looked up from the corner of her eye. "I thought you were a stuffy traditionalist then," she confessed.

The sparkle of a car flashed briefly upon them and they looked down and turned their heads, in time to see it pull with graceful dignity toward the gate of the Caliphal Palace, and he glimpsed its blazonry—black-white-green tricolor with a red triangle at the hoist containing a golden crown, the flag of the royal house of Iraq. He wondered if it were *Malik* Faisal, or just some of his people come to the betrothal party ahead of him. They should get back to the guests, he supposed. Then he took her in his arms and kissed her, and she responded ardently. It must have been all of five minutes since they'd done that before.

A slight cough behind them brought them apart and their heads around. It was *Amir* Nayef, the breast of his grey coat gleaming with orders and decorations and the emerald in the pommel of his dress-dagger twinkling.

"I thought I'd find you two here, Majesty." Tijan's father smiled. "You'll have many days ahead together, but may I remind you that today you have guests, and more coming every minute."

"Who came in the Iraq car?" Tijan asked.

"*Malik* Faisal and *Malika* Sabihah," Nayef said. Then he saw her bare head and was shocked. "Tijan, your *hijab*!"

Her hands went up and couldn't find it; she looked about in confused embarrassment. Amused, Tallal picked it from the short palm onto which she had tossed it and draped it over her head and shoulders, his hands lingering briefly. Then he gestured to the older man to precede them, and they entered the palmed walk.

Near Shammar Encampment, al-Basra, Iraq, August 1974

Tallal reined in his mare, watching Tijan gallop her horse through the slight depression, her unfurled *hijab* trailing behind her like green and black smoke in the morning twilight. Walid had been right. Her English riding lessons had not left her well-prepared to ride in the desert sands but she was doing a fair job. With time Tallal was certain she would be every bit his equal on horseback. She slowed her horse, turned to look at him. He gentled his mare in her direction.

Suddenly she laughed and flashed her reins. She and her horse sped away, sand flying into the air behind them. Tallal laughed too and urged his mare to speed. He caught up with her as she mounted the next dune and both reined in. Dawn was just breaking in the distance, a blue-orange glow as the disk of the sun peeked above the horizon. Tallal turned to watch the sunlight on Tijan's face, her brown eyes glistening and her black hair blowing softly in the cool breeze, dancing with her green and black veils.

"Beautiful," Tijan said, still watching the sunrise.

"Yes, beautiful," Tallal said, still watching her. She looked at him, glanced downward for just a moment, then looked up at him again and smiled.

"Thank you, beloved," she said. "For the compliment, for the riding, for the sunrise."

"You're welcome, beloved. Though I can take credit only for the compliment. The riding is yours." She started to object but he held up a hand. "Yes, I provided the horse but you do the riding, and have the desire for it. And the sunrise, of course, comes from the All Merciful."

"Thanks be to the All Merciful," she said with a giggle. Tallal turned his horse's head toward the rump of Tijan's and leaned forward to kiss her gently. Then a distant shout behind him brought him erect, and he turned his head around, following Tijan's gaze. A rider was approaching from the direction of the encampment, sand blowing behind him as he raced toward them. The man's head was bare, suggesting he'd departed in haste, and after a moment Tallal recognized him.

"It's Walid," Tijan said. "Did you not tell him he was not invited to join us?"

"I did. He was disappointed but it's not like him to interrupt like this. It must be something else. Come." Tallal urged his horse in the direction of the approaching rider. Tijan followed, matching Tallal's speed as he hastened to meet Walid.

After a few moments, they met on the other side of the depression, from where Tallal had admired Tijan only minutes before.

"My apologies, cousin," Walid said, as he pulled his horse to a stop. "And to you, *Amira*," he added, glancing at Tijan.

You have news?" Tallal asked.

"*Amir* Salim sent a helicopter but I told him I would find you first." Walid grinned.

"What news, Walid?"

"India has invaded East Pakistan!" Tallal looked at Tijan, then turned to look at the rising sun.

"So a greater war has come," he said, still looking into the distance. He turned back to look at Walid, reached a hand across to clasp Tijan's. "What news from the Saudi front?"

"No change when I rode out," Walid said. "But Salim expects a new offensive at any moment. The truce in Syria holds."

"We should return," Tijan said, releasing Tallal's hand to grasp her reins. Tallal nodded.

"Lead on, Walid," he said. Walid shook his head. Just then a distant, low-pitched roar became noticeable. Quickly it grew louder and a helicopter appeared over the low ridge to the southeast, about a kilometer off.

"I beat it here because I knew where you had headed, but I won't be able to beat it back," Walid shouted. Tijan's horse grew agitated as the small military helicopter circled above them and she struggled to keep it calm. It thrashed, turning left then right then left again. Tijan had given up trying to control it and was just trying to hold on. Tallal reached for the tossing reins but missed them and the horse bolted away, Tijan flailing about in the saddle.

Tallal kicked his mare, heading in pursuit.

Walid turned his horse toward the helicopter, trying to wave it off.

Again Tallal watched Tijan's *hijab* and long, brown hair trail behind her in the wind as her horse ran away. Tallal's mare quickly made up the distance between them. Tijan leaned forward, grasping for the loose reins but was almost thrown from her horse. Tallal pulled alongside, turning her horse to the right with his horse.

Tijan looked at him with wide eyes and open mouth. Her horse slowed and he continued to urge it right, turning it almost now in the direction from which they'd come. Tijan reached forward again, caught the reins and slowly pulled her horse to a halt. Suddenly, they were next to each other. Tears welled in Tijan's eyes but she smiled at Tallal.

Walid came up, leading his horse to the right of Tijan's. Her horse continued to calm, pressed between the other two horses. In the distance the helicopter had come to rest in a whirlwind of sand. As the sand settled three figures had already emerged from the helicopter and were running toward them. As they neared, Tallal recognized a captain of the Household Guard. His companions were both hostlers from *Sheikh* Hamid's stables.

"Our apologies, Majesty," the Captain said. "We did not intend to frighten the horses."

Tallal looked at Tijan. She smiled and nodded, reaching forward to grasp his hand.

"It was nothing, Captain." He glanced at Walid. "All is well."

The captain nodded slowly, while the hostlers came up behind him.

"Praise be to Allah, Majesty," the Captain said. Tallal nodded.

"You've come to take me to the palace?"

"Yes, Majesty," he said, glancing at Walid. "*Amir* Salim begs you to return at once."

"Thank you, Captain." Tallal dismounted, handed his reins to one of the hostlers, then helped Tijan from her horse. Once she was on the ground the other hostler took her horse. Holding Tijan's hand Tallal looked up at Walid, squinting in the morning sunlight. "I don't suppose you'll be coming with us?"

"With Your Majesty's permission I would ride back with these fine hostlers," Walid said, grinning again. Tallal nodded. Walid glanced at the captain. "Perhaps I will beat the helicopter again."

The hostlers both smiled but the captain frowned. Tijan laughed softly, and after a moment Tallal laughed too.

The Defence Ministry, Basra, Iraq, September 1974

"The reports are confirmed, Majesty," Salim said. "There have been nuclear strikes on both the eastern and western coasts of the United States, most likely against the rocketports in Florida and California."

"May Allah be merciful," Tallal said softly. "Do you know the origins of the missiles?" The defense minister shook his head.

"We do not have that information, Majesty. I am aware of intelligence from the Americans which believed the Florida rocketport would most likely be attacked from missile sites in the Urals and that in California by missiles launched from the Gobi."

"Have the Americans retaliated?" Again Salim shook his head.

"We do not know at this point, Majesty. Still, I would expect a retaliatory attack soon, if one has not been launched already."

Tallal turned his attention to Sabah. "Has there been a call for assistance from the Americans?"

"No, Majesty," the foreign minister said. "But they have called for the Federation Directorate to convene tomorrow. *Amir* Sharaf will attend."

Tallal nodded.

"It is unlikely that the Americans will ask us for specific assistance, Majesty," Yousef said. "They will expect us to continue to press the Saudis in Jordan."

"Then that is what we will do," Tallal said, looking around the table. The others nodded in turn. There was a quick knock at the door and then Nayef stepped into the room, followed by a military officer who moved quickly to confer with Salim.

"News?" Tallal asked. Nayef nodded. Tallal motioned for him to sit at the table.

"Additional attacks, Majesty," Nayef said. He looked at Salim who nodded to his aide. The aide quickly left the room, closing the door behind him. Salim turned to Tallal.

"Nuclear attacks in Alaska and Hawaii, Majesty," Nayef added. Tallal frowned. "Both back-up rocketports for the Lunar Base."

Tallal grimaced.

"There are also unconfirmed reports of attacks in Virginia, on the eastern coast and in New Mexico in the American southwest. Again, those are likely back-up rocketports for the Lunar Base."

"Then the Americans will need *al-Borak.*" Both Salim and Yousef nodded.

"I want to be there for the launch," Tallal said.

"No!" It was Nayef. "Majesty, you must not." Salim was shaking his head as well.

"It would be too dangerous, Majesty," Yousef said.

"The rocketport will become a target, Majesty," Salim added.

"I would expect so," Tallal said. "Surely you have plans to evacuate the facility after the launch?"

Salim looked at Yousef, who nodded softly.

"Yes, Majesty," Salim said, looking at his folded hands on the table in front of him.

"Then I will leave with the others, after the launch."

Yousef frowned.

"I am afraid I agree with *Amir* Nayef, Majesty," the Prime Minister said. "You are without an heir. Your death would create a succession crisis, Majesty."

"I will appoint *Malik* Faisal or *Malik* Hussein as Crown Prince," Tallal said.

Yousef shook his head. "Each would be opposed in the other's kingdom."

"And neither would be accepted in Syria," Nayef added.

"This is why it was your father who established the Caliphate, Majesty," Yousef said. "It was not only that his grandfather had proclaimed himself *Khalif* after the collapse of the Ottoman Empire. It was also that his father, unlike his uncles, had never ruled in Iraq or Jordan or Syria."

Tallal looked at Sabah.

"We would support either as *Khalif*, Majesty, as would the Emirates, but we are only a small part of the Caliphate," the Kuwaiti said.

"I understand the risks, uncles," Tallal said. "But what would my father have done?" Nayef would not meet his gaze. Salim and Sabah looked to Yousef.

"Your father would have gone to *al-Borak*, Majesty," Yousef said, after a moment. Tallal nodded.

"Your father had an heir," Nayef objected, now looking at him fiercely. Tallal rose from his chair, walked around the table to where Nayef was seated. He placed his hand on Nayef's shoulder.

"Uncle," he began. "Soon, it will be 'father.'"

Tears came to Nayef's eyes. "I must go. The world is at war. God willing, I must lead our people."

The Caliphal Palace, Basra, Iraq, September 1974

"No!" Tijan rose from the garden bench and grabbed Tallal by both arms. "You mustn't go!"

Tallal hugged her to his chest, reached up to stroke her hair.

"I must, beloved. Our people are about to enter an even greater war.

I'm their leader, their *Khalif.* I must lead the fight." Tijan sobbed, tried to push him away but he held her close.

"Walid says this '*al-Borak*' will be the most important target in all of the Caliphate." Tallal nodded.

"He's right. It is. But we will evacuate the personnel before it can be attacked."

Tijan looked up at him. "You promise to return to me?" she asked softly, her eyes glistening.

"That will be in the hands of the All-Merciful. My wish is that I return to you, that we be married, that we have many children and grandchildren." She hugged him.

"Walid says you'll take him with you."

"Yes. He's been to the facility. I'll need his counsel."

"Then take me too!"

"I will not. Nor would your father allow me." She pushed away again, breaking free this time. She turned and walked back toward the bench, paused and then continued down the path deeper into the garden. Tallal followed after her. She sat on the stone ledge of the small pool, dipped her hand into the water. Tallal sat beside her, looked at her rippling reflection in the pool.

"How long will you be away?" She was looking at his reflection too.

"No more than a few days. We'll leave in a few hours. The mission will not take long to undertake. The evacuation will come immediately afterwards."

"And you'll return to Basra?"

"Yes. There will be much to organize. It's likely the city will have to be evacuated. We'll flee into the desert." She looked up at him.

"Your people have grown accustomed to living in the city. They'll not be eager to return to the old ways."

"Our people," corrected Tallal. "We may have no choice. Allah willing, we'll be fortunate simply to return to our tents in the desert. There are much more horrible fates that could take us, that may yet take many of us."

"Has it truly come to that?"

"Praise be to Allah, I hope not," Tallal said. "But it may. We must prepare to save as many as possible."

"Then let's call the *imam* now," she said, she rose from her seat. "We can be married before you leave today!"

Tallal stood, took her in his arms again. "Beloved, you know there is more to the marriage ceremony than the rites performed by the *imam*, especially when you marry a *Khalif*. And then there's the joining of our families—"

"Bah!" she said. "Politics! Palace intrigue. I don't care about any of it."

Tallal reached out, took both of her hands in his.

"Beloved, I don't care either, at least when it comes to the two of us. If I were just a man, it would not matter at all." She looked up at him, her eyes bright now.

"Then let's be just a man and a woman...here, now, before God Almighty." Tallal nodded in agreement and bent down to kiss her.

Al-Borak Research Center, al-Dulaim, Iraq, October 1974

Again the plane landed at night. Again they were met by General al-Tay, but there were fewer in his escort this time. And the American air force officer, Miles, was not among them. Salim joined him in the first car, this time with al-Tay in the front seat. Again Walid was taken to another car.

"The Howard gyroscopes arrived from Portuguese Guinea this morning, Majesty," the General said, as the car pulled away from the plane. "The installation of the payload module is almost completed."

"When do you expect to launch?" Tallal asked.

"We will be ready before morning, Majesty," al-Tay said. "But we will not have a launch window until about noon. Of course, we will need the order from the Americans."

"How long will the launch window remain open," Salim asked.

"It will close shortly after sundown. If we don't launch before then we will wait another night."

The car pulled up before the small building. An airman opened the car door and urged them toward the small, concrete building. Walid and Salim's aide came up behind them and they stepped past the saluting guards and through the opened door. The guard inside had also risen to salute and another airman held the elevator for them.

"I have asked Colonel Miles to give you an update, Majesty," al-Tay said. "He's been overseeing the installation of the payload."

"Thank you, General," Tallal said. "My apologies for interrupting you and your men from your work."

"It is an honor to have you with us, Majesty," al-Tay said. "Though I wish the circumstances were such that we were not engaged in our mission."

"As do I, General. God willing, your mission will be successful and the fully-capable Lunar Base will bring hostilities to an end."

"God willing, Majesty."

There was a moment of deceleration and then the doors opened into the launch facility. General al-Tay led them up a gantry and into a hallway which lead to the launch control center. Several technicians were busy at their terminals. The main television display on the wall showed a similar scene of a somewhat larger group of technicians at similar terminals that Tallal recognized as an image of the U.S. launch control center in California. Another large display showed a map of the Earth upon which a series of orbital tracks moved slowly from west to east. Across the room the red-haired American colonel looked up from where he was bent over the shoulder of a seated technician and smiled. He spoke briefly to the technician, who nodded, and then moved quickly to the group.

"It's good to see you again, Your Majesty," Colonel Miles said, in English. "Has General al-Tay told you of our situation?"

General Al-Tay nodded.

"Shall we begin your briefing?" Tallal asked. Miles nodded and led the way to the conference room behind the control center. A large television monitor on the wall showed an image of the rocket; the nose cone had been removed and was held suspended in the air by a crane. Inside the opening three white-overalled technicians were crawling over a piece of equipment the size of a small car. As General al-Tay directed him to a seat Tallal noticed a smaller television monitor at the other end of the conference table, which showed what seemed to be an aerial view of a large area of blackened devastation, set amongst a background of rugged, snow-capped mountains.

"That must be one of the destroyed rocketports," Walid said in Arabic, taking a seat beside Tallal.

"It's what's left of the Kodiak rocketport in Alaska, Your Majesty," Miles said. It was the first time Tallal realized he must understand Arabic. "Those are the first aerial images we've had of the rocketport itself. It's been utterly destroyed. There were no survivors."

"Minister Salim has assured me there is an evacuation plan to assure the same does not happen here." Miles nodded, as did al-Tay.

"Colonel Miles will include details of the evacuation plan in his briefing, Majesty," al-Tay said. He nodded toward Miles.

"Thank you, General," the American said. "Welcome, Your Majesty, Minister Salim. We are just completing installation of the payload now and should be ready to launch in less than two hours. I can't share any more details about the facility but I can tell you that all but one rocketport in North America has been destroyed by the Eastern Axis attacks, meaning that it will be essential that our payload here is successful in reaching the Lunar Base...."

"Four...three...two...one!" Tallal could not tell if the voice on the public address system was excited or scared. The main television display, which had been showing the dark interior of the launch bay, intermittently illuminated by flashes of red light, went dark. Tallal noticed a dull roar that steadily increased in volume, accompanied by a soft rumble he could feel through the soles of his shoes.

"Rocket launch. We have rocket launch."

Tallal turned to look at Walid, who was smiling broadly. The main display activated again, this time showing a scene looking at an empty desert plain in the center of which was a growing fountain of broiling white cloud. Suddenly, as the rumble subsided he saw a flash of orange fire at the base of the fountain that was quickly hidden by the growing cloud. A moment later the narrow, pointed cylinder of the rocket itself emerged from the top of the cloud, the bright, orange fire flowing from its base.

"Rocket has cleared the rocketport." A small burst of applause erupted around the room.

"Congratulations, General," Tallal said.

"Thank you, Majesty," al-Tay said. "Your patronage is appreciated, as has been your presence here today."

"It is remarkable, Majesty," Walid said, standing beside him. "We have launched a rocket from al-Dulaim!" Salim nodded.

"Yes, a great day for our people," Tallal said. "And a horrid turn for humanity."

Again Salim nodded. Walid was silent.

Tallal turned to Miles. "Thank you, and your Government, Colonel, for your assistance here."

"I'm sure my Government appreciates the assistance of the Islamic Caliphate as well, Your Majesty," Miles said. "And it has been my honor to serve with your men."

Suddenly, two airmen stepped into the room and headed toward Tallal and the others.

"Majesty, it is time to leave," Salim said.

Tallal frowned. "Colonel Miles said the evacuation would not begin until thirty minutes after the launch."

"Your departure is scheduled before the formal evacuation, Majesty," al-Tay said.

"No, General," Tallal said, "I will stay until everyone has been evacuated."

Al-Tay frowned, looked to Salim.

"Majesty—" began the defense minister.

Al-Tay interrupted him. "We cannot evacuate personnel from the airfield control tower until your plane has taken flight."

Tallal looked from al-Tay to Salim.

"He's right, Your Majesty," Miles said. Tallal started to object, then sighed.

"Very well, gentlemen," Tallal said. "Thank you for your work. May Allah be pleased with your efforts." As Tallal stepped toward the waiting airmen General al-Tay and Colonel Miles saluted him.

Outside, a single car was waiting. To the southeast the long white trail of the rocket reached into the sky, a small orange spark just visible at its end. Then it was gone from sight and the wind continued to scatter the white trail. Tallal, Walid, and Salim were hustled into the car by the airmen and it sped toward the airfield.

As the car approached the airfield he noticed that the aircraft they had arrived in was nowhere to be seen. The plane they were headed toward was a larger aircraft, with four large, propeller-driven engines. It's markings were military but not those of the Caliphate Air Force.

"That's an American aircraft," Walid said.

"What is happening, *Amir* Salim?" Tallal asked. The defense minister turned to look at him.

"There will be two evacuations here today, Majesty."

"Two?"

Salim nodded. "We will evacuate our personnel from the rocketport...and we will evacuate the government—and your household—from the Caliphate, Majesty."

"What? No! Why have I not been informed?"

Salim winced.

"You would have been, Majesty, had you stayed in Basra. This evacuation has always been a contingency plan, to be initiated only if we had intelligence that Basra would be targeted by the Eastern Axis. That intelligence came, via the Americans, this morning. Your family, and *Amira* Tijan's family, as well as the Prime Minister and his staff, are aboard this transport, furnished by the Americans, which left Basra a short while ago."

"You brought Tijan—and my mother—to make sure I would go!"

Salim nodded.

"The Prime Minster made the decisions about who would be evacuated but I believe that is a reasonable conclusion, Majesty."

The car pulled to a stop near the aircraft. The driver got out and opened Tallal's door. The loud whine of the propellers made it difficult to hear. Walid and Salim came around the other side of the car. Two men who had been standing next to an open doorway on the side of the aircraft ran in their direction.

"Your Majesty," shouted the first man, a Caliphate airman, and motioned toward the plane. The other man, in an American uniform, also waved them toward the plane. Moving behind the rotating propellers, they approached the aircraft and climbed up the short, extended stairway into the open doorway. Another American airman, inside the aircraft, helped him through the portal. Yousef and Nayef were waiting inside.

"You should have told me," Tallal said as he ducked inside the aircraft.

"We did not know for certain, Majesty," the Prime Minister said. "We had hoped it would not be necessary." Tallal stepped aside as Salim and Walid, and then the two airmen entered the aircraft and secured the door. The large, open cargo bay was filled with rows of passenger seats which faced away from him, toward the rear of the plane. Most of them were filled, many with women and children.

"Where are we headed?"

"To Moçambique, Majesty," Yousef said. "The aircraft will refuel there before heading to the evacuation center, the provisional site of the American government."

"The Americans have evacuated their government?"

"Yes, Majesty," Yousef said.

"They have invited the governments of all Terran Federation members join them, Majesty" added Nayef.

"How many others?"

"Most, Majesty," Nayef said. "Only the Irish and Iceland have declined the invitation."

"Where?" Tallal asked. Yousef started to speak but was interrupted by a squeal of delight from behind Tallal. He turned around.

"Tallal!" Tijan rushed into his arms. His mother and sisters came up behind her, followed by Tijan's mother. Tallal kissed Tijan softly and then released her. He greeted his mother and sisters, kissing their cheeks, and clasped hands with Tijan's mother. Walid stepped around to greet them as well, kissing his aunt and clasping hands with Tallal's family.

Tallal turned back to Yousef. "Thank you for seeing to the safety of my family."

The Prime Minister nodded his head slightly.

"I am not pleased though to be surprised in this manner."

"Please accept my apologies, Majesty," Yousef said. "This is not how we intended you to learn of this course of action. We did not expect it would be necessary at the time you left Basra."

"You are forgiven," Tallal said. "But no more secrets." Again, Yousef nodded slightly. "Now, tell me. Where are we bound after Moçambique?"

"Antarctica, Majesty."

En route (by air) to Beira Air Base, Moçambique, October 1974

Tallal was sitting with Tijan and his family in part of two rows of seats near the midsection of the cargo bay. The prime minister approached from the aisle to their right.

"Majesty, if we could have a few minutes," Yousef said, with a gentle smile.

Tallal nodded.

"Of course." He rose from his seat, briefly clasping Tijan's hand he looked at his mother and sisters. "Excuse me, Mother." He stepped out into the aisle, beckoning to Walid to join him, and following Yousef's direction stepped toward the forward part of the cargo bay. Nayef and Salim and a couple of aides were standing around a small table separated from the last row of seats by a small, temporary partition. A telephone and a small television display were mounted on the bulkhead forward of the table. Tallal took a seat at one end of the table and the others seated themselves around it.

"News?" Tallal asked. Yousef nodded to Salim.

"Yes, Majesty," the Defence Minister said. "The first news is that the rocket from *al-Borak* has successfully left Earth orbit and is on its way to Luna." Tallal nodded and smiled.

"And the evacuation, was it successful?"

"All personnel had left the facility within an hour, Majesty," Salim said. "All have been accounted for and our American colleagues are already headed home."

"Praise be to God," Tallal said. "Thank you and your men for a job well done." Salim nodded but his face was grim.

"We also have word of the first attacks from the Lunar Base, Majesty."

"How can that be with—ah, I see. *Al-Borak* was not the only back-up rocketport."

"Apparently not, Majesty," Salim said. "In fact, it seems the first navigation components were launched to the Lunar Base from rocketports in the U.S. nearly two weeks ago. You will recall Colonel Miles mentioning that at least one rocketport survived but it now also seems that the rocketports in Alaska and Virginia were both able to launch payloads to Luna before they were destroyed, and that another rocketport in Canada also launched payloads to Luna several days ago—though that may be the rocketport Colonel Miles mentioned. And in the past few days there have also been launches from back-up Federation rocketports in Thailand and the Philippines."

"And the attacks?" Tallal asked.

"Several extremely powerful nuclear explosions have been detected in western Russia and in central Asia, Majesty. Others have been detected in northern China and in India. They began yesterday but the most recent we know of occurred just a few hours ago. All have been directed at leadership targets."

"May the All-Merciful forgive us," Tallal said.

Yousef nodded.

Nayef looked at Salim and then turned to Tallal. "There are also indications, Majesty, that these attacks are having an effect on the Eastern Axis," Nayef said.

Tallal raised his eyebrows.

"Yes, Majesty," Salim said. "The pace of Eastern Axis attacks has slowed, and their targets have become more sporadic, mostly shifting from coordinated attacks against military targets to seemingly uncoordinated attacks against civilian targets."

"Cities, you mean?"

"Yes, Majesty," Salim said. "This may also be why there has not yet been an attack against *al-Borak*."

"Basra?" Tallal asked quickly. "Baghdad? Amman?" Salim shook his head.

"Safe, for now, Majesty," Salim said.

"It has been much worse, Majesty, in North America and Europe," Yousef said. "Many cities have been destroyed."

"Cities have been attacked too in Japan, Majesty," added the Defence Minister.

"That means there will be substantial fall-out," Walid said.

Salim nodded. "Radioactive clouds likely reach across much of North America and Europe now. And with the attacks from the Lunar Base, they will move across central and eastern Asia and into the Pacific too."

"We see now, Majesty, why the Americans have evacuated to the southern hemisphere," Nayef said.

"What will be the impact on our people," Tallal asked.

Salim and Yousef shook their heads.

"We cannot know, Majesty," Salim said. "It may be though that we will count ourselves fortunate when all has settled if radioactive fall-out is the most serious challenge we are faced with."

"It seems the All-Merciful will hear many calls for aid," Tallal said.

En route (by air) to Antarctica, October 1974

The stop in Moçambique had been short, just long enough to re-fuel the aircraft. Tallal had taken Tijan outside for a brief stroll on the apron—accompanied by a squad of Portuguese marines—the tropical air was very new for them. Afterwards, when the plane was aloft again, Yousef had asked him to join him for another update. They were seated again around the table at the front of the cargo bay.

"The Eastern Axis attacks have nearly stopped, Majesty," Salim said. "Leadership across the Eastern Axis nations has been destroyed and it is unclear who remains in charge, either to continue to fight or to agree an armistice."

"Already, Majesty, there has been an offer of surrender from a new, provisional government in India," Nayef added. Salim nodded.

"The Commonwealth has asked the Federation for assistance in occupying India, Majesty," Nayef said.

"Has the Federation responded?" Tallal asked.

"No, Majesty," Yousef said. "We've had word from *Sheikh* Sabah that the Federation Directorate is preoccupied with getting its own occupying forces into Russia and China—and with recovery in Federation areas that have been attacked."

"He has been instructed to tell them we will participate?"

"We have been unable to do so, Majesty," Salim said. He looked at Yousef, who nodded softly.

"It may be, Majesty, that Basra has been attacked by the Eastern Axis," Salim said.

"No!" he cried.

Salim nodded.

"*Al-Borak* remains whole, Majesty," the defense minister said, but we have been unable to reach Basra."

"We have a civil defense plan in place, Majesty," Yousef said. "If there has been a nuclear attack it is expected that it would be difficult for them to communicate with the outside world." Tallal covered his face with his hands, dropped his head.

"Baghdad? Amman?" he asked after a moment, his voice muffled by his palms.

"Unharmed, Majesty," Yousef said. "And the Saudis have begun to retreat from Jordan. The Americans have announced that they will attack any foe engaged in hostilities with the Terran Federation."

Tallal dropped his hands, raised his head, his eyes red.

"We may be called upon soon, Majesty, to occupy the Saudi lands," Salim said.

"Including a return to protecting the Holy Cities, Majesty," Nayef added.

Tallal nodded. "But Basra...."

Mayflower Settlement, Antarctica, October 1974

It was cold. Much colder than any winter Tallal had experience in the English Midlands. And yet summer—and sunrise—was just beginning here. He stood with Tijan a few dozen meters from the nearest shelter. The sheet of ice extended nearly half a kilometer ahead of them to the sea. He counted nine ships at anchor. A steady stream of tracked vehicles trekked across the ice to the makeshift port at the water's edge, and a file of small, rectangular boats—troop landing craft, he guessed—slowly moved between the port and the anchored vessels.

They held each other's hand but he could feel no warmth through the thick gloves the Americans had provided. They had to face each other to see each other's faces through openings in the heavy hoods, and had to speak more loudly to be understood even though it was very quiet, with only an occasional shout or sound of heavy machinery reaching them from the quickly growing settlement behind them.

"It's beautiful, in its way, isn't it, beloved?" Tijan said.

Tallal nodded, then realized she would not see his head move.

"Indeed, beloved, though I'm eager to return to our desert sands and warm sunlight."

Tijan turned to face him, took his other hand in hers as well.

"The world has changed much more in thirty days than you imagined it would in a lifetime," she said. This time she could see him nod.

"Yes. The British in India again. Commonwealth and Federation forces in Moscow and more Americans in Peking. Praise be to God, our own soldiers to guard the *Masajid* in Mecca and Medina again. The devastation in Basra...and in so many other cities across the world...."

Tijan leaned forward, wrapped her thickly padded arms around his equally thick torso.

He caught a slight, pleasant scent of her as she pushed the opening of her hood toward his. They could not quite reach to kiss but she smiled at him such that he could not help but smile back.

"Omnilingual" is considered by many readers and critics to be H. Beam Piper best short story. I fully agree. In July of 1955, Piper made a note in his diary that he had: "Picked up a paperback copy of Edward Sapir's Language: An Introduction to the Study of Speech *at Doubleday's; will be useful in next story." It took another year before he wrote the story. However, Sapir's book sparked the genesis of "Omnilingual," which is about a scientific expedition to Mars and what happens when a team of archaeologists find some very interesting ruins.*

Piper does a good job of displaying a band of scientists, many of whom who are more interested in their personal gain and reputation, than in scientific investigation. The engine behind the story is the thrill of scientific discovery as the team finds more and more clues behind the lost Martian civilization. "Omnilingual" was published in Analog Science Fiction *in 1957, and also has the distinction of being the only Terro-Human Future History story written by Piper which takes place shortly after the founding of the Terran Federation.*

Unusual for the time, the protagonist, Martha Dane, is a woman scientist who is on equal footing with the male members of the archaeological team. Pursuing a line of investigation that the other members of the team shy away from, she makes a major discovery and has to convince the other members of the team. I suspect Martha was modeled after Elizabeth Hurst, Piper's wife: it's notable that his early stories Piper's women characters are mostly minor characters and stereotypes until after his marriage and divorce.

OMNILINGUAL

53 *A.E.*

Martha Dane paused, looking up at the purple-tinged copper sky. The wind had shifted since noon, while she had been inside, and the dust storm that was sweeping the high deserts to the east was now blowing out over Syrtis. The sun, magnified by the haze, was a gorgeous magenta ball, as large as the sun of Terra, at which she could look directly. Tonight, some of that dust would come sifting down from the upper atmosphere to add another film to what had been burying the city for the last fifty thousand years.

The red loess lay over everything, covering the streets and the open spaces of park and plaza, hiding the small houses that had been crushed and pressed flat under it and the rubble that had come down from the tall buildings when roofs had caved in and walls had toppled outward. Here, where she stood, the ancient streets were a hundred to a hundred and fifty feet below the surface; the breach they had made in the wall of the building behind her had opened into the sixth story. She could look down on the cluster of prefabricated huts and sheds, on the brush-grown flat that had been the waterfront when this place had been a seaport on the ocean that was now Syrtis Depression; already, the bright metal was thinly coated with red dust. She thought, again, of what clearing this city would mean, in terms of time and labor, of people and supplies and equipment brought across fifty million miles of space. They'd have to use machinery; there was no other way it could be done. Bulldozers and power shovels and draglines; they were fast, but they were rough and indiscriminate. She remembered the digs around Harappa and Mohenjo-Daro, in the

Indus Valley, and the careful, patient native laborers—the painstaking foremen, the pickmen and spademen, the long files of basketmen carrying away the earth. Slow and primitive as the civilization whose ruins they were uncovering, yes, but she could count on the fingers of one hand the times one of her pickmen had damaged a valuable object in the ground. If it hadn't been for the underpaid and uncomplaining native laborer, archaeology would still be back where Wincklemann had found it. But on Mars there was no native labor; the last Martian had died five hundred centuries ago.

Something started banging like a machine gun, four or five hundred yards to her left. A solenoid jack-hammer; Tony Lattimer must have decided which building he wanted to break into next. She became conscious, then, of the awkward weight of her equipment, and began redistributing it, shifting the straps of her oxy-tank pack, slinging the camera from one shoulder and the board and drafting tools from the other, gathering the notebooks and sketchbooks under her left arm. She started walking down the road, over hillocks of buried rubble, around snags of wall jutting up out of the loess, past buildings still standing, some of them already breached and explored, and across the brush-grown flat to the huts.

There were ten people in the main office room of Hut One when she entered. As soon as she had disposed of her oxygen equipment, she lit a cigarette, her first since noon, then looked from one to another of them. Old Selim von Ohlmhorst, the Turco-German, one of her two fellow archaeologists, sitting at the end of the long table against the farther wall, smoking his big curved pipe and going through a loose-leaf notebook. The girl ordnance officer, Sachiko Koremitsu, between two droplights at the other end of the table, her head bent over her work. Colonel Hubert Penrose, the Space Force CO, and Captain Field, the intelligence officer, listening to the report of one of the airdyne pilots, returned from his afternoon survey flight. A couple of girl lieutenants from Signals, going over the script of the evening telecast, to be transmitted to the *Cyrano*, on orbit five thousand miles off planet and relayed from thence to Terra via Lunar.

Sid Chamberlain, the Trans-Space News Service man, was with them. Like Selim and herself, he was a civilian; he was advertising the fact with a white shirt and a sleeveless blue sweater. And Major Lindemann, the engineer officer, and one of his assistants, arguing over some plans on a drafting board. She hoped, drawing a pint of hot water to wash her hands and sponge off her face, that they were doing something about the pipeline.

She started to carry the notebooks and sketchbooks over to where Selim von Ohlmhorst was sitting, and then, as she always did, she turned aside and stopped to watch Sachiko. The Japanese girl was restoring what had been a book, fifty thousand years ago; her eyes were masked by a binocular loupe, the black headband invisible against her glossy black hair, and she was picking delicately at the crumbled page with a hair-fine wire set in a handle of copper tubing. Finally, loosening a particle as tiny as a snowflake, she grasped it with tweezers, placed it on the sheet of transparent plastic on which she was reconstructing the page, and set it with a mist of fixative from a little spraygun. It was a sheer joy to watch her; every movement was as graceful and precise as though done to music after being rehearsed a hundred times.

"Hello, Martha. It isn't cocktail-time yet, is it?" The girl at the table spoke without raising her head, almost without moving her lips, as though she were afraid that the slightest breath would disturb the flaky stuff in front of her.

"No, it's only fifteen-thirty. I finished my work, over there. I didn't find any more books, if that's good news for you."

Sachiko took off the loupe and leaned back in her chair, her palms cupped over her eyes.

"No, I like doing this. I call it micro-jigsaw puzzles. This book, here, really is a mess. Selim found it lying open, with some heavy stuff on top of it; the pages were simply crushed." She hesitated briefly. "If only it would mean something, after I did it."

There could be a faintly critical overtone to that. As she replied, Martha realized that she was being defensive.

"It will, some day. Look how long it took to read Egyptian hieroglyphics, even after they had the Rosetta Stone."

Sachiko smiled. "Yes. I know. But they did have the Rosetta Stone."

"And we don't. There is no Rosetta Stone, not anywhere on Mars. A whole race, a whole species, died while the first Cro-Magnon cave-artist was daubing pictures of reindeer and bison, and across fifty thousand years and fifty million miles there was no bridge of understanding.

"We'll find one. There must be something, somewhere, that will give us the meaning of a few words, and we'll use them to pry meaning out of more words, and so on. We may not live to learn this language, but we'll make a start, and some day somebody will."

Sachiko took her hands from her eyes, being careful not to look toward the unshaded light, and smiled again. This time Martha was sure that it was not the Japanese smile of politeness, but the universally human smile of friendship.

"I hope so, Martha: really I do. It would be wonderful for you to be the first to do it, and it would be wonderful for all of us to be able to read what these people wrote. It would really bring this dead city to life again." The smile faded slowly. "But it seems so hopeless."

"You haven't found any more pictures?"

Sachiko shook her head. Not that it would have meant much if she had. They had found hundreds of pictures with captions; they had never been able to establish a positive relationship between any pictured object and any printed word. Neither of them said anything more, and after a moment Sachiko replaced the loupe and bent her head forward over the book.

Selim von Ohlmhorst looked up from his notebook, taking his pipe out of his mouth.

"Everything finished, over there?" he asked, releasing a puff of smoke.

"Such as it was." She laid the notebooks and sketches on the table. "Captain Gicquel's started airsealing the building from the fifth floor down, with an entrance on the sixth; he'll start putting in oxygen generators as soon as that's done. I have everything cleared up where he'll be working."

Colonel Penrose looked up quickly, as though making a mental note to attend to something later. Then he returned his attention to the pilot, who was pointing something out on a map.

Von Ohlmhorst nodded. "There wasn't much to it, at that," he agreed. "Do you know which building Tony has decided to enter next?"

"The tall one with the conical thing like a candle extinguisher on top, I think. I heard him drilling for the blasting shots over that way."

"Well, I hope it turns out to be one that was occupied up to the end."

The last one hadn't. It had been stripped of its contents and fittings, a piece of this and a bit of that, haphazardly, apparently over a long period of time, until it had been almost gutted. For centuries, as it had died, this city had been consuming itself by a process of auto-cannibalism. She said something to that effect.

"Yes. We always find that—except, of course, at places like Pompeii. Have you seen any of the other Roman cities in Italy?" he asked. "Minturnae, for instance? First the inhabitants tore down this to repair that, and then, after they had vacated the city, other people came along and tore down what was left, and burned the stones for lime, or crushed them to mend roads, till there was nothing left but the foundation traces. That's where we are fortunate; this is one of the places where the Martian race perished, and there were no barbarians to come later and destroy what they had left." He puffed slowly at his pipe. "Some of these days, Martha, we are going to break into one of these buildings and find that it was one in which the last of these people died. Then we will learn the story of the end of this civilization."

And if we learn to read their language, we'll learn the whole story, not just the obituary. She hesitated, not putting the thought into words. "We'll find that, sometime, Selim," she said, then looked at her watch. "I'm going to get some more work done on my lists, before dinner."

For an instant, the old man's face stiffened in disapproval; he started to say something, thought better of it, and put his pipe back into his mouth. The brief wrinkling around his mouth and the twitch of his white mustache had been enough, however; she knew what he was thinking. She was wasting time and effort, he believed; time and effort belonging not to herself but to the expedition. He could be right, too, she realized. But he had to be wrong; there had to be a way to do it. She turned from him silently and went to her own packing-case seat, at the middle of the table.

Photographs, and photostats of restored pages of books, and transcripts of inscriptions, were piled in front of her, and the notebooks in which she was compiling her lists. She sat down, lighting a fresh cigarette, and reached over to a stack of unexamined material, taking off the top sheet. It was a photostat of what looked like the title page and contents of some sort of a periodical. She remembered it; she had found it herself, two days before, in a closet in the basement of the building she had just finished examining.

She sat for a moment, looking at it. It was readable, in the sense that she had set up a purely arbitrary but consistently pronounceable system of phonetic values for the letters. The long vertical symbols were vowels. There were only ten of them; not too many, allowing separate characters for long and short sounds. There were twenty of the short horizontal letters, which meant that sounds like -ng or -ch or -sh were single letters. The odds were millions to one against her system being anything like the original sound of the language, but she had listed several thousand Martian words, and she could pronounce all of them.

And that was as far as it went. She could pronounce between three and four thousand Martian words, and she couldn't assign a meaning to one of them. Selim von Ohlmhorst believed that she never would. So did Tony Lattimer, and he was a great deal less reticent about saying so. So, she was sure, did Sachiko Koremitsu. There were times, now and then, when she began to be afraid that they were right.

The letters on the page in front of her began squirming and dancing, slender vowels with fat little consonants. They did that, now, every night in her dreams. And there were other dreams, in which she read them as easily as English; waking, she would try desperately and vainly to remember. She blinked, and looked away from the photostated page; when she looked back, the letters were behaving themselves again. There were three words at the top of the page, over-and-underlined, which seemed to be the Martian method of capitalization. *Mastharnorvod Tadavas Sornhulva.* She pronounced them mentally, leafing through her notebooks to see if she had encountered them before, and in what contexts. All three were listed. In addition, *masthar* was a fairly common word, and so was *nor-vod*, and so was *nor*, but *-vod* was a suffix and nothing but a suffix. *Davas*, was a word, too, and *ta-* was a common prefix; *sorn* and *hulva* were both common words. This language, she had long ago decided, must be something like German; when the Martians had needed a new word, they had just pasted a couple of existing words together. It would probably turn out to be a grammatical horror. Well, they had published magazines, and one of them had been called *Mastharnorvod Tadavas Sornhulva*. She wondered if it had been something like the *Quarterly Archaeological Review*, or something more on the order of *Sexy Stories*.

A smaller line, under the title, was plainly the issue number and date; enough things had been found numbered in series to enable her to identify the numerals and determine that a decimal system of numeration had been used. This was the one thousand and seven hundred and fifty-fourth issue, for Doma, 14837; then Doma must be the name of one of the Martian months. The word had turned up several times before. She found herself puffing furiously on her cigarette as she leafed through notebooks and piles of already examined material.

Sachiko was speaking to somebody, and a chair scraped at the end of the table. She raised her head, to see a big man with red hair and a red face, in Space Force green, with the single star of a major on his shoulder, sitting down. Ivan Fitzgerald, the medic. He was lifting weights from a book similar to the one the girl ordnance officer was restoring.

"Haven't had time, lately," he was saying, in reply to Sachiko's question. "The Finchley girl's still down with whatever it is she has, and it's something I haven't been able to diagnose yet. And I've been checking on bacteria cultures, and in what spare time I have, I've been dissecting specimens for Bill Chandler. Bill's finally found a mammal. Looks like a lizard, and it's only four inches long, but it's a real warm-blooded, gamogenetic, placental, viviparous mammal. Burrows, and seems to live on what pass for insects here."

"Is there enough oxygen for anything like that?" Sachiko was asking.

"Seems to be, close to the ground." Fitzgerald got the headband of his loupe adjusted, and pulled it down over his eyes. "He found this thing in a ravine down on the sea bottom—Ha, this page seems to be intact; now, if I can get it out all in one piece—"

He went on talking inaudibly to himself, lifting the page a little at a time and sliding one of the transparent plastic sheets under it, working with minute delicacy. Not the delicacy of the Japanese girl's small hands, moving like the paws of a cat washing her face, but like a steam-hammer cracking a peanut. Field archaeology requires a certain delicacy of touch, too, but Martha watched the pair of them with envious admiration. Then she turned back to her own work, finishing the table of contents.

The next page was the beginning of the first article listed; many of the words were unfamiliar. She had the impression that this must be some kind of scientific or technical journal; that could be because such publications made up the bulk of her own periodical reading. She doubted if it were fiction; the paragraphs had a solid, factual look.

At length, Ivan Fitzgerald gave a short, explosive grunt.

"Ha! Got it!"

She looked up. He had detached the page and was cementing another plastic sheet onto it.

"Any pictures?" she asked.

"None on this side. Wait a moment." He turned the sheet. "None on this side, either." He sprayed another sheet of plastic to sandwich the page, then picked up his pipe and relighted it.

"I get fun out of this, and it's good practice for my hands, so don't think I'm complaining," he said, "but, Martha, do you honestly think anybody's ever going to get anything out of this?"

Sachiko held up a scrap of the silicone plastic the Martians had used for paper with her tweezers. It was almost an inch square.

"Look; three whole words on this piece," she crowed. "Ivan, you took the easy book."

Fitzgerald wasn't being sidetracked. "This stuff's absolutely meaningless," he continued. "It had a meaning fifty thousand years ago, when it was written, but it has none at all now."

She shook her head. "Meaning isn't something that evaporates with time," she argued. "It has just as much meaning now as it ever had. We just haven't learned how to decipher it."

"That seems like a pretty pointless distinction," Selim von Ohlmhorst joined the conversation. "There no longer exists a means of deciphering it."

"We'll find one." She was speaking, she realized, more in self-encouragement than in controversy.

"How? From pictures and captions? We've found captioned pictures, and what have they given us? A caption is intended to explain the picture, not the picture to explain the caption. Suppose some alien to our culture found a picture of a man with a white beard and mustache sawing a billet from a log. He would think the caption meant, 'Man Sawing Wood.' How would he know that it was really 'Wilhelm II in Exile at Doorn?'"

Sachiko had taken off her loupe and was lighting a cigarette.

"I can think of pictures intended to explain their captions," she said. "These picture language-books, the sort we use in the Service—little line drawings, with a word or phrase under them."

"Well, of course, if we found something like that," von Ohlmhorst began.

* * * * *

"Michael Ventris found something like that, back in the Fifties," Hubert Penrose's voice broke in from directly behind her.

She turned her head. The colonel was standing by the archaeologists' table; Captain Field and the airdyne pilot had gone out.

"He found a lot of Greek inventories of military stores," Penrose continued. "They were in Cretan Linear B script, and at the head of each list was a little picture, a sword or a helmet or a cooking tripod or a chariot wheel. That's what gave him the key to the script."

"Colonel's getting to be quite an archaeologist," Fitzgerald commented. "We're all learning each others' specialties, on this expedition."

"I heard about that long before this expedition was even contemplated." Penrose was tapping a cigarette on his gold case. "I heard about that back before the Thirty Days' War, at Intelligence School, when I was a lieutenant. As a feat of cryptanalysis, not an archaeological discovery."

"Yes, cryptanalysis," von Ohlmhorst pounced. "The reading of a known language in an unknown form of writing. Ventris' lists were in the known language, Greek. Neither he nor anybody else ever read a word of the Cretan language until the finding of the Greek-Cretan bilingual in 1963, because only with a bilingual text, one language already known, can an unknown ancient language be learned. And what hope, I ask you, have we of finding anything like that here? Martha, you've been working on these Martian texts ever since we landed here—for the last six months. Tell me, have you found a single word to which you can positively assign a meaning?"

"Yes, I think I have one." She was trying hard not to sound too exultant. "*Doma.* It's the name of one of the months of the Martian calendar."

"Where did you find that?" von Ohlmhorst asked. "And how did you establish—?"

"Here." She picked up the photostat and handed it along the table to him. "I'd call this the title page of a magazine."

He was silent for a moment, looking at it. "Yes. I would say so, too. Have you any of the rest of it?"

"I'm working on the first page of the first article, listed there. Wait till I see; yes, here's all I found, together, here." She told him where she had gotten it. "I just gathered it up, at the time, and gave it to Geoffrey and Rosita to photostat; this is the first I've really examined it."

The old man got to his feet, brushing tobacco ashes from the front of his jacket, and came to where she was sitting, laying the title page on the table and leafing quickly through the stack of photostats.

"Yes, and here is the second article, on page eight, and here's the next one." He finished the pile of photostats. "A couple of pages missing at the end of the last article. This is remarkable; surprising that a thing like a magazine would have survived so long."

"Well, this silicone stuff the Martians used for paper is pretty durable," Hubert Penrose said. "There doesn't seem to have been any water or any other fluid in it originally, so it wouldn't dry out with time."

"Oh, it's not remarkable that the material would have survived. We've found a good many books and papers in excellent condition. But only a really vital culture, an organized culture, will publish magazines, and this civilization had been dying for hundreds of years before the end. It might have been a thousand years before the time they died out completely that such activities as publishing ended."

"Well, look where I found it; in a closet in a cellar. Tossed in there and forgotten, and then ignored when they were stripping the building. Things like that happen."

Penrose had picked up the title page and was looking at it.

"I don't think there's any doubt about this being a magazine, at all." He looked again at the title, his lips moving silently. "*Mastharnorvod Tadavas Sornhulva.* Wonder what it means. But you're right about the date—*Doma* seems to be the name of a month. Yes, you have a word, Dr. Dane."

Sid Chamberlain, seeing that something unusual was going on, had come over from the table at which he was working. After examining the title page and some of the inside pages, he began whispering into the stenophone he had taken from his belt.

"Don't try to blow this up to anything big, Sid," she cautioned. "All we have is the name of a month, and Lord only knows how long it'll be till we even find out which month it was."

"Well, it's a start, isn't it?" Penrose argued. "Grotefend only had the word for 'king' when he started reading Persian cuneiform."

"But I don't have the word for month; just the name of a month. Everybody knew the names of the Persian kings, long before Grotefend."

"That's not the story," Chamberlain said. "What the public back on Terra will be interested in is finding out that the Martians published magazines, just like we do. Something familiar; make the Martians seem more real. More human."

* * * * *

Three men had come in, and were removing their masks and helmets and oxy-tanks, and peeling out of their quilted coveralls. Two were Space

Force lieutenants; the third was a youngish civilian with close-cropped blond hair, in a checked woolen shirt. Tony Lattimer and his helpers.

"Don't tell me Martha finally got something out of that stuff?" he asked, approaching the table. He might have been commenting on the antics of the village half-wit, from his tone.

"Yes; the name of one of the Martian months." Hubert Penrose went on to explain, showing the photostat.

Tony Lattimer took it, glanced at it, and dropped it on the table.

"Sounds plausible, of course, but just an assumption. That word may not be the name of a month, at all—could mean 'published' or 'authorized' or 'copyrighted' or anything like that. Fact is, I don't think it's more than a wild guess that that thing's anything like a periodical." He dismissed the subject and turned to Penrose. "I picked out the next building to enter; that tall one with the conical thing on top. It ought to be in pretty good shape inside; the conical top wouldn't allow dust to accumulate, and from the outside nothing seems to be caved in or crushed. Ground level's higher than the other one, about the seventh floor. I found a good place and drilled for the shots; tomorrow I'll blast a hole in it, and if you can spare some people to help, we can start exploring it right away."

"Yes, of course, Dr. Lattimer. I can spare about a dozen, and I suppose you can find a few civilian volunteers," Penrose told him. "What will you need in the way of equipment?"

"Oh, about six demolition-packets; they can all be shot together. And the usual thing in the way of lights, and breaking and digging tools, and climbing equipment in case we run into broken or doubtful stairways. We'll divide into two parties. Nothing ought to be entered for the first time without a qualified archaeologist along. Three parties, if Martha can tear herself away from this catalogue of systematized incomprehensibilities she's making long enough to do some real work."

She felt her chest tighten and her face become stiff. She was pressing her lips together to lock in a furious retort when Hubert Penrose answered for her.

"Dr. Dane's been doing as much work, and as important work, as you have," he said brusquely. "More important work, I'd be inclined to say."

Von Ohlmhorst was visibly distressed; he glanced once toward Sid Chamberlain, then looked hastily away from him. Afraid of a story of dissension among archaeologists getting out.

"Working out a system of pronunciation by which the Martian language could be transliterated was a most important contribution," he said. "And Martha did that almost unassisted."

"Unassisted by Dr. Lattimer, anyway," Penrose added. "Captain Field and Lieutenant Koremitsu did some work, and I helped out a little, but nine-tenths of it she did herself."

"Purely arbitrary," Lattimer disdained. "Why, we don't even know that the Martians could make the same kind of vocal sounds we do."

z"Well, grant that. And grant that it's going to be impressive to rattle off the names of Martian notables whose statues we find, and that if we're ever able to attribute any place names, they'll sound a lot better than this horse-doctors' Latin the old astronomers splashed all over the map of Mars," Lattimer said. "What I object to is her wasting time on this stuff, of which nobody will ever be able to read a word if she fiddles around with those lists till there's another hundred feet of loess on this city, when there's so much real work to be done and we're as shorthanded as we are."

That was the first time that had come out in just so many words. She was glad Lattimer had said it and not Selim von Ohlmhorst.

"What you mean," she retorted, "is that it doesn't have the publicity value that digging up statues has."

For an instant, she could see that the shot had scored. Then Lattimer, with a side glance at Chamberlain, answered:

"What I mean is that you're trying to find something that any archaeologist, yourself included, should know doesn't exist. I don't object to your gambling your professional reputation and making a laughing stock of yourself; what I object to is that the blunders of one archaeologist discredit the whole subject in the eyes of the public."

That seemed to be what worried Lattimer most. She was framing a reply when the communication-outlet whistled shrilly, and then squawked: "Cocktail time! One hour to dinner; cocktails in the library, Hut Four!"

* * * * *

The library, which was also lounge, recreation room, and general gathering-place, was already crowded; most of the crowd was at the long table topped with sheets of glass-like plastic that had been wall panels out of one of the ruined buildings. She poured herself what passed, here, for a martini, and carried it over to where Selim von Ohlmhorst was sitting alone.

For a while, they talked about the building they had just finished exploring, then drifted into reminiscences of their work on Terra—von Ohlmhorst's in Asia Minor, with the Hittite Empire, and hers in Pakistan, excavating the cities of the Harappa Civilization. They finished their drinks—the ingredients were plentiful; alcohol and flavoring extracts synthesized from Martian vegetation—and von Ohlmhorst took the two glasses to the table for refills.

"You know, Martha," he said, when he returned, "Tony was right about one thing. You are gambling your professional standing and reputation. It's against all archaeological experience that a language so completely dead as this one could be deciphered. There was a continuity between all the other ancient languages—by knowing Greek, Champollion learned to read Egyptian; by knowing Egyptian, Hittite was learned. That's why you and your colleagues have never been able to translate the Harappa hieroglyphics; no such continuity exists there. If you insist that this utterly dead language can be read, your reputation will suffer for it."

"I heard Colonel Penrose say, once, that an officer who's afraid to risk his military reputation seldom makes much of a reputation. It's the same with us. If we really want to find things out, we have to risk making mistakes. And I'm a lot more interested in finding things out than I am in my reputation."

She glanced across the room, to where Tony Lattimer was sitting with Gloria Standish, talking earnestly, while Gloria sipped one of the counterfeit martinis and listened. Gloria was the leading contender for the title of Miss Mars, 1996, if you liked big bosomy blondes, but Tony would have been just as attentive to her if she'd looked like the Wicked Witch in *The Wizard of Oz* because Gloria was the Pan-Federation

Telecast System commentator with the expedition.

"I know you are," the old Turco-German was saying. "That's why, when they asked me to name another archaeologist for this expedition, I named you."

He hadn't named Tony Lattimer; Lattimer had been pushed onto the expedition by his university. There'd been a lot of high-level string-pulling to that; she wished she knew the whole story. She'd managed to keep clear of universities and university politics; all her digs had been sponsored by non-academic foundations or art museums.

"You have an excellent standing: much better than my own, at your age. That's why it disturbs me to see you jeopardizing it by this insistence that the Martian language can be translated. I can't, really, see how you can hope to succeed."

She shrugged and drank some more of her cocktail, then lit another cigarette. It was getting tiresome to try to verbalize something she only felt.

"Neither do I, now, but I will. Maybe I'll find something like the picture-books Sachiko was talking about. A child's primer, maybe; surely they had things like that. And if I don't. I'll find something else. We've only been here six months. I can wait the rest of my life, if I have to, but I'll do it sometime."

"I can't wait so long," von Ohlmhorst said. "The rest of my life will only be a few years, and when the *Schiaparelli* orbits in, I'll be going back to Terra on the *Cyrano*."

"I wish you wouldn't. This is a whole new world of archaeology. Literally."

"Yes." He finished the cocktail and looked at his pipe as though wondering whether to re-light it so soon before dinner, then put it in his pocket. "A whole new world—but I've grown old, and it isn't for me. I've spent my life studying the Hittites. I can speak the Hittite language, though maybe King Muwatallis wouldn't be able to understand my modern Turkish accent. But the things I'd have to learn here—chemistry, physics, engineering, how to run analytic tests on steel girders and beryllo-silver alloys and plastics and silicones. I'm more at home with a civilization that rode in chariots and fought with swords and was just learning how to work iron. Mars is for young people. This expedition is a cadre of leadership—not only the Space Force people, who'll be the commanders of the main expedition, but us scientists, too. And I'm just an old cavalry general who can't learn to command tanks and aircraft. You'll have time to learn about Mars. I won't."

His reputation as the dean of Hittitologists was solid and secure, too, she added mentally. Then she felt ashamed of the thought. He wasn't to be classed with Tony Lattimer.

"All I came for was to get the work started," he was continuing. "The Federation Government felt that an old hand should do that. Well, it's started, now; you and Tony and whoever came out on the *Schiaparelli* must carry it on. You said it, yourself; you have a whole new world. This is only one city, of the last Martian civilization. Behind this, you have the Late Upland Culture, and the Canal Builders, and all the civilizations and races and empires before them, clear back to the Martian Stone Age." He hesitated for a moment. "You have no idea what all you have to learn, Martha. This isn't the time to start specializing too narrowly."

They all got out of the truck and stretched their legs and looked up the road to the tall building with the queer conical cap askew on its top. The four little figures that had been busy against its wall climbed into the jeep and started back slowly, the smallest of them, Sachiko Koremitsu, paying out an electric cable behind. When it pulled up beside the truck, they climbed out; Sachiko attached the free end of the cable to a nuclear-electric battery. At once, dirty gray smoke and orange dust puffed out from the wall of the building, and, a second later, the multiple explosion banged.

She and Tony Lattimer and Major Lindemann climbed onto the truck, leaving the jeep stand by the road. When they reached the building, a satisfyingly wide breach had been blown in the wall. Lattimer had placed his shots between two of the windows; they were both blown out along with the wall between, and lay unbroken on the ground. Martha remembered the first building they had entered. A Space Force officer had picked up a stone and thrown it at one of the windows, thinking that would be all they'd need to do. It had bounced back. He had drawn his pistol—they'd all carried guns, then, on the principle that what they didn't know about Mars might easily hurt them—and fired four shots. The bullets had ricocheted, screaming thinly; there were four coppery smears of jacket-metal on the window, and a little surface spalling. Somebody tried a rifle; the 4000-f.s. bullet had cracked the glasslike pane without penetrating. An oxyacetylene torch had taken an hour to cut the window out; the lab crew, aboard the ship, were still trying to find out just what the stuff was.

Tony Lattimer had gone forward and was sweeping his flashlight back and forth, swearing petulantly, his voice harshened and amplified by his helmet-speaker.

"I thought I was blasting into a hallway; this lets us into a room. Careful; there's about a two-foot drop to the floor, and a lot of rubble from the blast just inside."

He stepped down through the breach; the others began dragging equipment out of the trucks—shovels and picks and crowbars and sledges, portable floodlights, cameras, sketching materials, an extension ladder, even Alpinists' ropes and crampons and pickaxes. Hubert Penrose was shouldering something that looked like a surrealist machine gun but which was really a nuclear-electric jack-hammer. Martha selected one of the spike-shod mountaineer's ice axes, with which she could dig or chop or poke or pry or help herself over rough footing.

The windows, grimed and crusted with fifty millennia of dust, filtered in a dim twilight; even the breach in the wall, in the morning shade, lighted only a small patch of floor. Somebody snapped on a floodlight, aiming it at the ceiling. The big room was empty and bare; dust lay thick on the floor and reddened the once-white walls. It could have been a large office, but there was nothing left in it to indicate its use.

"This one's been stripped up to the seventh floor!" Lattimer exclaimed. "Street level'll be cleaned out, completely."

"Do for living quarters and shops, then," Lindemann said. "Added to the others, this'll take care of everybody on the *Schiaparelli*."

"Seem to have been a lot of electric or electronic apparatus over along this wall," one of the Space Force officers commented. "Ten or twelve electric outlets." He brushed the dusty wall with his glove, then scraped on the floor with his foot. "I can see where things were pried loose."

The door, one of the double sliding things the Martians had used, was closed. Selim von Ohlmhorst tried it, but it was stuck fast. The metal latch-parts had frozen together, molecule bonding itself to molecule, since the door had last been closed. Hubert Penrose came over with the jack-hammer, fitting a spear-point chisel into place. He set the chisel in the joint between the doors, braced the hammer against his hip, and squeezed the trigger-switch. The hammer banged briefly like the weapon it resembled, and the doors popped a few inches apart, then stuck. Enough dust had worked into the recesses into which it was supposed to slide to block it on both sides.

That was old stuff; they ran into that every time they had to force a door, and they were prepared for it. Somebody went outside and brought in a power-jack and finally one of the doors inched back to the door jamb. That was enough to get the lights and equipment through: they all passed from the room to the hallway beyond. About half the other doors were open; each had a number and a single word, *Darfhulva*, over it.

One of the civilian volunteers, a woman professor of natural ecology from Penn State University, was looking up and down the hall.

"You know," she said, "I feel at home here. I think this was a college of some sort, and these were classrooms. That word, up there; that was the subject taught, or the department. And those electronic devices, all where the class would face them; audio-visual teaching aids."

"A twenty-five-story university?" Lattimer scoffed. "Why, a building like this would handle thirty thousand students."

"Maybe there were that many. This was a big city, in its prime," Martha said, moved chiefly by a desire to oppose Lattimer.

"Yes, but think of the snafu in the halls, every time they changed classes. It'd take half an hour to get everybody back and forth from one floor to another." He turned to von Ohlmhorst. "I'm going up above this floor. This place has been looted clean up to here, but there's a chance there may be something above," he said.

"I'll stay on this floor, at present," the Turco-German replied. "There will be much coming and going, and dragging things in and out. We should get this completely examined and recorded first. Then Major Lindemann's people can do their worst, here."

"Well, if nobody else wants it, I'll take the downstairs," Martha said.

"I'll go along with you," Hubert Penrose told her. "If the lower floors have no archaeological value, we'll turn them into living quarters. I like this building: it'll give everybody room to keep out from under everybody else's feet." He looked down the hall. "We ought to find escalators at the middle."

The hallway, too, was thick underfoot with dust. Most of the open rooms were empty, but a few contained furniture, including small seat-desks. The original proponent of the university theory pointed these out as just what might be found in classrooms. There were escalators, up and down, on either side of the hall, and more on the intersecting passage to the right.

"That's how they handled the students, between classes," Martha commented. "And I'll bet there are more ahead, there."

They came to a stop where the hallway ended at a great square central hall. There were elevators, there, on two of the sides, and four escalators, still usable as stairways. But it was the walls, and the paintings on them, that brought them up short and staring.

They were clouded with dirt—she was trying to imagine what they must have looked like originally, and at the same time estimating the labor that would be involved in cleaning them—but they were still distinguishable, as was the word, *Darfhulva*, in golden letters above each of the four sides. It was a moment before she realized, from the murals, that she had at last found a meaningful Martian word. They were a vast historical panorama, clockwise around the room. A group of skin-clad savages squatting around a fire. Hunters with bows and spears, carrying a carcass of an animal slightly like a pig. Nomads riding long-legged, graceful mounts like hornless deer. Peasants sowing and reaping; mud-walled hut villages, and cities; processions of priests and warriors; battles with swords and bows, and with cannon and muskets; galleys, and ships with sails, and ships without visible means of propulsion, and aircraft. Changing costumes and weapons and machines and styles of architecture. A richly fertile landscape, gradually merging into barren deserts and bushlands—the time of the great planet-wide drought. The Canal Builders—men with machines recognizable as steam-shovels and derricks, digging and quarrying and driving across the empty plains with aqueducts. More cities—seaports on the shrinking oceans; dwindling, half-deserted cities; an abandoned city, with four tiny humanoid figures and a thing like a combat-car in the middle of a brush-grown plaza, they and their vehicle dwarfed by the huge lifeless buildings around them. She had not the least doubt; *Darfhulva* was History.

"Wonderful!" von Ohlmhorst was saying. "The entire history of this race. Why, if the painter depicted appropriate costumes and weapons and machines for each period, and got the architecture right, we can break the history of this planet into eras and periods and civilizations."

"You can assume they're authentic. The faculty of this university would insist on authenticity in the *Darfhulva*—History—Department," she said.

"Yes! *Darfhulva*—History! And your magazine was a journal of *Sornhulva*!" Penrose exclaimed. "You have a word, Martha!" It took her an instant to realize that he had called her by her first name, and not Dr. Dane. She wasn't sure if that weren't a bigger triumph than learning a word of the Martian language. Or a more auspicious start. "Alone, I suppose that *hulva* means something like science or knowledge, or study; combined, it would be equivalent to our 'ology. And *darf* would mean something like past, or old times, or human events, or chronicles."

"That gives you three words, Martha!" Sachiko jubilated. "You did it."

"Let's don't go too fast," Lattimer said, for once not derisively. "I'll admit that *darfhulva* is the Martian word for history as a subject of study;

I'll admit that *hulva* is the general word and *darf* modifies it and tells us which subject is meant. But as for assigning specific meanings, we can't do that because we don't know just how the Martians thought, scientifically or otherwise."

He stopped short, startled by the blue-white light that blazed as Sid Chamberlain's Kliegettes went on. When the whirring of the camera stopped, it was Chamberlain who was speaking:

"This is the biggest thing yet; the whole history of Mars, stone age to the end, all on four walls. I'm taking this with the fast shutter, but we'll telecast it in slow motion, from the beginning to the end. Tony, I want you to do the voice for it—running commentary, interpretation of each scene as it's shown. Would you do that?"

Would he do that! Martha thought. If he had a tail, he'd be wagging it at the very thought.

"Well, there ought to be more murals on the other floors," she said. "Who wants to come downstairs with us?"

Sachiko did; immediately. Ivan Fitzgerald volunteered. Sid decided to go upstairs with Tony Lattimer, and Gloria Standish decided to go upstairs, too. Most of the party would remain on the seventh floor, to help Selim von Ohlmhorst get it finished. After poking tentatively at the escalator with the spike of her ice axe, Martha led the way downward.

The sixth floor was *Darfhulva*, too; military and technological history, from the character of the murals. They looked around the central hall, and went down to the fifth; it was like the floors above except that the big quadrangle was stacked with dusty furniture and boxes. Ivan Fitzgerald, who was carrying the floodlight, swung it slowly around. Here the murals were of heroic-sized Martians, so human in appearance as to seem members of her own race, each holding some object—a book, or a test tube, or some bit of scientific apparatus, and behind them were scenes of laboratories and factories, flame and smoke, lightning-flashes. The word at the top of each of the four walls was one with which she was already familiar—*Sornhulva*.

"Hey, Martha; there's that word," Ivan Fitzgerald exclaimed. "The one in the title of your magazine." He looked at the paintings. "Chemistry, or physics."

"Both." Hubert Penrose considered. "I don't think the Martians made any sharp distinction between them. See, the old fellow with the scraggly whiskers must be the inventor of the spectroscope; he has one in his hands, and he has a rainbow behind him. And the woman in the blue smock, beside him, worked in organic chemistry; see the diagrams of long-chain molecules behind her. What word would convey the idea of chemistry and physics taken as one subject?"

"*Sornhulva*," Sachiko suggested. "If *hulva's* something like science, "*sorn*" must mean matter, or substance, or physical object. You were right, all along, Martha. A civilization like this would certainly leave something like this that would be self-explanatory."

"This'll wipe a little more of that superior grin off Tony Lattimer's face," Fitzgerald was saying, as they went down the motionless escalator to the floor below. "Tony wants to be a big shot. When you want to be a big shot, you can't bear the possibility of anybody else being a bigger big shot, and whoever makes a start on reading this language will be the biggest big shot archaeology ever saw."

That was true. She hadn't thought of it, in that way, before, and now she tried not to think about it. She didn't want to be a big shot. She wanted to be able to read the Martian language, and find things out about the Martians.

Two escalators down, they came out on a mezzanine around a wide central hall on the street level, the floor forty feet below them and the ceiling thirty feet above. Their lights picked out object after object below—a huge group of sculptured figures in the middle; some kind of a motor vehicle jacked up on trestles for repairs; things that looked like machine-guns and auto-cannon; long tables, tops littered with a dust-covered miscellany; machinery; boxes and crates and containers.

They made their way down and walked among the clutter, missing a hundred things for every one they saw, until they found an escalator to the basement. There were three basements, one under another, until at last they stood at the bottom of the last escalator, on a bare concrete floor, swinging the portable floodlight over stacks of boxes and barrels and drums, and heaps of powdery dust. The boxes were plastic—nobody had ever found anything made of wood in the city—and the barrels and drums were of metal or glass or some glasslike substance. They were outwardly intact. The powdery heaps might have been anything organic, or anything containing fluid. Down here, where wind and dust could not reach, evaporation had been the only force of destruction after the minute life that caused putrefaction had vanished.

They found refrigeration rooms, too, and using Martha's ice axe and the pistol-like vibratool Sachiko carried on her belt, they pounded and pried one open, to find desiccated piles of what had been vegetables, and leathery chunks of meat. Samples of that stuff, rocketed up to the ship, would give a reliable estimate, by radio-carbon dating, of how long ago this building had been occupied. The refrigeration unit, radically different from anything their own culture had produced, had been electrically powered. Sachiko and Penrose, poking into it, found the switches still on; the machine had only ceased to function when the power-source, whatever that had been, had failed.

The middle basement had also been used, at least toward the end, for storage; it was cut in half by a partition pierced by but one door. They took half an hour to force this, and were on the point of sending above for heavy equipment when it yielded enough for them to squeeze through. Fitzgerald, in the lead with the light, stopped short, looked around, and then gave a groan that came through his helmet-speaker like a foghorn.

"Oh, no! No!"

"What's the matter, Ivan?" Sachiko, entering behind him, asked anxiously.

He stepped aside. "Look at it, Sachi! Are we going to have to do all that?"

Martha crowded through behind her friend and looked around, then stood motionless, dizzy with excitement. Books. Case on case of books, half an acre of cases, fifteen feet to the ceiling. Fitzgerald, and Penrose, who had pushed in behind her, were talking in rapid excitement; she only heard the sound of their voices, not their words. This must be the main stacks of the university library—the entire literature of the vanished race of Mars. In the center, down an aisle between the cases, she could see the hollow square of the librarians' desk, and stairs and a dumb-waiter to the floor above.

She realized that she was walking forward, with the others, toward this. Sachiko was saying: "I'm the lightest; let me go first." She must be talking about the spidery metal stairs.

"I'd say they were safe," Penrose answered. "The trouble we've had with doors around here shows that the metal hasn't deteriorated."

In the end, the Japanese girl led the way, more catlike than ever in her caution. The stairs were quite sound, in spite of their fragile appearance, and they all followed her. The floor above was a duplicate of the room they had entered, and seemed to contain about as many books. Rather than waste time forcing the door here, they returned to the middle basement and came up by the escalator down which they had originally descended.

The upper basement contained kitchens—electric stoves, some with pots and pans still on them—and a big room that must have been, originally, the students' dining room, though when last used it had been a workshop. As they expected, the library reading room was on the street-level floor, directly above the stacks. It seemed to have been converted into a sort of common living room for the building's last occupants. An adjoining auditorium had been made into a chemical works; there were vats and distillation apparatus, and a metal fractionating tower that extended through a hole knocked in the ceiling seventy feet above. A good deal of plastic furniture of the sort they had been finding everywhere in the city was stacked about, some of it broken up, apparently for reprocessing. The other rooms on the street floor seemed also to have been devoted to manufacturing and repair work; a considerable industry, along a number of lines, must have been carried on here for a long time after the university had ceased to function as such.

On the second floor, they found a museum; many of the exhibits remained, tantalizingly half-visible in grimed glass cases. There had been administrative offices there, too. The doors of most of them were closed, and they did not waste time trying to force them, but those that were open had been turned into living quarters. They made notes, and rough floor plans, to guide them in future more thorough examination; it was almost noon before they had worked their way back to the seventh floor.

Selim von Ohlmhorst was in a room on the north side of the building, sketching the position of things before examining them and collecting them for removal. He had the floor checkerboarded with a grid of chalked lines, each numbered.

"We have everything on this floor photographed," he said. "I have three gangs—all the floodlights I have—sketching and making measurements. At the rate we're going, with time out for lunch, we'll be finished by the middle of the afternoon."

"You've been working fast. Evidently you aren't being High-Church about a 'qualified archaeologist' entering rooms first," Penrose commented.

"Ach, childishness!" the old man exclaimed impatiently. "These officers of yours aren't fools. All of them have been to Intelligence School and Criminal Investigation School. Some of the most careful amateur archaeologists I ever knew were retired soldiers or policemen. But there isn't much work to be done. Most of the rooms are either empty or like this one—a few bits of furniture and broken trash and scraps of paper. Did you find anything down on the lower floors?"

"Well, yes," Penrose said, a hint of mirth in his voice. "What would you say, Martha?"

She started to tell Selim. The others, unable to restrain their excitement, broke in with interruptions. Von Ohlmhorst was staring in incredulous amazement.

"But this floor was looted almost clean, and the buildings we've entered before were all looted from the street level up," he said, at length.

"The people who looted this one lived here," Penrose replied. "They had electric power to the last; we found refrigerators full of food, and stoves with the dinner still on them. They must have used the elevators to haul things down from the upper floor. The whole first floor was converted into workshops and laboratories. I think that this place must have been something like a monastery in the Dark Ages in Europe, or what such a monastery would have been like if the Dark Ages had followed the fall of a highly developed scientific civilization. For one thing, we found a lot of machine guns and light auto-cannon on the street level, and all the doors were barricaded. The people here were trying to keep a civilization running after the rest of the planet had gone back to barbarism; I suppose they'd have to fight off raids by the barbarians now and then."

"You're not going to insist on making this building into expedition quarters, I hope, Colonel?" von Ohlmhorst asked anxiously.

"Oh, no! This place is an archaeological treasure-house. More than that; from what I saw, our technicians can learn a lot, here. But you'd better get this floor cleaned up as soon as you can, though. I'll have the subsurface part, from the sixth floor down, air sealed. Then we'll put in oxygen generators and power units, and get a couple of elevators into service. For the floors above, we can use temporary airsealing floor by floor, and portable equipment; when we have things atmosphered and lighted and heated, you and Martha and Tony Lattimer can go to work systematically and in comfort, and I'll give you all the help I can spare from the other work. This is one of the biggest things we've found yet."

Tony Lattimer and his companions came down to the seventh floor a little later.

"I don't get this, at all," he began, as soon as he joined them. "This building wasn't stripped the way the others were. Always, the procedure seems to have been to strip from the bottom up, but they seem to have stripped the top floors first, here. All but the very top. I found out what that conical thing is, by the way. It's a wind-rotor, and under it there's an electric generator. This building generated its own power."

"What sort of condition are the generators in?" Penrose asked.

"Well, everything's full of dust that blew in under the rotor, of course, but it looks to be in pretty good shape. Hey, I'll bet that's it! They had power, so they used the elevators to haul stuff down. That's just what they did. Some of the floors above here don't seem to have been touched, though." He paused momentarily; back of his oxy-mask, he seemed to be grinning.

"I don't know that I ought to mention this in front of Martha, but two floors above—we hit a room—it must have been the reference library for one of the departments—that had close to five hundred books in it."

The noise that interrupted him, like the squawking of a Brobdingnagian parrot, was only Ivan Fitzgerald laughing through his helmet-speaker.

Lunch at the huts was a hasty meal, with a gabble of full-mouthed and excited talking. Hubert Penrose and his chief subordinates snatched their food in a huddled consultation at one end of the table; in the afternoon, work was suspended on everything else and the fifty-odd men and women of the expedition concentrated their efforts on the University. By the middle of the afternoon, the seventh floor had been completely examined, photographed and sketched, and the murals in the square central hall covered with protective tarpaulins, and Laurent Gicquel and his airsealing crew had moved in and were at work. It had been decided to seal the central hall at the entrances.

It took the French-Canadian engineer most of the afternoon to find all the ventilation-ducts and plug them. An elevator-shaft on the north side was found reaching clear to the twenty-fifth floor; this would give access to the top of the building; another shaft, from the center, would take care of the floors below. Nobody seemed willing to trust the ancient elevators, themselves; it was the next evening before a couple of cars and the necessary machinery could be fabricated in the machine shops aboard the ship and sent down by landing-rocket. By that time, the airsealing was finished, the nuclear-electric energy-converters were in place, and the oxygen generators set up.

Martha was in the lower basement, an hour or so before lunch the day after, when a couple of Space Force officers came out of the elevator, bringing extra lights with them. She was still using oxygen-equipment; it was a moment before she realized that the newcomers had no masks, and that one of them was smoking. She took off her own helmet-speaker, throat-mike and mask and unslung her tank-pack, breathing cautiously. The air was chilly, and musty-acrid with the odor of antiquity—the first

Martian odor she had smelled—but when she lit a cigarette, the lighter flamed clear and steady and the tobacco caught and burned evenly.

The archaeologists, many of the other civilian scientists, a few of the Space Force officers and the two news-correspondents, Sid Chamberlain and Gloria Standish, moved in that evening, setting up cots in vacant rooms. They installed electric stoves and a refrigerator in the old Library Reading Room, and put in a bar and lunch counter. For a few days, the place was full of noise and activity, then, gradually, the Space Force people and all but a few of the civilians returned to their own work. There was still the business of airsealing the more habitable of the buildings already explored, and fitting them up in readiness for the arrival, in a year and a half, of the five hundred members of the main expedition. There was work to be done enlarging the landing field for the ship's rocket craft, and building new chemical-fuel tanks.

There was the work of getting the city's ancient reservoirs cleared of silt before the next spring thaw brought more water down the underground aqueducts everybody called canals in mistranslation of Schiaparelli's Italian word, though this was proving considerably easier than anticipated. The ancient Canal-Builders must have anticipated a time when their descendants would no longer be capable of maintenance work, and had prepared against it. By the day after the University had been made completely habitable, the actual work there was being done by Selim, Tony Lattimer and herself, with half a dozen Space Force officers, mostly girls, and four or five civilians, helping.

They worked up from the bottom, dividing the floor-surfaces into numbered squares, measuring and listing and sketching and photographing. They packaged samples of organic matter and sent them up to the ship for Carbon-14 dating and analysis; they opened cans and jars and bottles, and found that everything fluid in them had evaporated, through the porosity of glass and metal and plastic if there were no other way. Wherever they looked, they found evidence of activity suddenly suspended and never resumed. A vise with a bar of metal in it, half cut through and the hacksaw beside it. Pots and pans with hardened remains of food in them; a leathery cut of meat on a table, with the knife ready at hand. Toilet articles on washstands; unmade beds, the bedding ready to crumble at a touch but still retaining the impress of the sleeper's body; papers and writing materials on desks, as though the writer had gotten up, meaning to return and finish in a fifty-thousand-year-ago moment.

It worried her. Irrationally, she began to feel that the Martians had never left this place; that they were still around her, watching disapprovingly every time she picked up something they had laid down. They haunted her dreams, now, instead of their enigmatic writing. At first, everybody who had moved into the University had taken a separate room, happy to escape the crowding and lack of privacy of the huts. After a few nights, she was glad when Gloria Standish moved in with her, and accepted the newswoman's excuse that she felt lonely without somebody to talk to before falling asleep. Sachiko Koremitsu joined them the next evening, and before going to bed, the girl officer cleaned and oiled her pistol, remarking that she was afraid some rust may have gotten into it.

The others felt it, too. Selim von Ohlmhorst developed the habit of turning quickly and looking behind him, as though trying to surprise somebody or something that was stalking him. Tony Lattimer, having a drink at the bar that had been improvised from the librarian's desk in the Reading Room, set down his glass and swore.

"You know what this place is? It's an archaeological *Marie Celeste*!" he declared. "It was occupied right up to the end—we've all seen the shifts these people used to keep a civilization going here—but what was the end? What happened to them? Where did they go?"

"You didn't expect them to be waiting out front, with a red carpet and a big banner, *Welcome Terrans*, did you, Tony?" Gloria Standish asked.

"No, of course not; they've all been dead for fifty thousand years. But if they were the last of the Martians, why haven't we found their bones, at least? Who buried them, after they were dead?" He looked at the glass, a bubble-thin goblet, found, with hundreds of others like it, in a closet above, as though debating with himself whether to have another drink. Then he voted in the affirmative and reached for the cocktail pitcher. "And every door on the old ground level is either barred or barricaded from the inside. How did they get out? And why did they leave?"

The next day, at lunch, Sachiko Koremitsu had the answer to the second question. Four or five electrical engineers had come down by rocket from the ship, and she had been spending the morning with them, in oxy-masks, at the top of the building.

"Tony, I thought you said those generators were in good shape," she began, catching sight of Lattimer. "They aren't. They're in the most unholy mess I ever saw. What happened, up there, was that the supports of the wind-rotor gave way, and weight snapped the main shaft, and smashed everything under it."

"Well, after fifty thousand years, you can expect something like that," Lattimer retorted. "When an archaeologist says something's in good shape, he doesn't necessarily mean it'll start as soon as you shove a switch in."

"You didn't notice that it happened when the power was on, did you," one of the engineers asked, nettled at Lattimer's tone. "Well, it was. Everything's burned out or shorted or fused together; I saw one busbar eight inches across melted clean in two. It's a pity we didn't find things in good shape, even archaeologically speaking. I saw a lot of interesting things, things in advance of what we're using now. But it'll take a couple of years to get everything sorted out and figure what it looked like originally."

"Did it look as though anybody'd made any attempt to fix it?" Martha asked.

Sachiko shook her head. "They must have taken one look at it and given up. I don't believe there would have been any possible way to repair anything."

"Well, that explains why they left. They needed electricity for lighting, and heating, and all their industrial equipment was electrical. They had a good life, here, with power; without it, this place wouldn't have been habitable."

"Then why did they barricade everything from the inside, and how did they get out?" Lattimer wanted to know.

"To keep other people from breaking in and looting. Last man out probably barred the last door and slid down a rope from upstairs," von Ohlmhorst suggested. "This Houdini-trick doesn't worry me too much.

We'll find out eventually."

"Yes, about the time Martha starts reading Martian," Lattimer scoffed.

"That may be just when we'll find out," von Ohlmhorst replied seriously. "It wouldn't surprise me if they left something in writing when they evacuated this place."

"Are you really beginning to treat this pipe dream of hers as a serious possibility, Selim?" Lattimer demanded. "I know, it would be a wonderful thing, but wonderful things don't happen just because they're wonderful. Only because they're possible, and this isn't. Let me quote that distinguished Hittitologist, Johannes Friedrich: 'Nothing can be translated out of nothing.' Or that later but not less distinguished Hittitologist, Selim von Ohlmhorst: 'Where are you going to get your bilingual?'"

"Friedrich lived to see the Hittite language deciphered and read," von Ohlmhorst reminded him.

"Yes, when they found Hittite-Assyrian bilinguals." Lattimer measured a spoonful of coffee-powder into his cup and added hot water. "Martha, you ought to know, better than anybody, how little chance you have. You've been working for years in the Indus Valley; how many words of Harappa have you or anybody else ever been able to read?"

"We never found a university, with a half-million-volume library, at Harappa or Mohenjo-Daro."

"And, the first day we entered this building, we established meanings for several words," Selim von Ohlmhorst added.

"And you've never found another meaningful word since," Lattimer added. "And you're only sure of general meaning, not specific meaning of word-elements, and you have a dozen different interpretations for each word."

"We made a start," von Ohlmhorst maintained. "We have Grotefend's word for 'king.' But I'm going to be able to read some of those books, over there, if it takes me the rest of my life here. It probably will, anyhow."

"You mean you've changed your mind about going home on the *Cyrano*?" Martha asked. "You'll stay on here?"

The old man nodded. "I can't leave this. There's too much to discover. The old dog will have to learn a lot of new tricks, but this is where my work will be, from now on."

Lattimer was shocked. "You're nuts!" he cried. "You mean you're going to throw away everything you've accomplished in Hittitology and start all over again here on Mars? Martha, if you've talked him into this crazy decision, you're a criminal!"

"Nobody talked me into anything," von Ohlmhorst said roughly. "And as for throwing away what I've accomplished in Hittitology, I don't know what the devil you're talking about. Everything I know about the Hittite Empire is published and available to anybody. Hittitology's like Egyptology; it's stopped being research and archaeology and become scholarship and history. And I'm not a scholar or a historian; I'm a pick-and-shovel field archaeologist—a highly skilled and specialized grave-robber and junk-picker—and there's more pick-and-shovel work on this planet than I could do in a hundred lifetimes. This is something new; I was a fool to think I could turn my back on it and go back to scribbling footnotes about Hittite kings."

"You could have anything you wanted, in Hittitology. There are a dozen universities that'd sooner have you than a winning football team. But no! You have to be the top man in Martianology, too. You can't leave that for anybody else—" Lattimer shoved his chair back and got to his feet, leaving the table with an oath that was almost a sob of exasperation.

Maybe his feelings were too much for him. Maybe he realized, as Martha did, what he had betrayed. She sat, avoiding the eyes of the others, looking at the ceiling, as embarrassed as though Lattimer had flung something dirty on the table in front of them. Tony Lattimer had, desperately, wanted Selim to go home on the *Cyrano*. Martianology was a new field; if Selim entered it, he would bring with him the reputation he had already built in Hittitology, automatically stepping into the leading role that Lattimer had coveted for himself. Ivan Fitzgerald's words echoed back to her—when you want to be a big shot, you can't bear the possibility of anybody else being a bigger big shot. His derision of her own efforts became comprehensible, too. It wasn't that he was convinced that she would never learn to read the Martian language. He had been afraid that she would.

Ivan Fitzgerald finally isolated the germ that had caused the Finchley girl's undiagnosed illness. Shortly afterward, the malady turned into a mild fever, from which she recovered. Nobody else seemed to have caught it. Fitzgerald was still trying to find out how the germ had been transmitted.

They found a globe of Mars, made when the city had been a seaport. They located the city, and learned that its name had been Kukan—or something with a similar vowel-consonant ratio. Immediately, Sid Chamberlain and Gloria Standish began giving their telecasts a Kukan dateline, and Hubert Penrose used the name in his official reports. They also found a Martian calendar; the year had been divided into ten more or less equal months, and one of them had been Doma. Another month was Nor, and that was a part of the name of the scientific journal Martha had found.

Bill Chandler, the zoologist, had been going deeper and deeper into the old sea bottom of Syrtis. Four hundred miles from Kukan, and at fifteen thousand feet lower altitude, he shot a bird. At least, it was a something with wings and what were almost but not quite feathers, though it was more reptilian than avian in general characteristics. He and Ivan Fitzgerald skinned and mounted it, and then dissected the carcass almost tissue by tissue. About seven-eighths of its body capacity was lungs; it certainly breathed air containing at least half enough oxygen to support human life, or five times as much as the air around Kukan.

That took the center of interest away from archaeology, and started a new burst of activity. All the expedition's aircraft—four jetticopters and three wingless airdyne reconnaissance fighters—were thrown into intensified exploration of the lower sea bottoms, and the bio-science boys and girls were wild with excitement and making new discoveries on each flight.

The University was left to Selim and Martha and Tony Lattimer, the latter keeping to himself while she and the old Turco-German worked together. The civilian specialists in other fields, and the Space Force people who had been holding tape lines and making sketches and snapping cameras, were all flying to lower Syrtis to find out how much oxygen there was and what kind of life it supported.

Sometimes Sachiko dropped in; most of the time she was busy helping Ivan Fitzgerald dissect specimens. They had four or five species of what might loosely be called birds, and something that could easily be classed as a reptile, and a carnivorous mammal the size of a cat with bird-like claws, and a herbivore almost identical with the pig-like thing in the big *Darfhulva* mural, and another like a gazelle with a single horn in the middle of its forehead.

The high point came when one party, at thirty thousand feet below the level of Kukan, found breathable air. One of them had a mild attack of *sorroche* and had to be flown back for treatment in a hurry, but the others showed no ill effects.

The daily newscasts from Terra showed a corresponding shift in interest at home. The discovery of the University had focused attention on the dead past of Mars; now the public was interested in Mars as a possible home for humanity. It was Tony Lattimer who brought archaeology back into the activities of the expedition and the news at home.

Martha and Selim were working in the museum on the second floor, scrubbing the grime from the glass cases, noting contents, and grease-penciling numbers; Lattimer and a couple of Space Force officers were going through what had been the administrative offices on the other side. It was one of these, a young second lieutenant, who came hurrying in from the mezzanine, almost bursting with excitement.

"Hey, Martha! Dr. von Ohlmhorst!" he was shouting. "Where are you? Tony's found the Martians!"

Selim dropped his rag back in the bucket; she laid her clipboard on top of the case beside her.

"Where?" they asked together.

"Over on the north side." The lieutenant took hold of himself and spoke more deliberately. "Little room, back of one of the old faculty offices—conference room. It was locked from the inside, and we had to burn it down with a torch. That's where they are. Eighteen of them, around a long table—"

Gloria Standish, who had dropped in for lunch, was on the mezzanine, fairly screaming into a radiophone extension:

"...Dozen and a half of them! Well, of course they're dead. What a question! They look like skeletons covered with leather. No, I do not know what they died of. Well, forget it; I don't care if Bill Chandler's found a three-headed hippopotamus. Sid, don't you get it? We've found the *Martians!*"

She slammed the phone back on its hook, rushing away ahead of them.

Martha remembered the closed door; on the first survey, they hadn't attempted opening it. Now it was burned away at both sides and lay, still hot along the edges, on the floor of the big office room in front. A floodlight was on in the room inside, and Lattimer was going around looking at things while a Space Force officer stood by the door. The center of the room was filled by a long table; in armchairs around it sat the eighteen men and women who had occupied the room for the last fifty millennia. There were bottles and glasses on the table in front of them, and, had she seen them in a dimmer light, she would have thought that they were merely dozing over their drinks. One had a knee hooked over his chair-arm and was curled in foetus-like sleep. Another had fallen forward onto the table, arms extended, the emerald set of a ring twinkling dully on one finger. Skeletons covered with leather, Gloria Standish had called them, and so they were—faces like skulls, arms and legs like sticks, the flesh shrunken onto the bones under it.

"Isn't this something!" Lattimer was exulting. "Mass suicide, that's what it was. Notice what's in the corners?"

Braziers, made of perforated two-gallon-odd metal cans, the white walls smudged with smoke above them. Von Ohlmhorst had noticed them at once, and was poking into one of them with his flashlight.

"Yes; charcoal. I noticed a quantity of it around a couple of hand-forges in the shop on the first floor. That's why you had so much trouble breaking in; they'd sealed the room on the inside." He straightened and went around the room, until he found a ventilator, and peered into it. "Stuffed with rags. They must have been all that were left, here. Their power was gone, and they were old and tired, and all around them their world was dying. So they just came in here and lit the charcoal, and sat drinking together till they all fell asleep. Well, we know what became of them, now, anyhow."

Sid and Gloria made the most of it. The Terran public wanted to hear about Martians, and if live Martians couldn't be found, a room full of dead ones was the next best thing. Maybe an even better thing; it had been only sixty-odd years since the Orson Welles invasion-scare. Tony Lattimer, the discoverer, was beginning to cash in on his attentions to Gloria and his ingratiation with Sid; he was always either making voice-and-image talks for telecast or listening to the news from the home planet. Without question, he had become, overnight, the most widely known archaeologist in history.

"Not that I'm interested in all this, for myself," he disclaimed, after listening to the telecast from Terra two days after his discovery. "But this is going to be a big thing for Martian archaeology. Bring it to the public attention; dramatize it. Selim, can you remember when Lord Carnarvon and Howard Carter found the tomb of Tutankhamen?"

"In 1923? I was two years old, then," von Ohlmhorst chuckled. "I really don't know how much that publicity ever did for Egyptology. Oh, the museums did devote more space to Egyptian exhibits, and after a museum department head gets a few extra showcases, you know how hard it is to make him give them up. And, for a while, it was easier to get financial support for new excavations. But I don't know how much good all this public excitement really does, in the long run."

"Well, I think one of us should go back on the *Cyrano*, when the *Schiaparelli* orbits in," Lattimer said. "I'd hoped it would be you; your voice would carry the most weight. But I think it's important that one of us go back, to present the story of our work, and what we have accomplished and what we hope to accomplish, to the public and to the universities and the learned societies, and to the Federation Government. There will be a great deal of work that will have to be done. We must not allow the other scientific fields and the so-called practical interests to monopolize public and academic support. So, I believe I shall go back at least for a while, and see what I can do—"

Lectures. The organization of a Society of Martian Archaeology, with Anthony Lattimer, Ph.D., the logical candidate for the chair. Degrees, honors; the deference of the learned, and the adulation of the lay public. Positions, with impressive titles and salaries. Sweet are the uses of publicity.

She crushed out her cigarette and got to her feet. "Well, I still have the final lists of what we found in *Halvhulva*—Biology—department to check over. I'm starting on Sornhulva tomorrow, and I want that stuff in shape for expert evaluation."

That was the sort of thing Tony Lattimer wanted to get away from, the detail-work and the drudgery. Let the infantry do the slogging through the mud; the brass-hats got the medals.

She was halfway through the fifth floor, a week later, and was having midday lunch in the reading room on the first floor when Hubert Penrose came over and sat down beside her, asking her what she was doing. She told him.

"I wonder if you could find me a couple of men, for an hour or so," she added. "I'm stopped by a couple of jammed doors at the central hall. Lecture room and library, if the layout of that floor's anything like the ones below it."

"Yes. I'm a pretty fair door-buster, myself." He looked around the room. "There's Jeff Miles; he isn't doing much of anything. And we'll put Sid Chamberlain to work, for a change, too. The four of us ought to get your doors open." He called to Chamberlain, who was carrying his tray over to the dish washer. "Oh, Sid; you doing anything for the next hour or so?"

"I was going up to the fourth floor, to see what Tony's doing."

"Forget it. Tony's bagged his season limit of Martians. I'm going to help Martha bust in a couple of doors; we'll probably find a whole cemetery full of Martians."

Chamberlain shrugged. "Why not. A jammed door can have anything back of it, and I know what Tony's doing—just routine stuff."

Jeff Miles, the Space Force captain, came over, accompanied by one of the lab-crew from the ship who had come down on the rocket the day before.

"This ought to be up your alley, Mort," he was saying to his companion. "Chemistry and physics department. Want to come along?"

The lab man, Mort Tranter, was willing. Seeing the sights was what he'd come down from the ship for.

She finished her coffee and cigarette, and they went out into the hall together, gathered equipment and rode the elevator to the fifth floor.

The lecture hall door was the nearest; they attacked it first. With proper equipment and help, it was no problem and in ten minutes they had it open wide enough to squeeze through with the floodlights. The room inside was quite empty, and, like most of the rooms behind closed doors, comparatively free from dust. The students, it appeared, had sat with their backs to the door, facing a low platform, but their seats and the lecturer's table and equipment had been removed. The two side walls bore inscriptions: on the right, a pattern of concentric circles which she recognized as a diagram of atomic structure, and on the left a complicated table of numbers and words, in two columns. Tranter was pointing at the diagram on the right.

"They got as far as the Bohr atom, anyhow," he said. "Well, not quite. They knew about electron shells, but they have the nucleus pictured as a solid mass. No indication of proton-and-neutron structure. I'll bet, when you come to translate their scientific books, you'll find that they taught that the atom was the ultimate and indivisible particle. That explains why you people never found any evidence that the Martians used nuclear energy."

"That's a uranium atom," Captain Miles mentioned.

"It is?" Sid Chamberlain asked, excitedly. "Then they did know about atomic energy. Just because we haven't found any pictures of A-bomb mushrooms doesn't mean—"

She turned to look at the other wall. Sid's signal reactions were getting away from him again; uranium meant nuclear power to him, and the two words were interchangeable. As she studied the arrangement of the numbers and words, she could hear Tranter saying:

"Nuts, Sid. We knew about uranium a long time before anybody found out what could be done with it. Uranium was discovered on Terra in 1789, by Klaproth."

There was something familiar about the table on the left wall. She tried to remember what she had been taught in school about physics, and what she had picked up by accident afterward. The second column was a continuation of the first: there were forty-six items in each, each item numbered consecutively—

"Probably used uranium because it's the largest of the natural atoms," Penrose was saying. "The fact that there's nothing beyond it there shows that they hadn't created any of the transuranics. A student could go to that thing and point out the outer electron of any of the ninety-two elements."

Ninety-two! That was it; there were ninety-two items in the table on the left wall! Hydrogen was Number One, she knew; One, *Sarfaldsorn*. Helium was Two; that was *Tirfaldsorn*. She couldn't remember which element came next, but in Martian it was *Sarfalddavas*. *Sorn* must mean matter, or substance, then. And *davas*; she was trying to think of what it could be. She turned quickly to the others, catching hold of Hubert Penrose's arm with one hand and waving her clipboard with the other.

"Look at this thing, over here," she was clamoring excitedly. "Tell me what you think it is. Could it be a table of the elements?"

They all turned to look. Mort Tranter stared at it for a moment.

"Could be. If I only knew what those squiggles meant—"

That was right; he'd spent his time aboard the ship.

"If you could read the numbers, would that help?" she asked, beginning to set down the Arabic digits and their Martian equivalents. "It's decimal system, the same as we use."

"Sure. If that's a table of elements, all I'd need would be the numbers. Thanks," he added as she tore off the sheet and gave it to him.

Penrose knew the numbers, and was ahead of him. "Ninety-two

items, numbered consecutively. The first number would be the atomic number. Then a single word, the name of the element. Then the atomic weight—"

She began reading off the names of the elements. "I know hydrogen and helium; what's *tirfalddavas*, the third one?"

"Lithium," Tranter said. "The atomic weights aren't run out past the decimal point. Hydrogen's one plus, if that double-hook dingus is a plus sign; Helium's four-plus, that's right. And lithium's given as seven, that isn't right. It's six-point nine-four-oh. Or is that thing a Martian minus sign?"

"Of course! Look! A plus sign is a hook, to hang things together; a minus sign is a knife, to cut something off from something—see, the little loop is the handle and the long pointed loop is the blade. Stylized, of course, but that's what it is. And the fourth element, kiradavas; what's that?"

"Beryllium. Atomic weight given as nine-and-a-hook; actually it's nine-point-oh-two."

Sid Chamberlain had been disgruntled because he couldn't get a story about the Martians having developed atomic energy. It took him a few minutes to understand the newest development, but finally it dawned on him.

"Hey! You're reading that!" he cried. "You're reading Martian!"

"That's right," Penrose told him. "Just reading it right off. I don't get the two items after the atomic weight, though. They look like months of the Martian calendar. What ought they to be, Mort?"

Tranter hesitated. "Well, the next information after the atomic weight ought to be the period and group numbers. But those are words."

"What would the numbers be for the first one, hydrogen?"

"Period One, Group One. One electron shell, one electron in the outer shell," Tranter told her. "Helium's period one, too, but it has the outer—only—electron shell full, so it's in the group of inert elements."

"*Trav, Trav. Trav's* the first month of the year. And helium's *Trav, Yenth*; *Yenth* is the eighth month."

"The inert elements could be called Group Eight, yes. And the third element, lithium, is Period Two, Group One. That check?"

"It certainly does. *Sanv, Trav*; *Sanv's* the second month. What's the first element in Period Three?"

"Sodium. Number Eleven."

That's right; it's *Krav, Trav*. Why, the names of the months are simply numbers, one to ten, spelled out.

"*Doma*'s the fifth month. That was your first Martian word, Martha," Penrose told her. "The word for five. And if *davas* is the word for metal, and *sornhulva* is chemistry and/or physics, I'll bet Tadavas Sornhulva is literally translated as: Of-Metal Matter-Knowledge. Metallurgy, in other words. I wonder what *Mastharnorvod* means." It surprised her that, after so long and with so much happening in the meantime, he could remember that. "Something like 'Journal,' or 'Review,' or maybe 'Quarterly.'"

"We'll work that out, too," she said confidently. After this, nothing seemed impossible. "Maybe we can find—" Then she stopped short. "You said 'Quarterly.' I think it was 'Monthly,' instead. It was dated for a specific month, the fifth one. And if *nor* is ten, Mastharnorvod could be 'Year-Tenth.' And I'll bet we'll find that *masthar* is the word for year." She looked at the table on the wall again. "Well, let's get all these words down, with translations for as many as we can."

"Let's take a break for a minute," Penrose suggested, getting out his cigarettes. "And then, let's do this in comfort. Jeff, suppose you and Sid go across the hall and see what you find in the other room in the way of a desk or something like that, and a few chairs. There'll be a lot of work to do on this."

Sid Chamberlain had been squirming as though he were afflicted with ants, trying to contain himself. Now he let go with an excited jabber.

"This is really it! *The* it, not just it-of-the-week, like finding the reservoirs or those statues or this building, or even the animals and the dead Martians! Wait till Selim and Tony see this! Wait till Tony sees it; I want to see his face! And when I get this on telecast, all Terra's going to go nuts about it!" He turned to Captain Miles. "Jeff, suppose you take a look at that other door, while I find somebody to send to tell Selim and Tony. And Gloria; wait till she sees this—"

"Take it easy, Sid," Martha cautioned. "You'd better let me have a look at your script, before you go too far overboard on the telecast. This is just a beginning; it'll take years and years before we're able to read any of those books downstairs."

"It'll go faster than you think, Martha," Hubert Penrose told her. "We'll all work on it, and we'll teleprint material to Terra, and people there will work on it. We'll send them everything we can...everything we work out, and copies of books, and copies of your word-lists—"

And there would be other tables—astronomical tables, tables in physics and mechanics, for instance—in which words and numbers were equivalent. The library stacks, below, would be full of them. Transliterate them into Roman alphabet spellings and Arabic numerals, and somewhere, somebody would spot each numerical significance, as Hubert Penrose and Mort Tranter and she had done with the table of elements. And pick out all the chemistry textbooks in the Library; new words would take on meaning from contexts in which the names of elements appeared. She'd have to start studying chemistry and physics, herself—

Sachiko Koremitsu peeped in through the door, then stepped inside.

"Is there anything I can do—?" she began. "What's happened? Something important?"

"Important?" Sid Chamberlain exploded. "Look at that, Sachi! We're reading it! Martha's found out how to read Martian!" He grabbed Captain Miles by the arm. "Come on, Jeff; let's go. I want to call the others—"He was still babbling as he hurried from the room.

Sachi looked at the inscription. "Is it true?" she asked, and then, before Martha could more than begin to explain, flung her arms around her. "Oh, it really is! You are reading it! I'm so happy!"

She had to start explaining again when Selim von Ohlmhorst entered. This time, she was able to finish.

"But, Martha, can you be really sure? You know, by now, that learning to read this language is as important to me as it is to you, but how can you be so sure that those words really mean things like hydrogen and helium and boron and oxygen? How do you know that their table of elements was anything like ours?"

Tranter and Penrose and Sachiko all looked at him in amazement.

"That isn't just the Martian table of elements; that's *the* table of elements. It's the only one there is." Mort Tranter almost exploded. "Look, hydrogen has one proton and one electron. If it had more of either, it wouldn't be hydrogen, it'd be something else. And the same with all the rest of the elements. And hydrogen on Mars is the same as hydrogen on Terra, or on Alpha Centauri, or in the next galaxy—"

"You just set up those numbers, in that order, and any first-year chemistry student could tell you what elements they represented." Penrose said. "Could if he expected to make a passing grade, that is."

The old man shook his head slowly, smiling. "I'm afraid I wouldn't make a passing grade. I didn't know, or at least didn't realize, that. One of the things I'm going to place an order for, to be brought on the *Schiaparelli*, will be a set of primers in chemistry and physics, of the sort intended for a bright child of ten or twelve. It seems that a Martianologist has to learn a lot of things the Hittites and the Assyrians never heard about."

Tony Lattimer, coming in, caught the last part of the explanation. He looked quickly at the walls and, having found out just what had happened, advanced and caught Martha by the hand.

"You really did it, Martha! You found your bilingual! I never believed that it would be possible; let me congratulate you!"

He probably expected that to erase all the jibes and sneers of the past. If he did, he could have it that way. His friendship would mean as little to her as his derision—except that his friends had to watch their backs and his knife. But he was going home on the *Cyrano*, to be a big shot. Or had this changed his mind for him again?

"This is something we can show the world, to justify any expenditure of time and money on Martian archaeological work. When I get back to Terra, I'll see that you're given full credit for this achievement—"

On Terra, her back and his knife would be out of her watchfulness.

"We won't need to wait that long," Hubert Penrose told him dryly. "I'm sending off an official report, tomorrow; you can be sure Dr. Dane will be given full credit, not only for this but for her previous work, which made it possible to exploit this discovery."

"And you might add, work done in spite of the doubts and discouragements of her colleagues," Selim von Ohlmhorst said. "To which I am ashamed to have to confess my own share."

"You said we had to find a bilingual," she said. "You were right, too."

"This is better than a bilingual, Martha," Hubert Penrose said. "Physical science expresses universal facts; necessarily it is a universal language. Heretofore archaeologists have dealt only with pre-scientific cultures."

"The Satchel" by David Johnson takes place during the early Terran Federation and provides us with our first look at how things have turned out in the United States after the Third and Fourth World Wars. The Federation has been sending out Explorer Teams to locate and help the survivors; in this story they run into a tribe of survivors who help rewrite the early history of the war.

THE SATCHEL

David Johnson

162 A.E., Terra

When Lynne Nakazwe heard the deer crashing through brush and scuffling the dead leaves, she stopped and stood motionless in the path. She watched them bolt down the slope from the right and cross in front of her, wishing she had the camera, and when the last white tail vanished in the green-brown woods she drove the spike of the staff into the ground and took both hands to shift the weight of the pack. If she'd had the camera, she would not be leading this mission. She turned to her squad, who had stopped behind her on the trail, and motioned them to follow.

"It won't be long now," she said. "We're almost to the base of the bluff wall so the encampment must be near."

"Do you think they'll give us any trouble, arriving this close to dark?" Sergeant Hammadi asked, following behind her.

"Perhaps," she replied. "There've been Aid Teams from Baton Rouge Base in this region for a couple of years now so we're likely not the first Rangers they've encountered. Still, it's probably a good idea for us to make a bit of noise so we don't surprise them." The non-com nodded.

"Their sentries will likely see us before we see them," Hammadi added.

"I'm counting on it, Sergeant." Hammadi turned to the other rangers.

"You heard the Lieutenant," he said. "Make some noise." The others, two men, Esterhuizen and Calderón, and a woman, Stewart, did their best to move off the animal track they'd been following, stepping on small branches and kicking rocks in their paths. Calderón, the corpsman, began to whistle an off-key tune.

She smiled. She'd gotten a good squad for her first command. Then the smile turned to a frown. That had taken longer than it should have. She'd been out of the Academy at Canberra for almost a year now, and had been posted to the Reclamation Service base at Baton Rouge for over nine months. Most of her peers had had several command assignments, leading Explorer or Aid Teams into the morass their ancestors had created in the Northern Hemisphere. But the Explorer Teams were usually focused on identifying natural resources for exploitation, while the Aid Teams brought material assistance and development skills to survivor communities. Her specialty was history which, in the Terran Federation Reclamation Service, generally meant artifact recovery. In the early years, the Rangers had conducted missions into old military bases or research facilities or industrial plants or atomic power stations but most of those sorts of sites had been "reclaimed" years ago. Lynne had been on field missions throughout the lower Mississippi Valley since she'd arrived in North America but this was the first time she'd been in command.

Her squad's mission had been sparked by an Aid Team which had been in this area three months ago. While helping villages in the riparian region here on the east side of the Mississippi River with flood irrigation, the Rangers had heard rumors of "survivors" of the crash of President Bolling's airship, back during the debacle of 114 A.E., living in a small encampment near the base of the bluffs to the east. Bolling's body and those of most of the airship crew had been recovered in the old U.S. air force search-and-rescue operation but there had, in fact, been others with Bolling who had never been found.

In those years immediately after the War the radiation in a city that had been hit like St. Louis had kept most rescuers away. Indeed, it's likely there wouldn't have been a recovery effort at all if it had been anyone else beside the President aboard that crashed airship.

After being asked to research the details of the Bolling crash and recovery, Lynne had been assigned by Colonel Filho, the base commander, to lead a Ranger squad into the area to look for hard evidence. There would be no actual survivors—it had been nearly fifty years since Bolling's airship had crashed—but there could be villagers who had heard of the crash and, perhaps, had encountered survivors.

"Halt!" a voice cried, in North American-accented English.

The man appeared before Lynne, stepping from behind a tree a dozen yards ahead. An arrow was drawn in his small bow. His deerskin jerkin and trousers made it difficult to see him against the trees and brush.

Calderón had stopped whistling. Stewart, behind Hammadi, began to raise her carbine, but the sergeant waved her down. Around them Lynne began to see other archers, both men and women, dressed like the man before her.

"Looks like your plan worked," Hammadi said. Lynne couldn't help but grin.

Lynne pushed the staff into the ground again and slowly raised both of her arms, hands open toward the lead archer.

"There is no death here," she said, also in English, using the greeting common among the survivor communities in this part of the lower Mississippi Valley.

"You're Sky People." The archer did not lower his bow. Lynne nodded. The man was young, with the sparse beginning of a beard. Like most survivors in this area he was dark-skinned like her.

"If you know we're Sky People then you know we mean you no harm."

"Others have told us this about the Sky People."

"Have these others also told you of the help we've given them?" The young man nodded, lowering his bow. Lynne noticed that the other archers did not follow his lead.

"We have no need of help," he said.

"Of course," Lynne said. "But we still have help to give. Are there no children who are sick or injured? No elders who suffer?" The young man nodded.

"Yes, there are those who are hurt or suffer, both children and elders. It's always been this way in the Strict."

"Is it always that way for those who've told you about the Sky People?" The young man watched her for a moment then glanced at Hammadi and the rest of her squad. He gestured at the archer closest to him, his hand turning palm downward. The archer lowered her bow. Slowly, the others followed her example.

"Come," he said. "The Sup'intendent will want to speak with you." He turned and began to walk away. Lynne nodded to Hammadi then grasped her staff and turned to follow the young archer. The sergeant motioned for the squad to follow her. Around them, the other archers paced them, moving among the trees and brush. Lynne caught up with the leader. He glanced at her but kept moving at a brisk clip.

"My name's Lynne," she said, smiling.

"I'm Arin," he said, not turning to look at her.

"Thank you, Arin, for bringing us to your...Sup'intendent."

"It's my charge," he said. "I lead the hunters when strangers approach the Strict."

"Have you seen many strangers?" Arin shook his head.

"You're the first," he said. "Sometimes people come up from the river to trade but they're known to us."

"And before you led the hunters?"

"It was my father's charge, but he was killed last summer by raiders from the plains above the bluffs."

"I'm sorry," Lynne said.

Arin shook his head. "Death often walks among us," he said. "My father knew that, as I know it."

Lynne nodded. "Death comes too often to your people."

Arin glanced at her again but said nothing.

"And your mother? Brothers or sisters?"

"My mother died birthing me. I was her only child."

"Again, I'm sorry," Lynne said. "Perhaps we will be able to help other mothers and their children to survive."

Again he glanced at her.

"Sky People have helped the river-dwellers for several seasons but none have ever come to help us." Lynne nodded.

"There are many people who need help and too few of us to help them all but we help those we can."

"Liar!" Arin shouted. Lynne stopped. Behind her Hammadi motioned for her squad to stop as well.

After a moment Arin paused and turned toward her. Around them the other hunters had halted too. Arin looked at the ground. "Forgive me, Lin of the Sky People." After a moment, his eyes rose to meet hers.

It was difficult to tell in the growing darkness but Lynne thought they glistened with tears.

"I've been a poor host." He turned and continued on, moving at an even faster pace, his hand reaching up to brush his eyes.

Again, Lynne rushed to catch up with him. Hammadi and her squad followed and the other hunters again moved through the trees around them.

"I'm sorry to have offended you," she said after a few moments.

"I'm the one who has given offense," he said. "I've held a grudge against the Sky People since before you came to us."

"But you said you'd never met any Sky People."

"We've never seen the Sky People the river-dwellers speak of." Arin turned to look at her. "We've never seen Sky People like *you*."

"There are other Sky People?" Lynne asked.

Arin stopped. Again the hunters among the trees stopped.

Hammadi didn't need to motion to the squad; they had halted too. Stewart was not the only one to raise her carbine slightly.

"Careful, Sergeant," Lynne said.

Hammadi nodded, but he kept his hands on his own weapon too.

"I don't know," Arin said. He seemed to be staring intently at Lynne but his eyes were shrouded in shadow. "You're the first to come among us in my lifetime but you're not the first Sky Woman I've known."

Lynne shook her head, then realized he likely couldn't see the movement.

"I don't understand," she said.

"My grandmother's mother was a Sky Woman."

Arin said no more during the rest of the journey to their encampment. Sentries met them at the edge of what seemed to be a large meadow that Lynne guessed was just beyond bow range of the bluffs to the east. There were at least a dozen of the semi-permanent domed tents that were common among the peoples of this region. Lynne and her squad were escorted to where a small bonfire burned before one of the huts. There were many people about, including children of all ages, all wearing the same deerskin clothing Arin and the other hunters wore. Word of their arrival had apparently gone ahead. A small group of elders, three men and three women, sat on two large logs near the bonfire and Lynne and her squad were invited to sit on similar logs across from them. After they were introduced, Arin had Lynne asked to repeat her offer of assistance. He and a handful of his hunters stood behind the seated elders.

Sup'intendent Jerald, facing Lynne, reminded her of her grandfather. His beard and short, tightly-curled hair were greying and many weather-worn wrinkles lined his face. His voice had the same deep timbre as her grandfather's and though he spoke with an accent he spoke with the same, unhurried pace. Unlike her grandfather, the Sup'intendent—Superintendent, Lynne guessed—was missing a couple of teeth though Lynne thought he was a few years younger than Granddad.

"It is kind of you to offer to help our sick and injured," the Sup'intendent said. His features flickered in the firelight. "What will you ask of us in return?"

"You are correct that our help will have its costs for your people," Lynne said. "It will not be furs or salted meat or anything else that we will take away with us. We will want to help some of your people learn from us about healing and perhaps other things. This will take them away from the work they do now. When they have learned these new things some may not wish to return to hunting prey or gathering food." The Sup'intendent nodded and turned to look at the woman seated to his left.

"If all do not do their share of work, there will not be enough for all in the Strict to eat," the woman who had been introduced as Teenah said.

"This is true, but if the injured are healed and the sick do not die they will do work that would not have been done."

Teenah and a couple others nodded.

Devon, the man on the Sup'intendent's left, spoke up. "And they will eat food which would not have been eaten," he said.

Lynne nodded. "Some of what we will teach will help you not just to gather more and better food, but to grow food as well."

"Bah!" the man seated next to Teenah said. His name was Nik. "The river-dwellers grow food and then starve when the river floods!"

Lynne frowned and was about to respond when the Sup'intendent interrupted.

"The floods cause less damage to their villages and fewer river-dwellers starve since the Sky People have come among them," he said. Several of the elders nodded.

"That is another kind of help we can give," Lynne said. "We have helped the river-dwellers to build their homes so they are less threatened by the floodwaters. We are working now to build dams which will channel the flooding away from their growing places."

"What of the raiders who come down from the plains above the bluffs?" Alis asked.

"Other Rangers like us have gone among the people on the plains above," Lynne said. "The plains-people raid when they do not have enough to eat, when their homes have been knocked down by a storm, when the winter kills too many of the deer and cattle they hunt. We will help them too so they no longer need to raid."

"Why do you do these things?" That was Fred, seated next to Nik, the man who had been interrupted by the Sup'intendent.

Lynne looked to Hammadi on her left and to Esterhuizen seated beyond the sergeant, then to Calderón on her right and Stewart beyond him. She turned back to the elders, leaning slightly forward, her hands spread before her, palms turned up:

"We are trying to repair the damage caused by the Big War, to rebuild the civilization that has been lost," she said. "We know how fortunate we have been to have survived without having our homes destroyed, without having sickness ravage our families and neighbors, without losing the skills and tools to heal the sick and injured.

"Even now our sisters and brothers travel to the other worlds, where other people like you were left to fend for themselves after the War." She looked up at the waning three-quarters moon, visible even in the firelight in the cloud-free sky of early spring. "But our work, we Rangers, is here helping you and the river-dwellers and even the plains-people above the bluffs, and many, many other people across this land and other lands beyond the seas." She looked back at the elders. "We do this with gratitude, because we are able to do it."

The Sup'intendent nodded.

The Sup'intendent allowed Calderón to tend to a sick child that was brought to them. His illness was not serious but the corpsmen was able to give him something to ease his pain and help him to sleep. While Calderón treated the child, Hammadi and the others pitched their tents in a space near the edge of the meadow indicated by one of the sentries. Lynne had lost track of Arin as the encampment settled down for the night. The rangers gathered in the space between their three tents, a small lantern providing a bit of artificial light.

"The boy's father was pleased to see him resting calmly," Calderón said.

"Good work, ranger," Lynne said. "Hopefully, there'll be others we can help tomorrow."

The corpsman nodded.

"Do you suppose the hunter's great-grandmother was a survivor of the crash?" Esterhuizen asked.

"It seems a reasonable assumption," Lynne said. "Odd though that he seemed so troubled by it. It was difficult to tell but I think he was in tears."

"And nothing about it from the elders," Hammadi said.

"Perhaps she was the only one," Stewart said. "The elders might not draw the same connection as the boy between her and us."

"Or maybe her story is a fabrication," Esterhuizen said. "Some fanciful tale passed down in his family but not believed—or known—in the wider community."

Lynn nodded.

"Or perhaps the elders have some reason not to tell us," Hammadi said. "Perhaps they're hiding something."

"Or perhaps they're just being cautious," Lynne said. "In any event, we should speak with Arin again tomorrow. Each of you watch for an opportunity to do so."

A softly muttered "yes, ma'am" came from each of the rangers. "Calderón, you'll have a busy day, so no watch for you. The rest of you to bed." She placed her hand on Hammadi's shoulder. "I'll wake you in a couple of hours."

The sergeant nodded and the rangers made their way to their tents.

Esterhuizen woke them before sunrise. It would be another clear day. "People are up," he said.

Shortly, a young woman Arin's age came over to them. A bow and quiver were hung over her shoulders and Lynne tried to remember if she'd been among the band of hunters they had encountered yesterday.

"G'morning," she said. "The Sup'intendent asks you to join him for breakfast." She pointed toward the space near the still-burning bonfire where they had met the night before.

"Please thank the Sup'intendent," Lynne said. "We're grateful for his hospitality."

The young woman nodded and turned to leave.

"One moment," Lynne said. The young hunter stopped and turned. "Will Arin lead the hunters today?"

The woman frowned. "Yes," she said, after a moment. "We're about to leave."

"Please ask the Sup'intendent—and Arin—if I and one of my companions might join the hunt."

"You'd miss the Sup'intendent's breakfast."

Lynne smiled and nodded.

"I don't mean to give offense and will do as the Sup'intendent asks," Lynne said. "But I'd also like to join your hunting party."

"I'll bring your request to the Sup'intendent." The woman turned and headed back toward the bonfire.

The Sup'intendent seemed to take no offense, especially after Lynne detailed Hammadi and Stewart to stay behind with Calderón. Esterhuizen, the ecologist, would come with her. The hunters seemed less pleased, particularly when they learned the rangers carried no bows and could not shoot the ones they were offered. Arin himself refused to speak with her as the hunters made their way into the woods. As the sun climbed into the blue sky Lynne followed Esterhuizen near the rear of the line of five hunters, with the young woman who had first greeted them bringing up the rear. Her name was Bekah.

"What do we hunt today?" Lynne asked softly, once the sounds of the encampment had faded away behind them.

"Deer," Bekah said. "Perhaps a wild pig, if we're fortunate."

Lynne nodded, turned to call out softly to Esterhuizen walking in front of her. "What are our chances of finding any pigs, Ranger?" Lynne asked, in Afrikaans.

"Not good," Esterhuizen replied, also in Afrikaans. "As likely to come across a boar as a pig in this area."

"Why don't you speak so we can understand you?" Bekah asked. Lynne turned back to the hunter.

"I'm sorry," Lynne said. "My companion doesn't speak your language." That wasn't true, but the pretense gave them an excuse to speak in a way that the survivors didn't understand. It was standard Ranger practice. "I was telling him what it is we hunt."

Suddenly the hunters ahead stopped. Lynne paused.

Arin was making his way back from the lead position. He stopped before Lynne.

"Bekah shows you kindness," he said. "But your words scare off the game." He pointed back toward the encampment. "If you want to talk the Sup'intendent and the others will talk with you."

Lynne bowed her head briefly, then met Arin's gaze.

"Please forgive us," she said. She turned to Bekah, "And my apologies to you, Bekah." Looking back at Arin she said, "You'll hear no more from us unless asked."

After a moment Arin nodded, then turned and made his way back to the head of the line of hunters.

It was past noon when the hunters turned back toward the encampment. Before mid-morning they'd encountered several deer—Lynne wondered at the time if they were the same ones from the day before—and killed seven. (She and Esterhuizen had merely watched; it wouldn't do to have shot the deer with their carbines.) The quarters had been cleaned and hung from trees, out of reach of the foxes and the wolves, and they were headed back now to take them down and bring in the kills.

They paused near a small stream for lunch, a bit of venison they'd brought with them cooked over a small fire.

After the meal, Bekah had excused herself and gone into the woods while the others broke camp, putting out the fire and gathering their bows. Most of the hunters had been personable enough to Lynne—and to Esterhuizen when she'd "translated" their thanks to him for helping to clean the carcasses—but Arin still avoided her. Lynne moved around the small clearing, closer to where Arin sat on a log cleaning his knife. She thought she heard a rustling and snort in the distance behind her but ignored it as she approached the young hunter. A sudden shout brought Arin erect and she turned to see what was happening.

Bekah had emerged from the foliage several dozen yards from the camp but suddenly turned and began to run quickly to the left. To the right, where the other hunters had been pointing, a boar was racing toward her. A couple of hunters managed to loose arrows but they fell short.

Arin raced past Lynne and began shouting along with the other hunters, attempting to distract the boar.

Lynne lifted her carbine and stepped down to one knee. She released the safety and sighted along the short barrel, tracking the boar as it ran toward the spot where Bekah had disappeared into the brush. She fired, three quick shots in succession.

The first seemed to have no effect but the boar shuddered at the second shot and tumbled to the ground with the third, skidding into the brush where Bekah had run and disappearing in a cloud of dust and leaves. Lynne switched on the safety almost without thinking.

A couple of the hunters around her had dived for cover but Arin and another stood looking at her, their mouths open.

Then Arin turned to the others. "See to Bekah!" he said, pointing toward the place where the boar had fallen. The hunter ran off immediately and those that had sought cover followed apace. Esterhuizen came up with his own carbine in his hands.

"I'd sat it down to help break camp," he said.

"Not to worry, Ranger," she said. "Many of our friends here had done the same."

Arin, coming up behind him, looked from Esterhuizen to her.

"He's sorry he didn't have his weapon," she said. "I told him he wasn't the only one."

"Yes," Arin said, turning to speak to the ranger, a second bow in his hand. "Bekah left her bow behind too." Lynne "translated" quickly.

Arin pointed toward Lynne's carbine. "I'm not sure I believed what I'd heard about your Sky Weapons before but that's more powerful even than I'd imagined."

Lynne said, "That's why we use them only when necessary."

Arin nodded.

"So not to hunt?" Lynne smiled.

"No, not to hunt. Besides, you and your hunters did quite well this morning with your bows."

Arin frowned. "We could've done much better with Sky Weapons. Will your help include such things?"

Lynne shook her head slowly, then patted the carbine. "The bullets in this carbine are like the arrows in your quiver. When they're gone it's not much use, other than as a club."

Arin nodded and smiled.

"We'll give you some things," she said, "but what we most want to give you is the knowledge to make things for yourselves."

Again Arin nodded.

"That will take time," he said. "Our people must be taught, and stuff to make a thing must be gathered, and the things to make them with prepared, and we know nothing of any of this."

Now it was Lynne's turn to nod. "You're a skilled hunter, Arin. How long did it take you to learn to make an arrow, a bow, to track a deer or avoid a boar?"

"Why, my father and the other hunters of the Strict taught me from when I was a child!"

"And you will likely be an old man before your people can make all of these things."

"Yes, I see," Arin said. "We'll need your help for a long time."

At that moment Bekah came up with several of the other hunters. She stopped before Lynne.

"I'm in your debt," she said.

Lynne smiled. "I'm sure you would have done the same for me," she said, reaching out to place her hand on Bekah's shoulder, but the younger woman stepped forward and embraced her. Lynne returned the hug, looking at Arin over the hunter's shoulder. He was smiling broadly.

There was a feast that evening—which included the boar, followed by a celebration with dancing. Small drums, carved pipes and horns and rattles and other small, hand-made percussion instruments made music that was as unfamiliar as it was raucous. There were songs, sung as a group and others song by one or two people. At one point Bekah came to where Lynne was sitting near the bonfire and drew her into the dance. Lynne couldn't follow the form but enjoyed it nonetheless. Soon all of her rangers were up and dancing with hunters and others.

A small group of hunters broke away from the dancing and began wrestling. Both men and women wrestled with each other and at one point Stewart joined in. She bested every opponent, though the last bout was very close. A pair of hunters lifted Stewart onto their shoulders and paraded her around the meadow to the cheers and applause of the other wrestlers.

Then there was storytelling. First, the stories were meant for the children. The scenes were more primitive, the monsters were unusual, but the themes were the same as those she'd heard as a child from Granddad. As the children grew sleepy and were led away by their parents the tales became darker and more realistic. There were tales of great hunts, mostly told by the elders and others who were older than Arin and Bekah and the other young hunters. There were stories of battles with the plains-people and with warriors from other settlements in the river valley. One story told of how the first Sup'intendent had gathered the people of the Strict together after the Big War to protect themselves from the marauders and cannibals.

Some of the stories had mythical elements to them though it was clear they were not understood to be mere myths by the people. Lynne could recognize elements of the Christianity which had been common in this region before the War but she doubted these tales would fit well with what a Catholic like Calderón believed much less with the beliefs her Presbyterian Granddad or Esterhuizen's Dutch Reformed grandparents might have learned as children.

Eventually, Lynne and her rangers found themselves once again seated around the small bonfire with the Sup'intendent and the other elders. Again, Arin and his hunters were gathered behind the elders. Across the encampment, many people were making their way back to their tents.

"You and your people have already helped us in many ways," the Sup'intendent said. He looked at Calderón and nodded.

Hammadi had told her that the corpsman had been busy all day treating ill children and ailing elders. He and Stewart had even helped to deliver a baby in the afternoon. "You and your people have been generous too," Lynne said. "I hope you will allow us to bring others who might give more help than we have been able to give."

The Sup'intendent nodded, looked to the other elders to his left and his right. Teenah and Fred smiled. Alis and Devon and even Nik, after a moment, nodded softly.

"Yes," the Sup'intendent said. "We would be grateful to accept help from the Sky People."

Lynne smiled.

"Tell us more about what you plan."

"We have a tool, a *radio* which we can use to speak with other Rangers like those among the river-dwellers," Lynne said. "Some of them will come here in flying-things. They will build places to live and work while we are here."

"How will we feed all these Sky People"? Nik asked.

"We will bring our own food," Lynne said. "And the tools and other things to do our work."

The Sup'intendent nodded. "How much space will you need?" he asked.

"At first, perhaps a third of the meadow here," Lynne said. "Later, space will be needed for the growing of food, and a place for teaching, a *school* will need to be built, and other places to live and work. These will take more space than what's available here in the meadow."

"It will take much work to cut down trees," Alis said.

The Sup'intendent nodded.

"You must have tools that will help with that," he said.

"Yes," Lynne said.

"And then?"

Lynne glanced at Hammadi next to her, then looked across to Arin standing behind Teenah:

"There will be many other things that must be decided, but not tonight," Lynne said. "But I do have one more request."

The Sup'intendent opened his right hand toward her, palm upward. He raised his brows and widened his eyes a bit.

"I would like to know more about the mother of Arin's grandmother."

The Sup'intendent turned to look over his shoulder at Arin. "Come," he said, beckoning to Arin. "Sit." He indicated a space on the log next to Alis.

Arin looked at Lynne, then stepped around the log and seated himself next to Alis. The woman reached over, took his hand in hers.

"Arin's grandfather was my brother, Mat," Alis said looking up at the young hunter. "His wife's mother was a Sky Woman. Kara came from the sky in a great flying-thing that fell to earth near the Great River."

Lynne's heart jumped at the name. Cara Blanchfield had been among those whose bodies had never been found in the recovery of Bolling's crashed airship. She had been Bolling's military attaché.

"Most of her companions were killed. In those days the river-dwellers were savages; they still ate people."

"How did Kara come to your people?" Lynne asked.

"She and another man—I've forgotten his name—fled the savages," Alis said. "They met a party of our hunters. Kara's companion had been injured in the fall of the flying-thing and he died before the hunters returned to the Strict. There was some trouble about that. Kara wanted to bury the man in the earth but our custom is to place the dead upon the funeral pyre. Eventually, the hunters helped Kara to dig a grave."

Esterhuizen whispered something in Hammadi's ear.

"Could your hunters still find this grave?" the sergeant asked.

Alis leaned forward, looked over at Devon. The elder nodded.

"I came of age a few years after Kara came to the Strict," Devon said. "I believe I could find the place where Kara's companion was buried."

"When the other Rangers come they will want to visit the place where the man was buried," Lynne said, looking at the Sup'intendent, who nodded and the gestured again to Alis.

"Kara had been injured too. She was brought into our tent and my mother tended to her. Hyoo, who led the hunters when they found her, visited Kara often. She recovered quickly. When she was well she wanted to go back to where the flying-thing had fallen but Hyoo and the hunters would not take her. She had been fortunate to escape the savages once. He did not believe she would do so a second time."

"For many years Kara believed that other Sky People would come for her, but no one ever came."

Tears welled in Arin's eyes, sparking in the firelight.

Alis continued, "Kara and Hyoo grew fond of each other and eventually they were married. Kara was a great warrior. She could wrestle better than all of Hyoo's hunters, though partly this was because she moved in ways that were new to them."

Arin glanced at Stewart for a moment.

"In those days only men of the Strict were hunters but Kara taught her ways to both men and women and after a time there were also women among the hunters."

"There were many other new things that Kara taught us," the Sup'intendent said. "We are a different people from the people we were before Kara came to us."

Several of the other elders nodded in agreement.

"In time Hyoo and Kara had a daughter," Alis said. She turned to look at Arin. "Janis was Arin's grandmother. When Janis grew into a woman she and Mat were wed. They had a son, Jakob, who was Arin's father. Kara died when Arin was still a boy. She was lain on the funeral pyre, as she had asked."

"And Janis, and Mat?" Lynne asked, glancing from Alis to Arin.

"Matt was killed in a raid by the plains-people," Alis said. She reached out and put her arm around Arin. "Janis, who had cared for Arin since he was born, became ill and died last winter."

Arin sobbed beside her.

"I'm sorry, Arin," Lynne said.

He raised his hand, wiped the tears from his eyes. "Death often walks among us," he said.

Alis hugged him more tightly.

"Death has often walked too soon among your family, Arin," the Sup'intendent said. He turned to look at Lynne again. "Now you have the story of Arin's grandmother's mother. I am thinking that the Sky People have come for her after all."

Lynne said, "Not for Kara, specifically," she said. "But we had heard from the river-dwellers that there may have been Sky People who had come to your people many years ago. The bodies of those who fell out of the sky with Kara were gathered by Sky People not long after they fell. There were others who were never found and were presumed dead. Now we know that Kara survived."

Lynne explained to her team whom she believed Kara to be as the rangers returned to their tents for the night. Stewart wanted to know what Kara's airship had been doing flying over a nuked city in the wasteland that North America had become after the Big War.

"I thought the American capital had moved to Antarctica by then," he asked as he turned on the small lantern around which their tents had been pitched.

"It had," Lynne said. "It's unclear exactly why President Bolling traveled from Mayflower to St. Louis. Bolling had been a senator in St. Louis and had come to Antarctica when the U.S. government was evacuated in the early months of the War. She had recently been reelected president and was touring the ruins to see if it would be possible to return the government to the former capital. The crash itself was suspicious at the time."

"There was a coup or something, right?" Hammadi asked.

"Or 'something,'" Lynne said. "Before she was elected president Bolling had invited her chief political opponent to stand for office with her as her vice president. Given the devastation the United States had just suffered in the War she thought a 'national unity' government would be a good idea. There had been some kind of precedent for that sort of arrangement in the early history of the United States.

"It must have worked because Bolling won the election. Eventually, she opened negotiations with Argentina and Brazil and Australia and South Africa and the other Southern Hemisphere nations to re-form the Terran Federation—most of the original Federation nations had been devastated in the War—but on a more equal basis. Vice President Marshall strongly opposed her efforts but was sidelined because he was part of the government. After the crash many believed he was implicated in her death."

"Ah, now I remember," Calderón said. "That's when General Lanningham came to Montevideo with the atomic bomb plans."

"Right," Lynne said, nodding. "When Bolling was killed Marshall became president and withdrew from the negotiations but at that point the other nations decided to move ahead to form the new Federation—*without* the United States."

"I'd always wondered about that," Esterhuizen said. "Before I joined the Rangers I did a couple of tours in the Constabulary and spent some time in Mayflower and McMurdo. It was odd because many of the Americans had this strange appreciation for the old Federation even though it was clear they resented the occupation."

"There's irony there," Lynne agreed. "Marshall lived to see what remained of the United States be forced into the Federation, just as the former loyalist colonies on Mars had been taken over by the Free Republic after the War. If Bolling hadn't been killed it's possible the Americans could be playing a key role in the Federation today."

"So what do you think happened to her?" Stewart asked.

"Officially, the president's airship suffered some sort of technical malfunction," Lynne said. "That seems unlikely but there was no formal investigation at the time. St. Louis was still pretty hot back then and the recovery team didn't spend much time at the crash site—as the survivors we heard about this evening attest. The airship wreckage was destroyed by the recovery team, ostensibly to keep it from falling into hostile hands. Marshall, the vice president, was in charge back in Mayflower and so the official records—which I've seen—are conclusive about it being an accident.

"But the reactions of other officials who were in a position to know at the time, like Lanningham, suggest that may have been a whitewash. I don't know if Marshall had Bolling killed or not but it seems clear he took immediate advantage of her death."

"And left Arin's great-grandmother and that other man behind," Hammadi said.

"Perhaps," Lynne said. "We'll have to see if she had any family who still survive—that other man too, once his remains are identified. It could be that Arin is the long-lost cousin of someone in Antarctica."

The next morning, as Esterhuizen was preparing breakfast, Lynne asked Hammadi to help Stewart set up the satellite radio. Clouds had come in during the night and it looked like they might get some rain today. When the connection was made she spoke with the technician at Baton Rouge Base, telling him they had established contact with the survivor community and confirmed that personnel from the Bolling crash had taken refuge here. She also reported that the survivor community had agreed to accept Ranger assistance and asked that an Aid Team be dispatched as soon as possible. The technician told her that an Aid Team had already been mustered and would likely arrive by air in the next thirty-six hours.

As Stewart stowed the radio Lynne noticed Arin and Alis approaching. The old woman held the young hunter's arm for support as they slowly made their way across the meadow. In Arin's other arm was a large bundle wrapped in a heavy fur. A light rain began to fall.

"Good morning," Lynne said as the two survivors reached their tents. The old woman smiled.

"Good morning, Sky Woman," Alis said. "Arin has something he'd like to show to you."

Lynne turned to Hammadi but already the sergeant was pulling a tarp from a pack. He and Calderón quickly deployed the tarp, raising it on expandable poles to create a covered space near where Esterhuizen hunched over the portable stove.

"Thank you, Sergeant," Lynne said. She turned back to Alis and Arin. "Will you join us for breakfast?" Alis nodded.

"I'm sure Arin has already eaten but I would be happy share your meal out of the rain," Alis said. She took a seat on a small log, holding Arin's hand as he sat beside her. Stewart handed each of them a bowl of oatmeal and gave one to Lynne as well. There wasn't space under the tarp for all of her team so Stewart pulled the hood of her jacket over her head and returned to huddle with the other rangers around the stove. Alis took a spoonful from the metal bowl.

"Mmm," she said. "It's quite good." Beside her Arin held the bowl in his hand but did not eat. "Go on then, show it to her."

Arin nodded, placing the bowl on the ground between his feet. He shifted the bundle, laying it flat on his lap.

"Before my grandmother died she gave this to my father." He brushed his palms over the soft fur. "He died without telling me what it was but he did tell me that it had been my great-grandmother's." Arin began to unfold the fur covering. Underneath was a black leather satchel, clearly not something which had been made by the survivors. It had metal clasps which Lynne guessed would have still glistened had it been sunny. A thin leather strap was looped around the leather handle at the top, another loop large enough to fit around one's wrist dangled loosely at the other end.

Lynne's heart seemed to skip a beat. She thought she recognized this satchel. As Bolling's military attaché, Blanchfield would have carried the codes and instructions the president would have used to authorize a nuclear attack. In her research she'd assumed it would have been destroyed with the airship wreckage—there had been no record of its recovery with Bolling's body—but this satchel matched the description she'd scanned. If her memory served, it would have also contained a secure radio to allow Bolling to communicate with her military commanders. Why hadn't Cara Blanchfield used the radio to call for rescue?

"I believe it *was* your great-grandmother's, Arin," Lynne said. "She was a warrior who would have carried a satchel very much like this for the leader of her people, who was killed when their flying-thing fell from the sky. She would have protected it with her life."

Arin's eyes went wide. Beside him Alis smiled and squeezed his hand.

"You must open it," Alis said. "Let the Sky People see what is inside."

Arin set the fur covering aside and turned the satchel on his lap, the metal clasps facing upwards. The clasps clicked softly as he unlatched one and then the other and folded the cover over.

"I have never opened this before," Arin said, looking from Alis to Lynne. He reached inside and pulled out what seemed to be a large binder. It too was covered in black leather, like an old book. He handed it across to Lynne.

"Thank you," she said. She opened the cover of the binder. Inside were laminated pages, bound by three metal rings attached to the inner spine. Paging through the sheets slowly Lynne saw that they were lists in English of targets, mostly military facilities of the old World Commonwealth in Europe and central Asia and northern Africa. There were also lists of old Terran Federation military forces based in North America and in southwestern and eastern Asia. She even recognized listings for the old bases at Luanda and Beira.

Arin was pulling something else out of the satchel. It seemed to be a piece of electronic equipment. Lynne closed the binder as Arin handed it across to her. There was a small handset attached by a short cable and the tip of an extendable antenna poked out of one side. This must be the radio! She looked over at her team who were watching from just beyond the tarp. She motioned for Stewart to approach.

"Arin," Lynne said. "Do you remember me talking about a tool, a *radio* that we can use to speak with other Sky People who are far way?"

The young hunter nodded.

"This is a radio. May we see if it is still working?" Arin looked at Alis, who nodded softly.

"Yes," Arin said.

Lynne handed the radio to Stewart. "Check it out," she said and Stewart nodded.

"Can I take it into the tent?" the Ranger asked. Lynne looked at Arin, who looked again at Alis. She smiled and nodded. Arin looked at Stewart and nodded too. The Ranger ducked into her tent, where she had stored the satellite radio earlier.

Arin reached into the satchel again and pulled out a handful of small, laminated cards all bound by a single metal ring. He handed them across to Lynne. Each card was a different color and had a list of random words written in large capitals: SHARK, ARGONAUT, LEMONADE, INDRA, SILVER, etc. Lynne guessed they were part of some sort of challenge-response authentication process used to confirm the identity of the president.

"That's everything," Arin said, interrupting Lynne's musing. She looked up as Arin pulled his hand from inside the satchel. She put out her hands.

"May I have a look?" Arin nodded and handed the satchel to her. The satchel itself was built around an aluminum frame. There were no pockets on the outside or inside of the satchel, though there was a raised guide inside which seemed to create a space to hold the radio. It was undamaged, no burns or water stains and seemed relatively unused. That made sense for the original satchel but also suggested that Arin's father and grandmother had taken very good care of it and hadn't handled it much either.

Stewart returned from the tent, the radio in her hands. She stepped under the tarp and returned the radio to Lynne. The antenna, as long as Lynne's forearm, was extended.

"It works, Lieutenant," Stewart said. "The battery had discharged but I was able to connect it to our satellite unit and get it to broadcast a signal."

"You're certain?"

The communication technician nodded.

"Thank you, Ranger," she said frowning. Avoiding looking at Arin or Alis, Lynne pushed the antenna back into the radio and then slid it into the satchel. She placed the cards inside and then the binder. Carefully she closed and latched the cover. She handed the satchel back to Arin. Alis looked at Stewart, who had rejoined the other rangers around the stove, then back at Lynne.

"What did she discover?" Lynne looked up, glanced at Alis and then at Arin.

"It seems that you may have been right, Arin," she said. The young hunter' brow furrowed.

"What do you mean?" he asked softly.

"When you called me a liar when we first met," Lynne said. "I wasn't lying; I didn't know. But it seems that those other Sky People, many years ago, didn't come to help her when Kara called for them."

It was difficult for Lynne to explain to Arin and Alis what she believed had happened to Blanchfield. The intricacies of internal politics in the old United States of America and Antarctica made little sense to these descendants of its abandoned former citizens. The distinction between the United States back then and today's Terran Federation which had sent Lynne and her fellow Rangers here to North America was difficult for them to grasp. To them they were all simply Sky People. Alis helped even without fully understanding, again drawing the distinction between the cannibalistic river-dwellers from whom Kara had fled and the docile farmers of today who were held in more than a little contempt by the people of the Strict.

Eventually, Arin seemed satisfied that the Sky People who had likely refused to answer Kara's call for help were different from Lynne and her squad and, more importantly, from the Rangers who would come to help the people of the Strict in the weeks and months and years ahead.

In truth, Arin seemed quite pleased to learn that his great-grandmother had played such an important role among the Sky People. As a Sky Woman she'd always been regarded as someone special by the people of the Strict and by her acts she had come to be known as a great warrior, but now Arin realized—with no small bit of friendly help from his grand-aunt—that Kara had been special among the Sky People too.

Finally, Arin held out the satchel to Lynne again.

"I think my great-grandmother would want you to have this." Lynne reached out, took the satchel.

"Are you sure, Arin?"

The young hunter nodded.

"You and your...Rangers will want to look at it more closely, won't you?"

Lynne nodded. "Thank you very much, Arin. We will take good care of it."

Arin smiled as Alis put her arm around his shoulders.

While Calderón and Stewart continued their efforts to help those people who needed medical attention, Lynne and the rest of her team spent most of the day working with the Sup'intendent and a couple other elders and several of the hunters identifying tents which could be moved to make space for the Ranger Aid Team and marking out the likeliest bits of the forest to be cut down to provide lumber—and more space—to build the school.

Late in the afternoon a hunter came dashing into the clearing. "A flying-thing comes!" she cried.

The Sup'intendent, who had been speaking with Lynne and Hammadi, raised his arms and called out to the people in the meadow.

"Do not be afraid," he said. "These are the Rangers, companions to our friends here." He indicated toward Lynne and Hammadi.

Still, older women took the children into the forest and the hunters gathered their bows and knives.

Within moments a small, four-person aircar drifted slowly into view just above the treetops to the southwest, moving more slowly than a person could run. Its long shadow moved across the meadow as it descended to the ground. The Sup'intendent, along with Teenah and Devon, made their way toward the vehicle as it came to rest. Lynne and Hammadi followed immediately behind them. Arin and several of his hunters came along too.

A Ranger stepped from the aircar, removing his cap. Lynne recognized Netuno Rebelo who had been at the Academy with her. She'd thought the Brazilian ranger was still in Texas. She moved up beside the Sup'intendent as Netuno stepped forward to greet him.

"If I might make introductions, Sup'intendent?" she asked.

The Sup'intendent bowed his head.

She smiled at Netuno. "This is Sup'intendent Jerald of the Strict and his fellow elders, Teenah and Devon."

Netuno bowed slightly.

"May I present my colleague and friend, Lieutenant Rebelo of the Terran Federation Reclamation Service."

"Welcome, Lieutenant," the Sup'intendent said, reaching out to take Netuno's hand. "We are pleased to meet a friend of Lieutenant Nakazwe." Netuno smiled.

"It is an honor to meet you, Sup'intendent," he said. "With your permission, there is a larger vehicle behind us which we'd also like to bring down." The Sup'intendent looked at Lynne, who nodded.

"Yes, by all means, Lieutenant," he said. "We have been expecting you."

Netuno turned to the aircar driver, waved downward with his arm. As the driver spoke into his radio Lynne turned to Sergeant Hammadi.

"Please direct them to the place we agreed this morning, Sergeant."

"Yes, ma'am," Hammadi said, moving across the meadow as a larger contragravity vehicle appeared over the treetops. As it made its way down several hunters emerged from the forest, apparently having followed it to the meadow. Arin went to meet them.

"Please, Lieutenant," the Sup'intendent said. "Come tell us about your work." He turned and indicated the space around the small bonfire where the other elders had gathered. Around the meadow the older women and children began to re-emerge from the forest and people started to gather around the bonfire. As they made their way across the meadow Lynne stepped next to Netuno.

"I thought you were in Texas?" she whispered in Portuguese.

"My team just returned a few days ago," the Brazilian replied, also in Portuguese. "When I'd heard you were out here I volunteered to lead the Aid Team. Congratulations on your first command."

"Thanks," Lynne said. "You're not going to believe what we've found."

Netuno explained to the elders and the assembled survivors that his team would sleep in their tents tonight but would begin construction tomorrow on a semi-permanent shelter. The larger vehicle was a standard Aid Team air-lorry with accommodations for eight and a cargo of light construction equipment. It would also serve as a temporary infirmary and Calderón was successful in transferring two of his most serious patients, an older woman suffering from cancer and a child with meningitis, into the vehicle that evening. The survivors wanted to hold another feast for the new group of rangers but both Netuno and Lynne politely declined; they knew such hospitality would unnecessarily tax the resources of the community.

It was more than two hours after sunset before Lynne and Netuno managed to find some time alone together. They sat in the cramped cab of the air-lorry, with the hatch to the cabin-cum-infirmary closed. Lynne had brought along the satchel and had passed it to Netuno to examine. As he removed the radio, Lynne explained what Stewart's analysis had discovered.

"You think it was working after the crash?" he asked. Lynne nodded as Netuno took the binder and code cards from the satchel.

"There's no indication of damage; the discharged battery is to be expected after so many years."

Netuno nodded as he paged through the binder.

"So she probably used the radio to call for help," Netuno said, looking up at Lynne.

She said, "That's what I think."

"Why wouldn't they come to get her?"

Lynne explained briefly about the conflict between the dead American president and her vice president, about her plans to make the United States part of the re-formed Terran Federation.

Netuno raised his eyebrows. "So this device will answer some unanswered questions from that period of history. Lynne, this truly is remarkable." He put the radio back into the satchel.

"Well, my squad just stumbled across it," Lynne said.

"That may be true but you know how hard it can be to get some precious artifact from a survivor community like this," Netuno said. "Remember when Bowen found the film canister of *Ben Hur* among that survivor community in Baja California? They had no idea what it was but it still took her weeks to get them to part with it—and that was only after their 'shaman' had tried to burn it!

"Here they've just *given* it to you. From what I gathered speaking with these people today that's because you've done an excellent job here."

"Thank you," Lynne said. "It was touch and go for a bit."

"You're too modest, Lynne. Colonel Filho will be impressed!" Netuno said as he placed the cards and binder back in the satchel. "This is the most unusual artifact any of us have recovered in years—and could very well spark a political row in Antarctica! Given its added historical significance you're bound to get a citation. I'll wager Hammadi will make that recommendation in his report." He laughed. "You'll probably be the first in our class to make captain!"

The next morning Lynne and Sergeant Hammadi had breakfast with Netuno and his sergeant. Calderón and Esterhuizen would stay here with Netuno's team while Lynne, Hammadi and Stewart returned to base for their next assignments. Netuno's driver would take them to the larger

Ranger detachment in what had once been East St. Louis and they'd catch a regular transport from there to Baton Rouge.

Lynne had told the elders before Netuno's team arrived that most of her squad would be leaving but she imagined they'd still want to make some ceremony of the departure. And she wanted to say a personal good-bye to Arin. The young hunter deserved it.

Lynne and her squad spent most of the day helping Netuno's team lay the foundation for the Aid Team quarters. They cleared a small area of forest along the northeast edge of the meadow, shaping the felled timber into lumber. Calderón managed to move three more patients into the infirmary, another child and two older men. None of the three adults were expected to survive but the palliative care was appreciated by both the patients and their families. Hammadi and Esterhuizen had broken Lynne's squad's camp and packed those items which wouldn't be left behind with Netuno's team into the aircar. Calderón's and Stewart's packs and equipment were moved to the Aid Team's temporary camp. By mid-afternoon the raised foundation for the quarters was completed and a sewage pipe was run to the nearby stream, downstream from where the survivors gathered their water.

Lynne was taking a break with Hammadi, enjoying the late afternoon sunshine while Netuno and his engineer reviewed plans for the pump which would bring running water to the quarters building—and to the temporary infirmary in the lorry—when Arin led the hunting team that had gone out that morning into the meadow. After the hunters had placed their kills in the small smokehouse they gathered around the newly-constructed foundation, marveling at the amount of work the rangers had done in a single day.

As Arin and Bekah approached Lynne and Hammadi, the Sergeant rose and excused himself, exchanging friendly but brief greetings with the hunters. Lynne indicated for them to join her on the freshly-cut log.

"It looks like you had a successful hunt," she said. Bekah smiled and Arin nodded.

"Bekah shot a pig and we got two deer," Arin said. He looked over at the newly-constructed foundation for a moment, then added, "I am more impressed with what you've done here than I was when you shot the boar."

Beside him Bekah nodded. "I see there is much we will learn from you besides better hunting and wrestling," she said with a broad smile. Lynne nodded toward the wide platform.

"What you will learn in the school will help you and your people more than a gun that can kill a charging boar will help you," Lynne said.

Bekah smiled.

Beside her Arin nodded but frowned. "They won't teach us about Kara's...satchel in the...school, will they?" he asked.

Lynne shook her head. "No, but when we've learned more about it—and about Kara's companion who was killed—I will make sure that knowledge is shared with you."

"You'll come back?" Bekah asked.

Lynne pursed her lips. "I don't know," she admitted. She turned and waved her hand to the north. "There are many more people who need our help." She looked at Arin. "But I promise you that what we learn about the satchel will be shared with you by the rangers with you here." She wondered if she should tell Arin about the possibility that he might have relatives in Antarctica but decided against it. "I can't promise I will come back here but I can promise that."

Bekah leaned closer, reached out to hug Lynne. After a moment the hunter turned and pulled Arin into the hug as well.

"Thank you, Sky Woman," he said.

After the Fuzzies, the Thorians are one of Piper's more interesting intelligent alien lifeforms. Unfortunately, we never learn much about them, other than they have furry facial features. In "Ministry of Disturbance," which takes place in the Second Empire, we learn the Thorians make up the Imperial Household Guard. Piper describes them thusly: "Their bodies were covered with a stiff mat of black hair, and their faces were slightly like terriers'... They were hillmen from the southern hemisphere of Thor, and as a people they made excellent mercenaries. They were crack shots, brave and crafty fighters, totally uninterested in politics off their own planet, and, because they had grown up in a patriarchal-clan society, they were fanatically loyal to anybody whom they accepted as their chieftain."

In this fascinating story, David Johnson, explores the planet Thor and the Grandfather myths of its inhabitants. Here Roberto Hawkwood learns to his surprise that there may be more to the Grandfather myth than mere superstition.

GRANDFATHER ENCOUNTER

David Johnson

316 A.E.

Roberto Hawkwood watched through the small portal as the cargo lighter pushed away from the grey spheroid of the Trans-Space freighter *Mensa* and fell toward Thor. The irregular surface of the freighter's hull slid slowly out of view as the lighter turned and Roberto caught a glimpse of the blue-and-white planet. He was surprised how much it looked like Terra and his heart skipped a beat as he wondered for a moment if they'd never left the Sol System. Then he remembered the six months of boredom aboard *Mensa*, with just a handful of passengers and fewer than a dozen crew members for company. Roberto had kept to his small compartment, re-reading microbooks about the colonization of Thor and reviewing the recordings of interviews he'd conducted with Nsundu's descendants.

He usually took his meals in his compartment too and avoided the gambling and drinking games that were the usual fare in the ship's galley. Even his time in the ship's small gymnasium usually came late during the night watch when most of the others were asleep.

Three passengers had stayed aboard *Mensa*, headed on to Baldur. The two others sitting with him in the lighter's tiny passenger compartment, a man and a woman, were technicians employed by the Chartered Thor Company. For the thousandth time Roberto wished he'd been able to afford passage on a spaceliner. He'd nearly depleted his fellowship grant of sols making this trip to Thor to complete his research, though for reasons he didn't quite understand that didn't trouble him. Professor Forgeron had insisted he come to Thor to interview the old Thoran who—if he were truly who he claimed to be—was the last surviving member of Isaac Nsundu's band.

He'd learned about the Thoran, Ahrree—Nsundu had called him "Harry," by chance. A reporter with the *Tihrundheim Dispatch* had interviewed the Thoran "grandfather" as part of the seventy-fifth anniversary celebrations of Thor's settlement. Otherwise Roberto might never have heard of him; local interviews with native sophonts did not often make the news on Terra. At Forgeron's urging Roberto had contacted the reporter, a Miss Kitsune Marrom (whose father was the newspaper's editor), and asked for her assistance in speaking with the old Thoran rebel. She'd readily agreed and her last communication had urged Roberto to come to Thor as quickly as possible. The details weren't clear but apparently *Ahrree* was planning some sort of pilgrimage and wasn't expected to return to the Tihrundheim Native Reservation where he lived.

A splashing of red-orange light through the portal began to mask the arc of the planet and Roberto noticed an increasing vibration in his seat. The lighter was entering Thor's upper atmosphere. The two technicians hardly seemed to notice, their low conversation continuing on without interruption. Roberto closed his eyes and tried to ignore the shuddering by reviewing what had brought him here to Thor.

Isaac Nsundu had been one of the early colonists, a young metallurgist from Nyasaland employed by the Chartered Thor Company in its platinum processing operations. Often working in remote regions, Nsundu developed an affinity for the native Thorans employed as general laborers by the Company. His wife, Marianna, was a teacher in the Native Affairs Schools. Shortly after they were married they moved out of the married-employee housing provided by the Thor Company and—at the invitation of a local chieftain—built a homestead site on the Tihrundheim Reservation. Eventually, Marianna stopped teaching to care for their three small children but Nsundu continued to work for the Chartered Thor Company even as he chafed at the Company's treatment of its native workers and its slow encroachment into Reservation lands across the planet.

The infamous Úr Continent Resettlement, when several hundred thousand Thorans were forcibly removed after the discovery of large platinum deposits on land which had been designated as a Native Reservation, was a turning point for Nsundu. He left his position with the Thor Company and took employment with a local Thoran tribe trying to engage in its own mineral exploitation efforts. It was also in this period that he became associated with a group of Terran settlers who opposed the Chartered Thor Company's operations. Through various legal maneuvers first at the Native Affairs Commission, then in the Native Cases Court, and finally at the Planetary Supreme Court this group won several concessions on behalf of various Thoran tribes. But Nsundu was still dissatisfied and began to work clandestinely with a smaller group to offer training to Thorans in the use of Terran arms and military equipment.

When this group opposed Nsundu's efforts to plan armed attacks against Chartered Thor Company facilities Nsundu returned to his friends among the Thoran tribes and there finalized his plan to raid the Terran Federation armory at Tihrundheim spaceport.

The first thing Roberto noticed about Thor was how it smelled. This may have been the result of having just spent six months breathing recycled air aboard *Mensa*. It was heightened by the fact that he couldn't see much—it was nighttime when they emerged from the lighter. It definitely smelled different. It wasn't bad or good; it was just...subtly different, as if someone nearby were cooking with some unusual spices. Roberto wondered how long it would be before he didn't notice it any more.

The two Thor Company people followed the cargo handler who had opened the hatch out into the spotlighted darkness. Roberto grabbed his valise and ducked through the portal as well. The air was cool and dry. The hum of the lighter's idling drive made it difficult to hear much but he could see several figures and small vehicles moving about on the landing apron. He stepped down the portable stairway extending from the lighter and followed the two Company people, directed by the cargo handler toward a small building. He started when he realized that some of the people on the apron—and even a few of the vehicle operators—were Thorans.

Roberto had seen images of Thorans, of course, but had never before seen one in person. They tended to be shorter than the Terrans. All—Terran and Thoran—were dressed in work coveralls and it was difficult to see as they moved in and out of the spotlights from the lighter and on the cargo gantry but he could make out, here and there, the dark matted hair where their hands and necks emerged from the coveralls and under the caps on their heads. Thorans were often described as "dog-like" and Roberto could understand the comparison but their faces did not, in truth, look like any dog he had ever seen. Yes, their noses and mouths protruded from their faces more than did those of a Terran and their teeth were larger and sharper than a Terran's but their faces were hairless, like those of a Terran ape and their heads were much larger, in comparison to the size of their bodies, and more ovoid than those of any dog he'd ever encountered. Roberto had never noticed it from the images he'd seen but now he thought the Thorans were more "human-like" than "dog-like." Then he realized that this was an observation he'd read several times in Nsundu's diaries.

He stopped and looked around the landing apron. If this were the Tihrundheim Spaceport then the Armory building should be here somewhere. There were several buildings visible around the spaceport, some obviously cargo and service facilities for the spaceships and contragravity ships. The building he had been following the Thor Company people toward was a passenger terminal. Several other buildings were in the near distance, some well-lighted, others not, many with various sorts of vehicles parked on or around them, but it was impossible to tell in the darkness which of them might have been the Armory. Roberto turned and continued on toward the terminal. There were a handful of people outside the building; a uniformed porter approached him.

"Mr. Hawkwood?" the middle-aged man asked.

Roberto nodded.

"Welcome to Thor. Your baggage will be available inside the terminal building shortly." He turned and pointed with his hand to the open doorway behind him.

"Thank you," Roberto said.

"Will you need accommodations or transport into the city?"

"No, I don't think so," Roberto said, shaking his head. "Someone is supposed to meet me here."

The porter nodded.

Roberto moved through the doorway. Inside, a young woman approached him, followed by two Thorans. He recognized the woman from the films they'd exchanged. Kitsune Marrom smiled, her large, brown, almond-shaped eyes twinkling. Her short, black hair glistened in the terminal lights. She was dressed in slacks and a dark jacket. The taller of the Thorans wore a kilt and short jerkin, the other a sleeveless smock. Both native outfits were patterned in garish plaid. Stepping toward Roberto, the woman reached out her right hand. Behind her, the taller Thoran held a large camera-recorder.

"Mr. Hawkwood," she said, smiling more brightly. "I'm Kitsune Marrom. Welcome to Thor."

Roberto shook her hand, surprised at the firmness of her grip.

"Uh, thank you. Pleased to meet you, Ms. Marrom," he replied, almost with a stutter. Behind her, the shorter Thoran leaned toward the other, seemed to say something that Roberto didn't catch.

"You can call me Kitsune," she said. "Or Kit, like my friends do."

"Thank you, er...Kitsune," he said. "Please, then, call me Roberto." Looking at the camera he asked, "You're recording this?"

"Yes," she said. "We don't get many visitors from the University of Cape Town. We'll have a special edition on the morning telecast. I've been doing features all week. I hope you'll give us an interview once you've gotten settled."

"Why, yes, certainly," he found himself saying, though the idea appalled him. He was surprised to discover that he did not want to disappoint this woman.

Kitsune introduced the Thorans as they made their way to the baggage area. The taller one was Oorvahrr. He worked for the *Dispatch*. The shorter Thoran, Sahshtroo, was a female. Oorvahrr's hair was the traditional black but Sahshtroo's was deep brown, and seemed a bit lighter at her neck. She wasn't a news agency staffer but rather a friend of Kitsune.

Both Thorans spoke Lingua Terra, though it was difficult for Roberto to understand them. Any "th" tended to sound like "sh" and they rolled—Roberto resisted thinking "growled"—their "r's" but in a manner unlike the South Americans Roberto had grown up with.

Oorvahrr switched-off the recorder, handed it to Kitsune, and retrieved Roberto's luggage. Sahshtroo led them outside the terminal building to a small aircar. In the overhead lights he could see *Tihrundheim Dispatch* emblazoned on the car's side. It was in good repair but the model was of a style Roberto had not seen since his childhood in Norte Grande. As Oorvahrr placed his luggage in the cargo hatch at the front of the car, Kitsune opened the rear door for him and took his valise. He ducked and stepped inside as Sahshtroo got in the front seat. Kitsune walked around the front of the car, put the valise in the hatch, and got in the backseat from the other side. Oorvahrr sat at the vehicle controls in the front next to Sahshtroo.

"Hotel Riquelme?" Oorvahrr asked, looking at Kitsune in the mirror over the front window. Kitsune turned to Roberto and smiled.

"We've reserved accommodations for you. The Riquelme is a nice place but we'd like it if you'd consider staying with our family."

"The Marroms are wonderful hosts," Sahshtroo said, turning to look at him over the front seat. Kitsune winked at the Thoran, then looked back at Roberto.

"You'd have your own suite and Mother is a wonderful cook."

"It would be my pleasure," he said, after a moment. "Thank you very much." Kitsune grinned.

"Take us to the *Dispatch* Building, Oorvahrr," she said.

"You got it, Kit," the Thoran said. He activated the controls and the car lifted into the air.

"You said in your last message that Ahrree was about to make a journey?"

"He's gone to meet Ghu," Sahshtroo said from the front seat. Beside him, Kitsune nodded. "It's his Last Journey," she said.

"'Last Journey'?" Roberto asked.

"When a grandfather has reached the end of his life he makes a final pilgrimage into the wilderness to meet the Grandfather of Grandfathers."

"Nonsense," Oorvahrr said. "It's just a silly ruse to keep from becoming a burden on the clan. When my Grandfather Time comes it will be because some grandfather has shot me for paying too much attention to his granddaughter!"

Sahshtroo punched him and the aircar lurched slightly as he accidentally activated and then readjusted a control. Kitsune smiled as the bump pushed her toward Roberto for a moment.

"As you can see, the Journey has fallen out of favor with the younger generation but for a grandfather like Ahrree the Last Journey remains an important ritual."

"When will he return from this 'Journey'?"

"He won't," Sahshtroo said.

"Only if he fails," she said. "But if there's one thing I know about Ahrree it's that he's going to get his audience with Ghu."

Roberto frowned.

"I know Ghu is the Thoran Grandfather God," Roberto said, glancing at the Thorans. "But I didn't know he...held audiences."

"He doesn't," Oorvahrr said.

"No grandfather has ever lived to tell of it," Sahshtroo said.

"Since before anyone can remember grandfathers have ventured into the wilderness never to return," Kitsune said. "It's sacrilege to look for a grandfather's body but some have nevertheless been found from time to time, usually at the bottom of a ravine or in a calm pool downstream from treacherous rapids or frozen in the melting snows of spring."

"Once the charred remains of a grandfather were found in the smoldering ruin of a forest fire," Sahshtroo added.

"Grandfather Ghu is a cruel and merciless god," Oorvahrr said. Again Sahshtroo punched him but this time he didn't flinch and the aircar remained steady.

"Then I am too late," Roberto said. "If Ahrree has gone on his 'Last Journey' I won't get my chance to speak with him about his time with Isaac Nsundu." He frowned, looking down at his hands and shaking his head. He felt a soft touch on his shoulder, looked up to see Kitsune's hand there. A spark seemed to go through him.

"It's forbidden to seek out a grandfather's corpse but there's nothing that says we can't catch up with Ahrree before he meets Grandfather Ghu," she said. Her smiled evoked a smile from Roberto too.

"It is possible?" he asked.

Kitsune nodded.

"He's only been gone two weeks," Sahshtroo said. "He's not even had time to make it to the outer reaches of the tribes' hunting grounds."

"It may be difficult to track him," Kitsune said. "Particularly because we won't be able to take the aircar to his actual location—he'd never speak to you if we did that—but we can get close and then trek the rest of the way."

"Who knows?" Oorvahrr said, baring his teeth in what Roberto was coming to recognize was a Thoran grin. "Perhaps you'll get to meet Grandfather Ghu."

The Marroms made their home in the same building where they produced the news. Oorvahrr landed the aircar on the well-lit landing stage, eight stories above the ground. Kitsune, Sahshtroo, and Roberto got out and Oorvahrr lifted the car to the garage enclosure at the edge of the landing stage. Kitsune said Oorvahrr would bring the luggage down shortly as she led him to the elevator.

Even though it was well after midnight the elder Marroms were waiting in the main room off the household reception area. Kitsune made brief introductions. Her father, Inácio Marrom, was a small, wiry man whose black hair was greying. Mrs. Marrom looked like a middle-aged version of Kitsune. She thanked Roberto for accepting their invitation to stay with them and then quickly urged everyone off to bed, saying she would prepare brunch in the morning.

Roberto was grateful for this. *Mensa's* crew had been slowly adjusting the interior day-and-night cycle to the longer period of Thor over the course of the six-month journey from Terra, so Roberto was as tired as his hosts. Mrs. Marrom called into another room, in odd words that Roberto didn't recognize. When an elderly Thoran female appeared he guessed she'd been speaking Thoran. The Thoran servant led him down a long hallway and opened a door to a guest suite. The lights were already on and Roberto's luggage was sitting in a neat bundle just inside the door.

The Thoran female—no, woman—he told himself, bid him goodnight in broken Lingua Terra and closed the door. Roberto quickly made his preparations for the night and was asleep within minutes in the most comfortable bed he'd lain on in half a year.

A knock woke him. Soft light was coming in the shaded window glass and Roberto realized it was already daylight outside. He rose and opened the door. The elderly Thoran woman was standing in the hallway looking up at him.

"Lady say please join family eat in twenty minutes." Roberto nodded. The servant nodded in return and turned to walk down the hallway. Roberto closed the door and readied himself for brunch. In less than twenty minutes he was back in the main room where animated voices and a delicious aroma were coming from what he guessed must be the dining room through a doorway at the rear. As he stepped in that direction Kitsune appeared in the doorway and smiled. Roberto stopped short.

"Good morning," she said. She was wearing a short, green dress that highlighted her legs and trim figure. "Did you sleep well?"

"Yes, yes," Roberto said. "Thank you. Good morning to you too."

"You're just in time for brunch. Mother's been cooking all morning." She beckoned him toward her and turned and stepped back through the doorway. Roberto followed her into a small dining room. Mr. Marrom was seated at the head of the table. Sahshtroo sat at his left. The table was set and a large meal had been placed along the sideboard.

"Good morning, Mr. Hawkwood," Marrom said.

"Good morning, sir," Roberto replied. Two places had been set along the right side of the table. Kitsune stepped around to that side and Roberto followed her, moving quickly to hold her chair for her.

"Thank you," she said, indicating the chair next to her. "Please, have a seat." Roberto nodded and took the indicated chair. Just then Mrs. Marrom came through another doorway carrying a large serving dish.

Roberto began to rise but she waved him back in his seat.

"Oh, good morning, Mr. Hawkwood," she said with smile. "So happy that you've joined us." She sat the dish on the sideboard and stepped to the other end of the table, taking the seat to Roberto's right. The Thoran woman had followed her from what Roberto guessed must have been the kitchen and began serving from the sideboard.

"Did you sleep well?" Mrs. Marrom asked.

"Yes, quite well."

"Oh, I'm pleased!" Across from him Roberto noticed Sahshtroo winking—yes, winking—at Kitsune.

"My daughter tells me you've agreed to give us an interview," Mr. Marrom said. Roberto turned and nodded.

"Yes, sir," he said. "Though I really don't understand what it is I might to have to say that would be of interest to your readers."

"Well, I don't want to steal Kitsune's thunder but you must understand we don't get many visitors from Terra here," Marrom said. "Especially not Terran academics who are interested in our own history."

"I can understand that," Roberto said. "But surely your own history won't be news? I mean, I'm sure everyone learns the basic story at school." Across from him Sahshtroo made an open-mouthed sound that Roberto guessed was a laugh.

"They get some history all right," Marrom said. "But the schools here are all run by the Chartered Thor Company. As you might imagine they'd don't quite see the early history of the colony in the same way that you do."

Roberto frowned. He wondered again if there were more to the difficulty he'd had in gathering primary materials about Nsundu's life than just the distance between Terra and Thor. "I see," he said.

After brunch Kitsune led him down to the news level. Sahshtroo came along. Soon he and Kitsune were seated across from each other on a small set, with bright lights overhead and young men behind the two cameras. Sahshtroo was seated in the windowed recording room with the director.

"We'll get started in just a moment," Kitsune said, smiling. "Try not to let the lights and cameras distract you. We're just going to have a conversation. Try to focus on me." As far as Roberto was concerned, that last bit of advice was entirely unnecessary. Kitsune turned her attention to the camera behind him.

"This is Kitsune Marrom. The *Tihrundheim Dispatch* is very fortunate to be able to speak with Mr. Roberto Hawkwood, just arrived from Terra." She turned to Roberto.

Welcome, Mr. Hawkwood."

"Thank you," Roberto said, nodding. "I'm pleased to be here." Kitsune glanced back at the camera.

"Mr. Hawkwood is an historian at the University of Cape Town. What brings you to Thor, Mr. Hawkwood?"

"Well, I'm here to learn more about Isaac Nsundu's effort to start an uprising among native Thorans back in the last century. Specifically, I'm interested in his final raid on the Federation Army Armory in 240 A.E."

Kitsune nodded again, her attention back on him.

"I understand you have a particular interest in someone who was there."

"Yes, there was a member of Nsundu's band, a Thoran named Ahrree, whom I understand from your own reporting is still alive. I very much hope to speak with him to capture his account of the siege at the Armory."

Kitsune nodded, again turning her attention to the camera.

"Some of you will remember our reporting about Grandfather Ahrree during the seventy-fifth anniversary celebrations last year." She looked back at Roberto. "What do you hope to hear from Ahrree?"

"Many of the details of the raid, and of the capture of Nsundu and his raiders, and of his trial and eventual execution are already well known," Roberto said. "What I most hope to get from Mr. Ahrree are his impressions of Nsundu." Kitsune nodded.

"I hope you get your chance to speak with Grandfather Ahrree, Mr. Hawkwood."

"Uh, thank you," Roberto said, suddenly realizing that the extent of Kitsune's involvement in his efforts must not be known to her audience members.

"Can you tell us, Mr. Hawkwood, what has led to your interest in Isaac Nsundu and to the events surrounding his raid?"

"Well, Nsundu's effort represents the first attempt on any Federation colony world to spark an uprising among the native sophonts. It's a seminal event in Federation history."

"You mean there have not been native uprisings on other worlds like Yggdrasil or Loki or Freya?" Roberto nodded.

"Correct," he said. "It seems unlikely, of course, that the Khoograhs of Yggdrasil would be capable of an actual uprising on a large scale. The Lokians, on the other hand, are especially unwarlike, with little history of conflict even among themselves. And the Freyans, being so like Terrans, are quickly becoming fully-integrated members of Federation society." Kitsune nodded.

"I understand discussions are underway for Freya to become a Federation Member Republic, once the accession negotiations with Odin and Baldur are completed."

"Yes, that's my understanding too," Roberto said. "If they're successful, the Freyans will be the first non-Terrans formally to join the Federation."

"So do you think had Nsundu's uprising been successful, 'Member Republic' would be something we'd be talking about with respect to Thor today?" Roberto frowned. This was an unexpected turn of the conversation.

"I'm afraid, uh,...I can't imagine that," Roberto said. "Nsundu's raid was doomed from the beginning."

"Oh. Why is that?"

"Well, to begin with, the raid was poorly planned. Just twenty-seven raiders—Terran and Thoran—against a Federation Army garrison of several hundred soldiers. Even with control of the Armory Nsundu's band would not have prevailed against that force."

"What did Nsundu hope to accomplish?"

"Well, that would be my second point. It's generally believed—and my research has confirmed this—that Nsundu hoped to spark a wider uprising among the Thoran population. But that wasn't going to happen either."

"And why is that?"

"Well, from all accounts, Thorans are not averse to conflict but as we've seen in the decades since they're not particularly adept at cooperating in large numbers. To have been successful against the Federation Army—and Chartered Thor Company—forces at the time would likely have required a united Thoran force numbering in the thousands. Of course, that's not even considering the Terran Federation's eventual response had there been a successful uprising."

"It sounds like Nsundu was on a fool's errand," Kitsune said. "What leads you to be so interested in Nsundu if he never had a chance?"

"Nsundu was no fool but I think he was impatient. Before he led his raid against the Armory he had worked for some time with other Terrans who were interested in improving the lot of Thorans."

"Other Terrans?"

"Yes," Roberto said. "Other early colonists like Kyla Henriques and Florencio Wicks whom Nsundu had worked with for years, making gains on behalf of Thorans in the courts. Ultimately though, Nsundu abandoned these efforts."

"What led to the change?"

"That's what I'd like to speak with Mr. Ahrree about."

"Surely you must have an idea?"

"Well, there are likely many reasons. Some of it, I suspect, was simply due to personal differences among Nsundu and his colleagues. It was tough work fighting the Thor Company in the courts and many of them suffered professionally and personally because of it. It may also have been part of Nsundu's own heritage. His family had been at the forefront of opposition to Afrikaner rule in South Africa in the First Century, Pre-Atomic."

"Ah, but that turned out all right, no?"

"Yes, the anti-African policies of the Afrikaner government were eventually changed, in time for it to avert being expelled from the British Commonwealth—what we think of now as the World Commonwealth that was defeated in the Fourth World War. Still, Nsundu grew up hearing family stories of struggle by native peoples against more powerful colonizers."

"What is it you most hope to hear from Grandfather Ahrree?"

"I would like to know what it was that led Nsundu to turn to violence. That move caused most of his Terran colleagues to break with him. It also wasn't part of his own experience—he was a metallurgical engineer with no service in the Federation armed forces—who by all accounts was a peaceful and reserved man in person. He seems an unusual warrior."

"I hope you get your answers here on Thor, Mr. Hawkwood," Kitsune said, smiling again. "And I hope you'll come back and speak with us again before you return to Terra."

"Thank you," he said. "It would be my pleasure."

Kitsune turned to the camera:

"That was historian Roberto Hawkwood, from the University of Cape Town on Terra, hoping to encounter the last surviving member of Isaac Nsundu's band of rebels."

"Our best guess is that Ahrree is headed to Mount Tindoonahbohr," Kitsune said from behind the controls of the old airjeep. Roberto had difficulty understanding her. The day was sunny and warm and she'd left open the duraglass canopy but the fifty mile per hour wind coming over and around the windscreen whisked her words away as Roberto tried to listen from the back seat. Sahshtroo sat beside Kitsune in front, often leaning out over the left-side door to face into the wind. A tight yellow scarf covered Kitsune's head, mostly keeping her dark hair from being windblown. Clearly, she'd done this before.

"Is there a special significance to this mountain?" Roberto asked, his hand holding his fluttering new hat on his head. After the interview yesterday, Kitsune and Sahshtroo had taken him to a shop in downtown Tihrundheim and helped him to purchase the clothing he would need for a wilderness excursion. Sahshtroo turned to grin at him.

"It's a volcano."

Roberto wasn't sure he'd understood her correctly. "Home of the Grandfather of Grandfathers!"

"Tindoonahbohr is Ghu's traditional home," Kitsune added. "Only the bravest of Grandfathers will go there to meet him."

"Why's that?"

"The volcano's is pretty active," she said. "It's rare for there to be a full eruption—I've only seen two, and the first was when I was a child—but lava flows and seismic instability are common and gas releases are an almost constant occurrence."

"Most Grandfathers would rather meet Ghu in a less inhospitable location," Sahshtroo said. "It's a good thing Ghu likes to move about."

"How will we find Ahrree?"

"We'll set down about a day's hike from the base of the volcano," Kitsune said. "There is a trail to the crater at the summit and it's on this side of the mountain. That's where Ahrree will begin his ascent."

"Won't he have too much of a lead?" Roberto asked. "How will we ever catch up with him?"

"The Last Journey is a complicated ritual. There is much to prepare for along the way so Ahrree will be moving much slower than us."

"We may even catch him before he starts up the mountain," added Sahshtroo.

The airjeep set down less than three hours after they'd left Tihrundheim. Kitsune settled it into a small glade near a rushing stream. Mount Tindoonahbohr towered in the distance. A smoky plume rose from its snow-capped peak, illuminated by the afternoon sun to the west. It was part of a range of mountains to the northeast but its summit stood well above its neighboring peaks. The lush forest was new to him but the ragged peaks reminded Roberto of his childhood home. As the airjeep settled to the ground the mountain was hidden by the canopy of trees but he would have sworn he heard it rumble once the contragravity generator was powered off.

"We'll camp here tonight," Kitsune said as she climbed from the airjeep and opened the rear door for Roberto. Sahshtroo had already gotten out her side and was opening the forward cargo hatch. Roberto followed Kitsune to the rear of the airjeep where she opened the hatch and began pulling equipment out

"Shouldn't we get started as soon as possible?" he asked.

Kitsune stopped and turned to look at him. Her jaw was clenched but Roberto thought her eyes were still smiling.

"When is the last time you camped in the wilderness, Roberto?"

"Well…uh…it's been quite some time," he stammered.

"How long?" She was smiling now.

"When I was a teenager I went to camp each summer in Parque Lauco," he said softly, looking down at his new boots. Sahshtroo had come around the other side of the airjeep and stood watching them.

"That's what I thought," Kitsune said, her smile growing. She reached out, placed a hand on his shoulder. "Let's take it slow."

Roberto nodded.

"We want to get a sense of your trekking skills," Sahshtroo added.

"It will be a tough journey," she said, "especially if we don't catch Ahrree before he's headed up the mountain." Roberto's attention was still on her hand resting on his shoulder. "It's likely we'll have to climb part way up the mountain anyway. Ahrree won't stop just because we've caught up with him and certainly not to talk with you." Kitsune dropped her hand from his shoulder and returned to pulling equipment out of the airjeep's cargo hatch.

"Do you really think he won't want to talk with me?"

"No, no," Kitsune said, handing him a sleepsack. "Ahrree loves to tell stories; I'm sure he'll speak with you. It's just that he's not going to interrupt his Last Journey. If you want to talk with him you're going to have to make part of that Journey with him."

The first day of the trek went well enough. The weather was good—sunny but cool, with just a brief rain shower in the afternoon. Roberto had never spent enough time in the wilderness to develop any familiarity with the plants and animals of Terra so the Thoran forests seemed no more alien to him than he imagined one of the new-growth forests of the Northern Hemisphere would be. He impressed both Kitsune and Sahshtroo by not slowing their pace—his time in the tiny gymnasium aboard *Mensa* had been well spent—and he thanked Ghu for the good hiking books they'd selected.

Along the way today they'd found traces of small campsites which Kitsune and Sahshtroo believed had been Ahrree's, so it seemed they were on the right track. Sahshtroo even thought they might catch up with the old grandfather sometime tomorrow. For now, they'd made camp against a low rock outcropping, one of many that had become more apparent as they'd neared Tindoonahbohr.

Roberto was washing the dishes from the evening meal Kitsune had cooked, using a bucket filled with water from the nearby stream. Sahshtroo sat across the small campfire from him smoking an oddly shaped pipe, the first time Roberto had seen a Thoran—or any non-human—do so. Kitsune sat next to him on the fallen tree, sipping cider from a cup.

"Why are you interested in Isaac Nsundu, Roberto?" she asked. The firelight glistened in her dark eyes and soft shadows fluttered across her face and neck. "Surely he's not well known on Terra."

"No, he's not, at least not by anyone who isn't an historian." Kitsune waited for him to continue. "But I'd read about Nsundu before I went to university," Roberto said. "I had been interested in Federation history even as a teenager, and in the Federation colonial experience especially."

"Why was that?"

Roberto paused for a moment, a wet cloth in one hand and a tin dish in another. He looked closely at Kitsune but could not read her expression in the flickering firelight.

"I don't know how much you know of Terran history, but South America, and southern Africa, and Australia were not always the locus of Terran civilization."

"Of course," Kitsune said. "Everyone knows how civilization was destroyed in the Northern Hemisphere in the Atomic Wars." She glanced across the campfire. "Right, Sahshtroo?" The Thoran woman nodded, pulling the pipe from her mouth.

"That's what they taught us at the Commission School."

"Yes, but before the Atomic Wars, when Terran civilization was focused in the Northern Hemisphere much of the Southern Hemisphere had been colonized—conquered, really—by more powerful nations from the North. So the formative experience in places like South America—where I grew up—or southern Africa—where Nsundu was raised—was an experience of imperialism."

Kitsune frowned. "But that was hundreds of years ago! Surely you had no such experience of 'imperialism' as a teenager."

Roberto softly shook his head, returned his attention to the dishes. "No, I did not."

"There was something else?" Kitsune asked, after a moment.

Roberto nodded, though he continued with his dishwashing. "My family, well...my father's family—and, yes, parts of my mother's family—were not from South America originally. They had come from North America, as refugees after the Atomic Wars. Not like the fortunate ones, those Americans who resettled in Antarctica or the British and other Europeans who resettled in southern Africa and Australia before the worst of the destruction. My ancestors spent generations migrating south through Central America and northern South America—devastated like the rest of the Northern Hemisphere in the Fourth World War—and were treated as outcasts wherever they arrived, forced into the most desolate regions like the deserts of Norte Grande where my family ended up."

"Sounds like what it is like to be a Thoran after the Terrans arrived," Sahshtroo said.

Roberto nodded vigorously.

"Which is what Nsundu came to realize," Kitsune added.

Again Roberto nodded.

"My father is a miner, my mother a cook in the mining company kitchens," Roberto said. "I am the first among my siblings and cousins to go to university. That I was able to go to the University of Cape Town was almost unimaginable. There are other places—like the University of Adelaide—where there has been an emphasis upon the colonial history of the Federation but Nsundu is held in special regard at Cape Town. My professor, Dr. Forgeron, is a well-regarded historian of Federation colonization."

Roberto finished drying the last of the utensils. "He urged me to come to Thor to speak with Ahrree, after we learned of your interview with him last year."

"I see," Kitsune said, nodding softly. "But what is it about Nsundu himself that interests you? Surely you haven't come all the way to Thor simply because your professor told you to come?"

Roberto turned to her, watched the shadows frolic across her face. Again he nodded softly. "Nsundu came from a family which had endured the experience of imperialism, of having had their homelands taken from them by powerful outsiders," Roberto said. "Sure, that had been long before he was born, but not so long that he didn't hear the old family stories of the struggles as a boy, the same way I heard the stories of my own ancestors."

Kitsune looked closely at him. He almost felt as if he were falling into her dark, glistening eyes. "What is it that you hope to do here on Thor?" she asked finally.

Roberto met her gaze, reached forward and took his hand in hers.

"It is a crazy dream," he said, almost in a whisper. "I want to finish the work that Nsundu began."

"Great Ghu!" Sahshtroo said, from across the campfire. Kitsune placed her other hand over his hand and nodded. Her smile was like the sunrise.

It was raining softly when they broke camp the next day. The forest was thinner now, with ever larger rock outcroppings but the low clouds made it impossible to see Mount Tindoonahbohr. Even without being able to see very far ahead Roberto could tell the terrain was rising as he followed Sahshtroo between trees and over rocks, with Kitsune following behind him. About mid-morning, with Roberto hoping she would call for a break, Sahshtroo suddenly paused, crouched low while raising her left hand. Roberto stopped on the trail and, after a moment, Kitsune quietly stepped up next to him. It was impossible to tell what Sahshtroo had seen in the wet, grey light.

She took a few steps forward, motioning with her hand for them to come forward. Kitsune stepped ahead and as Roberto followed her he began to notice a strong odor which he did not recognize.

When they reached Sahshtroo, she had picked up a large branch and was poking at what seemed to be the carcass of a short-haired animal. There was a great deal of blood about—Roberto guessed that was the odor he was smelling—and so much of the carcass had been eaten that it was impossible for Roberto to tell what sort of animal it had been.

"Fahndwee," Sahshtroo said, turning over what seemed to remain of the head with her branch. Kitsune nodded, turning to look at Roberto.

"Sort of like a goat," she said.

Roberto nodded, looking out at the forest around them.

"What would have done this?" he asked.

Kitsune turned back to look at Sahshtroo.

"Stumble-dactyl?" she asked. The Thoran woman nodded, stepping back from the carcass and letting her branch fall to the ground.

"Not long ago," Sahshtroo said. "We may have scared it off. Not all of the fahndwee has been eaten."

Roberto followed Sahshtroo's gaze as she scanned the trees around them, looking up into the branches above.

"What's...uh, what's a 'stumble-dactyl'?"

Sahshtroo looked at Kitsune.

"It's difficult to explain," she said. "It's a large predator, obviously, but there's nothing like it on Terra."

Sahshtroo continued to watch the branches overhead.

"A bird of prey?" Roberto asked.

"Sort of, but it can't actually fly. A stumble-dactyl can glide from a perch in a tree or on a rock, but on the ground they waddle-around on the elbow joints of their wings."

"How big are they?" he asked.

Now Kitsune was looking upward too.

"Larger than any Terran bird of prey. The largest can be the size of a small Thoran. Gliding, their wingspan can be wider than you are tall."

"Are they dangerous?"

"Only when they're hungry," Sahshtroo said. She looked at Kitsune. "We should move along." Kitsune nodded and Sahshtroo moved to the left, making a wide detour around the dead fahndwee. Kitsune smiled and indicated that he go ahead. Roberto hitched up his pack and started out after Sahshtroo. After a moment, Kitsune followed. Roberto kept looking upward, leading him to stumble on the trail. He thought he was being silly until he realized Sahshtroo was still watching the trees and rocks above them, too.

They had lunch in a broad, rocky clearing. The rain had stopped but it was still impossible to see Mount Tindoonahbohr or even to tell where the sun was in the sky. The dead *fahndwee* was more than an hour behind them but Sahshtroo had chosen the spot because it provided no perch from which a stumble-dactyl might swoop down upon them. As they continued on after lunch the path grew more steep and the forest had thinned to just an occasional tree. The ground was mostly rocky, though small plants grew here and there from the cracks and crevices. Even though it continued to rain on and off it seemed to Roberto that it was getting warmer, which was odd. If anything the clouds were lower and thicker and Roberto would have guessed it would get colder.

He started to catch wisps of an odd odor and after a while he recognized it smelled like rotten eggs. Sulphur he realized. They must be nearing the base of the volcano.

Roberto began to notice bits of steam rising here and there from between the rocks. By now it was clear they were climbing. He often had to use his hands to navigate between the rocks as they climbed. Their pace slowed and Roberto had to concentrate on his footing, stepping carefully to avoid a deep crack or sharp rock. Sahshtroo called a halt as they came up against a high outcropping.

Kitsune came up behind him, taking a sip from her canteen. She nodded as Sahshtroo pointed to the right. "We'll have to get around this ridge before we can continue upward...."

For a quick moment Roberto thought he had slipped but then he realized the ground was shaking. His arms flailed out as he reached for the rock wall behind him. Kitsune dropped her canteen and took a step in his direction as bits of gravel and dust began to fall around them. There was a deep, grumbling roar. Roberto watched Sahshtroo crouch low against the rock wall and followed her example. Kitsune stood between them, back against the wall.

A sharp, high-pitched whistle made Roberto flinch and then he saw a tall plume of steam burst from the ground practically in front of them. It smelled terrible, worse than the sulphurous odor to which he'd grown accustomed. The ground stopped shaking and the plume dissipated in a cloud that drifted over them. Roberto began to feel light-headed and nauseous. Kitsune took a step toward him and he reached out to grab her offered hand. Sahshtroo came up behind her but Roberto had to shake his head.

He was seeing double. Sahshtroo, partially obscured by the fading cloud and swirling dust, was also standing behind herself, a tall staff in her hand, the brown hair on her head now oddly mixed with gray. Roberto's eyes went wide, and Kitsune turned to follow his stare. Sahshtroo too turned around to look at herself. The Thoran woman barked something Roberto did not understand.

"Ahrree!" Kitsune cried.

Roberto sat on a small rock, Kitsune sitting beside him. Ahrree had led them around the rock outcropping to a small clearing of volcanic gravel and a few hardy trees, swept by a soft breeze. Kitsune had explained that it was the chemicals in the plume that had made him ill but guessed there would be no lasting effects. Already the fresh air was helping him to feel better.

Ahrree stood across the clearing, leaning on his staff and watching them. Sahshtroo paced along the edge of the clearing, looking down at the thick forests below. Roberto wondered if she were still looking for the stumble-dactyl.

"So," Ahrree said. He voice was deeper than Sahshtroo's, and even Oorvahrr's, and shook a bit in a way which suggested anger more than age. "You are the man from Terra who has questions about the Kahnree."

Roberto frowned, he'd never heard that word before but after a moment recognized it as one he'd read many times. The word for "ally" in the Thoran dialect of the Tihrundheim Reserve. Roberto nodded and rose to his feet.

"I'm very pleased to meet you…Grandfather."

Ahrree's eyes narrowed, he turned away, looked up the mountain.

"You should not have followed me, Kit."

"I know, Ahrree," Kitsune said, standing as well. "I'm sorry."

"She told you she would bring him to you before you left," Sahshtroo said. "She asked you to wait." Ahrree turned to glare at the younger Thoran, then looked at Kitsune.

"You are fortunate I realized it was you after calling upon Grandfather Ghu to stop those who followed my path." Sahshtroo laughed softly—provoking a glare from Ahrree—but Kitsune bowed her head.

"My thanks, Grandfather," she said. "You are kind to have interceded with Ghu on our behalf. Our apologies for interrupting your Last Journey." After a moment Ahrree waved his staff in dismissal and turned once again to look up the mountain.

"You have always been an impetuous child, Kit."

Kitsune smiled, glanced at Roberto, lifted her hand toward Ahrree, palm up.

"Would you permit us to journey with you a bit, Grandfather?" Roberto asked. When Ahrree did not respond Roberto turned to look Kitsune. She lifted her hands, palms out, and nodded. Roberto looked back at the Thoran. After a moment Ahrree turned around.

"Grandfather Ghu will not be happy," he said.

Roberto started to respond but Kitsune shook her head quickly. Ahrree turned back to the mountain, raised both hands, the staff rising above his head. "I will ask his forgiveness." He continued in Thoran, his voice rising.

After a moment, Kitsune leaned close to Roberto, whispering softly in his ear.

"He asks Ghu to allow 'these outsiders' to accompany him on his Last Journey."

A low rumble interrupted Ahrree and the ground shook softly once again. There were a series of red flashes in the clouds above, where the peak of the mountain would be. Ahrree kneeled, his staff placed on the ground beside him, his head bowed. Kitsune kneeled as well, motioning for Roberto to do the same. When Sahshtroo remained standing Kitsune waved at her hurriedly, motioning for her to kneel too. After a moment, she lowered herself to one knee.

There were no more flashes or rumbling but Ahrree remained motionless for some time. After several minutes Ahrree raised his head, reached for his staff and used it to help him rise to his feet. He turned and nodded, indicating that they should rise as well.

"Ghu is a compassionate and generous god," he said. "He assents to you joining my Last Journey for a time. But you must follow my commands along the way, and depart when I say, or you will feel the power of his wrath."

"Yes, Grandfather," Kitsune said beside him. She looked at Sahshtroo, then back at Ahrree. "We will heed your command and depart when you say we must."

Ahrree nodded. "You must leave your Terran weapons and tools here," he said.

"We have none, Grandfather," Kitsune said. "Just cooking implements and knives."

"No guns?" Kitsune shook her head.

"Not even a radio, Grandfather." Ahrree looked at her closely, then glanced at Sahshtroo who touched the right side of her chest with her left hand.

"Then let us continue," he said, turning back toward the mountain. "There are many more steps before us." They picked up their packs and began to follow the old Thoran up the mountain.

Ahrree had little to say the rest of the afternoon, other than to give direction as they made their way slowly up the mountain. Roberto wouldn't have admitted it but he was pleased that the old Thoran kept a somewhat slower pace than Sahshtroo had kept, especially because he stopped at several points to engage in what seemed simple but inscrutable rituals. He would come upon a particularly large rock or maybe a small stand of trees or some place where steam arose from the ground and stop. Turning he would order Roberto and the others to sit quietly. Then he would slowly move about whatever natural feature had caught his interest, speaking softly and performing what seemed to be an odd, slow dance that was never the same.

Sometimes when Ahrree stopped Roberto wondered what it was about that particular place which led him to him to conduct his ritual there, for there didn't seem to be anything particularly remarkable about. After the second or third time of this Roberto began to suspect that he chose these spots precisely to confuse his unwanted audience.

Each time Ahrree's ritual would end with several minutes of still silence, the old Thoran sitting on the ground, his staff across his knees. Roberto came to enjoy these rests, sitting quietly beside Kitsune, listening to the wind blowing across the mountain, the sounds of the occasional animal in the brush or air, a distant rumble or hiss of steam. They encountered no more tremors, nor plumes of acrid gas. Roberto told himself this was mere happenstance, not because Ahrree had actually induced his god earlier to frighten them at their first encounter.

Ahrree chose a campsite as the grey skies darkened. The rain had stopped and a slight breeze kept the small clearing he'd chosen free of the unpleasant odor of the mountain. The old Thoran assented when Kitsune asked if they could build a fire. Roberto helped her with the kindling and in preparing their meal. Sahshtroo took out her pipe but after a glare from Ahrree she put it back into her pocket and began to pitch the tents.

Ahrree had only a small sleepsack which he spread on the opposite side of the clearing from the fire. As Roberto helped Kitsune with the cooking he watched the old Thoran perform another complex ritual, almost like some sort of martial art form. After a few minutes he returned to the fire, taking a seat across from Roberto. Kitsune dished out the simple stew she'd prepared. Ahrree took a bowl and accepted the piece of bread which Roberto offered as well. He declined a cup of cider, sipping water from his small canteen instead.

"Let us give thanks to Ghu for these gifts tonight," he said, looking at each of them in turn. Roberto watched the others but there seemed to be no response that was required. He nodded when Ahrree looked at him again.

"Why have you come to Tindoonahbohr, Mr. Hawkwood?"

Roberto was taken aback.

"Why...why to speak with you. And please, call me Roberto."

Ahrree nodded. "Roberto, then. Yes, you want to know of my time with the Kahnree, but why have you come here, Roberto?" He turned and gestured around him, to the clearing, to the mountain itself it seemed.

"I don't understand," he said. "I've come here because this is where Kitsune said we would find you."

Kitsune grinned, looked across the fire to Sahshtroo.

"He's asking why Ghu brought you here," Sahshtroo said.

Kitsune nodded, still smiling.

"I...I didn't know...Ghu brought me here," Roberto said.

"He's new to our world, Ahrree," Kitsune said. "He is a guest who does not know our ways."

Ahrree shook his head.

"This man, I'm certain, knows many things about our world you younglings do not know. Great Ghu! I imagine he knows things about the Kahnree, about the early days of the Terrans in this world that I do not know."

"That may be, Grandfather," Roberto said. "Kitsune is right though. I do not know your ways. I must admit that before today I had always considered Ghu to be...a myth." He was ashamed that he had been about to say "joke."

"You're not alone in that," Sahshtroo said.

"Was it a myth that nearly threw you off the mountain today?" Ahrree asked.

Roberto look at Kitsune. After a moment she turned to Ahrree. "You know what most Terrans believe about Ghu, even those who grew up on our world."

"Yes," he said. "I know. Too well I know. But no Terran has ever climbed Tindoonahbohr looking for an old Grandfather on his Last Journey." He looked again at Roberto.

"Why have you come here, youngling?"

Roberto shook his head.

Ahrree watched him for a few more moments, then added, "Think on that this night. Tomorrow we will talk about the Kahnree. But only after you have answered my question." He took a bite of bread and returned to eating his stew.

Kitsune reached down and took Roberto's hand in hers, giving it a gentle squeeze.

Of course Roberto had difficulty falling asleep that night. Why was he here? To speak with Ahrree just as he had spoken with so many others who had known Nsundu or those around him. Why, he had even managed to speak with Nsundu's granddaughter in Blantyre last spring! True, none of the people he'd spoken with had ever met Nsundu personally but many of them, like the granddaughter, knew others who had. Of course he was here to speak with the last person living to have known Nsundu himself. Why else would he be here?

It was even more absurd to ask why Ghu had brought him here. Ghu was a figment of Ahrree's imagination! There was no Thoran Grandfather God moving Roberto around in the universe, from Terra to Thor to the shoulder of this volcano. It would almost be funny if Roberto had not come so far to speak with the one person alive who had known Nsundu. And now that person refused to speak with him about Nsundu until he had an answer to his outrageous question.

As he finally fell asleep Roberto was half-dreaming of a huge, hairy hand picking him up from the plateau atop Table Mountain and placing him beside a huge plume of whistling steam halfway up Mount Tindoonahbohr....

When Roberto awoke the next morning the sun was already peeking over the eastern horizon. He sat up in his sleepsack. Kitsune was sitting near the fire, stirring a small pot of cider. She smiled at him.

"Good morning," she said. "Cup of cider?"

"Yes, please."

Sahshtroo was sitting on a nearby log, puffing softly on her pipe.

Suddenly he started, looking wildly about. Ahrree was nowhere to be seen, though his wrapped up sleepsack was sitting near where he'd unrolled it the night before. Kitsune pointed back down the path that had brought them to this clearing.

"Nature called," she said. She stepped over to Roberto, handed him a cup of warm cider. "Breakfast will be ready in a few minutes."

"Thank you." Roberto took a sip of the cider, sat the cup on the ground and slid out of his sleepsack, kneeling to roll it up. After putting on his shoes he rose, glanced at Kitsune, pointed down the path. She nodded, and turned her attention back to the fire. Roberto went to find a tree.

Walking down the trail so that he could no longer see the clearing he looked about for a spot where he might answer nature's call. Suddenly Ahrree stepped up from behind a low rock, hitching his kilt around his waist.

"Sorry," Roberto said, looking away.

Ahrree seemed to chuckle.

"It is a good spot," he said. "Except I found it first." He smiled and pointed to his left. "Try over there."

"Thank you," Roberto said, not moving. Ahrree moved toward him, then stepped around him and up the trail.

"I will return to the camp and await your answer to my question."

Roberto cursed to himself silently.

When he returned to the clearing Ahrree was sitting with the others around the campfire. Kitsune waved him to a seat beside her and handed him a bowl of hot cereal. Roberto ate heartily, happy for the distraction from any conversation.

"I hope we have not slowed your Journey, Ahrree,"

Kitsune said. Ahrree paused from his cereal and shook his head softly.

"How much longer to the crater?"

The old Thoran paused again. "Three days, I think." He took another spoonful of cereal. "You will not be permitted to join me at Ghu's

Hearth." He turned to look at Roberto but Roberto would not meet his gaze.

"I... I had a dream...of Ghu...last night," he said finally.

Across the campfire Sahshtroo's eyes widened.

"Grandfather Ghu is not in the habit of visiting when one is sleeping," Ahrree said.

"But I did have a dream," Roberto said. Kitsune placed her hand on his upper arm.

"Perhaps Ghu speaks differently with Terrans," she said. Ahrree glanced at Kitsune, then back at Roberto.

"That may be," he said, nodding slowly. "And what did Ghu have to say in your dream?"

Roberto shook his head. "The dream...was only...that he...brought me here."

Ahrree smiled.

"Well," Ahrree said, rising from his seat. "That's a start." He reached to take Sahshtroo's empty bowl. "Let me do the washing and we can get back to the Journey."

The trail steepened. Patches of snow appeared, often covering the loose rocks which formed the trail, and grew larger as the morning wore on. The sky had cleared and the bright sun made it difficult to see at times. Far above the snow-covered peak of the volcano released dark swirls of smoke into the air. Roberto found himself forced to pay closer and closer attention to his footing, often stumbling and having to resort to using his hands many times. By the time they stopped for their first break of the morning the only patches of ground not covered by snow were the occasional, foul-smelling patch heated by the mountain.

He sat with Sahshtroo on a large rock, the smoke from her pipe swirling around them. Kitsune was standing with Ahrree on the trail ahead, speaking in soft tones that Roberto could not hear. He looked at Sahshtroo.

"Whatever can he mean, 'Why am I here?'" Sahshtroo watched him through the twirling smoke.

"Ahrree wants to tell you his stories," she said after a moment. "He would not have let us come along if he didn't." She pulled the pipe from her mouth and grinned. "Or rather, he would not have asked Ghu for permission for us to accompany him."

"You...you don't believe in Ghu?"

"Ghu has been a powerful figure in my life since I was a child in the widows' camp outside the Federation Army base. I believed in Ghu then, but I'm not sure what I believe now. I've learned lots of remarkable things from you Terrans, especially from people like Kitsune and her family." She took another puff of her pipe. "I do know that Ahrree loves a spectacle and giving Ghu a 'little help' is something he's fond of doing."

Roberto nodded, shading his eyes with his gloved hand while he looked out at the forest spread in the distance below them.

"What does he want from me?"

"He wants to know why telling you his stories will matter. Not just to you and your studies. Not just to your colleagues and teachers back on Terra."

"I'm not sure it does."

Sahshtroo pulled the pipe from her mouth, looked sharply at him. "Truly? What about what you told Kitsune the other night?"

"About wanting to carry on Nsundu's work? But I'm no soldier."

"Neither was Nsundu, at least not in the beginning," Sahshtroo said. "Ahrree's time with Nsundu and his rebels was a very important time in his life. He almost died in the battle and afterwards only escaped being executed like the handful of other survivors because of his young age." She pulled on the pipe again, exhaled a long wisp of smoke. "In the years since there have been many clashes, Thoran tribes attacking Terrans pushing into their territories, or a clan on a reservation will slaughter some Terran colonists or Company people or a constable, before they are beat down by the Company troops and the Army.

Ahrree has always sought out the stories of these battles, and can recount them in detail himself." She took another draw on the pipe. "But in none of these fights have there been Terrans fighting with the Thorans."

Roberto turned to look at her. "No allies? No Kahnree."

Sahshtroo nodded. "Ahrree has told the tales of this travels with Nsundu many times, to anyone who will listen. Ghu! I must have heard them all dozens of times. Now he goes on his Last Journey. He is old, he is dying. He wants to know that his time with Nsundu mattered."

Kitsune called out to them, indicating with her hand that it was time to get back on the trail. Ahrree had already turned his back and was once again slowly leading the way up the mountain.

"I don't suppose an historical article published in some academic microbook on Terra matters," Roberto said as he stood and pulled his pack onto his back.

Pulling her own pack on Sahshtroo nodded and stepped toward Kitsune. She looked back over her shoulder, her eyes twinkling and a wide smile on her face.

"Why have you come to Tindoonahbohr, youngling?"

They had trekked around to the north face of the mountain and were climbing in shadow now. Roberto was following Ahrree with Kitsune behind him and Sahshtroo father back down the trail. The mixed snow and rocks here made the trail treacherous, though the switchbacks allowed them mostly to walk rather than climb. A wide swath of snow-covered talus spread below them, the snow disturbed by a winding trail that marked their path for the last half hour or so. Suddenly Sahshtroo called out and Roberto saw a huge shadow fall out of the sky toward Ahrree!

Ahrree raised his staff, struck at the shadow. It gave a sharp cry that reminded Roberto of animated pterosaurs he'd seen in films. The creature flapped its great wings at Ahrree, almost covering him entirely. Ahrree continued to strike at it with his staff. The creature struck back with its sharp beak and the staff fell from Ahrree's hands. A red stain began to grown on his shoulder.

Suddenly Ahrree was lifted from the trail and the creature flew toward Roberto, Ahrree dangling from its claws and flailing about, striking at it with his hands.

The great wings flapped, sounding like a sail luffing, their wash pushing Roberto's hat from his head. The creature was carrying Ahrree less than six feet above the ground and Ahrree's thrashing feet rushed at Roberto's head. He leaped, trying to grapple with Ahrree as the Thoran's legs crashed into him. He was forced backward and failed to get a grip on Ahrree.

He fell off the trail, tumbling head over heels into the snow and loose rocks below. He reached the bottom of the talus and his head hit a large rock as he tumbled down into larger rocks and sparse brush. He head throbbed and he could no longer see. A sharp pain tore at his thigh....

Oblivion was slowly replaced with pain. Pain unlike anything he'd felt before. Something stabbed at his leg, again and again. He tried to pull away but he couldn't move. Something pounded at his head. Somewhere far away a voice was calling his name. He wished it would go away, would let him fall back into the darkness. It seemed for a bit like it did, but the pain didn't go away. Then he recognized the voice.

"Roberto," Kitsune cried. "Roberto. Roberto." He opened his eyes but the pain blurred his vision and he closed them again.

"Roberto!" He opened his eyes again.

Kitsune looked down at him. "Oh, Roberto," she said. Tears trickled down her checks.

"What...what happened? Ahrree!" He tried to sit up and the pain forced him down. Kitsune cradled him in her arms.

"Lie still," she said. "You're hurt. Badly." The pain punctuated her words.

"I'm here," Ahrree said, from above him, or behind him. He couldn't tell. He opened his eyes again. Kitsune tried to smile at him.

"I am only slightly injured," Ahrree said.

"He's very injured," Sahshtroo said, also beyond his vision. "The stumble-dactyl tore his shoulder pretty badly."

Ahrree's lack of argument confirmed her assessment.

"Your leg is broken," Kitsune said. "Compound fracture of your thigh. It must hurt terribly." Roberto nodded unsteadily. "We've managed to stop most of the bleeding but you're in bad shape."

"What happened?" he asked.

Kitsune frowned, looked above him. Behind him, he realized. He was lying on his back.

"The stumble-dactyl wasn't able to lift Ahrree away," she said. "It dragged him into you and knocked you off the trail. Your leg was broken in the fall and you were knocked unconscious." She paused, looking behind him again. "Ahrree managed to...convince the stumble-dactyl to release him, and Sahshtroo and I caught him before he fell off the mountain too."

"What happened to the...the stumble-dactyl?"

"Glided away, down the mountain," she said.

"What do we do now?" he asked.

Kitsune shook her head, began to cry again. "You can't walk," she said. "And we'll never be able to carry you down the trail." She closed her eyes, turned her head upward. "Ahh! I wish I had hidden a radio in my pack!"

"You must go and bring help," Ahrree said.

Before they left, Kitsune and Sahshtroo pitched two of the tents and pulled Roberto into one, propping him up so he could see out the open flap. They built a campfire and gathered kindling, perhaps enough for three nights if it were used sparingly. They'd recovered Ahrree's staff and with it he was able to move about the small camp, though even Roberto could tell that he was hurting. As Sahshtroo and Kitsune were repacking their packs Ahrree wandered off, saying he would be return shortly. Kitsune ducked into the tent, knelt beside Roberto. She brushed the hair from his forehead, straightened the blanket which covered him.

"We'll be back with the airjeep in two days," she said. "Three at most."

"We will be okay," Roberto said. "I'll miss you, Kit."

Kitsune's eyes seemed to fill with tears and she looked away quickly.

"Your bleeding has stopped. If you stay still the bleeding shouldn't start again. It's Ahrree I'm most worried about. He needs more than the crude compression bandage Sahshtroo's fashioned for him. The stumble-dactyl wounded him badly; he may not last three days."

"We'll be okay," Roberto repeated. He tried to ignore the pain in his leg which called him a liar. "I'll take care of Ahrree."

"I will need no care-taking, youngling," Ahrree said, squeezing into the tent. He had some dark, bulbous nodules in his hand. "Eat this!"

"What is it?"

"Kowleen root. It will help with the pain." Kitsune took a nodule, held it to Roberto's mouth. It was cold and tasted like dirt. He bit into the nodule and nearly spit it out. The pain lanced his leg. The root was horribly bitter.

"Eat!" Ahrree said. He ate. Ahrree handed the nodules to Kitsune and she helped him to eat three more. Roberto thought he was going to be sick, but wasn't.

"Thank you," Kitsune said, laying her hand on Ahrree's arm. "Now go outside and rest!"

Ahrree grunted, but did as she said. Kitsune bent low, kissed Roberto on the brow, then softly on the lips. His heart jumped.

"Three days," she said, rising. Roberto tried to smile.

Ahrree sat on the ground, just outside the tent, tending to the small fire. He looked up at the sky.

"Maybe three more hours of daylight," he said. "The women-folk won't get far this day, even headed downhill and without an old grandfather and a Terran scholar to slow them down."

"Will they be all right?" he asked. The pain had begun to recede. "Kitsune said the stumble-dactyl had flown down the mountain too."

A strange glow, which couldn't be from the small fire, seemed to paint Ahrree in an odd, purple and red light. "Stumble-dactyls are day-hunters. The women-folk will not be prey tonight." He poked his staff at the fire, moving in what almost seemed like slow-motion to Roberto. "The beast must have been very hungry to attack a person. It is likely she has already eaten something else by now. Fahndwee perhaps." He looked up at the sky again, spoke softly in Thoran in what was almost a whisper. After a few moments he said, "I have asked Ghu that they travel without peril."

"Thank you," Roberto said. "I hope that Ghu watches over them."

Ahrree looked at Roberto, smiled broadly. "So, why are you here, Roberto Hawkwood?"

Roberto shifted his body slightly to the left, tried to sit up a bit straighter. After a moment he was surprised that doing so hadn't resulted in the sharp stab of pain to which he'd almost become accustomed. Must be something to that foul-tasting root after all.

"I'm still not sure why I am here, Ahrree," he began. "Or why Ghu has brought me here—though I'm glad now it wasn't, it seems, do die falling off Mount Tindoonahbohr!"

"Ghu has not finished with you, youngling. You have yet to make it off his mountain with your life!"

"Yes," he said. "And that terrifies me. Perhaps though, that is why I am here." Ahrree raised his thick eyebrows, nodded slowly. "I came here to hear about your time with Isaac Nsundu, to bring your story back to Terra to share with my fellow historians, to complete my studies at the University and launch my career as a professional scholar."

"And now you believe something different?"

Roberto nodded. "I cannot go back to Terra."

Ahrree nodded. "Why is that?"

"Because I am in love with Kitsune Marrom." Roberto expected the Thoran to be surprised, disappointed even, but Ahrree simply smiled.

"Kitsune has never seen a visitor from Terra who was not on Company business—or with the Army—and that novelty was the source of her interest in you," he said. After a moment, he continued, "But now I believe Kitsune may love you too."

"Really?" Roberto asked. He didn't jump but he did try to sit up. He felt the pain this time, but it subsided quickly.

Ahrree nodded.

"I have lived among Terrans my whole life," Ahrree said. "I have known Kitsune since she was a small child and have watched her grow into a woman. The woman looks at you now like the girl-child looked at her father."

Roberto smiled widely, feeling slightly dizzy.

Ahrree frowned. "But this is not why Ghu has brought you here."

Ahrree prepared a small meal, some bacon and bread and a pair of corn-apples. He brought a plate into the tent for Roberto and waited to make sure he needed no help eating before returning to the campfire. He had warmed two cups of cider too, leaving one with Roberto. Ahrree closed his eyes and sat silently for a few moments, before sipping from his own cup. The sky had darkened, not night yet but a deep twilight. The odd purple-red glow had vanished with the sun and now shadows and orange firelight flickered across his face. Roberto began to eat as well. Still he had no answer for Ahrree.

After the meal the Thoran scrapped the dishes—no washing now—and helped Roberto make preparations to sleep. When Roberto was back in the tent and bundled up in the blanket Ahrree gave him more of the kowleen root which he washed down with the last of his cider. Ahrree spread his sleepsack out alongside the campfire and lay down.

"Perhaps Ghu will visit you in your dreams again this night," he said after a bit.

"Perhaps," Roberto said, already drowsy. "Good night, Ahrree."

Roberto slept fitfully, awaking whenever he tried to roll over. Each time the small campfire still burned, and once or twice he noticed Ahrree tending to it. When he did sleep he had the sense of great turmoil, though the nature of the turmoil eluded him. At times he seemed to be falling down the mountainside again, blows raining upon his head and pain tearing at his leg, though when he awakened the pain was not there. Eventually he noticed the sky outside the tent getting brighter. He had no sense of having rested at all. The fire had fallen to embers and Ahrree lay unmoving on his sleepsack. Fear caught at Roberto and he tried to listen for the Thoran's breathing but heard nothing. There was no apparent sign of movement in his prone form.

"Ahrree," he cried. His voice louder than he'd intended. As he inhaled to shout again Ahrree's head moved and his eyes opened. He lay there quietly looking up at the sky.

"What would you ask of me today, Grandfather?" Ahrree asked softly.

Roberto smiled. "That wasn't Ghu," he said. "It was me!"

Ahrree turned to look at Roberto, slowly sat up. He smiled. "Good morning," he said. "The Grandfather of Grandfather's has given us another day on his mountain!" He looked at Roberto. "Do you have an immediate need?"

Roberto shook his head and Ahrree nodded in response. He began to stoke the fire again.

It became clear that the day would get no brighter. Apparently they'd slept well past sunrise. Clouds had formed overnight and again it looked like rain. It was colder than it had seemed the night before.

Later, after Ahrree had prepared bowls of warm cereal and was sitting once again next to the campfire and eating, he turned and looked squarely at Roberto in the tent.

"If you will not go back to Terra what will you do here on Thor? Become a teacher in the Company schools?"

Roberto shook his head. "Perhaps one day, but not now," he returned Ahrree's stare. "One time, while we were following you here, I told Kitsune I wanted to continue Nsundu's work."

Ahrree's eyes widened and he pulled his head back a bit.

"You are not a warrior," he said.

"No, I'm not. But neither was Isaac Nsundu. He was a scientist, a scholar as I am really, who looked for stories in rocks and stones as I look for them in people...including Thoran grandfathers."

"Yes, that is true."

"Besides," Roberto said. "There are many warriors on Thor. What Nsundu brought was leadership, not the fighting prowess of the warrior."

"But the Company is stronger now, and there are more Federation troops in Tihrundheim than there were on all of Thor when the Kahnree led us in the raid upon the Armory."

"They are still small in number compared to all the warriors among the Thorans. And I believe I have something Nsundu did not have."

"And what is that?"

"Patience."

Ahrree nodded again. He looked up at the sky, spoke softly to Ghu for a few moments. Then turned back to look at Roberto again.

"I met the Kahnree the day my mother was killed in the widow's camp," he began.

Ahrree talked all morning, telling of his early days with Nsundu, after Nsundu had taken Ahrree in as an orphan. The Thoran clan which controlled the territory where the Nsundus had made their homestead objected to a Thoran youth living with a Terran family so Nsundu brought Ahrree with him as he gathered his band of rebels. For three years Nsundu traveled among the Thoran tribes of Fé Continent—and once they visited the Thoran refugees on Úr Continent—seeking allies, raising funds to buy weapons, and recruiting fighters for his band.

Ahrree's tales of their encounters with the many chieftains and grandfathers of different tribes confirmed one of Roberto's basic beliefs about Nsundu: he failed to see the Thoran tribes as distinct social units. His model was the jumble of modern tribal communities of southern Africa and so he could not recognize the Thoran tribes for what they were: sovereign communities, who often saw other tribes as their adversaries more than they did the Terrans.

Ahrree also described many clandestine meetings with Terrans who were sympathetic to Nsundu's cause. In truth Ahrree had not understood much of what had happened in these encounters but Roberto was able to ask him questions about details which allowed Roberto to make sense of them. The details that Ahrree was able to recall these many decades since—in spite of the fact that he often had not understood the larger context at the time—suggested a remarkable capacity for observation. Roberto desperately wished he had a recorder.

To Nsundu's frustration and eventual dismay, his sympathizers among the Terrans were largely unwilling to support an active rebellion. For some this was a position based in principle: they saw the Thorans as more noble, more decent than the Terran colonists, and the Chartered Thor Company in particular, and were not prepared to urge them to open conflict. For others the reluctance to support Nsundu's rebellion was purely practical: they understood the vast power of the Terran Federation and recognized that the Federation would never allow the Thorans to prevail over the Terran settlers.

Roberto had come to believe that here was one of Nsundu's greatest errors. Even if his rebellion had been successful, even if the Thoran tribes had been able to overcome their differences and unite against the Terrans, against the Company, he had no plan for dealing with the Federation on Terra. He was too much of an idealist it seemed, believing that somehow the Federation would accept a fait accompli on Thor.

By late-morning, not long after Ahrree had gone to fetch water from the snow-fed runnel which ran below their campsite, Roberto realized he was dozing off as Ahrree recounted another tale. Gently, he called a halt, insisting that the Thoran take a rest too. When Ahrree didn't argue with him Roberto realized that the grandfather's injuries were taking their toll. Roberto fell asleep almost before Ahrree had finished laying out his sleepsack.

He awoke to the aroma of more bacon. Ahrree was huddled over the campfire, preparing another meal. It was getting dark again. They'd survived their first day. When Ahrree noticed he was awake he turned and rummaged among the foodstuffs he'd laid out for the meal. After a moment he entered the tent, more kowleen in his hand.

"Eat some more," he said.

Roberto reached for the dark nodules, then paused. "How much is left?"

"This is the last of it."

Roberto frowned. "You must have it then, Grandfather."

Ahrree shook his head, slowly.

"You must do as I say, youngling. It is Ghu's command."

"Please, Ahrree." Ahrree looked at him, then turned and left the tent, eating the kowleen.

"I have never head Ghu speak through a Terran before," he mumbled to himself as he returned to his cooking. Soon he was handing Roberto a small plate of food.

"There is no more cider," he said, passing Roberto a canteen he'd refilled in the streamlet.

"The water is good," Roberto said. "Thank you—and Grandfather Ghu—for this meal."

Ahrree nodded and turned his attention to his own plate. After a few moment he looked up. "Tell me how patience would have helped the Kahnree."

Roberto paused briefly to collect his thoughts. "Patience would have helped Nsundu to understand that the Thoran tribes were not ready to cooperate against the Terrans. He needed to help them to recognize their shared adversary before bringing the battle to the Terrans."

Ahrree nodded at this.

"Patience was also needed to solve the problem of the Terran Federation. Nsundu knew but failed to accept that the Terran Federation is much more powerful than all of the tribes of Thor even if they were united across the planet."

"What hope is there then for our people?"

"The Terrans will never leave Thor," Roberto said. "This world is much like Terra and worlds like Terra are rare. So the Thorans need to work toward an outcome which includes the Terrans. Nsundu should have known this too. Indeed, it was what his own grandfathers and their grandfathers had done on Terra."

"Now I know, Roberto Hawkwood, why you are here."

Again Ahrree cleaned up after the meal and helped Roberto to make his preparations to sleep. It began to rain and after a few minutes Ahrree gave up on trying to keep the fire going. He pulled his sleepsack into the other tent, then returned and crawled inside the tent with Roberto.

"I will sleep in the other tent this night," he said. All Roberto could see was Ahrree's silhouette against the night sky coming through the tent flap. "Rain means the night will not be too cold." Roberto nodded, the realized Ahrree likely could not see him.

"Call to me once you are inside your tent," Roberto said. Ahrree grunted and crawled out of the tent. After a few minutes he called out in a loud voice.

"Good night, Roberto Hawkwood." Roberto smiled.

"Good night, Grandfather." His leg was hurting again. He wished there had been more kowleen. The rain beat down on the tent, a steady patter. Darkly, he wondered if Ahrree would make it through the night. He realized he would miss the old Thoran terribly.

A low howling woke him. It was steady. Artificial. It was getting louder. Nearer, he realized. He called out to Ahrree but there was no answer. The howling increased and after a bit he thought he saw a light flash across the rain-drenched trees across the clearing. It flashed again, this time briefly illuminating the side of the tent. The howling stopped and all he could hear was the rain falling on the tent. Again he called out to Ahrree. Again no answer. Another light flashed outside the tent. A voice called his name.

"Roberto! Ahrree!" It was Kitsune.

How could it be? A light shone on the tent flap and it was pulled aside. A flashlight shone in his eyes, then the beam was turned up over his head.

"Roberto!" Kitsune said, ducking into the tent and wrapping her arms around him. He held her as best he could, tried to ignore the pain in his leg as her weight shifted against him. She was wet and dripping all over him, but he didn't mind a bit.

"How did you get here so quickly?" he asked, once she had released him and sat back.

"It was Sahshtroo's doing. We talked that first night and she told me she could make much better time than I could. So this morning she started out ahead of me. She quickly outdistanced me. I stuck to the open areas as I continued to make my way down and by shortly after sunset she found me with the airjeep. We talked about camping for the night but I could not wait." She leaned forward and hugged him again. "Where is Ahrree?"

"In the other tent," he said. It was then he noticed Sahshtroo in the distance calling Ahrree's name.

"Let me go see," she said, taking the flashlight and crawling out of the tent. She called to Sahshtroo and after a moment he could see a second flashlight lancing about in the darkness outside the tent. Sahshtroo had looked in the other tent but Ahrree wasn't there. He didn't seem to be anywhere about the campsite, though his sleepsack was still in the tent. Kitsune stuck her head back into the tent.

"We're going to get you into the airjeep and then take it up to look for Ahrree. He can't have gone far." She stepped out again and spoke with Sahshtroo and after a couple of minutes the headlights of the airjeep were shining on the tent. Kitsune climbed in and after a moment Sahshtroo stuck her head inside as well.

"It's good to see you," he said.

She nodded. "Was Ahrree all right?"

"He was weak but he seemed to be okay. He was sleeping in the other tent to get out of the rain."

"Ready?" Kitsune asked.

"Ready," he said. Sahshtroo pulled at the end of the sleepsack he was lying on as Kitsune tried to lift his torso toward the opening. They made little progress and after a moment Sahshtroo said something he didn't understand but which sounded like a curse. She stepped outside the tent and there were a series of quick snaps along the side of the tent. Suddenly the side lifted from the ground and flipped over their heads, the tent collapsing as the rain began to fall on them.

Kitsune and Sahshtroo kneeled on either side of him and helped him to stand on his good leg. Pain jabbed at his other leg. Slowly they helped him to the airjeep and lifted him into the rear compartment. Quickly they climbed into the jeep, Sahshtroo on the right at the controls. After a moment the jeep lifted into the air as twin spotlights illuminated the campsite in bright circles that grew as they gained altitude. Kitsune turned to look at him.

"Sahshtroo called the Air Patrol before she picked me up. It won't be long before they're here."

They searched for an hour but had found no sigh of Ahrree when the first search and rescue vehicle arrived.

"He doesn't want to be found," Sahshtroo said.

The constable in the airjeep's screen asked them to set down so they could attend to Roberto's injuries. Roberto wanted to remain aloft, to keep searching but Kitsune would have nothing of it. Once on the ground the constables transferred Roberto to their vehicle. Sahshtroo quickly took the airjeep back to the air to continue to look for Ahrree.

Kitsune watched as the medic began to examine Roberto's leg. She held Roberto's hand, softly stroking his hair with her other hand. Finally, the medic administered something for the pain. In the cab the other constable was talking on the screen to a second search and rescue vehicle which had just arrived. Roberto's vision blurred. He was suddenly very sleepy.

When he awoke, Kitsune was still holding his hand. She was still wearing her trekking clothes though they were dry now and Roberto was lying in a bed wearing only a thin gown. They were in some sort of hospital, in Tihrundheim he guessed. His leg was immobilized in a bandage. Daylight shone through the window though they were too high for him to see anything but another building in the distance.

"Ahrree?" he asked. Kitsune began to cry.

"Sahshtroo and the constables searched for several more hours." She shook her head softly. "The Air Patrol has sent two search and rescue teams out again today but so far no word. It continues to rain on Tindoonahbohr."

"He's finished his Last Journey," Roberto said.

Kitsune nodded. "I very much hope he got to meet Grandfather Ghu.

"Did he ever tell you about his time with Nsundu?" Kitsune asked after a moment.

Roberto laughed. "Yes! He talked for hours. I wish I had had a recorder. I learned many, many things."

Kitsune's eyes narrowed and her brow furrowed. "So you must have been able to tell him why you are here."

Roberto nodded, glanced at the open doorway to the room. "Patience," he began.

CHARTERED COMPANIES OF THE TERRAN FEDERATION

John A. Anderson

1. Chartered Companies in the First Terran Federation?

Piper connects the early extraterrestrial colonization with the settlement of the Americas. "And when Mars and Venus are colonized, there will be the same historic situations, at least in general shape, as arose when the European powers were colonizing the New World..."[1] Many of these New World colonies had royal charters; particularly those of the British and French, and it is known that the Terran Federation is modeled on the British Empire. So although he does not say, his chartered companies may have their beginning early in the First Federation's history, soon after WWIII (AE 31). This is the 'interplanetary age', paralleling the early transatlantic age. Terra is superficially united under the Federation, but we know that nation-states still exist, because "The Future History" mentions colonies being planted on "Mars, Venus, Asteroid Belt and Moons of Jupiter" by various "member states" of the First Terran Federation. [2] So the postulated companies are apparently sponsored by nations (as in the New World historical model), rather than the Federation.

As well as serving national pride and prestige, the extraterrestrial colonies would certainly have a strong economic motive. Somewhere, Piper also mentions "rising birthrates," even with the interruption of nuclear war. According to the logic of those days, more and more people on Terra meant that the finite global resources would have to be divided into smaller and smaller shares per person. (The only alternative would be fighting among themselves, but the global Federation Government—backed by the nuclear missile fortress on Luna—presumably keeps everyone in check. At least for a while.)

Any spacefaring nation would certainly seek off-world resources to support its rising population. In the real world, Terra had 3.5 billion people in 1965, so in Piper's Future History, it is probably 4 or 5 billion by the time of the Cyrano Expedition to Mars in 1996 (AE 54). This is at least two times too many. Because in *Space Viking*, Marduk has "almost two billion" people, which in Beam's universe seems to be the most a fully civilized Terra-type planet can support. [3]

Having a chartered company develop the off-world resources would save the national government (that is, the taxpayer) from having to foot the bill. Private enterprise is always more efficient than government. So at least some of the original extraterrestrial colonies (particularly American and British) would be chartered companies, employing capitalism to support their respective peoples back home, as well as develop new worlds and promote the emigration of excess population. These factors may also be a driving force in the "First Terraforming" on Mars.[4]

However, since nation-states are subordinate to the First Federation, I presume that some portion of these off-world resources have to be turned over to the world government on Terra (either directly or through corporate/national taxes), to support the rising populations of non-spacefaring nations.

2. "I Claim this Planet…"

Though they probably cannot claim entire planets, these postulated chartered companies may lay claim to whole moons. Their precedent for this would be Luna. In "The Future History", Beam mentions the "Collapse of UN owing to disputes as to *national sovereignty over*, and militarization of, Luna."[5] As the first people to land, the Americans apparently assert 'national sovereignty over' the Moon; in other words claiming it as US territory. In "The Edge of the Knife", this prompts the USSR to demand the "internationalization" of their lunar base.[6] But that demand presumably also means internationalizing Luna as a whole. The Soviets would certainly protest against America's right to own the entire Moon, when they have only established a single base. Lunar annexation by the first to arrive is also seen in Piper's non-THFH tales. In "The Mercenaries", Suzanne Maillard mentions that "After the spaceship is built, and Luna is annexed to the Western Union..."[7]

The assumed sweeping nature of early extraterrestrial claims would parallel the New World historical model. For in the Treaties of Tordesillas (1494) and Zaragoza (1529), Spain and Portugal divided all newly discovered lands outside Europe into Spanish (western) and Portuguese (eastern) hemispheres.

But this dual partition of the Earth ignored the French, Dutch and English—among other Europeans—who soon began sending out their own expeditions, chartering companies (indeed, the French, Dutch and English all had East India Companies) and planting colonies in the Hispano-Portuguese zones. This claim-jumping included the Americas (which mostly 'belonged' to Spain), as well as the African coast, India and the East Indies (mainly 'Portuguese'). In a similar manner, early interplanetary explorers such as the United States and Great Britain may stake some pretty broad claims—such as whole moons, and possibly whole hemispheres on Mars and Venus—which are disputed by later-arriving spacefaring nations.

Over-broad extraterrestrial claims could therefore be a factor in the "colonial claims and counter-claims" mentioned by Piper in "The Future History".[8] For example, an American exploratory expedition could land on Ganymede and stake its claim to the moon, after which a "Ganymede Company" is organized and incorporated on Terra, and a ship sent to develop the Jovian satellite. Initially of course, this would be located in one small section of Ganymede (like the US base on Luna), and later expeditions by, say, the Chinese and Indians could land in other sections and assert their own claims to Ganymede. They're all member states in the Federation; share and share alike, right? Unless the Americans want to go to war to enforce their claim (an extreme step the Federation Government would undoubtedly oppose), they could only defend it through effective occupation; planting more bases and settlements in other parts of Ganymede. China and India would follow suit, and you might then end up with a fearful jigsaw, like a patchwork quilt. Especially if other major nations, like Britain, France and Japan, join in a 'scramble' for Ganymede. Similar situations could occur on the other moons of Jupiter, the Asteroid Belt (Ceres in particular), or planets like Mars and Venus—not to mention Titan and the Twilight Zone of Mercury, mentioned in *Four-Day Planet*.[9]

Thus, maps of all these celestial bodies could wind up resembling the map of Africa, after the famous 'Scramble' of the late Nineteenth Century divided it between the British, French, Germans, Spanish, Portuguese, Italians and Belgians. (Incidentally, territories ruled by Great Britain were exploited by royally-chartered entities like the British East Africa Company, British South Africa Company, Niger Company and the African Lakes Company.) Rivalries between five of these seven nations eventually led to the First World War, and "The Future History" informs us that rivalries among the nations with extraterrestrial colonies end up causing the Fourth World War.

From the First Federation and interplanetary age, we now turn to the Second Federation and the interstellar age.

3. Uniting Whole Planets

Unlike the deduced chartered companies of the First Federation, which were sponsored by individual nations, the chartered companies of the interstellar age are sponsored by the Second Federation—mainly because nation-states no longer exist. The interstellar companies control whole planets, like the Chartered Zarathustra Company in *Little Fuzzy*. This means they were probably instituted not long after the Second Federation is established. Why? Because ruling whole planets begins with Terra, which only becomes a "Completely unified world" after WWIV (AE 106-109).[10] The war destroys the entire Northern Hemisphere, thereby eliminating all the nations which sent out the original chartered companies. Several decades later (AE 174), the Venusian colonies unite their planet to oppose Federation rule. That appears to be the second planet to be completely unified; the independent but short-lived Republic of Venus later becoming the "Federation Member Republic of Venus".[11]

Furthermore, in "The Future History", we read "Wars of colonial pacification and consolidation; the new [Second] Terran Federation imposes system-wide pax."[12] 'Pacification' means that Venus (and any other extraterrestrial colony in rebellion) is defeated, while 'consolidation' seems to mean planetary unification. Although the Venusian colonies are unified by the Venusians themselves, I assume that the colonies on Mars are the first to be 'consolidated' by the Second Federation into the Member Republic of Mars. Consolidations would then follow on Mercury, Ceres, the Moons of Jupiter and Titan, though whether these newly-unified celestial bodies are self-sufficient enough to become Member Republics is questionable. (Planets, yes; moons and asteroids, no.)

Incidentally, this scenario suggests that after WWIV destroys all the Northern nations of Terra, their various extraterrestrial colonies are left in the patchwork quilt state by "the new civilization" in Southern Terra. During its Secession six decades later, Venus may be joined by some of these other colonies, meaning that after they are 'pacified' (defeated), the Second Federation decides to clean up the entire mess. All human-inhabited celestial bodies will henceforth be single political or commercial entities.

4. Population Pressure

According to Piper, WWIV causes the "Complete devastation of Northern Hemisphere of Terra."[13] In "When in the Course" (circa AE 250), "reclamation projects" are mentioned as being underway in North Terra,[14] but these are still not complete three centuries later. Because in *Uller Uprising* (AE 526), Carlos von Schlichten says that "much of it is wasteland to this day."[15] Since it takes a very long time to make the Northern Hemisphere of Terra habitable again, population pressure might again be a driving force. If we again assume rising birth rates in Southern Terra after WWIV (just as in North Terra after WWII and presumably

WWIII), the development of hyperdrive a few years after the Secession of Venus would be a godsend. In order to encourage economic growth to support an increasing number of people back home (possibly the Solar System as a whole this time, not just Terra), and promote emigration to lessen the burden, companies with broad powers are encouraged to find whole new worlds to colonize.

That would be a big incentive for people to invest; who wouldn't want to be 'king' of their own planet? It would also avoid the 'patchwork quilt' situation which I theorize occurred in the First Federation. Learning from past mistakes, the Second Federation has unified the celestial bodies in the Solar System, and now ordains that only one chartered company per planet will be allowed in the extrasolar systems. With rare exceptions like the Uller Company, which is forced to develop a second whole planet, Niflheim.[16]

5. "We Can Do Anything We Want"

The powers of these planetary companies appear to be near-absolute. For example, after the murders of Governor-General Sid Harrington and Lt. Governor Eric Blount, General von Schlichten appoints himself Governor-General of Uller; his authority to do so is pulled out of his holster.[17] The main reason appears to be distance. Von Schlichten says that "The Uller Company…is six and a half parsecs away" on Terra, which is six months travel-time one way.[18] Not only is it impossible for Terra to rule the extrasolar planets directly from that distance in space, it would take at least a year for a distress call to reach Terra and bring back reinforcements to Uller. The Terrans ruling Uller are on their own, and even though the general is forced to put down the Uprising with nuclear weapons, it is probable that his self-elevation to Governor-General will be ratified by the Company and the Federation.

The 'distance' element is repeated in *Little Fuzzy*, where Terra is again six months away, and the Chartered Zarathustra Company is headquartered on Terra. The CZC "owns" the planet Zarathustra and its moon Darius "outright", only omitting the other moon, Xerxes, due to the strategic needs of the Federation. Victor Grego, who runs the Company on Zarathustra, says that "Xerxes was the one thing about Zarathustra that the Company didn't own; the Terran Federation had retained that as a naval base. It was the one reminder that there was something bigger and more powerful than the Company."[19]

Just below the Federation Government are the Chartered Companies? That's pretty powerful! And in fact, the CZC has "a very liberal charter", with Grego stating that "*We can do anything we want* as long as we don't violate colonial law or the Federation Constitution." [20] "Anything" actually includes "genocide" (mass murder; similar to the nukes used on Uller), which Grego initially plans for the Fuzzies when their probable sapience threatens the company's charter, including its "import-export monopoly." [21] He has a year to make the problem disappear, before news of the discovery of the Fuzzies reaches Sol and an investigative team is sent to Zarathustra. "By the time Rainsford's report brings anyone here from Terra, we may have [the Fuzzies] all trapped out." [22]

Furthermore, since corporations aren't generally democratic, the chartered companies may be more powerful than regular colonies or Member Republics, which are democracies. Though the power of these planetary corporations probably decreases once a world has developed enough population and infrastructure to graduate into a Colony or Member Republic of the Federation. Victor Grego suggests this when discussing the results of losing the company's charter. "[A] Colonial Governor General would move in, with regular army troops and a complicated bureaucracy. Elections, and a representative parliament, and every Tom, Dick and Harry with a grudge against the Company would be trying to get laws passed—And, of course, a Native Affairs Commission, with its nose in everything." [23]

The chartered company system would therefore be the first stage; the 'spearhead' of extrasolar expansion, moving ever outward.

6. Claiming Whole Systems

I don't believe that there is any mention of the CZC exploiting other planets of the Zarathustran system. Thus, it appears to be the System States Alliance that takes this authority to the next level, in which each member State (human-inhabited planet) claims sovereignty over its whole system. Though the defeat of the Alliance makes this a short-lived policy (from AE 839 to 854), it seems to be the unofficial norm after the Federation dissolves. On Marduk, "nobody ever thinks about Abaddon for any reason,"[24] but Marduk's sovereignty over the outermost planet of its system is seemingly implied. Similarly, Lucas Trask is Prince of Tanith, but he sends ships to investigate the outer, uninhabitable planets in the system just in case Prince Viktor of Xochitl is hiding ships there, waiting to strike Tanith. [25] Trask's authority over his own system also seems to be vaguely suggested.

But the 'single-system state' concept seems to be officially adopted by the Galactic Empire. In "A Slave is a Slave", Prince Trevannion declares to the Adityans that "I think we'd better make the limits of your sovereignty the outer orbit of the system."[26] This may be standard practice, since under the Imperial Constitution, the Empire controls all hyperspace vessels.[27] Interstellar space (via the Dillingham drive) is therefore ruled by the Galactic Empire, while interplanetary space (via Abbot drive) is left to the individual planets.

Piper is not explicit about their shape on a star map, but I assume that any single system state—from those in the Alliance to the People's Commonwealth of Aditya—would be displayed in the shape of a disc; from the innermost to the outermost planetary orbit, along (and to a certain distance above and below) the system's Ecliptic. They could be spherical, centered on their respective stars, but unless there's an oblique planet in the system (like Pluto in ours), there would be little reason for, say, any Adityan interplanetary ship on Abbot drive to voyage too far from the Ecliptic. For one thing, it would take too long; Captain Rainer says that a normal-space vessel "would take almost a year" to go from Marduk to Abaddon.[28] And patrolling a huge spherical volume of sovereign space would probably require a huge fleet of ships, not to mention hyperdrive. Aditya has neither, although the System States presumably have both.

Speaking of the System States, Piper also includes chartered companies in *The Cosmic Computer*.

7. Chartered Companies in the Alpha Gartner System

If the 'disc shape' theory is correct—particularly for the system states of the Alliance—this would tie in the chartered companies on Poictesme. When Litchfield Exploration and Salvage takes over Force Command Duplicate, they stake a claim to the area, out to a radius of ten miles.[29] And when Koshchei Exploitation and Development takes over Port Carpenter, they file "the usual ten-mile radius" claim.[30] On maps, the claims by these and other companies would then be disc-shaped, separated by tens or hundreds of miles, similar to the deduced disc-shaped system states of the Alliance or the Empire, separated by tens or hundreds of light-years.

The newly-organized companies on Poictesme have to file an "application for charter" with the Planetary Government,[31] and register discoveries like Force Command to the Claims Office in Storisende.[32] I presume this procedure is very similar to how the Chartered Companies of the Second Federation acquire whole planets (with an 'Extrasolar Claims Office' on Terra), as well as how the postulated chartered companies of the First Federation acquire parts of moons and planets in the Solar System (presumably an 'Extraterrestrial Claims Office', also on Terra. Indeed, the ETCO may evolve into the ESCO.).

Incidentally, Rodney Maxwell says that "We can't claim exclusive rights to the whole planet [Koshchei], like the old interstellar exploration companies did before the War."[33] The reason why is not given, but probably because Koshchei is not a newly-discovered planet, being part of the Alpha Gartner system which was colonized several centuries previously. It has already been developed, although abandoned for the last forty years. Another possibility is that the Federation Government no longer provides 'very liberal charters' as was the case on Zarathustra. If so, the effect would be to discourage more expansion, contributing to the later decline and fall of the Terran Federation.

The Fourth World War is also called the First Interplanetary War, so combat probably occurs on Mars, Venus, etc. between the extraterrestrial companies/colonies of rival Terran powers. This aspect links them to the competition between some companies on Poictesme, which claim different parts of the planet, in at least one case resulting in serious combat. "One battle, between two regularly chartered prospecting companies, lasted three days, with an impressive casualty list."[34]

Another aspect of Poictesme parallels the Second Federation. At a meeting in Storisende, the leaders of all the major companies get together and decide to "partition the Alpha Gartner System."[35] The interplanetary chartered companies agree to concentrate on certain planets, and not stake counter-claims against each other.[36] That means Koshchei Exploitation & Development effectively gains a monopoly on the planet, and could then be called 'the Koshchei Company', rather like the chartered planetary companies of the Terran Federation. And in fact, the planet follows Federation practice, by quickly becoming "Koshchei Colony", with Luther Chen-Wong as chief executive.[37] One then wonders if Piper meant for Koshchei to later progress into a Member Republic in "the new (Poictesmean) Federation" envisioned by Conn Maxwell.

So assuming I'm analyzing Piper right, the process is gradual. From claiming whole moons (starting with the US and Luna) to uniting whole planets (Terra, Venus); then from owning whole planets (like Zarathustra under the CZC) to claiming sovereignty over entire systems (the short-lived SSA); and then theoretically controlling whole systems (Marduk, Tanith) to officially controlling them (Aditya).

ENDNOTES

1. H. Beam Piper, *Empire* (New York, NY: Ace Books, 1981), p. 55
2. John F. Carr, *H. Beam Piper: A Biography*, (Jefferson, North Carolina: McFarland & Company, 2008), p. 212
3. H. Beam Piper, *Space Viking* (New York, NY: Ace Books, 1963), p. 155
4. Piper, *Empire*, p. 54
5. Carr, *Piper Biography*, p. 212, emphasis added
6. Piper, *Empire*, p. 30
7. H. Beam Piper, *The Worlds of H. Beam Piper* (New York, NY: Ace Books, 1983), p. 54) Beam may have included a subtle connection between Suzanne Maillard and Paul Meillard, the main character in "Naudsonce". Their similar last names parallel a similar purpose. Suzanne is involved in a project to annex Luna to Terra (or part of Terra, anyway; the Western Union), while Paul is involved in annexing Svantovit to the Second Terran Federation.
8. Carr, *Piper Biography*, p. 212
9. H. Beam Piper, *Four-Day Planet/Lone Star Planet* (New York, NY: Ace Books, 1961), p. 31
10. Piper, *Empire*, p. 21
11. Piper, *Four-Day/Lone Star*, p. 7
12. Carr, *Piper Biography*, p. 213
13. Ibid., p. 212
14. H. Beam Piper, *Federation* (New York, NY: Ace Books, 1981), p. 213
15. H. Beam Piper, *Uller Uprising*, (New York, NY: Ace Books, 1983), p. 64
16. Ibid., p. 16
17. Piper, *Uller Uprising*, p. 99
18. Ibid.
19. H. Beam Piper, *Little Fuzzy* (New York, NY: Ace Books, 1962), p. 13
20. Ibid., p. 11, emphasis added
21. Ibid., pp. 45, 47
22. Ibid., p. 47
23. Ibid., p. 45
24. Piper, *Space Viking*, p. 220
25. Ibid., p. 200
26. Piper, *Empire*, p. 88
27. Ibid., p. 89
28. Piper, *Space Viking*, pp. 220-221
29. H. Beam Piper, *The Cosmic Computer* (New York, NY: Ace Books, 1983), p. 80
30. Ibid., p. 146
31. Ibid., p. 122
32. Ibid., p. 78
33. Ibid., pp. 145-146
34. Ibid., p. 85
35. Ibid., p. 190
36. Ibid., p. 194
37. Ibid., p. 245

In "The Sample," Jonathon Crocker explores the bureaucratic nightmare that has ensnared the inhabitants of the planet Baldur. We learn that while the Federation can be a tool for repression, it can also be a force for liberation from local tyranny and misrule.

THE SAMPLE

Jonathon Crocker

March 19, Year 396, A.E.

The speakers came to life again, echoing through the large chamber. "Number seven hundred twelve to desk K4! Number seven hundred twelve to desk K4!"

Mercedes sighed as she stood, gathered up her carryall and walked towards the 'K' row of desks as quickly as she could without running. Still, the officious voice had time to repeat twice before she got to the number four desk, and for a brief moment she wondered what would happen to her if she got lost. She walked past the first three desks, and stopped at the one with the large '4' on its front.

The desks were higher than the supplicants standing in front of them, of course, so the clerks could look down on the newcomers. She wondered what children travelling alone, or the really short, did to get papers all the way up to desk level.

It was at most thirty seconds from the time she had been first paged, but already the person sitting underneath the hat with the large 'Inspector' badge looked bored and impatient and unhappy.

"Name," he said, "and passport." His hand was out, and he was looking at his own paperwork, not her.

"Mercedes Lee," she replied, giving him the passport.

He opened the passport, and then frowned. "Which is your family name?"

"Lee is my family name," she said.

"Then why did you say it first?"

She paused. "I don't think I did."

"Humph. An attitude like that, miss, you might end up in official custody. No more games, please! What is your business on Baldur?"

She had been warned about this, so she'd practiced a few times during the last week of the trip. She passed him another stack of papers and forms.

"My name is Mercedes Lee, I have a doctorate in physics and a master's degree in engineering, copies of both degrees are there. There is a copy of a letter from the Chancellor of Engineering at the University of Paris-on-Baldur to my employer, Hyperspace Motivators Incorporated (also known as HMI), inviting me personally to a joint research project between HMI and the University. The next letter is from HMI attesting both to my employment, and that I am the best qualified for this project as per Baldur Industry Ministry Title 4 regulations. There is also a copy of Baldur Economic Directorate form 3062, stating that this project has been placed in the 'potential direct economic benefit to Baldur' category countersigned by the Administration Chancellor of the University. There is also a copy of form 199 for the Baldur Family Directorate stating that I will not be a burden on Baldur social services for the duration of my stay, which, as you can see in both the letter from the University and the attached form TRA-404 from the University, could be as long as two years. And a letter from HMI that shows my pay will continue while I am here."

She took a breath. "And this," she passed over more forms, "includes a copy of a letter from my bank, the Bank of New Christchurch, that I have a balance over 3000 sols, here is the form 88-36 from the Baldur Finance Ministry stating that the Baldur Consul at Melbourne approved my bank's separate letter of credit for deposit at the Academics Bank of Baldur. Oh, and here is a letter from the University with attached form TRA-A13, stating that I have accommodations lined up here on Baldur. You can see the letters have been notarized as per Baldur regulations." She still remembered the way the notary's eyes had lit up when she mentioned "a little paperwork for Baldur," it was like an early Christmas for the woman.

The Inspector paused, eyes sweeping over the array of papers.

"Directorate," he finally said.

She paused again. "Excuse me?" she finally said, having no idea what he meant.

He smiled grimly. "Earlier you called it the 'Industry Ministry,' that is incorrect. The proper name is the 'Industry Directorate,'" he said.

"Ah. Of course," she said. When he continued to stare at her, she added "My apologies." She hoped she sounded sincere.

The Inspector poured over the paperwork for quite some time, reading carefully, cross checking facts, looking important. He actually seemed unhappier now that he did not have something to complain about. After a while, her thoughts drifted, as she tried to tune out the people around her in their own bureaucratic interrogation sessions.

"And what is this?" he asked, pointing at something on the desk.

It took her a moment to read what he was pointing at, it being awkward to read official documents upside down, and almost at eye level.

"Oh, yes, it is a copy of my birth certificate, from the city of Christchurch in New Zealand on Terra."

"Why is it here?" he asked.

"I brought it because the Baldur Immigration Ministry wanted to see a copy in addition to my passport." Which was silly, she'd needed the one to get the other.

"No, why is it not attached to your passport, as requested in the Immigration circular 307 distributed on the ship?"

"Because the circular said that it was to be stapled to page three below the photo, but the passport has big letters that state "no other forms are to be attached to this passport" right below the photo on page 3 and I didn't want to put staple holes in the it."

The Inspector put on a sardonic smile. "Here, miss, you are subject to the laws of Baldur, not the whims of the Terran Federation." Sure enough, he had a stapler, a big one from a desk drawer, and now two official forms that were not supposed to have holes in them, did.

"Doctor," was all she said.

"I am not a doctor," he replied, "I am an Inspector for the Government of Baldur." You could hear the capital letters when he spoke.

"But I am. Not 'miss', I am 'Doctor Lee.' And I'll remember the laws here."

That earned her a stormy scowl, as he flipped open his inkpad and manfully plied his official stamp over many documents, before stacking them all as sloppily as possible in a lose pile and wordlessly returning some to her.

"Thank you," she said as she turned and followed the yellow arrow on the floor.

It took a few minutes to walk to the baggage area, then thirty more to wait for her case to appear on the luggage return belt, now sporting several official approval stickers. Inspector K4 had forgotten to give her the blue form that allowed her to reclaim her baggage, but a mere twenty minutes talking to the man under the "Supervising Inspector" headwear got her permission to leave the concourse with her own property again.

It took another ten minutes to make her way to the main entrance of the terminal.

"Doctor Lee!" Someone called and waived from beside the green pillar on the right, just as they had arranged. She made her way over.

"Doctor Beck! It is good to see you."

"And you. We can't really talk here; our car is just this way." He seemed to be in a bit of a hurry to get away.

"Is something wrong?" she asked.

"No. Well, yes, our parking is about to expire, I'd rather not pay more."

It took only a minute to get to the aircar, load it and pile in, with her taking the seat behind the driver. She started to say something but a sharp shake of Dr. Beck's head made her stop.

Finally they were up and away, and after a couple of "just one moment" hand gestures to her, Dr. Beck asked the driver, "So, how is traffic today?"

She thought that an odd question, this model aircar had plenty of windows through which to see traffic. Then she noticed the driver wasn't answering.

Then a soft chime sounded from the front of the car. "Okay, Doctor Beck, we are clear, light is green," the driver said.

"Thank Ghu. Doctor Lee, I would like to introduce one of my grad students, Gloria Heath."

The driver waved a hand. "Pleased to meet you, Doctor Lee. Sorry for the abruptness, we just needed to get clear of their monitoring field."

"Whose monitoring field?"

"There are a lot of them in public areas, sadly," said Doctor Beck. "They're run by the Ministry of Public Safety, but any business secrets that get discussed are quickly passed to the relevant Department or Ministry or Inspectorate. So the last thing we want are discussions of any, ah, trade secrets."

"What about complaints about the ancestry of people that thought Kafka was writing an instruction manual for government bureaucracy, who do those get forwarded to?" she asked rhetorically.

"Public Safety and a visit from the police, that's why we shushed you."

She was stunned. "For complaining about inefficiency?"

"They call it 'sedition'," Gloria said. "A fine of a thousand francs for a first offence, it goes up pretty quickly to jail time from there."

Lee paused. "And you're certain we're not being monitored here?" she asked. When they nodded, she exploded, "This is on a Member Republic of the Federation? That is insane!" They nodded again.

"Yes, it is," Beck said. "There's an election coming up in a couple of months, and they're running scared. Since President DuPaul took office, he's been busy growing the bureaucracy, putting up hurdles for people he doesn't want on the planet. Our only growth industries are ministries and inspectors. GDP is down, productivity is down. Our population should be about a million higher, but he's trying to set the planet up as his own private sandbox, and he doesn't want a lot of outside influence, so he keeps as many people out as he can. That's why all of our correspondence had to be paper copy, no audiovisual, it's easier for them to copy and check."

Lee paused. "I thought that seemed a bit odd. I did send a couple of my own audiovisuals as well as the paper copy, did you get them?"

"No," Beck said. "We did get notice from the Post Office that the envelope had broken open in transit, and they couldn't guarantee that all the contents were still inside, but if we wanted to submit an itemized list, anything found matching that description would be forwarded on to us."

Lee shook her head. "Why isn't there a travel advisory on this planet? How can they let him get away with this?"

Beck shrugged. "There's a lot of high-level politics going on between here and Terra. We don't know the whole story yet, but everyone is waiting to see how the elections turn out."

"You mean they're not going to be rigged? Isn't that a safe conclusion?"

"Everyone hopes not. Turnout is expected to be high."

"I can imagine. I'll bet the graveyards vote, too."

"We're on final approach," Gloria said. She took the aircar over a small landing stage, touched it down perfectly, and quickly shut down all the car systems.

Lee took a chance to look around the campus before they got into the lift. "I'm sorry for being so fixated on that, but I have to admit, I was thrown for a loop. I should have been asking about the project. I'm actually looking forward to finding out more about it; everything up until now has been top secret."

Beck and Gloria exchanged a look. "It's just as well we didn't discuss the project much. We're heading right to the lab now," Beck said. "Normally we'd give you a day touring scenic Baldur, especially after a long trip like yours, but time is pressing, I'm sorry to say. We've been trying to get you here for years; we really need your help. And not to be rude, but we were hoping for a team of six, as we requested in our letters."

"No offence taken—if half of what you're hinting at is true, a team of six would be hard pressed to manage." She took a few steps toward the lift, and then paused.

"I would like to take a moment," Lee told them.

"Of course, go right ahead," Beck said.

Lee looked around the campus, a series of low buildings in the middle of parkland at one edge of the city, set apart from the larger towers of the city. Normally she'd have used the term "greenspace" but there were mostly native trees that were reddish. Combined with the light from Baldur's primary, which was a bit more orange and slightly dimmer than Terra's, the effect was of an autumn afternoon, even though it was closer to noon in mid-summer.

They got in the lift. "The other five couldn't get clearance from the Baldur Consulate. We're still trying, but every time they deny someone, the paperwork starts over." The doors closed, and the lift started descending.

"Are we secure now?" Lee asked. "Some hints at what I'll be spending the next year or two working on would be most appreciated."

"A few years ago, an expedition from the university found something interesting. It took us a while to appreciate how interesting. With your work at Hyperspace Motivators, you'll be in a position to judge this better than we can. So we'll take you to it, but we'll leave the description at that, so you can come at it without preconceptions. Is that acceptable, Doctor?"

"All right." It came out sounding guarded, even to her ears. "I've got to say, you folks on Baldur really know how to throw a doc a party, after six months on a ship in hyperspace. I hope it's worth it."

"Don't worry," Gloria said with a smile. "It sounds ominous, but it should all be clear in a little while."

The lift doors opened, and there was a small open car waiting for them, of the type used on golf courses. The three of them got on and drove down a tunnel.

This time Beck was driving and Gloria was beside Lee. "Please understand, Doctor Beck can be a little dramatic, but with the political… climate these days, I think it's deserved. We landed across campus from the lab, right now we're going through some of the maintenance tunnels so we can't be picked up by any observers."

Lee nodded. Silence seemed the best option to her, right now.

It was another fifteen minutes before they came to a large door labelled "Auxiliary Sewage Control." Doctor Beck took a key off his belt, unlocked the door and opened it, let them in, and locked it behind them. Lee made certain to note that it had the 'crash bar' style exit handle that let someone out of a locked door.

A short hallway and two ninety-degree turns later, there was a larger anteroom with storage closets along one wall, a large unmarked door on the other, and two locks on walls either side to the door, placed far enough apart that one person would be unable to use both at the same time. Beck and Gloria both took keys from around their necks, and went to opposite walls. Without a word, Beck nodded to Gloria, they turned keys simultaneously, and a light over the doorknob went from red to green with a click. Beck opened the door, and let them in.

Whatever it was she was expecting, it wasn't this: a bright room that could have been a well-equipped lab at a university anywhere in the Terran Federation. This one had a heavy-duty workbench in the middle of the room with some strange equipment on it, shelves and storage closets around the edge of the room, and magnifiers and circuit testers and wrenches and drivers and other useful tools on the shelves.

"This is The Sample," Doctor Beck said. "As I've indicated, I want you to have a fresh opinion of it when you look at it. We'll tell you more later, but we are very interested in your opinion. Now," he said as he crossed the room to one shelf, picked up a meter and switched it on, "as you can see from this Geiger counter there is no radiation above background, there's an atmosphere tester on that bench if you want a look, but The Sample is pretty stable. So please have a look at it, don't worry about your safety for any reason. Gloria will stay here with you, if you have questions about the materials it's made of she can show you the testing reports.

"There's a bathroom around the corner if you need one, Gloria can let you back in here. When we had this lab remodeled, we put in monitors to see if The Sample was going to do anything toxic, or explode. It's been quietly inert ever since, and we're not afraid of explosions any more, but the monitors are still there and local law says I must advise you of this.

"I have to report your arrival to the Chancellor of Engineering, I'll be back in about an hour to pick you up. The Chancellor is taking us to dinner in the Faculty Club, they have an excellent chef. See you then, Mercedes!" Then he turned, and walked out, the door buzzing itself locked when it closed.

Slowly, Lee turned from where she had been staring at the closed door, to look at Gloria. Gloria smiled helpfully.

"So, do I need gloves and safety goggles to handle "The Sample" or is contamination not a concern?" Lee asked.

"If you want them, they're right over here," Gloria said. "Gloves are a good idea, it is a little grungy, and it's hard to get your hands clean afterward."

Doctor Lee took a look at The Sample. The main body was a piece of metal, about a yard long and half that wide, concave, with a bunch of odd-looking bulky electronics along the inside face. The overall effect was as if someone had ripped out about a quarter of a thick metal drum and thrown it on the table.

"Doctor Beck said that you had results on the materials?"

"Yes," Gloria said, reaching over to a rack to pull a clipboard out. "Right here."

"Great." Doctor Lee put her blonde hair in a ponytail, up out of the way. She picked up gloves, and said, "Let's see if I can earn my pay."

A group of people were waiting at a table in the Faculty Club, which was trying very hard to look like one of the famous clubs of London, or perhaps New York, with wood panels and cozy lighting. There was a distinguished looking gentleman with white hair that was probably the Chancellor, a lady in her mid-thirties who looked like she thought running mere marathons was for wimps, and another lady who looked as equally distinguished as the gentleman, but with only a touch of grey at the temples. Doctor Beck led them over, and was obviously about to start introductions when he was beaten to the punch by the distinguished gentleman.

"Ah, Doctor Lee!" he said. "Welcome. Well, what do you think of the project?" He beamed, obviously waiting for her enthusiasm.

"Doctor Lee, may I introduce Chancellor MacLeod, head of the engineering department," Beck said. "Actually, Chancellor, we did discuss this. I've told her nothing so far, so she can approach it tabula rasa."

"What!" The Chancellor seemed shocked, and Lee liked him better already. "Oh, no, have you been paraded around down there on that little golf cart for 'security reasons?' All those keys? Oh my. Doctor Lee," he said, "you have my abject apologies. But let me introduce Detective Maria Napolitano, with the University Security department, and this is Doctor Bondar, Assistant Chancellor for Engineering. We are all going to be seeing a lot of each other on this project, so I thought it only fitting that we should take this chance to get to know each other a little better."

Everyone appeared pleased to meet Doctor Lee, and they all sat. They all looked at her, waiting expectantly. There was a glass of wine in front of her, so she had a sip, and it was very good. Part of her wanted to gulp it—it wasn't every day one had one's worldview upended—but that wouldn't be professional.

"Once or twice today," Doctor Lee began slowly, "I was told to hold my opinion until later. Is that the case now? Or can we speak freely?" She gestured around the Faculty Club with her wineglass.

The Chancellor looked at Napolitano, who nodded. "Yes," he answered, "our security sweep showed no monitors of any sort. As long as you keep your voice down, we can speak with complete candor."

Lee nodded. "First, I'll give you a bit of my background, to lay out my qualifications. In my work at Hyperspace Motivators Incorporated, I have been involved in research, design, manufacture, and accident analysis of Dillingham drives for over fifteen years. I am very familiar with all of the types of drives produced by my company, and almost as familiar with the ones built by our main competitor, Drax Power Systems. Those two companies account for around ninety eight percent of the hyperdrives built in the Terran Federation—which is to say, in known space.

"The rest are small companies doing custom ship orders, heavy on the chrome, for people that usually have more money than sense. It would be poor salesmanship to admit this in front of a potential customer, but the HMI and Drax models are very comparable. Ours cut travel time through hyperspace by a few percent, a fact which our sales people brag about to no end, but since ships almost always get delayed in normal space anyway through normal port operations, it's almost an academic distinction.

"The Keene-Gonzales-Dillingham drive was first available in the year 183, which was 213 years ago. The patents have long expired, and pretty much anyone can get a copy of the plans for a nominal fee. Therefore all hyperdrives are extremely similar except for a few small proprietary subsystems and cosmetic differences.

"So I should be able to look at pretty much any hyperdrive engine built in the last century, and even without reference to the standard markings that are required to be on the housing by law, I should be able to tell you what company built it, and roughly when." She paused for effect, taking a sip of wine.

"I have never seen a hyperdrive of the design I was just shown before today."

A waiter came to take their order. She selected roast beef and vegetables.

Once he was gone, she continued. "To start with, yes, I am certain that it is a fragment from a hyperdrive engine; there were three gadolinium cells, so there isn't much else it could be.

"There are seven technical aspects and one legal aspect that lead me to conclude that 'The Sample' was not made in the Federation. The legal part I've mentioned—all hyperdrives are required by law to have a serial etched into the housing multiple times so that in case of a disaster, when only part of a unit is recovered, the investigators don't have to waste time figuring out where it came from. A section that size should have five or six complete serial numbers on it, but there are none.

"As for the technical aspects, here's the executive summary: It has a titanium case, which no one uses. It has silver power cabling, and while silver is a better conductor than the copper we use, it is much more expensive, so no one uses it. The gadolinium cells are very close to the industry standard design, but in these the metal is alloyed with tantalum and lanthanum—everyone uses pure gadolinium. It has a rubidium atomic clock, a small one the size of a credit card, when standard silicon microchip timing circuits are used by every manufacturer I've ever heard of.

"Next, the electronics. There is a forest of diodes and transistors, made of germanium, and the resistors seem to be carbon powder construction. Germanium is used in newer electronics, but in the form of pathways on germanium–silicon compound microchips, down in the ten-thousand-per-human-hair range. These are big things the size of a grain of rice, gigantic in comparison. As far as I know, germanium diodes have specialized uses commercially, but shipboard electronics isn't one of them. And carbon powder resistors, again, have specialized uses, but most everyone uses the newer disk method when they're needed—most of the time, resistors are just carbon stampings on integrated circuits, but there isn't a single integrated circuit in The Sample, and there really should be—or housings where the chips or their boards have been knocked out, there aren't any of those either.

"Point six, the hardware isn't standard. The screws and brackets and mountings are all just a little off, not quite imperial measure, not even metric. Some of the nuts have six faces, the larger sized ones have seven. And the screws aren't designed for a Phillips-head screwdriver, or a Roberts-head, or even a flat blade. They're built for a screwdriver that has an oval head.

"But here's the big one, technical point seven. There are dozens of things in there that are circular, about three inches in diameter, and about a sixteenth of an inch thick. A few have damage on the outer casing, so we can see they have three layers inside, and that those three layers are incredibly thin. The outer two are silver, which is used in The Sample instead of copper, fair enough. But the middle layer is collapsium—either solid collapsium or collapsium plated something, I don't know yet."

"Three layers arranged like that sound like a capacitor," Gloria said.

"Exactly," Lee replied. "But no one in Federation space has come up with a collapsium dielectric yet, unless this is a recent breakthrough when I was on the way from Terra." A few people shook their head negatively.

Lee was surprised when Napolitano was the first to speak. "Dialectic? I thought that was a political term?"

Lee thought for a moment. "Oh, yes. It is, but an archaic one, I thought. No, in a capacitor, there are three layers. The outer two are good conductors, the one in the middle is not. The middle layer is called 'di-electric.'"

The Chancellor nodded. "Yes, the political term has come up a great deal of late, as the election approaches. Supposedly used by enemies of the state, which has caused a lot of careful enunciation and clarification in the introductory classes for physics and electrical engineering this academic year. But, Doctor Lee, we concur with your analysis; we reached it ourselves after a week of heated discussion, so we are impressed that you came up with the same conclusion after only an hour. What we do need to know, however: Is this a sample of a drive that could be in the next generation of hyperdrives, but with some advances beyond the current standard?"

"I don't see how," she said at once. "The capacitors are a completely unique materials combination, and that could be a real find. But the diodes and the rest are very much 'old school' compared to a standard chipset. Those circuits are tens of thousands of times larger than the integrated variety, and I don't see how that helps anyone at this point. Not to mention the resulting circuit architecture is so huge, you really do need an atomic clock to keep the thing running in synch.

"While you might be able to explain away two or maybe even three features as 'different for the sake of being different', taken as a whole, there is no way that it could be a commercial product."

"For the sake of argument, what about a hobbyist?" Doctor Bondar asked. "Someone like those 'sail-around-the-world-alone' enthusiasts that we hear Terra has so many of? If anyone can get plans, could they tweak it to their own design?"

"That is one hell of a rich hobbyist," Lee said. "No chipset, so custom germanium diodes? None of the industry-standard markings on anything? Collapsium capacitors? Even the smallest collapsium-plating setup runs around a million, and the power requirements are immense. It has to be a mid-size company at the very least— even the small custom houses building yachts for the more money than sense crowd don't do their own collapsium work, they order hull plates from the same suppliers the big shipyards use.

"Since every ship that wants to qualify for ships' papers must pass an inspection, the lack of that serial etched into the casing dozens of times would be an automatic fail, with a mandatory fine and re-inspection in 90 days to ensure compliance with the Federation Safety in Celestial Navigation Act of the year 183, Atomic Era."

"Oh, and I almost forgot. That thing has been sitting outside somewhere, and for a long time. There are tiny bits of fine dust in it, even the titanium is showing its age, and you would not believe the tarnish on the silver. Some of the smaller connections are just gone. I would say it is a few hundred years old at the very least."

The Chancellor said, "One piece of information that no one besides myself, and the geology professor that recovered The Sample has known about until now, is the age of the rock formation where it was found. Doctor Lee is quite right, it has been there a while. On the order of nine hundred years, plus or minus three hundred."

Doctor Bondar gave the Chancellor a dirty look. "And you complain about theatrics, Arthur? I've never known someone to play cards as close to the vest as you."

The Chancellor seemed to take it as a compliment. "But back to those capacitors for a moment. Gloria, I know you did all of the materials work. What are the middle sections made of?"

"We're not certain yet. The first scans were inconclusive and gave conflicting results. We've working on a full series of tests now."

"How do you think it got here?" Maria asked.

"That is an excellent question," Lee said. "Was anything else found with it?"

The Chancellor shook his head. "No. When it was found, the rock and gravel were cleaned out as carefully as possible, and brought into the lab as you see it. There were no other parts with it."

"It must have come from off-planet," Beck said. "Any society that built that thing here would have carved up the surface of this planet pretty thoroughly, and we'd have found their ruined cities the moment the first explorers hit orbit."

They paused for a moment as the food arrived. Lee looked at her plate, with roast beef, green and starch vegetable, and something like a stuffed apple on the side. She took a bite, then a moment to savor it.

"This is the best meal I have had in many light-years," she said to the waiter. "Possibly the best meal ever. My heartfelt compliments to the chef." The man smiled, and asked if there was anything else. When there wasn't, he gracefully withdrew.

"It wouldn't hurt to go over the crash site again," Lee said. "You probably weren't looking for three-inch sections of collapsium the first time."

"Very true," the Chancellor said. "I shall have to have some discussions with some geologists soon, I see. It was checked for anything more mundane, but I doubt they were looking for that."

"After six hundred to twelve hundred years, if the rest of it landed in a river, say, there wouldn't be much else left. Possibly an elevated titanium level in the local soil, but even that might have washed away by now."

"Wait a moment," Napolitano said. "Aren't the hyperdrives right at the core of a ship? Shouldn't there be piles of wreckage lying around where this was?"

"There were some early starship designs that had the engines outside the core of the ship, some were out on the ends of wings," Gloria said. "The laws of physics don't make spheres mandatory, we've just found them the best way for a number of reasons."

"Were there any signs of atmospheric entry on The Sample?" Napolitano asked.

"No. Unless we find a copy of the accident report carved in granite somewhere, we'll probably never know exactly what happened. For all we know, the alien version of the transportation safety board policed up everything else."

"Very well. What next, Doctor Lee?" the Chancellor asked.

"Tomorrow, I'll try to trace any of the circuitry between the electronics, see if I can nail down what the circuits were for. I'll have to wait for the new report on the collapsium, see if we can figure out its composition, and if it's just collapsium plating over a mundane core or if it is a solid piece. If you can arrange it, another sweep of the recovery site might be in order, there could be more of the collapsium plates that were missed on the first go. But first?" Lee paused.

"Yes?" the Chancellor asked.

"I am going to enjoy this food, it really is incredible."

The next few days passed in a blur. Lee got settled into her apartment on the University campus, almost a long-term hotel, but a businesslike one. She ran errands to the nearby Academics Bank, and to a grocery store a block away from the students' residences. At one point she looked into what it would take to get her Balduri aircar license and rent a vehicle, but the copious regulations the Citizen's Licensing Ministry (Temporary Offworld Visiting Sophonts Department) had brought into play, and the quite good public transit on and near campus, made her decide to buy transit tokens instead.

Maria Napolitano stopped by for another quick sweep of the premises, and let her know that she'd be visiting weekly. She gave Lee a few quick security tips, a few legal ones, and Lee took the time to ask a few questions about the city.

Most of her days were spent in the lab. Gloria handled the materials research, and between them they worked on deciphering the circuits. The wiring in the circuits was too far gone physically to say with absolute certainty what the circuits did, but the general layout conformed to the usual suspects—power regulation, timing and control. The only unusual thing about them seemed to be the total lack of integrated circuits of any kind.

Six days after her arrival, Doctor Lee thought it was a good time for her to take a break. She and Gloria decided that since it was Friday after many ten-hour days, it was only fair that they go for lunch at a place downtown, and then take in a museum or a park. They locked up the lab just after eleven and were on the transit airbus fifteen minutes later, sitting and chatting and watching the city outside the window.

"For your first day outside, it's too bad it's so cool and breezy," Gloria said. They were both wearing light jackets against the breeze, and it looked like it might rain.

"I do have another stop I want to make," Lee warned Gloria. "I tried to get information out of the Tourism Ministry for Greater Baldur. All I got were lists of forms they wanted me to fill out, so I want to stop by the Federation Building since we're downtown, maybe get some information on some good sights to see while I'm here."

"Oh," Gloria said. "You need a form to get access to the building. They can't block the entrance, or anything like that," she added, "but a couple of years ago they walled off the plaza in front of it, and put a checkpoint there. Without a 'day pass' you probably won't be able to get past it."

"We're in luck. I found out about that last night, and printed up a couple." Lee patted her coat pocket. "I brought a couple of spares, if you want to come along."

"Why, thank you! It's all offices around there, I may as well go in with you. I can always try to get some newspapers from home."

"Oh, you're not from Baldur?" Did Lee imagine it, or did several people's heads turn slightly?

"No, from Gimli, it's the next world out. It's a nice place, but not much besides a couple million people, mines, and the Navy base. Baldur's got a much better University. In a couple years I should be able to go home and get a top-rate job. Or start a business fabricating spares for mine equipment, or the Navy."

"You're a grad student, how much longer do you have until your doctorate?" Lee asked.

"Oh, any day now, I just need to set a date to defend my dissertation. This project has been keeping me busy."

"Even with this, you shouldn't wait," Lee said. "There's always going to be something there to eat your time. And once you're a doctor, they have to pay you better."

"True enough," Gloria said. "I just hope—"

They were interrupted by a sudden loud noise from outside, and yells from the front of the airbus. There were too many people standing, holding handrails, to see what the yelling was about, but it was several voices.

Lee reached in a pocket and got a recorder out, switched it on, and quickly said the date, time, and location, "public airbus on route 260 downtown."

The disturbance rippled back quickly through the airbus. It was so crowded it took a moment to realize that it wasn't a fight; it was reaction to something outside, people were pointing out the windows on the same side of the bus that they were on, but as they passed buildings, the view was interrupted. Then they were clear again.

"Good Ghu!" someone said. It might even have been her.

"The demonstration!" someone else said.

Lee turned to Gloria. "What demonstration?" she asked.

Gloria was ashen-faced. "Some of the student groups from the University, colleges, and some other groups, they called it a 'peaceful pro-democracy rally' but—"

In the large public square in front of the Capital Building, there had been a large demonstration that had just been broken up, and a cordon of zebra-striped aircars with police strobes flashing. But there were other cars, dark green combat cars, and as she watched and recorded another one made that loud noise again.

Miniguns have a distinctive noise, it is true, but Lee hadn't expected to hear it in the heart of downtown Paris-on-Baldur, which is why she hadn't recognized it at first. There was no mistaking the muzzle flashes, or the tracers, or the people wiped out when the bullets impacted.

Then a building got in the way of the view.

There was a moment of very profound silence on the bus, before it was broken by several quiet sobs and whimpers. Then the 'next stop' chime rang about a dozen times in quick succession, as people hit the stop-request button, and the bus slowed and turned for the next stop.

Lee frantically pulled a paper map of the city out of her pocket, checked their current location against the stops she had marked. "It's too soon," she muttered.

"What?" Gloria asked, still shaken.

"If they expand the cordon, we could get caught up in it if we get out here," Lee said quietly and urgently. "Wait for the next stop, we'll be clear."

Most people weren't waiting, as soon as it came to a stop at a landing stage on the tenth floor, there was a general exodus of almost everyone. Some were starting to panic.

Lee expected the airbus to pull off instantly, instead about a dozen people got on, some of them plainly bemused by the behavior of some of the departing passengers.

"Good, this is good for us, these people haven't heard. So we have a chance to mingle with the crowds at the next stop." Gloria nodded weakly.

Still, it was a long three minutes until the next stop, at the Munin Building. A few people got off with them, and Lee looked around for the way to ground level.

They made good time to the checkpoint outside the Federation Building where there were only a pair of policemen and their parked aircar. Baldur officialdom's natural habitat seemed to be under hats with large badges, she thought, it wasn't just at the starport. Best of all, they seemed fairly relaxed and the car's strobes were off, not what you'd expect if martial law had just been declared. She approached with a smile and a "Hello, I'd like to get to the Federation Building, please," and her printed passes in her extended hand. The checkpoint itself consisted of waist-high concrete barricades with a gap a yard wide, and a yellow line painted across the gap.

The younger officer took the passes, and actually looked pleasant. "State your business, please."

"I'm on Baldur for business, and I'm hoping to visit the tourist desk here."

"You should really go to the Tourist Bureau," the other officer said. "They'd have everything you'd want to see."

"I'm sure they do, but I haven't had a chance to do all the paperwork yet, and I was hoping to see something this weekend. Do you know, are the museums downtown open weekends?"

"Yes, the main ones are—" the younger officer began.

"But if you contact them directly," the other finished for him, with a pointed look at his partner, "they can give you the hours. But sure, step right through. And when you get the paperwork done for the Tourist Bureau, they'll have more information for you than these—wait, why is your friend crying?"

The officer seemed more alert now.

"Oh. Well, she just had a big fight with her boyfriend. And she was feeling really down, so I thought it might do her some good to get her out and about for a bit. We'll go have lunch after this; I hope that will cheer her up."

"I'm sorry to hear that," the younger officer said. "You must be feeling bad if a trip to the Federation Building will cheer you up."

Gloria managed a weak smile at that. The older officer regarded them both for a moment, and waived them though.

They made it inside the lobby before Gloria started sobbing openly.

It was about forty minutes before they came out again, and by then, the original two officers had been joined by several more police cars. At least six officers were standing around, and the cars all had their strobe lights on, sweeping the bare plaza in red and blue light.

Lee saw the younger officer from earlier answering questions of a much older man with a much larger badge on his hat. The young officer did a double take when he saw the two of them, and Lee heard him tell his superior, "That's them, right now."

The older man turned, and Lee was able to read "Detective Inspector" on his badge. "Stop there, now," he said after they had crossed the yellow line pained on the pavement. "What was your business in that building?"

"Like we told the police officers on the way in, I'm on Baldur for business, and wanted to see some of the sights this weekend. I didn't have a chance to do the paperwork for the Baldur Tourist Board, so I came here. Is there a problem?"

"I'll ask the questions. So why did it take almost an hour for you to get tourist information?"

"Was it that long?" Lee made a show of checking her watch. "By the time you find the right desk on the right floor, it's fifteen minutes already. Asking about what to see, finding out what's close to the transit line, coming back out, it all takes time. Then my friend is from Gimli, they had some Gimli style puffed-rice pudding at the cafeteria, we stopped for that."

The Inspector gave them a hard stare. "What tourist information did you get?"

Lee pulled some papers and pamphlets from her jacket pocket. "They gave me some brochures to look through; do you want to see them? We were going to go to the Baldur Natural History Museum and have a look; they said that it had a nice gift shop."

The Inspector turned to Gloria. "What brand of pudding was it?"

Gloria reached in a pocket, and pulled out a folded up label. "Valhalla," she said, showing him the label. "I'm a student from Gimli, it's hard to find here. I was going to try to see if anyone carries it or maybe special order some."

The Inspector looked them over, and seemed to decide something. "Very well. I am sorry to say that you will have to cut the day short, there was an industrial accident not far from here and large areas of downtown are being evacuated as a precaution. Please make your way home now." Then he left.

The original young officer guided them through the vehicles blocking access to the square. "You said you were a student? Are you at the University?" When Gloria nodded, he added, "The main line to campus has been diverted, it was near the accident site. You can still catch it at the Munin Building, it's that way, two blocks."

"Thank you," Lee said to him, as he nodded and went back to his post.

The two of them were silent all the way back. Already there was a heavy police presence on campus, but no checkpoints had been set up. They stopped at the grocery store and picked up a few things, then went to Gloria's room in the post-grad dorms.

Gloria collapsed in a chair and stared blankly out the window. Lee made a few calls to check in with Beck and Napolitano. Beck acted surprised that they were checking in on a Friday afternoon, so he probably hadn't heard. Napolitano tried to keep the conversation light, but seemed relieved that they were safe, so she probably had heard. By that time, the news channels were announcing a 'safety curfew' for the unnamed industrial accident downtown, and were asking people to stay in their homes for the weekend. It was effectively martial law.

Lee switched off the news, and turned to Gloria. "Is there anyone else you want to call, or to check on?"

Gloria shook her head dully. She stood suddenly and went to a shelf, and pulled down a book. Behind it was a small device that she switched on.

"It isn't safe to use this for long," she said. "My…friend made it, a Ph.D. candidate in electrical engineering. He's from Baldur; he was at the demonstration today. I was planning on going, but I got wrapped up in the work and lost track of time. We went past his room on the way here—he's not back."

"I'm sorry." There wasn't much more she could say.

"You left me in the cafeteria for a while," Gloria said. "What were you doing?"

"I really was getting tourist info," she said. "But I also gave them a copy of my recording. I'd been told to carry a personal recorder in case of problems with traffic cops, I certainly wasn't expecting that."

Gloria nodded. "What will they do with it?"

"Probably nothing yet, if they start something now, it would just cause more rioting and more massacres. But you can bet it will go to Terra and the Navy as soon as possible. They'll probably get a few more recordings together, but we were the first people to walk in with one."

"I thought we were dead at that checkpoint. How did you bluff them so well?"

Lee smiled. "If you believe my grandmother, there was an ancestor back in the First Century that was a famous actor. But once you make doctor, you'll have to say all kinds of impossible things at faculty staff meetings. Industry's the same way; you'll have plenty of practice soon enough."

Gloria thought for a moment. "Our project. What sort of improvements do you think we'll get out of it?"

"It's too soon to say for certain. Lately the main technical limitation has been hyperdrive field density—the denser the field the hyperdrives can maintain, the quicker the journey. There are a few approaches to that, but the industry has hit technical roadblocks at each one; a field strong enough to drive the ship faster keeps burning out big sections of the drive electronics. Drax is farther behind than we are, thank Ghu.

"But no one on Terra has tried collapsium capacitors. It might be a critical breakthrough. It might be chrome for the rich, as useful as fuzzy dice hanging on the bridge. But we'll start looking at that on Monday."

"How about we start tomorrow? No, I need a day. Sunday. Can we start Sunday?" Gloria asked.

"Of course." Lee reached out and switched the device off. "I picked up some ice cream for later. Or honey-rum, your choice. But first, you're going to have some genuine Kiwi Lasagna."

"What is that?" Gloria asked.

"Frozen lasagna heated up by someone born in New Zealand. I picked up extra cheese, and a green salad. Well, it's local, so it's more red than green. We'll need a couple of bowls for the salad, and where is your cooker?"

* * * * *

A couple of hours later they were both surprised by a knock at the door. Gloria paused the movie and walked to the peephole. "It's the Chancellor!" she said as she opened it.

"Ah, it is good to see you, Gloria," said the Chancellor. "May we come in?" He and Napolitano entered, closed the door and Napolitano set a small device on a shelf and switched it on. Lee decided that she was going to have to get one too.

"I hear that you both were far too close to a very unfortunate event, and I am glad that you are both safe," he said. "Normally, of course, your business is your own, but since it might involve the University, I have to ask if you were on your way to join the demonstration."

"No, I hadn't heard of it," Lee said. "We had been putting in ten hour days, and we broke for lunch and were going to see the sights downtown. It's just bad luck this was the day the regime decided to start shooting its own citizens."

The Chancellor nodded, but Napolitano spoke. "We've already had calls from security services about you," she said. "Did you really go to the Federation Building?"

"Yes," Lee said. "I printed up the 'day passes' last night. I wasn't going to spend six hours filling out Tourist Ministry paperwork, and they have a tourism section there. But then we saw part of the massacre, and I happened to have a recorder going and got some footage of it. The building was only a few blocks away, so we went straight there to deliver it to Federation security."

"That was brave. It might make it hard on you, though," Napolitano said.

"We had to get the word out. They can't be allowed to shoot people at will."

"Doctor Lee, I certainly agree with you, but our options at this point are limited," the Chancellor said. "Any further demonstrations would only serve to get people killed."

"True, but you don't have to riot, just show that you're not going to buckle under. Have they admitted to the shootings?"

"No, it was a tragic unspecified 'industrial accident' and there is nothing else available at this time," the Chancellor said. "We don't know how many were killed."

Lee thought for a moment. "Well, I know universities don't normally do this, but you could take attendance at classes next week. Try to reach those students not in class, see if you can confirm numbers at least."

"You know," the Chancellor said, "that is a good idea. It is both practical, and certainly not overstepping our authority in any way. Yes, I shall so order it in my department, and I shall make a few calls to the other Chancellors." He nodded at Napolitano, who turned off the device on the shelf and pocketed it. "I am sorry to have interrupted your well-earned break this afternoon," he said, "and I know how hard you two have been working. If you need a few days off to recover, that would be fine."

"Actually Chancellor," Gloria said, "we're quite eager to go to work. Tomorrow afternoon I'll be back at the lab."

"Outstanding. In that case, we'll have a small committee meeting on Wednesday afternoon; say two, in my office. It will be informal, just to give everyone a chance to keep tabs on the project. We shall see you then."

By Wednesday, they had a good idea of the technical specification of the collapsium capacitors. The silver plates sandwiched a layer of collapsed perovskite, a mineral that oddly enough had been used in uncollapsed form back in some of the early capacitors on Terra, back in the first century pre-atomic, when science was learning to tame electrons for its own uses.

To complicate matters, the university didn't have its own collapsium plant; like everyone else, when they needed something plated, they ordered it from the shipyard supplier. Not that they ever needed very much. And a shipyard supplier would be set up to make collapsium armor for ships—plates of high-quality steel to be skinned with shimmering collapsium and placed around the spaceframe of a ship. Since an average hypership was a globe about a thousand or even fifteen hundred feet in diameter, the plates were huge, measuring hundreds of feet by dozens of feet. Placing a special order for round plates three inches in diameter, based on a mineral and not steel, would attract far too much attention.

"So we'll have to build our own plating workshop," Doctor Lee said in the meeting the next day. It was the same six people that had met for dinner that first night.

"It could be very expensive," Doctor Bondar said dubiously.

"Yes, but not as bad as you think. We'd need a setup that could produce collapsium on an area of about 7 or 8 square inches, not the,"—she paused while she worked some numbers on a piece of paper—"over one point three million square inches of a regular shipyard plant. I haven't costed it out, I admit, but HMI has some of its own money sitting in a bank not far from here. I'm sure someone can come up with a reasonable university program that this equipment would be a reasonable expenditure for, and HMI can be seen to contribute to it. Nice and aboveboard, and when no one is looking, we make a test batch of plates for the collapsium capacitors."

"Perhaps," the Chancellor said. "But what about the ones you have now?"

"You mean, from The Sample? They're a thousand years old, the silver is badly degraded."

"True, but we have some silver in the metallurgy lab that you can use, and that's easy enough to obtain. Can you strip down a few of the original collapsium plates, use them to build a small batch of test units? If that yields promising results, we could proceed with this plating workshop of yours. It would give us time to get the cover story right, and to be seen working on it for the next academic year."

Lee pondered for a while. "I don't see why not. There are fifty-seven capacitors in The Sample. Say we rebuilt five in silver, five in copper. That would give us a better idea of what they could do. We might need a little midnight requisitioning on some of the labs on campus, but given, say, two weeks we should have some solid information."

"Excellent. When can you start?"

* * * * *

The door buzzer sounded, and Doctor Lee got up from her lab bench, and crossed to the intercom. "What's the password?" she asked, half seriously.

"Doctor Beck's password is a string of thirty-seven random words, but I can never remember them. My password is, I left my green coffee mug on the blue tile, and I really need coffee, so please open up."

Lee smiled, confirmed that Gloria's green mug was on the blue tile on the other bench, and hit the button to unlock the door to the lab.

It took a moment for Gloria to maneuver a handcart into the lab. "Special delivery," she said once the door was closed. "Please pass my mug."

"Sure," said Lee. "You look winded; do you want it warmed up?"

"No, cold is better." Gloria had a good drink. "Hmm. Thanks. As promised, only a couple of days late, one pair alien-based reverse-engineered collapsium capacitors. One in stylish silver, the other in stylish copper." She started opening the locked case on the handcart, and removing packaging.

"Fabulous. Have they tested them yet?"

"Not yet." Gloria paused to get a better grip on it. "Hang on. These things weigh at least fifty pounds each." Carefully, they got both units onto a side bench.

They weren't much to look at: two disks, each about three inches diameter, very thin, and coated in the same tan resin sealant to protect it from the elements. A pair of thick wires protruded from one side of each capacitor, one pair copper, and the other silver.

"I can see why you're winded, we'll have to build a carry unit if we're going to move them much," Lee said as she hooked up a test unit to each, turned the selectors, and switched them on. The dials barely flickered at first, and then the needles both very slowly moved towards the 'infinity' mark.

"That looks promising," Lee said. "Let's try to see how good a capacitor you really are." She adjusted the settings on both units. She frowned at the result and made some changes. No matter what she did, the 'undefined' light stayed on.

"Here, let's try one we know that works," Gloria said. She opened a drawer, pulled out a capacitor from a tray, and tested it on both units. "The test units are fine," she said after a minute. "Results show within 1% of the number printed on the case."

Lee thought for a moment. "We're going to need a bigger tester."

None of the labs on campus had a test unit of the right type. Finally, they found one in a small factory on the outside of town. An alumnus of the University had a small yet successful company building electronic components, and the specialized machine for testing the company's supercapacitors was exactly what they needed. Doctor Beck was worried sick over the potential security breach, until the Chancellor pointed out that the owner was very trustworthy. And also his son-in-law, and father of his grandchildren.

By that point, all ten test units were built, and all ten had been run through their paces in the Quality Control lab at the factory—after hours, by the factory owner himself with Doctor Beck having kittens over his shoulder. The "Sample Committee Six" were discussing the results over coffee at the Chancellor's house with Craig, the factory owner.

Craig was puzzled as he looked at the spec sheets. "Dad, you've got to let me in on this," he said to the Chancellor. "Those things are individually the most potent capacitors I have ever seen, and until tonight I thought I'd seen everything in the industry. It's got triple the capacitance of the best unit I've ever heard of. About five times what I can make here, there isn't much call for the really high-end stuff on Baldur yet, and they're expensive to build." He paused.

"Yesterday, if a customer came to me and said they needed something with these specs, I would have told him I can build a nice little bus with a bunch of my top units wired into it. It would measure about a foot long by six inches wide, weigh about sixty pounds, and cost about twenty-five thousand francs. Which is around seventeen thousand sols with the exchange," he added for Doctor Lee's benefit. "Today, I see a unit that can do the same work and is three inches diameter and a sixteenth of an inch thick. I'm not certain I want to know how much it cost. How you managed to cram all of that in there, I admit, I am dying to know that."

"Well, you won't have to die to find out, Craig," the Chancellor said. "How would you like to be able to build them? We could use your expertise for production. It would have to be kept as secret as possible, of course. The paperwork for the patent will take a while to clear, and I wouldn't want your competitors getting this before it's completed."

They'd discussed this beforehand at a meeting, and agreed that the factory would be much better suited to production than anything the university could set up. "There would be confidentiality agreements, secret handshakes, the lot. Of course, I want you to be able to turn a profit on them—I don't want my grandchildren to starve—but some of the equipment you'd need would be a little out of your ordinary."

"Just how far out of my ordinary?" Craig asked.

The Chancellor had been waiting, and passed a piece of paper to Craig, who took it, frowning.

"Hmm. Never worked with collapsium before. So that's the magic ingredient! My compliments to whoever cooked that up." He pondered the sheet, took a pen out of his pocket and did some figuring.

"All right, ballpark figures, so there could be corrections later. About a million to set up, if you have any of this equipment used at the University and you're looking to sell it, I'll make you a fair offer. I'm pretty sure all of it is available locally, I could get it all delivered within, say, three or four days. For setup and teething problems, I'd allow about two to three weeks. After that, I could probably get you batches of six capacitors a week in your choice of flavor, silver or copper—making the collapsium will be the slow part of the process. That's for a pilot project. I have no idea what demand would be. Cost per unit at a very rough estimate would be twelve thousand francs for materials and labor. But then I have to cover the cost of the equipment and overhead and all that business stuff that you claim bores you, dad. If you need it, I can get you a half-dozen in a month, but if it's just going to be those six, I'll need to recoup the whole million on them, and the last I heard, that was outside of the scope of the University's budget."

"I can help with that," said Doctor Lee. "My company would be willing to fund the setup of the pilot project; that is, pay for the equipment. We'd need a contract stating that, in return for funding the equipment, we would get to purchase no less than twenty of the new capacitors for the cost of materials plus one thousand francs, each. After that initial batch, we'll have the information to renegotiate a fair valuation for a price per unit for the follow-up contract. Your company would deserve a fair profit, but of course we have to answer to the shareholders, and must keep expenses down.

"Now, don't go hiring a staff of hundreds just yet. I can sign this preliminary contract, and the follow-up, but head office on Terra would have to figure how many units we would need. HMI will insist on the right of first refusal for at least four hundred units the first year. That will give us more than enough to have a bunch of test hyperdrives built for optimization purposes, and the verification-and-safety trials, and give us a leg up on early production. But it might stay at just those four hundred for a year or more, what with travel time and due process at headquarters.

"Now, if the University has the patents in place, of course, and you can convince all of the companies here that collapsium capacitors are the cat's whiskers, you can sell them as many as you can make. Just as long as you know that when word comes back from HMI, we would get priority."

Craig looked like he couldn't decide if he was going to be insulted or not. "So I have to drop everything else when the Lords of Terra say I have to?" he asked mildly.

"No, when the Terran Federation Navy finds out that we'll be able to provide a hyperdrive engine than can cut travel time by, say, ten or even fifteen percent, they'll invoke several priority clauses in their contracts with us. The Navy wants the shiny new toys before the private yacht crowd gets them, after all. Do you know the amount of the last 'big speed increase' that anyone was able to deliver? It was less than one percent, a lot less. Once we get this optimized, HMI is going to be incredibly busy. And your company could be a part of that.

"I am not going to insult you by asking for a signature now. Here are copies of the contracts, and the confidentiality agreement. Take them to your legal department, or your law firm, and go over them carefully. Someone from Legal was supposed to make the trip with me, but they were denied a visa so I've retained a local law firm instead: Contreras, Miller, and Leek—no relation. If you agree, or if you have points to discuss, we can set up a meeting. The minute we sign, we can start the purchase orders."

"Contreras, Miller and Lee is probably the biggest firm on the planet that doesn't have ties to the government," Craig said. "I've dealt with then a few times, they are very good at what they do." He paused, and seemed to consider something. "There is one thing I want to ask first," he finally said. "What happened on Volund, Doctor Lee?"

"You'll have to be more specific," Lee said. "Volund is a pretty busy place."

"What happened to the BVE Company? I received a letter that stated HMI had its factories hit by arsonists."

There was a cry of surprise from a few people at that.

"No," Lee said. "BVE was a supplier to HMI, but they were always late with orders and asking for extensions. We'd already decided to not renew anything with them, when we heard they'd ceased operations when the owner was arrested. It turns out that the owner had been diverting funds to build himself a nice little dacha in hunting country. Too bad he got cheap on the construction, it burned to the ground and worse, attracted attention. By the time the fire department airboats arrived they were asking questions about how this huge residential complex had been built in a nature preserve, things like that. After the trials and lawsuits went through the local courts, there wasn't anything left of the company.

"But the factory is still there, Volund Trade Goods, Incorporated picked it up for a song. It's all a matter of public record, it happened about six years ago. Your lawyers can research it if you want; all the Federation worlds send out routine legal updates. But please, tell me where you got this story, HMI has grounds for a lawsuit."

Craig shook his head. "It was an anonymous letter sent to my office yesterday afternoon." He pulled it out of his pocket and passed it to her. "I didn't believe the story, but I wanted to hear your take on it. There is no stamp or postmark on the envelope."

"This meeting was arranged yesterday morning," Napolitano said. "I knew they'd be unhappy with you for going to the Federation Building," she said to Lee, "but I wasn't expecting this. I don't think they were ready for the meeting, though, it's too desperate."

"And too easy to disprove," Lee said. "Plain paper, typed, no signature. I'll pass it to our lawyers, but it's too easy to deny. Of course, this means we have to work out where the leak was. You sweep for bugs at the offices?" she asked Napolitano.

"Of course, and this is the reason why," Napolitano said. "Probably someone is monitoring your screen frequencies, watching your screen calls that way. You see?" she asked the Chancellor. "Sometimes there really are monsters hiding under the bed."

"Yes, I have been forced to agree that you have been right on many occasions," the Chancellor said. "Sadly enough, the rate is increasing over the last few years. That is why we are meeting here, in a room without screens, or even windows to the outside, why music is playing in another room, and my lawn-mowing robot is working right now, when even a cursory scan will show how badly it needs a tune-up and maintenance to prevent such profligate static discharges across the neighborhood." He smiled. "Even if they inspect it, I doubt they'd find the security generators. But unless you have any other rumors that you need dispelled, Craig, I should walk you to the door. If you leave now you'll still be in time to tuck the girls in tonight. Please give them my love."

It wasn't long before he returned. "So," the Chancellor said, "we have the new miracle part in hand. Or at least, on order, and will have it in hand in four or five weeks. What is the next step?"

"Are you certain that he'll agree?" Beck asked. "He seemed a little put out by some of the terms of the contract."

"Oh, I think he will," the Chancellor said with a smile. "I wouldn't have asked him otherwise. If he declines: so be it, I will find you someone to build them. But what about testing?" he asked Lee. "Our labs are excellent for some things; testing functional hyperdrives is not one of them."

"When I came to Baldur, I brought several tons of equipment. Specialized testing gear for one, everything we need to bench-test the new part. Also components to build several complete hyperdrive engines. We'll leave out the standard capacitor units, and put in the new ones. On a couple we'll just do a straight swap, others we'll use all the extra space to maximum potential by uprating everything else, gadolinium cells and power supplies. There's also equipment to bench-test the completed drives before we let them stretch their legs."

Gloria frowned. "Where is all of this gear? Before you arrived, I checked with the spaceline in case we needed to have a truck to pick up equipment. I was very surprised there wasn't any."

"It's stuck in customs," Lee said. "It's been almost a month now, that's one of the reasons I secured the law firm. I've been stonewalled when I try to get it released."

"Well, you have a plan, that's the main thing," the Chancellor said. "It looks like the legal and production fronts will be the busy ones for a while. A perfect time for Gloria's announcement. Tell them!"

Gloria smiled awkwardly. "I've set the date for my thesis defense," she said.

"And about time, too!" the Chancellor beamed. "If all goes the way I expect it should, this time next week I'll be calling you Doctor Heath, and finding room in my budget to pay you more for this project." He checked his watch. "Oh, dear, almost time. I do not wish to seem rude, but there is a demonstration outside that we need to see. Come to the backyard please, everyone."

"It's a nice backyard, Arthur," Doctor Bondar said, "but I don't see anything for a demonstration of any sort."

"Just a moment, I'm going to turn off the lights." He did, and closed the door. "Now, look up."

There were a few clouds, but many stars were visible, even from the city. Most cities in the Federation had light-pollution guidelines that would have made astronomers from the twentieth century weep with jealousy. Far above, a satellite or two swept past. Or were they ships, she wondered?

The Chancellor's watch light glowed for a moment. "If everyone would look to the east, please," he said.

A very bright light came up about the trees, right on cue. At first, Lee thought it was an aircar.

"That isn't one of the usual objects," Napolitano said. "It's big enough for a couple of ships in a close orbit. What are you demonstrating,

Chancellor? About four Ministries are having a cow about this, right now, and I don't think you'll get bail."

"Oh, this isn't mine, Detective. No, I only overheard two people talking about this, and they slipped into the crowd before I could act. One of these people claimed that the Navy was building an orbital outpost here, despite official protests from the Baldur government, but you know how those rumors go, so I'd pay it no mind. I merely wanted to see if there was something overhead at this time. I should think that there were a few telescopic screens at the University that might catch a look at it, whatever it might be, and wonder if the automatics were left on so that pictures might be obtained."

"'Orbital Outpost' isn't the usual Navy nomenclature," Lee said.

"No," agreed the Chancellor. "If it were true, however, that would make this the Baldur Orbital Outpost. BOO for short. I can only speculate what the effect of such a visible reminder that the rest of the Federation is watching would have on those with a guilty conscience, and rest confident that no one of that sort is on this world."

They watched in silence as it cruised overhead, and finally sank below the horizon. "Whatever it was," Lee said, "I don't think it will make them release my equipment any sooner."

* * * * *

"Good morning, Doctor Heath," Lee said as she entered the project office, setting a couple of boxes down on her desk.

Gloria smiled. "Good morning to you too, Doctor Lee. Tell me, how long did it take you to get used to the title?"

"About ten minutes, but I have a very large ego. How is it going?"

Gloria, now Doctor Heath, looked like she didn't know if her fellow doctor was joking, until she saw the wink. "No major problems, they're making good time."

The lawyers had gotten the equipment released from customs, and the latest phase of the project had been moved to a workshop, one that was above ground and thankfully had windows. Four grad students had been recruited to help assemble the hyperdrives. Since the casing, power cells and components had all been shipped in ready-to-assemble form, and with matching assembly robots for the heavy work, it was essentially building hyperdrives from a kit – but one that had some fantastically precise detail-work.

"I've had a look at the schedule," Lee said, "and I want more redundancy. We'll have time to go ahead with building one more unit of each type, bring it up to nine total."

"Shouldn't it really be more, for the optimization program?"

"It should be, but I don't think that we'll be able to do that here." The week after the Navy deployed its prefab platform in low orbit; new regulations prohibiting any craft from in-system runs had been enacted. The freighters and liners would move between systems as always—"unlawful interference with interstellar trade"—was a good way to get your government removed by the Federation, and whatever the shortcomings of Baldur's government, they weren't stupid enough for that. "I wonder if the new restrictions were for the BOO station, or for us?"

"Either way, we're dead in the water," Gloria said. "If we can't get off-world, into the outer system, there's no way to test them. You'll have to crate them up and take them back to Terra. And Baldur will have lost a big opportunity."

"Why Doctor Heath," Lee said mock-reproachfully. "Don't give up the ship yet. I might have something to contribute at the weekly project meeting tomorrow, we'll see."

"All right," Heath said. "Oh, and some of the students are asking if there are collapsium components in the electronics because some parts are so heavy, and since they've never heard of that before, they want to know more."

"Some of the students are asking? Only some? Which ones?" Lee asked.

"Well, all of them, actually," Heath replied.

"Good, I'm glad we're paying for smart people," Lee said. "I'll go over it with them and remind them of the non-disclosure slash confidentiality agreements that they signed. If they blab about it, or worse let another company jump the gun on us, we'll be able to rescind their academic qualifications."

Heath looked apprehensive. "How far back would that go?" she asked.

"Back to preschool, I asked the law firm to be nasty on the 'stick' side of things," Lee said. "But I hope that it won't become necessary. In fact," she picked up one of the boxes she had brought in, "I'll head down there now with coffee and donuts and play good cop about it. I got coffee for you too, let's go have a look."

"Thank you all for coming," the Chancellor said as they settled into chairs in his office the next morning. "So, with our usual free form agenda, where do we stand? Doctor Heath, how goes assembly?"

"Yesterday afternoon the grad students finished assembly of hyperdrives number five and six. Doctor Lee asked for another one of each type, for a total of nine, the other three should be done by the end of the week."

"I'll be helping with the bench-testing," Beck added. "All nine should be fully rated by the middle of next week."

"But then we'll have nine hyperdrives and no way to test them, with the new law they just brought in," Bondar said. "And if we have to ship them to Terra for testing, won't that weaken the case for manufacturing the parts here on Baldur, and add months to the test program?"

"As long as the patents are in place, I suppose from that point of view it doesn't really matter where the parts get made," the Chancellor said. "The University would still get its royalty no matter where in the Federation they get built. It does seem a shame, though, I'll hate to tell Craig that he won't get the big orders he was hoping for."

"We might not have to disappoint Craig just yet," Lee said. "What if there was a way to run at least the preliminary tests here in the Baldur system?"

"But they've banned all civilian flights in-system," Beck said. "Well, ships can still fly out to the jump points for interstellar travel, but nothing else, and a merchant ship or a liner isn't going to sit there, ready to jump for a week while we do our tests."

"The key word there is 'civilian,'" Lee said.

"You mean, go to the Navy?" the Chancellor asked. "Wouldn't that be considered interference in local affairs?"

"It might have been, before the protesters were massacred. How many students of this University were killed, Chancellor?" Lee asked.

"From what we can determine, between three and four hundred. Our best guess is that total casualties at the demonstration were on the order of eight or nine hundred from all the schools involved, plus the general population."

"Those were all Federation citizens. I don't think it's any coincidence that the orbital station went up so soon afterward. Have you seen it lately?"

At first it had just been the prefabricated station and one ship. It was impressive in the night sky, especially when the ship was plated in collapsium which was a very good reflector. Then another ship had joined the formation.

"Well, it was cloudy last night," the Chancellor allowed. "But yes, in the evening sky the two ships are very impressive."

"I checked with one of the telescopic screens that track it," Lee said. "Have you seen the latest from before dawn this morning, when the clouds cleared?"

"No," the Chancellor said. "Has there been a development?"

Lee passed him a photograph.

"My word," the Chancellor said. "Is that five, or six ships?"

"I think it's seven," Lee said. "It's going to look very impressive tonight, if they keep flying in formation like that. Now, this all must have been ordered before the word of the shootings got out. The nearest Navy base is at Gimli, there hasn't been enough time for a ship to go straight there and back. Regardless, we still have a month until the elections, and every one of those Navy ships has at least one pinnace onboard, usually two or three. I would like to make a couple of calls."

* * * * *

"I've never been on a Navy ship before," Doctor Heath said.

"I have a secret to tell you," Lee said. "Don't tell Baldur Intelligence. My uncle is in the Navy. When I was a kid he took us for a tour of his ship when he was a commander. But these won't be ships tonight, just small craft."

They were waiting in an airlorry about a thousand miles from the city, parked in an alpine meadow. The University had a large tract of land that their Observatory was built on, far away from any cities or light pollution. The astronomy department loved it, and the geology and botany and zoology departments all took field trips to the area.

"Still, it will be something new. But I'm surprised that you got permission to visit Baldur if your uncle is Navy brass. How did intelligence miss it?" she asked.

"Probably because he's my mother's brother, his last name is Sanderson."

"And if he was a commander when you were a kid, say twenty years ago…"

"Very wise of you, to—oh wow, look!"

The formation of orbiting Navy ships came into view over the mountain range, and in the sunset it was an impressive sight. Each ship was about a quarter mile in diameter and flying very close to its neighbors. With this many ships in the formation, it was bigger than a full moon as seen from Terra, and each was very bright.

"I think the ships got here from Gimli," Heath said quietly.

"I think you're right," Lee said, awestruck.

Last night, there had been about nine, staggered like runners about to run a sprint. Tonight there were many more – there was a box formation around the fainter bar of the station, and the station had a ship at either end. It looked like a box around a squiggle.

"Is that a picture of something?" Lee asked. "Why are—"

"Oh, my great Ghu," Heath said, "it's the opposition logo."

"What?" Lee's knowledge of Baldur politics was almost infinitely more than it had been six months ago, but there were still some gaps.

"Each party has its own little symbol of course. The main opposition party uses something like a box with a squiggle in it. I don't know why,"

Heath added. "But it looks like those ships!"

"That has to be over twenty ships, maybe twenty-four," Lee said, "but it's hard to say. They're going behind those mountains too quickly-"

Sure enough, they were gone again.

"There are going to be some seriously vexed people at the Presidential Palace tonight," Heath said.

"You have a gift for understatement, Gloria," Lee said. "Still, I don't know what they can do about it."

"You know, the people were starting to call the BOO a different name."

"Oh? What?" Lee asked.

"Mistletoe station."

"Ouch. Nothing like a little gallows humor."

"I hope no one starts shooting."

"Me, too."

There was a long quiet pause.

"So now we wait," Heath said.

"It should be soon," Lee replied. "At least I got to see some of 'scenic Baldur' with the rushing rivers and mountains that always make the postcards."

"This is the same area where they found The Sample, isn't it?" Lee asked.

"About ten miles west of here," Heath said. "Speaking of The Sample," she added, "I found something on it that I wanted to show you."

"Oh, no, not more golf carts and locked doors when we go back," Lee said weakly.

"I actually have it here," Heath said, and pulled a clear plastic baggie out of an inner pocket, passing it to Lee.

It was a fragment of metal, about an eighth inch thick and about an inch and a half long. Most of it was the same silvery-white color, but there was a thin band across the middle that caught the light differently, one so thin you thought you had imagined it. She held it up to the light for a better look.

"You've seen it, good," Heath said.

"What is this?" Lee asked.

"That is a cross section of the casing, most of it is titanium. That thin stripe across the middle? Gadolinium," Heath answered. At Lee's look, she continued. "Some of the numbers on The Sample didn't add up, the gadolinium cells were slightly underweight from what we were expecting." There needed to be a minimum amount of gadolinium present in the hyperdrive, or else the drive simply wouldn't work. "It was possible it had weathered away, of course, but I had a hunch. It turns out that the edges we can see were all deformed mechanically by the original accident, whatever it was, and you can't get an accurate look. So I cut out a sample."

"I'm surprised Doctor Beck signed off on that," Lee said.

"We'd learned all we could from visual examination. The cross-section shows that layer, though, I did a few test cores; it seems to be a gadolinium layer all the way around the casing, right in the middle of the titanium. It's a very thin layer; it looks like about one-sixty-fourth of an inch everywhere I've sampled it. So by calculating the gadolinium mass that was missing from the cells, we can get a good estimate on the size of the original intact unit." She passed some papers to Lee.

"Good work, Doctor Heath. You've filled in a few blanks."

"Thank you. Will we need to find a company that can make these casings?"

Lee pondered that. "That might take a few months to get right, and buying gadolinium might be problematic right now. I am going to include these findings in my reports, of course. But when we're optimizing, it will be best to work with just one variable at a time. All of that depends on how well these test flights go."

"Here's our ride," Heath said, pointing out the two sets of descending lights.

It was two Navy pinnances, marker lights strobing as they set down in the high alpine meadow. As each pinnace cracked a large cargo hatch open on its side, the doctors got out of the cab of the airlorry.

"Ahoy the Navy!" Lee yelled as they walked the fifty yards to the landed craft, a pair of people from each walking towards them.

"Doctor Mercedes Lee? Doctor Gloria Heath? We are looking for Doctor Livingstone!" a young officer called when they were within twenty yards.

"That's us! We were told to ask for Captain Courage, from blue delta nine." Captain Courage was the hero of a kid's show popular all over the Federation. Lee heard a couple of snickers from the Navy party, and guessed that not everyone had been briefed on the contact countersign.

"Well, that would be us, ma'am, we reply red tango. I'm lieutenant Reuel." He had an Australian accent, and pronounced the rank 'leftenant'. "We are here to help with your test project. If you want to pull your truck over to the craft on your left, we'll help you transfer what you need, and then we'll be on our way."

Pulling the airlorry up beside the large hatch took a minute, and Navy personnel from both pinnaces helped move the crates. Lee noticed that none of them were wearing large hats. There were a few small crates and nine big crates, but the big ones each weighed several hundred pounds, so it took a little coordination to use the lifters to tranship them. The cargo area on the pinnace was about thirty feet long by fifteen wide, so there was plenty of room. One smaller crate of control equipment was sent to the other pinnace, but most of the crates went into the first. Finally it was done.

Reuel looked around. "Do you have a driver to take the lorry back?"

"No, someone from the Observatory will be here in the morning; I've been told it should be safe until then."

"Excellent. Please step aboard then, doctors. I noticed that you're both armed against the local bush-dragons, which is a fine precaution, but I will have to ask you to check your weapons in the locker for the duration. What make are they?"

"Ten millimeter Colt Argentine," Lee said.

"Nice choice, ours are Mars Consolidated, so we won't get them confused despite the same calibre. If you'd be so kind?" The lieutenant took the belts, holsters and all, and gave them to an enlisted man for safe storage. "Normally, I'd have to give you a chit, but I have orders that this all never happened. This way please to the control room."

It didn't take long to get there. Along the way, Heath asked "I thought they called it the bridge?"

"Actually, that term is reserved for ships, not small craft," someone said from behind them. They turned to see a man in his mid-thirties with a pleasant face and wearing the uniform of a lieutenant-commander. "This is a standard one-hundred-foot pinnace, so we don't rate that term, even though we can travel through hyperspace as quickly as a capital vessel."

"Ah, there you are, sir. May I present Doctors Lee and Heath of the University of Paris-on-Baldur? Doctors, I have been told to call this man Lieutenant-Commander Smith, of Federation Navy Intelligence. Chief, are we all set?"

"Ready to lift at any time, sir," a man said from across the control room.

"I don't want to be late for voting day," Lieutenant Reuel said. "Raise ship, initiate departure vector, ahead best speed."

"Aye, sir."

They'd hoped to see more of the take-off, but as dramatic as the mountains were in daylight, in the dark there simply was nothing to see. There was a mild sensation of acceleration, but that didn't give them enough to go by. The crew quietly went about their jobs, and after a couple of minutes, they began to see stars.

"How high are we?" Heath asked.

"Wentworth, what is our altitude?" Lieutenant Reuel asked.

"Just passing one hundred and fifty miles, sir," a man at a control station said.

Heath was shocked. "That's amazing! I thought we'd see a sunrise or something."

Reuel smiled. "Normally we would, ma'am, but our orders were to expedite dust-off. We kept to the planet's shadow and well away from the starport's radars. And we met out in the mountains so that we wouldn't have to play jamming games with the Baldur ground defenses again."

Now Lee was shocked. "You mean, they've been targeting the ships of the Federation Navy with fire control radars? Isn't that an act of war?"

"Not quite," said Commander Smith. "They've made a point of staying just on the side of legality. The election is in nine days, we don't need to start shooting when all indications are the voters want a new administration."

"If DuPaul's people haven't been busy printing up fake ballots," Lee said, "I've got a few bridges to see you. On Terra. In the northern hemisphere."

"We'll worry about that next week. For now, what would be the best way to proceed? We've got two pinnaces, some hyperdrive message drones, and platforms for your test drives. Where do you want us?"

Lee thought for a moment. "Originally I was going to suggest you put both pinnaces in the outer system, just a few light-hours apart just so we didn't die of boredom waiting for confirmations and timings. But if you've got message drones, we could go to the opposite ends of the system, and that would give better results."

"Sounds good. Lieutenant?"

"At this speed, sir, we'll be clear the planet's gravity well and be able to jump for the outer system in just over ten hours. We'll coordinate with the other pinnace and head for opposite sides of the system."

"Thank you, lieutenant. I'll be in the cargo bay assisting with the assembly."

"Aye sir."

They headed back to the cargo bay.

"If the Navy has hyperdrive message drones," Heath asked, "why do we have to wait for the freighters and liners to carry news, why don't they set up a network of mail drones?"

"The drones are too small for an interstellar run," Lee answered. "Over a few light-hours, single drive units work fine. After about a light-year, they experience Keene Turbulence and a proportion just never show up."

"What is Keene Turbulence?" Heath asked.

"We don't know, exactly. Ships mount ten drives and work fine, something as small as a pinnace use three and work fine, so there hasn't been much motivation to do research that costs you a high fraction of expensive equipment. If you can find a backer, though, could be good for another doctorate. Maybe a hundred sols a year book royalties."

"We'll have to connect your test drives to our mobile platforms," Smith said, "but from the information you sent, it should work out not too badly. We have extra engineering crew aboard, so we should be all set by the time we are ready to jump."

Since liftoff, more crates had been moved into this part of the cargo bay, and a crew was finishing setting up several hoists and test benches. Several officers and men walked over to meet them as they entered the bay.

"Doctors, this is Commander Contreras, he's the chief engineer of one of the ships orbiting Baldur right now. He and his men will be assisting us."

Unlike the other officers, Commander Contreras wanted to shake hands. "Doctors," he said, "a real pleasure. I'd love to go over the specs with you if we have the time. Until then, we'll get your test drives mounted."

"Mounted onto what?" Heath asked.

"Come have a look." Contreras led them over to a set of crates with Navy markings on the side. "This is a screen-guided unit, complete with a full set of lift-and-drive engines, so we can get your test drives into position and jump them. Each unit also has navigation lights, so we can tell which type of test drive we're looking at, the moment it comes out of jump."

"Why, that's perfect!" Heath said. "That's exactly what we need! How did the Navy know to have these?"

"Well, normally they carry fifty-megaton warheads," Contreras explained. "Without the bombs, the weapons bay is a bit larger than what we were told you need, but we've got a little machine shop on board and plenty of braces and spacers. We borrowed spare units from some of the ships over Baldur."

Heath looked pale. "Are they standard equipment?" she finally asked, quietly.

"Oh, yes, it's nothing to worry about," Smith said. "Every ship in the fleet has one when it's on active duty, and the reason we were able to borrow these is because no one wants to start blowing up cities on Baldur." Heath looked slightly relieved, but still like someone who'd had too much information for one day.

"You said they had navigation markers," Lee asked. "Can you change the color of the strobe lights?"

"Of course," Contreras said. "What do you need?"

"These three crates," Lee said, pointing them out, "are standard drives for comparison purposes. We could mark those as green. The next three are ones we have some new components that we're testing, just straight replacement, new for old. We could mark those as yellow.

"These last three, right here, we also replaced the components, but since the replacements are a lot smaller, we have maximized the content of the hyperdrives by cramming every bit of equipment into the drive we could. We could mark those as red."

Contreras nodded. "No problem at all."

"Please remind me again," Heath said, "since my field is the materials end of things. If a faster drive is just a matter of fitting in more equipment, couldn't you just build a bigger engine?"

"Well," Lee said. "You've probably noticed how when people talk about ships, they talk about 'hyperdrives' in the plural?" Heath nodded. "There's something called the prime node: when a hyperdrive sets up the drive field, all the equipment generating the field has to be within the prime node. It's pretty small, just over a yard in diameter is the biggest reliable size we can make right now. But the rest of the field propagates through the ship, until it is effectively contained by the collapsium skin of the ship.

"Just one engine wouldn't make a very strong field, though, and it would make a journey through hyperspace take even longer that it does now. So even this pinnace would have at least three drives, and a capital ship would have at least a dozen.

"Since it's a function of field strength, there is a point of diminishing returns. Much more than that just won't make the ship go any faster. The mass of the ship is also a factor, which is why a civilian ship loaded with freight like the *City of Windhoek* that brought me to Baldur can't quite make the same travel time as a Navy ship. Usually the difference is relatively small, about one part in eight or ten, since any ship a quarter-mile in diameter isn't going to be a lightweight."

"Thank you," Heath said.

"Unless there are any other questions?" Contreras asked. "Let's get to work."

"It's a pretty little constellation we've built," Heath said, peering at the repeater viewscreens. They were in the cargo hold: indeed, except for the three people manning the control room, everyone on board was in the cargo hold, watching the large repeater screen, all twenty six of them.

The screen showed an even dozen strobing lights, three each of the red, yellow and green test drives, and three more blue ones on the standard Navy message drones. The magnification was stepped way down, since the drones and the test units were spaced out enough that their hyperspace jumps wouldn't interfere with each other.

Lieutenant Reuel listened to the control room on his headset. "Sir, all is set," he said to Smith. "Anytime you're ready."

Smith turned to Lee and Heath. "Doctors, would you do the honors?" he asked, gesturing to the control board.

Lee and Heath smiled at each other as they stepped forward. Like a lot of potentially dangerous industrial equipment, the 'start button' was actually two large red buttons about a yard apart on the control panel, both clearly labelled with a red light over it, and both covered with transparent plastic flip-covers

The covers went up. "Okay," Lee said, "press on 'go'. Three, two, one, go."

There was a buzz from behind the panel, the two red lights turned green. Two of the blue strobes on the screen winked out as their drones jumped, and a sixty-second countdown clock beside the repeater screen sprang to life.

It was the longest sixty seconds of Lee's life. When the sweep hand hit 'zero' all nine of the test strobes vanished from the screen.

"If you thought the last minute was tense, wait for the next ten!" Smith said. "The soonest anything should come back is ten minutes from now," he said to the crowd. "If all goes to plan, we should get two message drones back first, then any surviving test drones a minute later. Then we'll see. By the Lieutenant's kind permission, smoking lamp is lit."

At that, more than a few of the crowd drifted away and started smoking.

"Won't that tax the life support?" Heath asked quietly.

"No, we can carry five hundred ground troops for a few days if we have to," Smith said. "We're only running less than thirty, so we're good for a few weeks."

"If things go well with the tests, we should be able to start back in a day or so," Lee said. "I don't want to miss the election."

"Why Doctor Lee," Smith said, "thinking of voting your own graveyard?"

"The thought had crossed my mind," she said, "but I want to show solidarity with everyone at the University."

"What do you think the results will be, Doctor Lee?" Commander Contreras asked.

"Bench tests were promising," she answered. "I like to aim low to as not disappoint people, so I'll go with as much as a five percent reduction in travel time. I hope for more, but if we get five percent, it would still be worthwhile."

"And to think," Contreras said, "all this from using collapsium in something as ordinary as a capacitor. I wonder why it took us so long to think of doing that."

"I suggest one factor was the backlash against the Buenos Aires event," Smith said. In answer to Heath's blank look, he added, "When the Christian Anarchists detonated a homemade atomic bomb in the year 378."

"Oh, of course, that was horrible," she said.

"The bomb maker was certifiable," Smith said. "He wasn't a well man, and he'd had a run of bad luck made worse by his own bad decisions. His new political friends had their own agenda for his talents, but at the end of the day, he was a one-off event. A lot of people that should have known better overreacted, either for empire-building, or to be seen to be 'doing something.' Or just out of fear. But a lot of technical education was sidelined, in a lot of areas, and even though it was twenty years ago, some fields are just getting back to a more normal footing."

"I think you have something there," Lee allowed. "But perhaps events like this will be a shot in the arm for technical research and education again."

Something started buzzing on the control console. "Hey, they're early!" someone shouted, pointing at the screen. Sure enough, there were three blue strobe lights showing there once more, and the one-minute countdown clock had restarted automatically.

There was a rush as people around the periphery of the cargo bay disposed of cigarettes and headed for the repeater screen. The sweep hand crawled toward zero.

Long before it reached zero, three red strobes appeared in the screen. Then the yellows and greens arrived in a photo finish. But the reds were first.

It had worked.

* * * * *

"That averages out to almost fourteen percent!" Contreras said. They were on the way back to Baldur, going over test data after sending the test drones back and forth for about a day. After thirty-two jumps the power cells on the test drives were exhausted. The engineering crew was almost done unshipping the test drives from the Navy's frames, and returning everything to crates.

"We'll have to check everything down to a sub microscopic level," Lee said. "It will be a few months of careful study here, and more work at Terra to optimize things, that can run concurrently. But even if we can't squeeze any further improvements out of it, we will have cut travel time between Terra and Baldur from six months down to five. Which isn't bad."

"That will be the single biggest efficiency gain in, what, thirty years?" Contreras said.

"At least," Lee said. "This will make the shareholders of HMI very happy. It would be insider trading for me to recommend anyone buy any shares in the company I work for. So I won't." She let that hang for a moment. "But in the crate marked 'delicate' that we loaded, there are some very fine drinks that my company would like to see distributed as a thank you to all involved."

"Well, doctor, that is very generous of—" Smith began.

"Sir!" Lieutenant Reuel ran into the cargo bay. "Commander Smith, you're wanted on the priority channel!" Smith quickly headed forward.

"At this range?" Contreras wondered. "There's at least a ten-minute delay."

"Well," Heath said slowly, "we do have a lot of detection gear."

"Commander," Lee asked, "would it be alright if we tried a news channel?"

"Of course, I'll even pipe it through to the control room."

They were able to get a faint signal from several of the commercial networks—only sound at first, then once they had hooked the amplifiers into the circuit, visual as well—a spokesperson in Federation Navy uniform. If it was election night coverage, they all agreed that didn't look good for the incumbent.

It was election coverage. *"After voting closed, all polling stations were sealed off by state security forces, and fake ballots brought in for counting. In operations across the city of Paris-on-Baldur, Federation Marines and Navy personnel were able to secure all polling stations to find the duplicate voting registers, fake ballots, and the genuine ballots. Admiral Cunningham of the Federation Navy has declared President DuPaul and his cabinet under arrest for malfeasance in office, electoral fraud, and ordering the massacre of the student protesters almost three months ago. Formal charges will follow.*

"Planetary forces of Baldur are ordered to remain in their barracks. Navy and Marine forces have secured the Capital Building, the Palace of the President of the Republic, Baldur Ministry of the Army, and all barracks within an hour's flight time of the city."

There were brief video clips of some of the sites, with a fifteen-hundred-foot Navy ship hovering scant dozens of feet over the building so 'secured'—the top of the aerial-mast of the Presidential Palace was actually bent by the ship bearing down on it, which got a lot of applause from the audience.

"But the election was supposed to be next week," Heath said. "What happened?"

"Probably DuPaul moved it up once he saw the formation flying the other night," Contreras offered. "Not that it mattered, rigged or not, after he ordered that massacre."

"It doesn't sound like there was much shooting, though, which is a good thing," Lee said. "Of course, a quarter-mile of battleship on the roof tends to discourage that."

Contreras had to laugh at that. "How did DuPaul take over in the first place?"

Lee shrugged. "Unscrupulous actions and distance from oversight, mostly."

"Well, it is a problem," Contreras said, "and it will be, even with an improved hyperdrive. You can bet that the next few years we'll see armies of monitors and agents fanning out to worlds all over the Federation to keep the next DuPaul from power."

"With a new government, do you think that Baldur will get some of the production of the new hyperdrive?" Heath asked.

"It should, I will recommend that," Lee said. "Of course, with the reports I've been sending to head office, and the copies of the hardware, I would imagine that a lot would be done on Terra. But every collapsium part built anywhere will mean a royalty for the University, and with so many ships routing through Baldur to Marduk and beyond, plus the Navy base at Gimli right next door, I'm pretty sure the Chancellor's grandchildren will be in no danger of starvation. If you want, I could recommend you for a senior position at HMI Baldur."

Heath's eyes widened. "Really?"

"Think it over; I don't need an answer today."

"How long do you think it would take to start production?"

Contreras asked.

Lee thought for a moment. "Six months for information to get back to Terra, an intensive optimization program. I could even jump-start things by shipping a couple of tons of parts back to Terra from the production line here, but at best it would be a year from now to start full-scale production, then equipping ships as they came in."

"The way things operate in the Federation, that's not bad, Doctor."

"I'll probably be out this way again in a year or two. Who knows, the ship might only take five months, or with luck and new engine casings, maybe even four."

* * * * *

It was ten months before Lee made it back to Terra: four months to wrap up, and six on the ship. Since it was Terra, three ships had landed at once from different points in the Federation, so Alice Springs Spaceport was busier that Baldur's spaceport had been on the outbound leg. Since it was Terra, she had only five forms to give the customs officer, not twenty, and the customs officers didn't live under oversized headgear.

Papers, please," the bare-headed customs officer asked, sitting at a desk that was desk-height, not bumping the ceiling. She passed him the papers and waited.

She wasn't expecting him to burst out laughing. She must have looked worried.

"No, it's Okay," he said, opening her passport to page three and pointing at the staple holes through page three right below the photo where it said in large letters, 'no other forms are to be attached to this passport.'

"So," he said, still chuckling, "I know you arrived at Baldur before they removed DuPaul. And the rest of your paperwork"—he checked each page—"...seems to be in order. Welcome home to Terra, Doctor Lee."

The End

www.ingramcontent.com/pod-product-compliance
Lightning Source LLC
Chambersburg PA
CBHW060553310726
48982CB00008B/1107/J
* 9 7 8 0 9 3 7 9 1 2 7 0 6 *